Z.L. COFFMAN

THE AETHYRGUARD

ZLC
STORYTELLING

THE AETHYRGUARD

ECHOES OF THE VEYRTH'KAEL SAGA
BOOK ONE
THE AETHYRGUARD: INITIATE

Table of Contents

About the Author

Copyrights

A Note from the Author

Acknowledgment

Dedication

Map of Aelinthar

Chapter 1: The Beyond Stirs

Chapter 2: Brothers

Chapter 3: The Initiate's Path

Chapter 4: The Weight of Routine

Chapter 5: Shadows of Home

Chapter 6: The Shape of Duty

Chapter 7: Into the Breach

Chapter 8: The Breach

Chapter 9: Awakened

Chapter 10: Return to Training

Chapter 11: Bonds

Chapter 12: The Echoes of Freedom

Chapter 13: The First Mission

Chapter 14: Threads of Power

Chapter 15: Battlemage's Station

Chapter 16: The Path Ahead

Chapter 17: On the road again
Chapter 18: Witherfield
Chapter 19: The Second Disappearance
Chapter 20: Reckoning
Chapter 21: The Weight of Return
Chapter 22: Echoes and Consequences
Chapter 23: Cracks in Stone
Chapter 24: The Mid-year Trial
Chapter 25: Knightmares
Chapter 26: Warden's Price
Chapter 27: Buried Tethers
Chapter 28: Caelen
Chapter 29: Storm-Tide
Chapter 30: Doubt and Dust
Chapter 31: The Gift
Chapter 32: The Gate Between
Afterword

A bout the Author
My name is Z.L. Coffman, though most people just call me Zach. I was born and raised in Indianapolis, Indiana, where I learned the value of stubborn hope and the healing power of a well-told story. If you ask me what shaped my heart, I'd point to my Midwestern roots and a lifelong love of '80s and '90s country music, the kind you belt out in the car, windows down, when you need to remember where you came from.

By day, I work in Medicaid management, leading teams dedicated to expanding access to care for people who need it most. I believe everyone deserves a chance at healing, and I hope one day to bring that passion for service into the world of politics. By night (and sometimes far too early in the morning), I write fantasy novels about found family, resilience, and the simple belief that even one small light can break through the dark.

My stories are inspired by the sweeping worlds of J.R.R. Tolkien, Naomi Novik, Jim Butcher, and Patrick Rothfuss. By the fierce wisdom of Maya Angelou, and the conviction that we are all, every one of us, striving to become our best selves, even when the road is broken. For me, fantasy isn't an escape; it's a lens to see what's possible, a safe place to wrestle with our shadows and find hope anyway.

When I'm not writing, you'll usually find me surrounded by a mess of pets and houseplants, rolling dice at the D&D table, or sharing laughter and late-night conversations with my found family in California. I love hearing from readers, swapping stories, and building the kind of community where everyone is welcome.

If you want to connect, talk craft, or just say hi, you can find me at www.zlcstorytelling.com or on social media, (@zlcstorytelling).

As the old man said, every remarkable story deserves a little embellishment.

Copyrights

Book Cover by O'Kenneth Designs

First edition 2025

A Note from the Author

Welcome to *The Aethyrguard: Initiate*.

Whether you've stumbled upon this book by chance or sought it out with intention, I'm grateful you're here. You're about to step into a world shaped by hope, haunted by loss, and held together by the fragile strength of chosen family.

This story was born from a belief that fantasy is more than magic and monsters. It's a place to ask challenging questions, to chase light through darkness, and to remember that our wounds can become windows into our souls.

Within these pages, every bond costs something. Every victory leaves a mark. And every hero, no matter how powerful, is still human.

You'll meet characters wrestling with legacy, loyalty, and the burden of becoming who they're meant to be. Their world is not a gentle one, but that is what gives it beauty.

The Aethyrguard fight to protect what remains. Not because they are perfect, but because they refuse to let darkness win.

I hope you see yourself in their struggles, their doubts, and their stubborn hope.

You can expect magic that exacts a price, battles that leave real scars, and relationships that matter more than any single victory. You'll find moments of tenderness tucked between the trials and, if I've done my job, candle burning against the dark.

Thank you for choosing to walk this path with me.

Acknowledgment

There are a great many people that have helped The Aethyrguard: Initiate come to life.

I hope you know, how much I appreciate you. I, truly, could not have done this without you.

To my Beta Readers. Your constructive words and passionate insights gave my story a needed scalpel, you understand the goal and helped see it through.

To the artists, your art is tremendous. The cover and Map have brought this world to life in a way I'd only dreamed.

To my editors, thank you both for the countless hours, storyboarding and red lines.

Thank you. All of you. I hope you know that I will always be grateful.

Dedication

Brother. I finally did it. I told you I would one day.

Here's the story I told you when we were kids, well, inspired by anyway.

I'm sorry you don't get to see how it ends.

This one is for you Ryan.

Until we see each other again.

<3

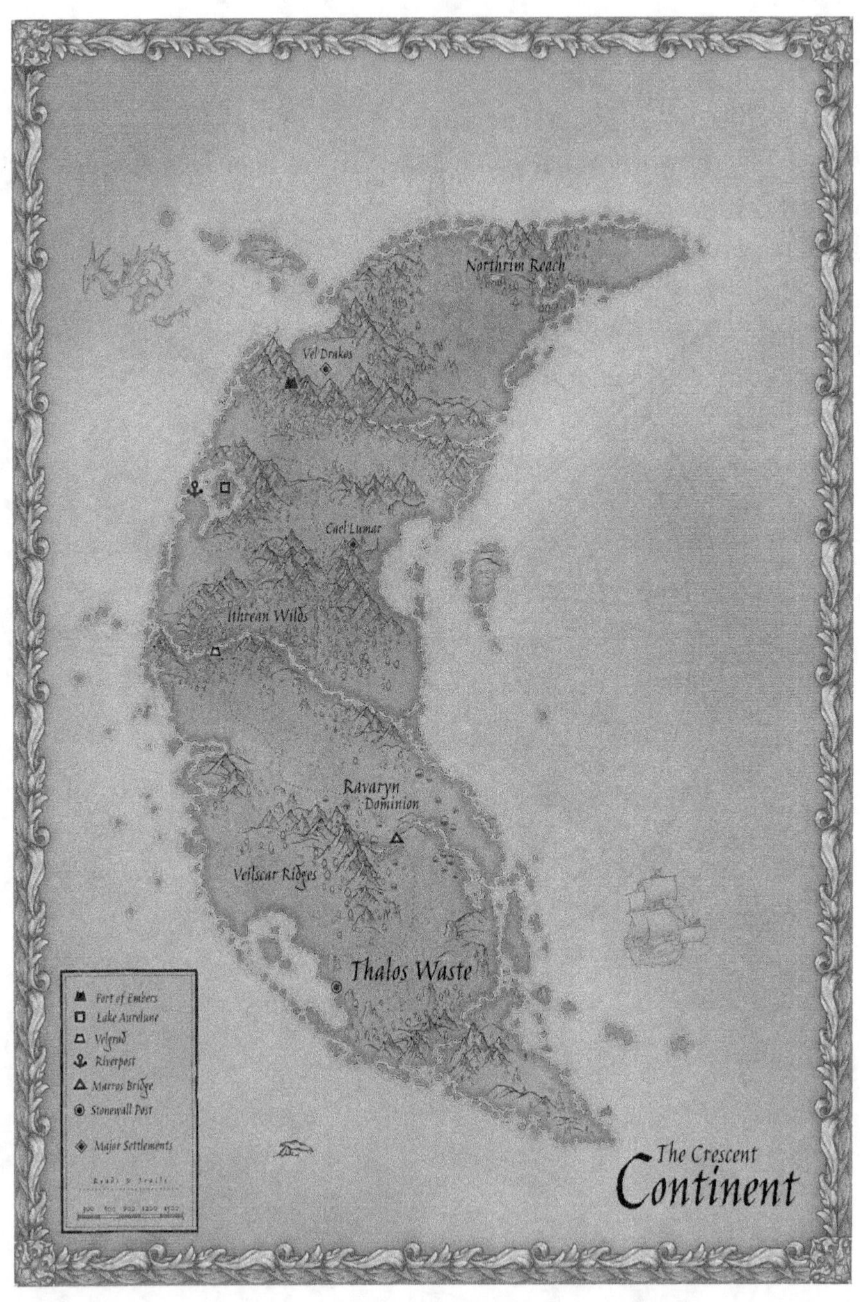

Northrim Reach
Vel Drakos
Cael Lumar
Ithrean Wilds
Ravaryn Dominion
Veilscar Ridges
Thalos Waste
Port of Embers
Lake Aurelune
Velgrad
Riverpost
Marros Bridge
Stonewall Post
Major Settlements
The Crescent Continent

Chapter 1: The Beyond Stirs

The waiting was the worst part.

Korvan stood in the antechamber beneath the Crown Keep, blacksteel pillars polished to a mirror's edge hemming him in. Five others shared the circle, chosen from a thousand hopefuls. Storm-blue cloaks hung stiff, sunburst clasps pressed to their chests. No one spoke. The walls held their breath.

Beyond the heavy doors, an Aethyrgate pulsed with a deliberate, ancient pull. This was the Initiate's Trial. It would separate the worthy from the not. Most returned changed. Some never returned.

Korvan took to the edge of space the way he always had.

The Gate watched without eyes. The Aethyr that poured through it felt observant, raising gooseflesh, crawling the skin of every Initiate present.

Beside him, Brusk shifted. Shorter than a boar at the shoulder and twice as broad, the Bulwark was slabs of living stone laced with copper fire. Garnet eyes swept the room with patient calm. His clubbed tail whispered across tile. He bore the smell of rain on rock and sun-warmed iron.

Korvan's fingers traced the Soulmarks along his forearms. Not a tattoo or birthmark but Brusk's loyalty etched in living Aethyr. The runes pulsed with the color of the sky, a second heartbeat under his skin.

He hadn't earned Brusk the way the Aethyrguard preferred. No glyph-seal, no overseer. It was instinct. He needed a protector. Brusk had answered.

His bond made him a question in a hall built for answers. His Soulmark burned a shade wilder than the others. Brusk's certainty cut through it, rooted in something older than approval.

The pulse answered steady. A second breath alongside his own.

A voice rose from memory, cold as iron: *Your mother died for you, boy. Don't forget that.*

Varnrik. A haunting that was always there.

His mother had left a gift and a debt. The spark cost her everything. Caelen had taken the shadow of it. A strange sickness, the frail echo of power that she should've left behind.

Korvan's fists closed. He would not waste what she gave him. He would survive this, Trial. He would climb high enough to carry Caelen free. Free from Varnrik's reach, from the grip of small fates.

A thin sound cut the silence. A soft whimper. An Academy boy shook, shoulders trembling, eyes wet.

Korvan started toward him. Brusk checked him with weight through the bond. *He needs courage. The Beyond breaks you.*

Korvan's jaw set. "Then he'd better find it fast."

Ancient gears stirred in the dark. Metal on metal. A throat clearing after centuries.

Light bled through a widening seam. Older than sun, wilder than lamp. Colors crossed and shifted, magic breathing in waves. Each pulse struck the rhythm etched into Korvan's skin.

Backs straightened. Korvan went last.

He looked at Brusk. Copper veining flared; plates flexed; the tail tip flicked like a banner. "We go together. Hold the line."

Brusk shouldered beneath his shadow. Warm assent pressed through the bond: *I go if Korvan go.*

They stepped.

Pressure hammered Korvan's ears. His throat rasped raw. He went anyway.

The Aethyrgate took them whole.

***

Force pressed from Aethyr into his Fyrstrand, burning across his Soulmark. Blue to gold to violet to colors without names. Each hue struck like a thunderclap. The Gate hungered.

He stepped again, and the world let go.

Silence surged. Flavor, texture, memory shook loose. Only the hum remained, a deep rattling in the bone.

Impact.

He staggered. Boots skidded on not-quite-stone. The air stank of acid and storm.

The Beyond or a chamber shaped by its logic. Sky gone. Glass shards veined in gold and bruised violet. Sideways trees. Stones adrift. Rules bent, not broken.

Brusk's claws scraped tile and twisted root. The bond thrummed low, a grit-deep warning. *Hate this ground.*

Korvan wiped sweat from his lip. "Tight to me."

His Soulmarks flared not only reacting but watching.

Attention settled the dust around them. Heavy. Patient. Ancient.

A gurgling roar climbed from the far basin. A wolf-shaped Veyrkin lumbered forward, broad as a cart, hide split and scorched. Violet seeped from its wounds, slick and wrong.

Their first test.

Dust leapt. The wolf hit like a falling wall. Tile lurched. Old blows rang in Korvan's ribs. His teeth sang. Bile rose sharp and mean.

Rage stayed in its place as a promise rose: *I won't fail him.*

Korvan slid, boots grinding along moss-slick tile. Heat rose along his forearms as his Fyrstrand met the beat within his chest. Brusk's thrum matched. Korvan's Soulmark flared hot and alive.

"Get'em Brusk," he rasped. One breath shaved into words.

Brusk feinted wide. The beast lowered its head, shifting weight to meet the charge. Pain had taught it.

Korvan's palm ignited with Aethyr. "Kinetic Pulse."

The shove landed ugly and hard. Stone barked his wrist on recoil. The beast's foreleg folded at the wrong angle. Brusk hit broadside, tusks carving deep. Black-violet ichor hissed and smoked.

Korvan moved through the opening summoning his glaive of light. Auryn's Edge bit through the eye. Jelly and bone grit slicked the guard. The haft jolted. His molars hummed.

Stillness fell as cold pressed behind his heart.

His hands shook. Heat braided the mark. Edges swam, then cleared. Copper crept across his tongue.

A boy screamed. A girl shouted above the hiss. Her bond bucked and would not answer. Korvan kept forward. Brusk pressed back to him. Their breaths matched.

***

The second ring bared its teeth.

Two hunters slid out sleek and low. One licked a ragged tongue of fire. The other prowled sideways, spine bowed like wire.

Korvan counted one-two-three. Brusk matched, chest low in moss. No signals. Only the old rhythm.

Fire roared. Claws snapped. Air burned sweet and bitter.

Korvan pivoted early, misread the silent one's line. Brusk's armored shoulder clipped his shin.

Heat kissed his thigh. Skin bubbled tight. Burnt hair stung his mouth. He swallowed the sound.

His fear hardened. Kinetic Pulse roared as he exhaled, shoved the silent hunter wide. The flamer curved for Brusk instead. Clever.

"Left. Cut it off," Korvan breathed.

Brusk knifed diagonally, tusks low.

Korvan took the high lane and aethyr pulsed again. A short, but mean blast, enough to stall the creature. Brusk hamstrung the flamer; a tendon twanged. Korvan took the throat. The silent one lunged blind into his follow-through and met steel. Ribs skated, edge bit. Breath left the beast in a wet fold.

They held while sound drained from the air.

The mark burned hot–cold–hot. Vision narrowed, then steadied. He rolled one shoulder. Bruised bone answered.

Ahead, a gate pulsed.

Korvan took a few deep breaths and the tremor in his hand subsided.

"Not done yet Brusk. Let's keep moving." He said.

***

One step, and the world exhaled him into blankness.

Brusk vanished. Bond, heartbeat, magic, stripped to quiet.

Flat land stretched unbroken. A low rise, with a spire at its crest.

He climbed. Each step heavier. Silence pressed on his chest and slowed his joints.

At the summit, truth waited: bone. White, cracked, worn by time. A faint Aethyrlight moved beneath its surface. His fingers brushed—

—and the yard behind their house erupted. Dust, splinters, a fence warped by rain. A practice stick broken. Knuckles split, old scars opened anew.

"You call that a guard?" Varnrik's slurred voice boomed from the porch. The bottle swayed on the steps. Bare feet on warped boards. Blade where the bottle had been. Caelen small at the step, arms locked around knees attempting to hide in plain sight.

Shame burned hotter than pain. Shame for being seen weak. But worse, that Caelen had to watch.

"You want to protect him, boy?" Spit hit dust. "Stop pretending you're strong."

Air cindered. The porch burned out. His Father's blade hung in the space Korvan's memory left open.

He tore his palm from the monolith. Breath sawed. Ash clung to skin that had never left the bone-field.

The Beyond emptied memory and made him lift the pieces.

For a heartbeat, Caelen's voice came small behind him. He turned into fog.

Truth, then. What the Aethyrguard wanted.

He set his palm to the burning mark. "I'm not him."

The line lay flat on stone. Something in him steadied. The same hands that once couldn't lift a branch. They lifted now.

The gate thrummed. He stepped, and silence took everything.

***

Wind thinned. Voices dulled. Beasts quieted. Even his own breath sounded wrong. Boots crunched on dust bright as powdered stars.

Walls and the sky fell away. A horizonless plain of mirrorstone warped distance. It felt venerable, something that remembered light.

He felt the difference in the Aethyr of where he was It was too potent, too overwhelming. This was not the chamber of the Initiate's trial, the manicured room that the Aethyrguard promised. This was a wound in the weave.

This was The Beyond.

The surface rippled, water disguised as earth. Each step sent a shimmer outward, as if he disturbed memories not stones. Breath fogged without cold. His heartbeat echoed like a far drum.

He reached for Brusk, for Fyrstrand spark. Nothing answered.

A shape formed at the plain's edge. Immense. Deliberate. Silence decided to walk. Its wings were folded. Limbs coiled with withheld power.

A myth with patience intact.

Hide caught light the way slate polished by river centuries would. It was streaked with the color of dawn and starlight. Not shining but storing the light. The heaven's memories soaked into scales.

Eyes found him. A deep radiance he had no words for. His body locked. Breath stilled. He stood at the eye of a storm not yet loosed. He knew it wanted him to bend.

An unknown feeling swelled within him. Like a cork popping from wine, an unknown strength flooded him. In the face of this unknown creature, Korvan's legs straightened, his back and shoulders relaxed, and he reached his full height.

He refused to kneel.

The dragon approached. One talon touched mirrorstone. Ripples moved outward. No spell-glow. Something truer or older he didn't know.

He raised empty hands. No spell. No shield. No blade. Only breath and the weight of being seen.

The great head lowered. Curiosity, not menace.

You would name me.

The voice moved through bone and marrow, where fear bends toward faith.

His throat tightened. "Why?"

The head tilted. Warmth gathered in star-bright eyes.

Because you see. Because you are a protector. Because you should not be here. Yet here you stand.

Truth passed through him like wind through fir. There, then gone.

Wings opened, sovereign. Space fractured with light. For one breath he stood inside it, not beneath.

Warmth tingled his skin. His Soulmark throbbed and felt alive, flush with magic, more than he'd ever felt. It was part of him, it tied him together and made him strong.

Far away, a wardstone cracked. The weave rippled, quiet and wide.

The dragon leaned close. Breath stirred the inches between them. Old wind. Warm stone. Endless sky.

Grief lived in those eyes. Wonder, too.

Caelen's fevered whisper rose from memory: *You always protect me. But you can't do it alone.*

He steadied on that.

Another voice came, older than the dragon, weight like tide. *Beware those who name too easily.*

Familiar but still foreign.

The dragon turned and walked back into the light.

White took the world.

***

The Aethyrgate shimmered like a wound, faint and insistent, pulling Korvan forward one heavy step at a time. Each stride weighed more, as if the forest clung to bone.

Brusk walked at his side, steady as quarried stone, one broad flank bracing him. Armor scored and dented. Copper veining flickered with worn defiance.

Korvan looked back once: the clearing, the fractured monolith, ash spiraling slow.

He left changed.

Pressure coiled his chest, collapsed breath and shape, then released. Fresh air rushed in. Crisp. Real.

The Ritual Atrium opened.

Rune-etched stones glowed softly underfoot. Overhead, a stained-glass dome held constellations in brass and crystal, burning a silent welcome.

His knees buckled. Brusk shouldered him upright with a grunt.

Sweat. Copper. The cold tang of Aethyrglass. Magic thrummed through the fortress.

The Aethyrguard stood in a circle: Champions, Arcanists, Knights. Deep blue and black, silver trim, sunbursts bright.

They watched with a held respect.

Most had trained since childhood, heirs of houses and domes, oaths taught with letters. Korvan came from dirt, from silence in another man's rage.

He had passed.

The only one from his group.

His Soulmarks, once radiant, lay faint now. Alive and fragile but utterly spent.

He straightened. He would not fall here.

A clear voice carried. "Korvan, of House Aric."

The name cut wrong. A father's scar pretending to be a banner.

Across the chamber stood a battlemage in immaculate black, onyx braids neat over one shoulder, gaze steady. "Welcome," she said. "To the Aethyrguard."

Relief ran hot and mean. His legs threatened to fold. Brusk edged close.

Korvan caught his reflection in the polished blacksteel pillar. He still looked eighteen, tall, wiry from lean years. His chestnut hair refused to be tied. His face had already paid its tithe: a bent nose, square jaw. The cloak around his shoulders fit too neatly, borrowed from a better-fed life.

His eyes were older. They still held the grey of dawn, but behind something else burned there, something new. A stubborn, quiet flame that refused surrender.

He touched the Soulmarks at his shoulder. Lines thrummed under skin like Brusk's but far deeper and he felt it throughout his body. It was sacred. But also unfinished.

The Trial had ended.

His true fight had only begun.

Chapter 2: Brothers

Five years earlier...

Korvan's hands were rough from chores, splintered and cold. Working beside Caelen, he barely felt them. Each nail he drove, each brace he set, each knot he tied carried more than labor. It carried defiance in the shape of a glider.

Caelen sat cross-legged, fingers on frayed rope, tongue caught between his teeth. Ten, and tying each knot as if his weight already hung from it. For him, it did.

Korvan steadied his brother's hands, his larger fingers guiding the smaller, paler ones. "Here. Like this," he murmured. "Tight enough to hold but loose enough to breathe."

Silver hair tossed in the ocean wind; Caelen's cheeks flushed. "You always make it seem easy, Korv."

Nothing came easy. At thirteen, Korvan's shoulders carried their father's temper and the ache their mother left behind. Caelen didn't see it because Korvan kept it from him.

"It's easy because I already made the mistakes," he said, tugging canvas straight. "You get to learn from mine."

Caelen laughed a bright, quick noise. The hitch followed; shoulders rose too fast.

"Maybe we rest," Korvan said, hand light on his shoulder. His chest tightened.

Caelen shook his head, eyes steady and hopeful. "No. We're close, Korv. Please. Just a little longer. I want to see it fly."

He weighed the clockwork of his brother's lungs against the wind's promise. The light in those eyes, all stubborn and alive, deserved its chance. This was the closest they'd ever come.

He nodded, and they tied the last knot.

The glider was patchwork: driftwood bones, scavenged canvas, rope that didn't match. Held by little more than gumption and will. But it might fly.

They carried it to the bluff. The sea breathed below. Wind tugged cloaks and rattled canvas like a promise. Korvan steadied the frame and glanced at Caelen, whose wide eyes shone brighter than surf.

"You ready to fly, Little Hawk?" he asked.

Caelen nodded, his slight frame taut with anticipation. "You should fly it, Korv. You built most of it."

Korvan shook his head. "No way. Your dream. Your flight."

A heartbeat of hesitation, then Caelen gripped the bars. Excitement, not fear.

Korvan filled his lungs with salt and sun-warmed wood. "Ready?"

"Ready."

Korvan ran.

Wind caught the canvas. The frame lifted. Caelen rose, weightless. Korvan's feet hammered grass, heart leaping to follow.

It flew.

For that bright instant their father's rage, their mother's absence, even Caelen's sickness fell away. Caelen's laughter lifted the sky and the world was right. Korvan let himself smile.

Then the nose tipped.

"Caelen!"

Wind shifted and the canvas bucked. Gravity took its due.

Caelen hit and rolled. The glider fractured around him. Splinters scored his arms. A cut opened at the knee; bright blood ran.

Korvan was already moving.

"Caelen!" Breath burned his throat. His pulse blurred the world.

He slid to his knees. Caelen pushed upright, dirt-smudged, eyes wide. And laughing.

"I flew, Korv," he said, full of wonder. "Did you see? I really flew."

Relief washed over Korvan as he pulled him close.

"Yes," he said, voice raw. "You flew, Little Hawk."

By the time they carried the wreck home, the wind had softened. The splintered frame tapped Korvan's shoulder every few steps, off-beat. Caelen kept close, knee bandaged, pride warm beneath the bruises.

Their cottage hunched at the Commons' edge: salt-worn beams, a leaning porch, rust veining the chimney. Smoke curled from the flue, thick and acrid.

Smoke meant one thing. Varnrik was home.

Korvan paused at the door. The glider's weight shifted wrong. Caelen's fingers found his, small and tight.

"Will he be mad?" Caelen whispered.

"When isn't he mad... but I'll take it," Korvan said.

They went in.

Heat and sour drink pressed over scorched food. Varnrik slouched near the hearth, bottle slack in one hand. Shoulders that once filled doorways had caved. Gray threaded his hair the way rust threads old chain.

Red-rimmed eyes found the broken frame. "What's this?"

Caelen flinched. Korvan stepped first, set the glider between them like a wall. "It's mine. We built it from scrap. I wanted to see if it would fly."

Varnrik's jaw ticked. "Yours."

"It didn't cost anything."

The lie burned. Caelen couldn't afford truth.

Varnrik rose slow, menace uncoiling. "A man's decision at thirteen?" Drink thickened the words. "You waste food money on trash while your brother's sick?"

Caelen edged forward. "Papa, it didn't—"

The hand came fast, an iron vice clamped on Caelen's shoulder. Not a strike but close enough.

"Quiet," Varnrik said, voice low and broken.

Korvan moved on instinct, sliding between them. "Don't touch him. It was my idea. I built it. I brought it home."

A memory echoed in Korvan's head. *Hold the line.*

And he would. Even against his father. Especially to protect Caelen.

Varnrik's stare glassed. Anger found a deeper vein.

"Your fault," he whispered. "Your mother gave everything to you, and you drag us under."

His chin flicked toward Caelen. "He rots because of you."

The words cut deeper than the bottle.

"You stole her spark," Varnrik said. "You left him sick and hollow."

Eyes up, breath tight.

"Then punish me," Korvan said, steady.

"Leave Caelen alone."

Grief braided to rage until they wore the same face.

"So be it."

The backhand landed heavy. Cartilage clicked in Korvan's nose; copper filled his mouth. A body shot found rib, breath-stealing. A cross raked the ear so sound snapped white. He angled his stance, keeping Caelen behind him, feet set to stay between.

"Stop!" Caelen cried.

Korvan shook his head once. Stay.

The blows kept rhythm; the words kept edges. Then Varnrik sagged back into the chair. "Useless," he muttered, bottle drooping.

Korvan straightened in pieces. Blood tasted like coins. Caelen reached him, tears bright on a too-pale face.

"I'm sorry," Korvan said, rough.

Caelen shook his head and wrapped him in small arms. "Don't. You always protect me."

However far their father fell, whatever the world asked, this he could answer.

Night slid in. Hearth-light turned his bruises, both the old and the new, oil-dark. Varnrik snored by the fire. The broken glider leaned in the corner, a wing that would never fly.

At the cot, Korvan pressed a damp cloth to his darkening ribs. He kept his face easy while Caelen watched.

"Korv," Caelen whispered. "You shouldn't have done that."

Korvan glanced over. Caelen looked smaller than normal in the bed, eyes ringed, skin drawn tight over bone.

"That's what big brothers do," he said.

"You always do," Caelen coughed, wet and worrying. Korvan's gut pulled tight. "Even when he's not drinking. You always stand in front of me."

"That's what I do," Korvan said. "I can bear it." He believed it, but he hated it too. Hated that he had to protect him.

Caelen's mouth trembled. "Why are you stronger? Why do I get tired and you don't?"

"I don't know," Korvan said.

Their mother burned bright at the end; something passed through and left them uneven. Korvan gaining an aptitude for magic that made him special. If he'd ever had the chance to work with it. It left Caelen sick, something inside him twisted and broken, something no healer ever could figure out.

"But I'll find out." Korvan forced his intent into the words, swearing it.

"I don't want you to fix me," Caelen whispered. "I want you to be happy, like when Mom was still here, before dad changed."

That slipped past Korvan's armor. He drew him close and held on.

"You make me happy," he said. "And when I'm strong, nothing will touch you. Not him. Not this. Not the world."

Caelen's breathing evened. Sleep smoothed the worry from his brow.

Korvan watched embers dull. The ache in his jaw had an old name and a new map. His vow burned hotter than any of the bruises.

Present…

Brusk's slow breathing grounded him at the foot of the cot.

Warmth moved under Korvan's ribs through the bond. *Brusk here.*

Leather, oiled metal, the ache of the Initiate's Trial. The echo clung like smoke from a long-dead fire.

Yeah, you flew, he thought, Caelen's laughter bright and close.

He turned a sliver of driftwood between his fingers, the last fragment of the glider he kept. Season after season, trial after trial, it rode in his satchel. Age had polished it smooth. More memory than wood now.

The new uniform felt foreign: storm-blue linen too clean, too fine; the bronze pin heavy at his chest. A symbol earned without mercy. In its shine he saw Caelen's smile.

And he heard her voice again, gentle, and final. Keep him safe.

She had whispered it; he swore back with a split lip and blood on his tongue. He swore after each bruise, each night of shaking hands, each silence pressed into bone.

He slid the driftwood into the hidden pocket over his heart. A small, hard promise under bone. A place no one would find.

Outside, bells chimed the third hour past dawn, their voices drifting over Cael'Lumar's rooftops like thin rain. In the Arc-Tower Barracks of the Fourth Ring, Initiates drilled and sparred and recited oaths. Duty threaded the stone halls and woke the city.

Korvan breathed deep. One count in. One count out. Lungs filled steady.

Caelen lived. Still fought.

Whatever The Beyond had shown, whatever came next, Korvan held the line. He would be the shield. He would become what he promised Caelen he would be.

Maybe, someday, he would look back with shoulders unburdened and say, with pride, *Yeah. We both flew.*

Chapter 3: The Initiate's Path

The bells tolled before dawn. Mortar rattled in the Arc-Tower Barracks of Cael'Lumar's Fourth Ring. Cots creaked. Blue cloaks lifted. Slit windows held a stripe of gray.

Korvan rose as the world found its edges. Soulmarks along his arms and shoulder glowed faint, pale runes swirling with his breath. A quiet reminder of how near the Trial had cut.

At the foot of the cot, Brusk heaved a warm breath. Copper veins across his hide pulsed steady. Hairline cracks still laddered the club of his tail. The Bulwark blinked slow, unbothered.

Korvan smoothed a hand over the ridged brow.

"Let's survive this too."

We will. Brusk responded as heat pressed beneath Korvan's ribs through the bond.

The corridor thickened with Initiates. Buckles cinched. Laces bit. No time for jokes. The line moved as one body toward the outer yards, nerves bridled. Down here there were war vaults, beast holds, guardian runes sunk deep in old stone. The place where the Aethyrguard shaped its future ranks.

The Beyond Trial proved his courage and potential. Today was the Assessment. This would decide the rest. Guard the Aethyrgate beneath the Crown Keep. Patrol the Crescent's cities. Bond as Tamers or take the necessary work no song remembers.

The yard opened under a slate sky. Statues of past Champions ringed the dirt, rain-chewed eyes set on nothing and everything. Real Champions stood beyond them: Battlemages and Knights in gold- or silver-trimmed cloaks, faces precise and poised.

Korvan took a place drawing a steadying breath. Brusk rumbled in at his flank like a wall that could walk. Eyes slid toward him. Some curious others cutting.

Word had already spread: he alone had passed the Beyond Trial. But he'd learned what that meant, the Trial was for those who did not have a sponsor or a legacy. It was for the untested to prove their worth. Almost no one ever did. Especially not an outsider with no House and no coin.

He stood here on the only rights that mattered—his bond and the Aethyr that hummed in marrow.

A tall, severe woman stepped forward. Metallic rings braided into her tight warrior's plaits. Her voice cracked.

"Step forward when your name is called."

Initiates were measured: balance, strikes, spell-shaping, bond control. The Academy boy who had trembled at the Aethyrgate trembled again; his Veyrkin turned its head and refused him. A coastal girl moved like water over stone; her bond answered with merciless clarity.

"Bren Halver—Bladesworn."

A ripple of approval. Bladesworn anchored lines and broke charges. When civilians needed a wall, they were there. Rok, Bren's Bulwark, made the point for him. Bulwarks took the hit so others lived; Bladesworn learned to breathe inside that weight and drive it back.

"Sera Mylen—Aethyrward."

A Quieter respect. Aethyrwards mended bodies and kept wardlines from collapsing while the fight still burned. Fennik, her foxlike mender, glowed at her heel, runes breathing silver warmth. With a touch and an oath, Sera could knit flesh and hold a failing sigil for one minute longer. One minute often decided a life.

"Thalen Ryst—Gloamblade."

An approving hush. Gloamblades cut threats before they grew teeth. His Veyrkin is a panther-like Shadebound. Midnight's eyes moved along the crowd, assessing everything. Thalen did not grandstand; he didn't need it. He drew clean geometry with his stance. His name was famous. House Ryst had their hands in everything, including the Aethyrguard.

"Ryn Dacre—Veilwarden."

"Javek Dacre—Veilwarden."

A sharp stir came from the crowd. Twins who moved like mirrors until choice forked them. Veilwardens read the world's skin, the seam-lines where The Beyond pressed thin. Ryn worked with a bright-gazed kite, a Seerbound that saw danger across a maze of alleys. Javek partnered a peregrine-fast falcon, a Pathcarver that cut clean lanes through wind and ward to find the opening no map showed.

Then:

"Korvan Aric, son of Varnrik."

A House that was no House. He stepped anyway. His heart calm, surprising himself.

Drills came first. He moved through them controlled and exact. Pain flared in his ribs with each pivot, a raw echo from the Ironmarked beast from the Beyond, but he did not falter. His body spoke this language: street fights and survival, lessons he shouldn't have had to learn.

Next was spell-shaping. Korvan called Auryn's Edge. Pressure gathered from Aethyr into his Fyrstrand, then burned along through his Soulmark. A radiant-glaive bloomed, razor-thin, but alive. He cut through the forms. On a tight turn the haft bit his palm; blood slicked his grip. He kept the line. Quills scratched. Judges watched, unread.

Last was the bond trial.

Brusk stepped into the ring. A granite golem woke with a grind of clockwork park and an Aethyrglass core. Korvan reached through the bond and drew from Brusk's modest reserve, shaping Halo Veil, a golden shield.

The construct hammered its arms slow yet relentless. Each impact rattled bone and pressed air from sore lungs. Stone spalled; a shard nicked his cheek and warm blood tracked along his jaw. Halo Veil thinned to honey at center.

The golem adapted, high feint, low hammer, testing their timing. Korvan slid his back foot a hand-width, breath riding the blow. The second strike came late by design; he let it glance, reset the arc, and met the third with full force.

"Hold the line," he muttered for himself.

Now. Brusk surged. The clubbed tail thudded once. The bond flared bright. Together they caught the next hit and rolled the weight away. Stone burst to dust and sparks of dying rune-fire. Grit salted his tongue. The yard smelled of hot rock and something new to Korvan, but distinctly arcane as the core bled power.

Breath returned in pieces. He flexed his hands. Blood winked in the grooves at his thumbs. The cheek cut ticked with each heartbeat.

Their was a moment of silence followed by the rapid scratching of quill on parchment.

Footsteps approached and a woman stopped before him.

Tall, at eye level with Korvan, and he was nearly a head taller than most. She was Midnight-haired. She held an aura of controlled strength. Posture as rigid as true steel. Eyes like set glass, sharp and measuring. Her armor was adorned with golden filigree and her authority was without question.

This was Eris Vale. The Gilded Knight. Hero of the Aethyrguard.

"One final measure," she said, calm and clear. "Why are you here?"

Earlier Initiates had mumbled legacy and rank, a desire to be the best, to prove themselves.

Korvan straightened. Every bruise ached. Ribs cinched. Caelen's fragile smile rose to him in an exhausted, unbroken memory. His mother's face dimmed with the spark she had given. His father's voice scraped an old wound. He rolled his shoulders a hair.

"To protect what I love," he said, voice low but solid. "Even if no one else will."

The silence that weighs a thing followed his words.

Eris tilted her head a fraction, then gave the smallest nod. Not praise. Acknowledgment. Whispers stirred. Too raw. Too unorthodox. Hard to file. Some jaws tightened.

The verdict came.

"Korvan Aric," Eris said, her voice adopting a tone that brooked no disagreement, "you are assigned to the path of the Aethyrbound."

Gasps rippled the line. The rarest path. Reserved solely for those born-attuned who could work the Disciplines on instinct and had immense potential Pride and dread turned together in his chest.

"Yes, Battlemage."

Brusk's tail thudded once—approval, solid as the stones they stood upon. Behind him someone scoffed, a smear of fear and envy.

Names rolled on.

"Kes Mora—Grounds Detail."

"Pellan Soot—Kitchens."

"Archivist's Clerk—Dome Two."

More names were called to the infirmary wing, to launderers, to kitchen hands. Bandages did not fold themselves. Pots did not clean themselves, and meals didn't magically appear.

All positions were important. While being bonded meant you had an affinity to work with the Aethyr, it didn't imply you could fight with it. Few could fight with their Veyrkin, let alone weave their magic and swing a blade too. Those chosen for such roles were already among the most elite of the citizens.

Cael'Lumar ran because someone hauled water, and someone counted arrows. The Aethyrguard held because a hundred kinds of labor met in one order, to serve one purpose.

Korvan did not turn. The path had opened. He stepped onto it and began the Initiate's path.

Chapter 4: The Weight of Routine

Korvan stood in the Arc-Barracks corridor of the Fourth Ring, spine straight, Brusk at his side sold as stone. Dawn poured through the clerestory, gold and shadow banding the darkstone floor. His Soulmarks ached from the Assessment. It was more a thrum than pain.

Soft footsteps drew his attention down the hall.

Battlemage Eris Vale stepped from the far arch, posture forged from dusksteel and years of drills. Presence moved before her like a blade unsheathed. Kaelith, the golden-winged pegasus, followed in spectral silence.

Korvan bowed his head. "Battlemage Vale."

"Korvan. Brusk." A single nod, curt, but kind.

Brusk dipped his tusked head, rumble low in his plated chest. He mirrored Korvan's tension.

"Today," Eris said, voice clipped and clear, "you begin your life as an Aethyrbound."

"Few walk this path. Fewer finish it." Her gaze held his, sharp the frost cuts across glass. "You will train and you will be spent: spell work, weapons, beast bonds, endurance, Beyond navigation, terrain, veil craft, our history, and doctrine. You will work alone when required. Your bond must become instinct, not based only on instruction."

She opened a palm to the halls. "This is your home now her within the Fourth Ring. The Arc-Tower Barracks are your quarters. War Vaults for bladework. Vaulted Chambers for theory. Beast-holdings for bond drills. The Sealed Hall is off-limits."

She handed him a brass slate, script etched neat:

Dawnsday—Soulmark stabilization, Fyrstrand breathwork

Moonsday—Weapon forms, paired drills

Ironday—Bond sync, beast harmonics

Forgesday—Discipline spellcasting

Stormsday—Terrain movement, flanking maneuvers

Veilsday—Rift exposure, illusion combat

Loresday—Magical theory, beast taxonomy

Restday—Recovery, journaling, duels, silence

"This training will shape you," Eris said, voice a fraction softer. "Or break you. What you become here is less strength than will."

Her eyes softened, "Fail with dignity Aric. Learn."

She turned and was gone.

Korvan let out a long breath. One thread in his shoulders eased.

Brusk stirred. *We no quit.*

A thin smile. "No. We won't."

They stepped into the morning light of the Fourth Ring toward iron, fire, and promise.

***

The week opened like the edge of a new blade, sharp and un-kind.

Dawnsday: under amberstone pillars, instructors paced with burnished staves. Korvan's Fyrstrand woke slow, sunlight behind cloud. Brusk's calm steadied him. His Veyrkin's pulse gave him a metronome to calm to and each breath worked wonders.

Moonsday hammered the War Vaults. Steel spoke in grueling repetition. Clean weight, clean timing, clean intent. Paired forms clicked like clockwork gears. Blades clattered. Beasts lunged. Corrections cracked from the instructors until voices rasped and muscles shook.

Eris always watched like a hawk. Kaelith stood quiet at her flank, wings folded neat.

Occasionally her voice would utter one word, "Again."

To Korvan's right, a lean Initiate flowed with panther precision. His Veyrkin, a shadow-cat with ember eyes, threaded his steps.

"Thalen Ryst," someone breathed. "Old money."

Another said. "More than that, his family built these halls."

Korvan studied the lines Thalen made: all clean timing and dangerous elegance. He was polished above all

In a pause Thalen caught his look. "Hope you last the week, common-born."

Korvan didn't blink. "I didn't realize you were so worried about me."

The smirk slipped, a fraction.

Further down, laughter lifted.

Sera Mylen knelt beside a fox-like Veyrkin, it was more magic than beast. She called him Fennik, red-furred, bright-eyed, and runes that glow with each exhale. A Mender. The rarest Veyrkin type.

She didn't flaunt him, she just moved with a comfortable grace, her hand to his fur, making his ears flick in answer. A true synergy. She caught Korvan's gaze and offered a grin that steadied anyone who saw it.

"Don't mind Thalen," she murmured as she passed. "He already thinks he runs the Fifth Ring."

At the yard's edge a broad-shouldered Initiate stumbled. Korvan caught his arm.

"Thanks!" the boy huffed. "I'm Bren. That's Rok."

The bear-built Bulwark chuffed, bumping Korvan's sleeve with an armored snout.

Instructors hunted flaws without mercy. Champion Torvin Kael gave corrections like lashes. His bronze-horned Pathcarver stared molten and unblinking. Spellring trials followed. Arcanist Mareth drifted like smoke, an owl blinking slow from his shoulder. Each failure earned a neat scratch of his quill.

By Ironday's close Korvan's thoughts blurred with fatigue. Then the bond trial.

He stepped inside the warded circle. Eris a cold weight at his back, Brusk square before him.

Aethyrglass-tipped arrows launched. Korvan raised his hand, breath locked to Brusk's.

The first shield shattered.

"Again," Eris demanded.

He closed his eyes. He looked inward past the pain, past his pride. He found Brusk's heartbeat within him, guiding him deeper. Finally he came that wellspring of power within his Fyrstrand.

He opened his eyes and focused, the Halo Veil erupted from his hand a brilliant dome that caused others to shield their eyes from the light.

The second shield held. Ten full seconds. Arrows sparked to ash against the golden barrier.

When his knees buckled, the barrier thinned.

He rose slow, lungs sawing, and let himself a small, true smile.

He had held, one of the few who could make a shield, and his held the longest.

***

Night settled on the Arc-Tower dorms. Bunks lined stone alcoves like teeth. Armor settled to hooks with ritual sounds. Soulmarks dimmed. Someone whispered to the Twin Pantheon, Kael'Thir for memory, Atheris for renewal.

Korvan sat on the cot's edge, boots still on.

Brusk rested beyond the aethyr-woven gate, glyphs faint along the bars. The bond hummed low, grounding as wind in a mountain pass.

He flexed his hands. Marks along his forearms pulsed.

"Tomorrow's Stormsday," Bren muttered. "Trees or cliffs first?"

Sera's voice, muffled, bright: "If we're lucky, we'll get both."

Laughter rippled. Even Thalen let a breath through.

Korvan stayed quiet. He watched the lines faint at his wrists, inked in light, still burning under skin.

Aethyrbound.

That was the name. Spellcraft and solitude. Weight and watch. A role never promised to gutter-born boys.

He lay back.

Above, an illusion dome scattered stars, set by some patient Reservoir. Nearly beautiful.

A question slid behind his ribs like flint.

A voice had spoken in The Beyond.

Name me.

He hadn't answered. The words tugged still. A vow he hadn't made, already carried.

Floorboards clicked. Brusk stirred. Two molten eyes opened.

Korvan worry lots, the bond murmured.

A breath that almost became a laugh. "I know."

He reached through the bars. Brusk pressed brow to palm, hide and skin meeting with quiet certainty.

"Do you think I can do this?"

The tail thudded once, slow, final. *Korvan do anything.*

The sound snagged in his throat. Something inside settled. That certainty felt like a lifeline.

Beyond the windows, Cael'Lumar glimmered. Lanterns like stars. Watchful.

He pictured Caelen curled beneath threadbare blankets. He had sworn to return changed. Strong enough. Worthy. Able to save them both.

I won't fail him. Korvan knew it was his purpose. He had to be strong for the brother that couldn't be.

A few deep breaths steadied his mind. The fire in him calmed.

Tomorrow would come. Another trial and another step toward his goal.

Brusk breathed in the dark, a slow and certain sound.

Sleep rose.

Korvan let it take him.

***

The light shifted.

Stars bled across a sea of glass.

He stood in a void. No sky. No floor. Only a shimmering reflection. Overwhelming silence. Light rippled underfoot.

A voice broke the stillness that felt threaded with age.

You are not alone.

He spun but found nothing.

Only silver and gold drifting like fireflies in the night.

A warmth he had never experienced and somehow remembered burned within him, it was foreign but also right.

When you fear... remember the flame within.

He tried to answer. His mouth would not move. Words caught behind years of practiced silence.

Light folded around him, lacing his hands, dousing ache, lifting bruise from bone. Recognition, not comfort.

Name me... when you've earned me.

Softer, but edged with iron.

He gasped, and the world cracked.

***

Korvan jolted upright. His breath ragged bursts, chest tight and skin damp.

His eyes adjusted to the stone ceiling. Night pressing against the glass of the barracks.

Brusk shifted beyond the gate, eyes ember-soft. *Bad dream?*

He scrubbed his face. The sting in his eyes wasn't only tiredness. "I... I don't know."

On the shelf, the letter sat unopened. Wax seal whole.

He looked to the lantern over his bed. Its light held steady.

"Tomorrow," he said, firmer.

He eased down, ribcage rising slow, breath finding the count again. Let the dark take him once more.

Chapter 5: Shadows of Home

The sun had only begun to crawl over the eastern cliffs when Korvan rose. He'd chased sleep, but it was a ghost that never settled. A tired frustration coiled under his ribs, tight and unshakable.

The letter waited on the shelf above his cot, sealed in dark-blue wax. Unbroken. Untouched. It had arrived the morning after the Trial and haunted the air like smoke ever since.

Brusk shifted beside the cot, stone plates rasping. Warmth pressed under Korvan's sternum. *Read it.*

"I have to," Korvan said.

His fingers felt thick. The seal snapped like bone. Paper bit his fingertip; a bead of red welled and ran. Heavy stock, self-important and wasteful. His father's taste.

Korvan,

Your place is here. Your brother needs you. He grows weaker, and still you chase glory in the city while he withers. What good is an oath to strangers if your family crumbles? I cannot keep paying the healers. You will send coin, or you will return. I will not starve for your foolish dreams.

Varnrik

His jaw locked until pain throbbed in his teeth. Each word a chain, dragging him back to narrow halls and colder nights. Back to that house. Back to that man.

Your place is here.

His hands trembled. Then he saw the second hand in the margin. Light strokes, uneven, but all too familiar.

Kor... Don't worry. I'm still smiling. I know you'll be great! Don't let him pull you back. You just be happy. That's all I want. I'm proud of you.

A drawing was beneath the script, crooked and earnest: two boys on a hill, a glider caught by wind between them.

Korvan pressed a hand to his mouth. One tear slipped free, hot, and defiant.

Gravel rolled warm along the bond. *Family break you?*

"Yeah, they already did," he whispered.

The paper shook. He tore Varnrik's letter down the spine with careful cruelty. Caelen's margin he folded small and slid into the hidden pocket over his heart.

"I won't go back, I'll get Caelen out, but I can't go back." he said.

Brusk lowered his tusked head and nudged Korvan's thigh. His tail thudded once. *We go Forward.*

***

The first bell rang across the Vaults, sharp and final.

Korvan stood. Night slid from his skin like old ash. His pulse found a slower, harder count.

I will be stronger. For Caelen. For me.

The yard churned with steam and breath. Cloaks clung to backs; boots sank in torn earth. Korvan's chest heaved, but the rhythm steadied to Brusk's presence at his side.

Knight Alrik raised a gauntleted hand. The run stopped. One whistle, one gesture, the Initiate line snapped into place.

"You want to command a Veyrkin?" There was iron in his tone. "Understand what you bonded with."

A Seerbound perched on his shoulder, glass-eyed, blinking wrong.

"The Veyrkin are born of the Aethyr, they aren't just animals or livestock. That is a Stoneback Urson." He gestured at Bren's Veyrkin Rok. "Another of you has a Mosscrag Taurhorn. You might mistake them for a Bear or an elk, but that would be your doom."

Knight Alrik continued. "Veyrkin are much more than pets, more than mounts. More than any tool. They are your partners; they are your strength. If you're lucky, they are your truest friend."

He halted before a girl with a jackal-lean Veyrkin, its tongue bobbed, and a small puddle had formed. A smile spread across the Knight's face.

"There are eight Aspects. They define how they fight, where they move, what they offer. Bulwark shields the line, takes the hit, keeps others breathing. Howler hits came hard and fast. Mender heals; the only type that can do so. Wyrdkin: able to bend the disciplines. Reservoirs are named for what they are, a reservoir of magic. Seerbound: eyes beyond just sight; senses what you miss, hear what you don't. Pathcarver: masters of movement; and able to run for days on end. Shadebound: stealth and illusion, you look away, and they are gone."

Silence drew tight as a bowstring.

"Aspect isn't a choice. The Aethyr cast them that way, and they never change. The Beyond molded them that way."

Korvan glanced at Brusk. He was a Bulwark through and through a protector first.

Alrik moved on. "Another truth: Prestige." He stopped by Fennik, where red fur breathed rune-light. "Prestige tells how much the Aethyr poured into a Veyrkin's blood. It defines their power, legacy, and potential. The Prestige Tiers are: Verdant: common, loyal, entry tier; they bleed easy and obey without question. Iron-marked: stronger, often element-kissed, rarer, smarter. Obsidian: scarce and tricky; they know more than they should and have more raw power than most people. Starlit: elite; each carries a gift of one of the elements. You ask them to do things, you don't command. Mythborn," his eyes ticked toward the Vault towers ",are one of a kind. If you ever meet a Mythborn, hope you survive them."

A ripple moved the yard.

Alrik's gaze lingered on Korvan longer than courtesy allowed. Korvan gave him nothing back.

"Know your Veyrkin. Know their limits. Know your own." He turned, cloak snapping. "Now to spar with blade and beast. Show me the bonds you made were worth it."

***

Drills ended in a sprawl of panting limbs. Bruises bloomed dark. Korvan's shoulder throbbed from a bad tumble. Brusk wore a fresh nick on one tusk, a cost paid to catch a blow that should have been Korvan's.

Alrik lifted a hand. The yard tightened.

"You've shown how you fight," he said. "Now show what you are bonded with."

He unclipped a round of polished Aethyrglass, rune-etched at the rim.

"This is a cadence Lens. It shows what the Beyond poured into your beasts. More bands, higher Prestige. Battlemage Eris Vale reads the weave with naked sight; a few of you may learn in time, if you have that gift."

He let silence weigh on them. "Let the bond flare."

The Lens passed first over a pair of Verdant Howlers. A single bright ring formed, clean and shallow. "Verdant," Alrik said. Honest light flared, then faded.

Sera moved. Fennik stepped with her. Topaz rippled his flanks, whole and bright. Two bands resolved in the Lens with a thin elemental line strung between, like a cool pulse at the wrist.

"Ironmarked Mender," Alrik said. "Very Rare and sorely needed. Keep this one safe Initiate Mylen."

Bren followed, Rok thudding steady. Their flare came low, earth's beat. One ring, thicker than the Howlers.' "Verdant Bulwark," Alrik said. "Relatively common, but a lasting specimen."

Thalen entered smooth as smoke. Midnight slid with him, dusk in motion. Illusion curled at his boots. Two crisp bands cut the glass, one edge frayed where darkness tried to lie.

"Ironmarked, Shadebound," Alrik said, near a twitch. "A fierce companion, Initiate Ryst."

Thalen gave nothing. The cat blinked once, unimpressed.

The rest held. So did Korvan. Brusk planted deeper, weight gathering under Korvan's boots.

Alrik brought the Lens near. Two rings glowed marking Brusk as Ironmarked, steady as a drumbeat. Knight Alrik's eyes flicked from the glass to Korvan, as if listening for something the tool couldn't name.

Korvan's Soulmark flared beneath his sleeve, once, then twice. A second note answered under the bond.

He held still while faint bands began to form.

Alrik turned away, but his gaze lingered.

The bell rang, sharp and cold.

Korvan rolled one shoulder.

"Hold the line," he murmured.

Brusk answered with a thrum through the bond. *Always.*

Chapter 6: The Shape of Duty

Eris set them in formation as dawn split the horizon over the Sapphire Sea. Wind off the cliffs worried her cloak. Kaelith stood behind her, half glimmer and half shadow, a golden sentinel.

"Today," Eris said, voice cutting the haze, "you begin city-familiarization drills." No one moved. "If you think an Aethyrguard's duty ends at the walls, you're already lost. The city is more than stone and seals. Its people are its pulse. Its rings are its blood. You will know both. You will defend both."

She paced the line, testing for weakness. Kaelith matched every step without sound, eyes like mirrored flame. "You will memorize all five rings of Cael'Lumar. Where you sleep. Where you kneel. Where you eat. Sacred, all of it." Her voice dropped lower, nearly reverent. "But where you bleed is holy."

Korvan's Soulmark warmed. Something in him stirred, it felt like answering a promise.

They started in the First Ring at Lantern Harbor. Noise and tide braided into one: skyships lashed to iron pylons, sails dripping, fishmongers calling through steam, rigging popping overhead. Dockhands swung coils of brine-stained rope through alleys slick with morning dew. The Night Bazaar slept with one eye open, arc-lanterns blinking in the mist.

"Riot lines start here," Eris said, never slowing. "A cutpurse can start a riot in a worried community. You're not only aiming to stop thieves, you're aiming to keep the peace."

Korvan mapped turns and choke points as they walked. Brusk moved behind, hooves quiet on warped boards, presence steady as ballast.

By midday they passed through the Gate of the Forge into the Second Ring, along Artisan's Row. Aethyrglass lanterns spun color in blown whorls. Forges rang against the city's ribs. Steam hissed from vents under the cobbles. Sigil-ink signs flickered at the edge of sight.

"Artisan's Row is as critical to the city as the Harbor. All the goods transported from the harbor come from here. If I were an assailant or a saboteur, this is where I'd strike," Eris said, nodding to a balcony hung with glowing filaments. "If you lose the heart of the population, it's livelihood, you lose the ring. Mind the ward barriers, some of our strongest are here."

Korvan scanned each overhang. Each collapse point. The city shifted in his mind: both a haven and its mighty heartbeat.

In the Third Ring the streets climbed and the sky narrowed. Walkways crowned with crystal and rune linked spires. The Temple of the Twin Pantheon took the heart of a square. Mirrored towers for Atheris and Kael'Thir, the gods of Creation and Memory. Across from it, the Twilight Basilica swallowed light under dusk-glass domes. Scholars drifted from Dawnspire College; familiars trailed mist and sparks like whispers.

Eris stopped them at the Square of Ascendants.

"Here," harder now, "you face beasts from The Beyond. Spellfire can break loose, but worse, people lose their faith, they lose their trust. It'll make a crowd turn feral. Sometimes the very people you swore to protect will turn on you." She let it settle.

By late afternoon they climbed to the Fourth Ring. Granite halls stepped up in tiers. Aethyr conduits ran along the walls like lit veins. The Arc-Tower Barracks flanked one side. Opposite, a sealed dome shimmered behind layered wards, the Vault Beast Chambers. Korvan noticed that though most of the initiates had glistening beads dotting their arms and faces, they all struck a smile at their home.

Containment drills followed. Evac codes shouted hoarse. Barricades hauled. False officials shielded from staged threats.

"Our seat of power lives here," Eris said, nodding toward chained gates that hummed with restrained force, the Sealed Hall of Lost Bonds. "But power rots if it isn't tested. We cannot rot. I will not allow it. "

Korvan's legs burned. He kept moving behind Eris who refused to show even the slightest bit of fatigue.

At last, the Fifth Ring. Crown Keep sat above the city, the way a monarch gazes out at their kingdom, with naught but authority and regality.

Aethyrglass bridges arced between towers. The White Gallery spilled rainbows across long colonnades. The Mirrorview Promenade set the whole of Cael'Lumar beneath their feet. Beautiful the way cliffs are beautiful, majestic because they were dangerous.

Before them, the blackstone doors of the Throne Rotunda stayed shut.

"You bleed here last," Eris said, low and final. "If you must bleed at all."

Her voice continued softer, a tempered steel lining it. "The worst things try to break us here. The Beyond sends monsters. But men... men send traitors. If it comes to it, if our city were ever truly besieged, this is our ultimate defensive position. In the nearly two thousand years our city has been here, it has remained the pinnacle of the Crescent Continent. This citadel has never been breached. It will not be so long as I draw breath."

She paused and took all their measure. Breaths came ragged, initiates swayed slightly and her eyes fell somewhere between Korvan and Thalen. Korvan turned to look at Thalen as Eris continued.

"But I will not be here forever, and I expect one of you to take my place." A smile spread wide on her face, "Eventually."

Eris dismissed them to return to the Barracks. She continued inside for a meeting she had with the High Warden and Archmage.

Korvan and Thalen looked at each other again, brows damp and legs twitching from exertion.

Neither could tell who she was talking to.

***

By nightfall Korvan's body screamed under his armor. Muscles throbbed. Breath scraped through lungs that had carried dust all day. He stood anyway. Maps burned behind his eyes. Routes, choke points, sacred places set by memory. Cael'Lumar was a massive city, he realized they'd only walked a small portion of it and it still took the entire day.

He stood.

Brusk pressed to his flank, warm and immovable as always. *We stand.*

"We stand." Korvan said.

Far below, dusk bells rolled the city. It's harbor, forges, temples, vault, spire. Life was carved into the stones. It was alive. Every clockwork machine, ever aethyr lamp, every child chasing gulls in the streets. It all had a purpose. To make the city stronger.

It found him as he looked at the city. A pressure deeper than the bond he shared with Brusk. A latch giving in a place he had never named, as if a missing piece remembered its way home. He glanced along the line of his comrades. Sera wiped sweat from her brow. Bren fixed a vambrace. Thalen kept his mask tight. The White Gallery bled spelllight; a soft aurora moved high mirrored on the twilight clouds.

Korvan felt that something watched him, curious and without malice. His Soulmark kicked once beneath the collarbone, sharp and sudden.

He shivered.

Brusk's ears twitched and settled. Whatever moved passed like breath on a mirror.

He left the bridge without a backward glance. The city breathed under him, unaware of his promise.

***

The following morning bit harder than any of the recent days. His steel was heavier. The air tasted thinner.

Korvan had favored the reach of a glaive, until the last couple of years he had been short, and liked the reach of a polearm. He didn't have to fight a lot, but he used a scythe on crops enough that a glaive felt second nature when he had to fight his first wild Veyrkin before he found Brusk. After finding Brusk it only made it easier and more sense to use a weapon with reach. The fact that Korvan gained over a foot and a half didn't hurt.

But swordwork came first. Discipline before instinct the instructors insisted. He ran forms until his shoulders trembled and fingers numbed on the grip. He did not pause. Ache cuts a cleaner edge, or so the instructors said.

Brusk paced the ring without much motion, anchor to Korvan's weather. The Bulwark would send a pulse and a quick, *Here*, to guide him.

Eris watched from shade. Kaelith wings flitted in the wind, dancing at the breeze's tug. When he staggered, Eris lifted one brow.

They moved to sparring. A shadow stepped through the ropes: Thalen Ryst. His poise was worn like a birthright. Midnight padded at his heel, black as poured ink, or maybe pitch. Her eyes catching violet light.

Thalen measured Korvan the way a blade studies bone. "Let's see if the Trial's little pet can dance," he said, low and precise.

Korvan answered with a defiant stance.

The bell rang.

Thalen moved like a man trained to draw first blood. He was measured and ruthless. Midnight traced the ring's edge; illusions slipped at the corners of sight. Korvan blocked high, then low.

Don't chase.

Breathe.

Hips.

Eris's lessons lived in his spine.

Feint.

Slip.

Thalen's shoulder hit a beat later. The mat caught Korvan's back. Air left in a rough grunt. Thalen leaned over, knee set to pin him.

Sweat cut his smirk thin. "That's all? I expected more from the Aethyr's golden prick."

Korvan bared his teeth and found breath around the rib ache. "I'm not beat yet. Again."

The second pass changed. Brusk held place, yet Korvan felt a steady pressure through the bond, scattered pieces falling into line. The Soulmark along Korvan's forearm warmed.

Thalen lunged, hunting the next opening. Korvan met him. A flicker ran under skin. Auryn's Edge ghosted bright for half a breath and was gone. Pressure gathered from Aethyr into Fyrstrand and slid down his palm with the exhale, turning steel aside. He stepped through the lane and drove his shoulder into Thalen's chest with bone-true weight.

Body.

Mat.

Thud.

Thalen was quicker, but Korvan was taller and wider, if only just.

A thin cheer cracked the yard. For a heartbeat Thalen's eyes went wide. Then anger tightened across his face.

He rose without a word. Midnight flowed with him, frustration made motion. The air tightened, as he pulled on his own Soulmark.

Eris lifted a hand. "Weapons of choice. One pass. Stop at the bell." The ring shrank.

Korvan opened his palm. Light gathered along bone and remembered itself as a blade. Auryn's Edge came bright and honest, a glaive of captured daylight. Heat ran his mark. The world narrowed and steadied.

Across from him, Thalen advanced with unhurried calm. He drew a longsword that carried its wealth in balance, not gems: It had a brushed guard, pitch leather wrap, and a discreet maker's mark at the ricasso. His stance settled into clean geometry. A duelist through and through.

The bell gave a piercing shriek.

Korvan measured his speed against Thalen's with reach, long arcs of the glaive meant to own the ring.

He rode each exhale, Force braided into every swing.

Thalen refused the lanes the glaive set. He folded inside the circle, feet cutting diagonals, shoulder passing light without letting it kiss cloth or his own blade. Midnight laid false lanes on the floor. A throat that wasn't there. A shin that was.

Korvan ignored ghosts and watched Thalen's hips, not his blade. Brusk weighted his feet to earth.

Anchoring, not chaining him down.

They touched once, then twice. Metal sang up Korvan's bones. Thalen's face stayed calm, but his eyes were wide and rapid.

Korvan shifted. Let the next breath carry more weight. The glaive flared; a bright crescent sheared shadow-mist thin. Gasps pricked the rail. Heat raced his forearm. The yard leaned a degree before it clicked true.

Thalen adapted without blinking. He killed distance and made it a knife fight at glaive range. Point kissed leather and was gone. Timing like a razor.

Korvan pressed. Two-beat feint high, third cut low. Force tucked under the edge like muscle. Thalen's heel kissed chalk. For a breath, the ring belonged to Korvan.

That was when Thalen stole it back. He let Auryn's Edge slide along his steel as if yielding the lane. The custom blade bit and held, something few blades could do against the magical weapon.

A turn of his wrist became a lever; the shaft collapsed. Midnight flicked a veil of darkness in Korvan's eyes. Thalen stepped through the gap the distraction bought and drew a straight line to collarbone.

Korvan turned late by a fraction.

The Point of Thalen's blade met Korvan's pulse.

Bell.

They held there, breathing.

Thalen looked down at the Glaive blade slightly pressed into his stomach.

A draw.

Sweat salted Korvan's mouth. Light trembled along the glaive and dimmed by degrees. Thalen eased back a step. No taunt. No smile. His gaze cut to the glaive, then to Korvan's hands. Something like acknowledgment clicked into place. It was spare but real.

Midnight's tail lashed and stilled. Brusk snorted, a heavy exhale that sounded like enough.

A thick hand thumped Korvan's back. Bren boomed, "You made him look like a piss-soaked mortal. Nobody moves him off his mark, let alone fights to a draw!"

Voices rose, surprise plain.

Eris didn't raise her voice; it cut clean anyway.

"Enough. This is the Aethyrguard, not a brawling pit." Her glance clicked from glaive to grip. "Aric, back hand too high on the recovery. Ryst, lose the flourish; take the angle without hesitation. Both of you did excellent."

A beat as she turned to the others. "If you have breath to cheer, you have breath to drill. Reset."

Benches scraped. Steel lifted. The line re-formed. Boots to chalk. Shoulders square. Eyes front. The murmur died. Sera slid to Korvan's flank and, before facing forward, let a quick, contained smile tilt, there and gone in a blink.

Blisters pricked under the callus ridge. A purple bloom gathered along his ribs. He flexed his wrist and felt where Thalen's blade had bitten.

He wondered if he'd bruised Thalen's stomach, or just his ego.

The expression Thalen shot at him said neither.

***

The mess hall hummed with warmth. Tin bowls knocked stone counters. Herbed root stew, spiced flatbread, roasted seabream. Steam climbed into the arches of the hall with the smells of coastal food.

Korvan sat across from Bren and Sera near the windows. His bowl sat half-finished. The broth carried pepper and lemon peel. Brusk dozed at his side, a snoring mountain. He'd seen his reflection in the dorm basin that morning, less hollow than when he arrived. Training and meals had begun to put him back into himself.

"If the food gets any better, I'm defecting to the kitchens," Bren said, grinning.

Sera arched a brow. "You're already bonded to a bear. Becoming one is a short walk."

"Rok would be proud to call me brother."

Korvan smiled then stilled as whispers moved down the benches.

"Another breach?"

"South of Lantern Harbor. A section of The Beyond swelling."

The words landed hot.

"a Breach in the Wards?" Bren asked.

"How rare is that?" Korvan asked.

Sera set her spoon down. "In the city? Extremely, I can remember once in my lifetime. Sometimes The Beyond heaves, like a wound under a bandage. Normal in places with high Veyrkin density, its just a serious amount of raw Aethyr. But Breaches are different. Usually something strong trying to get out of the Beyond into our plane. If the Wards thin too fast and there aren't enough Knights on rotation..."

"They send Initiates to contain it," Korvan said.

She nodded. He glanced at his forearms. Soulmarks still faint, still raw. The sovereign voice from the Trial lifted behind his eyes. Nothing like what he felt with Brusk, no push, only waiting.

Across the room, Thalen set his tin cup down hard enough to slosh broth. "If they send us to hold a breach," he said, "some of you won't come back." His stare found Korvan.

"We'll make sure everyone does," Korvan said.

Thalen paused. Just enough. His lip curled. He turned away.

"They've done it before?" Bren asked.

"It's how they separate those who survive from those who serve, that's what I heard one of the Knights say anyway," Sera said, voice low.

"If it comes, we face it," Korvan said.

We stand. Brusk added, a soft quake through the bond.

"Together," Korvan said.

***

Outside, stained-glass towers glowed against the night. Somewhere beyond white-ringed cliffs, the world heaved. They lingered in the warmth. Laughter followed them only to the doors.

Thalen stood alone under the arch to the training yard. Torchlight threw his shadow long across flagstone. Midnight curled at his feet, she was smoke given a spine. He kept his silence. So did the cat.

Above, the sky went indigo. Stars hid behind a slow drift of Aethyr haze. Cael'Lumar lay in glasslight and moving silhouettes. Far below, the sea whispered and kept its cold.

Thalen's jaw worked. Midnight's tail brushed his calf. Where it passed, shadow flared and narrowed.

"I should have ended it already," he muttered, voice like flint. "Or let one of Father's men handle it."

The cat blinked her eyes twin cuts of void. Heat lifted along Thalen's forearm. His Soulmark answered a distant echo.

Wind curled off the far wall. Too cold for summer. Midnight raised her head. Something stirred, but there was no shape to fix, no shadow to follow. Only a silence that folded thought inward.

Thalen turned from the wind and walked into the dark.

Midnight followed.

Chapter 7: Into the Breach

Korvan stood under a sky that didn't belong. Too many twilights layered at once. Runes pulsed underfoot, like breath moving through stone.

He knew this yard behind the old barracks, and knew it was changed. Wind stopped. Voices fell away.

He noticed there was just Thalen standing across the chalk.

He was alone with only the sound of exhales and the distance between them.

Thalen's voice broke the hush. "You think strength is deserved because you bled for it?"

Korvan's throat tightened. "I never asked for any of it."

"No, of course not," Thalen said, stepping in closer. "And yet you keep getting it. Power. The affirming looks. Praise." Wind curled where no trees stood; pale leaves drifted like ash.

"This isn't real," Korvan said.

"Sure it is," darker now. "Either way, you're afraid of me."

A hairline crack split the earth at Korvan's feet and widened. The light that poured out was blinding.

"I don't fear you," he said, and heard the lie, and the ground split more.

Thalen watched the fault open.

"We could have been brothers."

Korvan flinched.

Thalen continued, "You're a fraud, you don't deserve to be here. You don't deserve to be among us."

The line cut old bruises and the light twisted. Gold to red to smoke. The runes guttered.

Something vast stirred at the edge of his awareness. Both turned to look...

The bells did not chime. They screamed, high and sharp, knifing the stone halls.

Korvan jolted upright, lungs hauling air like he'd been drowning. Brusk was already up, plates sliding as he moved for the door.

Korvan didn't waste words. He moved trying to put the nightmare from his mind.

Practice leathers felt thin. Buckles were slow to fasten. Each motion a count toward impact.

The mess hall roared. Half-dressed Initiates slammed into ranks, armor half-fastened, eyes wide. Fear braided with fire.

Eris strode to the front, her armor shimmering with the dawn. Aethyrsteel cuirass. Midnight braids ringed in silver. Her presence drawn taught like a bow.

Three Veyrkin paced with her:

Kaelith, her pegasus, wings folded tight.

Talmar, the owl Reservoir , spelllight sliding over ageless feathers.

Coryn, dusk-coated Howler, prowling the edge like a four-legged storm.

Power danced between the three Veyrkin and Eris to such a potent degree that there was the illusion of the walls flexing as she walked past.

Eris didn't raise her voice. "Lantern Harbor. Outer Ring. A breach."

The words cracked the room.

"Three pulsing sites. Corrupted Veyrkin crossing over in droves. The Crown Guard are outmatched; Too many Knights and Champions are away on critical endeavors. Initiates..." Their title harkened all of them, "You will assist."

Cold slid through Korvan's gut. Eris never moved with all three bonds on display. He felt it with utter certainty.

This was no drill.

Around him: Sera's jaw set; Fennik's runes pulsed; Bren crushed the handle of his hammer with a white-knuckle grip white while Rok held steady. Thalen's smirk thinned, but Midnight paced with a glint in her eyes.

"A few Knights and a Champion will lead several of the squads. The largest group is with me, we will take the largest Breach," Eris said. "You will all support us. Bladesworn and Furybrands anchor our lines. The rest of you, your duty is the civilians: shield, extract, protect them. We must stall the breach until the ward stabilizes, and we can seal it."

Silence thickened and anxious eyes flitted.

Eris' eyes found Korvan. "Expect corrupted Verdant and Iron-marked tiers. Howlers, Shadebounds, Bulwarks of their own."

Kaelith shifted, the war horse eager for what comes next.

A young Knight shouldered forward in slate armor. "Aric, Ryst, Mylen, Halver, Dacre Twins. North wharf. Harbor Team Three, you are the tip of the Battlemage's spear."

"Yes, Knight." They responded in unison.

Korvan's jaw set. Brusk settled at his flank. And a warm readiness came over their bond steadying them.

Eris's last order came honed. "Prove your Soulmarks mean more than ink. Show that the Aethyrguard flourishes. Prove that you are damn fine warriors."

She turned. Her Veyrkin turned with her: gold, dusk, and spelllight flickering like war banners.

Today would draw blood. All the training they had been through led to moments like this.

The room surged with motion, galvanized by the Battlemage.

Straps cinched tight. Blades buckled. Breath quickened. Korvan stood as a heartbeat in the eye of it. He took a steadying breath, ignoring the slick of his palms as he worked more buckles, and adjusted his bracer. Heat threaded through his collar; his Soulmark thinned to a bright line. His Fyrstrand was full, he was as rested as he could be.

Sera touched his shoulder, pulling his attention back.

"North wharf is the worst of it. You ready?"

"Yeah, yeah I'm ready."

Bren tugged a strap tight. "Don't die, you prick." The easy tone cracked.

"You too, you big ass," Korvan said back with a wink.

Brusk snorted, warmth through the bond. *We hold.*

He didn't feel brave. But he knew he was ready, and from all their lessons he knew, ready was more important. But ready wasn't a feeling.

Ready was a choice.

He caught his satchel, heart ticking like a fuse, and went with the group.

In the courtyard light, his marks shimmered, pale flame threading his arms. Deep in his chest something cold pulled tight.

A presence waited past the breach. Wild and watchful. A hunger that didn't blink.

Korvan breathed once.

And he stepped into the dawn.

***

Lantern Harbor burned. Where fishwives had barked and dockhands slung rope, panic clawed the lanes now. Overturned stalls. Screams. Salt and smoke thick on the wind. Barrels rolled free, crushing ankles. Nets snagged legs like traps. A caged bird keened, high and thin, a ship's bell answered, harbor to harbor, as if the docks themselves cried alarm.

Korvan cleared the gate, and the world lurched. The Aethyr here ran thin, frayed like an old rope. Every breath tasted hollow, cracked at the edges. The ambient magic wasn't just weak, it was wrong. Twisted.

Above the roofs, a gash hung open in the sky, golden as the Aethyrgate beneath the Crown Keep but veined with Aethyrblight. Things crawled through it, many-eyed and slick with rot, their movements all wrong, like broken marionettes.

Ahead, He thought he name was…

Nessa dropped to her knees, her falcon-kin screeching in distress. Another initiate's sword clanged against stone, the sound too late, too desperate. Brusk pressed against Korvan's flank, his bulk hot as a forge. Korvan anchored to that heat, to the steady rise and fall of Brusk's breath, the weight of his blade.

Eris cut through the chaos like a blade through silk. Her cloak burned in Kaelith's light, the Starlit Pegasus hovering above, her wings casting a hush over the rift. The tear in the sky stuttered, as if hesitating.

"Initiates. Form on me." Her voice cut through the noise, and even in panic, they obeyed. Dockhands fell back behind the line of shields. Mothers dragged children into doorways, their hands shaking. Shutters slammed like drumbeats, a frantic rhythm marking the harbor's fear.

Korvan ran. Bren fell in at his shoulder, his face white but his jaw set. Sera crouched beside Fennik, her palm pressed to the fox-kin's chest, breathing him steady. Her eyes never left the breach, never wavered.

A brachyuran beast punched through the side of a warehouse, its carapace puffed with ichor, claws dripping black venom that sizzled where it splattered the cobbles.

"Form the line!" Eris barked. Shields locked into place, ragged but unbroken. Spear points lifted, trembling but ready.

Auryn's Edge answered Korvan's grip, the glaive flaring to life, humming with intention. The first beast came at them, and the impact shook the ground. Bren and Rok took the brunt of the charge, their shield and shoulder slamming into the earth. Korvan slid into the gap, Force riding his exhale as he cut. The glaive sheared through a leg, and ichor hissed as it sprayed his boot, the heat biting into his ankle. The shock of the blow ran up his arm, setting his molars humming. He stepped forward anyway because that was the only choice.

A shriek tore from the south. A second breach.

A howler burst from a shattered storefront, its mirror-shard scales flashing like broken glass. It lunged for a cluster of civilians, its jaws wide, its hunger palpable.

Korvan's gut turned to ice.

He and Brusk traded a glance, no words needed. Stone hooves hammered the cobbles as Brusk charged, slamming the beast sideways into a stack of crates. Wood exploded into splinters, and a board punched into the howler's hide with a wet, meaty pop. Korvan followed, his marks flaring as Auryn's Edge cut low. Tendon twanged, and the foreleg folded wrong. Brusk's tusks rang like a bell as they drove through flesh and glass-bone. The howler twisted, its shriek warping into a choke. Blood arced across the cobbles, dark and glistening. Glass-scales pinged off Brusk's plates like freezing rain. Korvan pinned the creature's skull, and the shudder of its death ran up his wrists as it crumbled to ash.

He staggered back, light trembling along his jaw. The horizon slipped, then steadied. Frost pain bloomed behind his eyes, and his ankle burned where the poison had kissed his skin. Brusk planted himself between Korvan and the wound in the sky, his plates flaring in warning.

Enough.

Kaelith struck like a sunstrike, her light searing through the crab-thing that had clawed its way into the harbor. The creature cracked under the assault, its carapace splitting like overripe fruit. Eris moved through the wreckage, her three Veyrkin a seamless extension of her will. The breach pulsed again, hungrier this time, its edges writhing like a living thing.

Korvan drove his legs forward, answering the call.

A quiet radiance swept over the harbor, a warmth rising from deep wells, moving over the stone like a tide. Talmar unfurled above them, his gold-silver feathers drifting down like offerings. Strength returned. The knife in Korvan's ribs dulled, the bright pain losing its teeth. The ice behind his eyes thawed a degree. His hands steadied.

Someone retched, then stood. An older Guard touched his brow in silent thanks and turned back to the fight.

Across the quay, the Initiates straightened. Some staggered. Some sobbed. But they stood. Clarity returned like the first light of dawn, fragile but unyielding.

Korvan exhaled hard and turned. Sera was already moving, Fennik glowing beneath her hands as she knelt beside Javek. His arm was gashed from shoulder to elbow, blood soaking through the fabric of his sleeve.

"Don't speak. Breathe. Let it take hold." Sera's voice was calm, her hands steady as silver thread-light braided from Fennik's runes to her palms, sealing the wound. Javek's trembling eased, and color crept back into his lips, slow but sure.

Korvan looked at his own hands. They were still shaking, but warm. Steady enough.

Brusk huffed steam, his tusks wet with ichor. *She buys time.*

"Let's spend it well," Korvan said.

Eris stood tall, her cloak was torn, but her eyes clear and un-yielding. Kaelith hovered above, her wings casting pale light over the devastation. Coryn paced the corpse-littered edge of the quay, his form low and grim. Talmar held the hush, his presence a balm against the chaos.

"You held," Eris said, her voice low and certain. "This was the first. Others will follow. Reform the lines."

Fear climbed Korvan's spine, cold and familiar. His thoughts turned to the Trial, Varnrik's porch, the silences that had tried to crack him open. He looked at Sera's steady hands, at Bren hauling an initiate upright, at Brusk, unshaken and immovable. Resolve tightened in his chest. He drew a breath, and it stung like winter air.

"We stand."

We hold, Brusk answered, the word resonating ground-deep.

They turned toward the wound in the sky, toward the fight that wasn't over yet.

The harbor scattered, moving as it was only driven by its fear. Fish stalls burned to blackened skeletons, the scent of rotted catch and lamp-oil thick in the air. Cries echoed from every alley. Mothers calling for children, sailors cursing and praying in the same breath. Ropes snapped under panicked hands, and gulls wheeled overhead, their cries sharp and frantic. Korvan braced himself against a half-fallen arch, his lungs burning. The shield wall wavered. Too many green eyes behind dented helms, too many hands shaking around spear shafts. Brusk held immovable beside him, his copper plates streaked with ash, catching the stray flickers of Aethyrlight. He was a wall, and he did not yield.

A hawk-kin shrieked from above, its wings shredded, its feathers twitching with taint. A violet film sealed its eyes, and it dove like a blade hurled from the sky.

"Hold the line!" Korvan's voice cut through the noise, sharper than he'd intended. But it was heard.

Steel rose. Shields locked. The hawk-kin struck, its beak carving a groove through the rim of a shield, shearing off two fingers that clattered to the ground like wet coins. The boy behind the shield went down, his legs giving out beneath him.

Brusk moved first. His tail arced, slamming the hawk-kin upward. Korvan met its descent, Auryn's Edge biting deep. Feathers charred, and bone gave way with a sound like sugar crushing underfoot. Hot ash and scorched keratin blew back into Korvan's face, stinging his eyes. The hawk-kin's scream cut off abruptly, its body coming apart in a shower of fire and cinder. The boy stared, his face pale, his body shaking. Korvan hauled him to his feet.

"Back in line."

The east side of the harbor screamed. Howlers poured from the collapsed remains of a warehouse, their mirrored ichor slicking the ground. Jaws frothed, and their eyes burned with a light that wasn't right, that wasn't natural.

"Form lines. Now!"

Steel met stone. Sera slid into place at Korvan's flank, casting a net of cool light over the fallen. Thalen strode past them, his laughter too sharp for the hour, too bright. Midnight blurred through the ranks of howlers, a shadow given form, her movements a dance of death. Illusion pooled at Korvan's boots, slipping off him like water, a trick of angles and hunger.

"The last pair feinted for the shields, then went under," Korvan said, his breath tight. "They're learning."

"Damn it...move!" Thalen barked, driving his blade forward, only to stumble as two howlers cut toward his exposed side.

Korvan shifted, his Halo Veil shield breaking one charge while Auryn's Edge split the second at the collarbone. Ichor flashed to steam, leaving behind a dark, stinging bloom. Thalen's eyes cut to Korvan, surprise and anger warring in his gaze.

"I don't need—"

"Save it," Korvan snapped, already turning to the next threat. For a breath, they stood back-to-back, steam rising from the ruin around them. Then they split, covering the angles. There were too many mouths, too many ways in. But the line held.

Heat crawled across Korvan's skin, prickling like a warning. He looked toward the rift and froze. The light around it stuttered, bending around a shadow pressing from the far side. It was tall, streaked with amethyst, its form shifting like smoke. The scent of ozone threaded through the blood and salt, sharp and electric.

Korvan's heart slipped a beat.

It sees me.

A second wave hit the square. Shields cracked under the assault, and a boss tore free, its maw punching a purple welt into the arm of the initiate behind it. Armor flashed, sticking to skin like molten metal. The scent of cooked oil and singed hair filled the air, acrid and choking. The pack altered course, veering toward the healers with cruel, calculated precision.

"Aethyrguard, advance!" Eris's voice cut through the storm, iron wrapped in fire. Kaelith surged skyward, her wings a blaze of light, checking the pack by inches.

Korvan lifted his glaive, pulling breath from the fear that had once ruled him. The ring of power sang in his bones, and he answered its call.

The taste of blood and burned fish filled his mouth, the drumming of panic and pain a relentless rhythm in his ears. Initiates staggered into place, their bodies bleeding, their breath too fast, their eyes wide with shock. Brusk loomed beside Korvan, his copper plates flexing with each step, a bulwark as strong as the walls of the city itself. A woman stumbled past them, clutching a girl to her chest, both cloaked in ash. The child's elbow clipped the stone, leaving a smear of red on the gray cobbles.

Korvan broke ranks, catching the woman's arm. "Temple square. Healers. Go."

A fresh impact cracked the arch behind them. "Now."

They ran, their feet skidding on blood-slick stone.

Korvan turned back too late. A corrupted wolf, its body twisted by the blight, barreled toward a group of sailors shielding their families, its jaws snapping, its eyes wild.

"Brusk." The word was a vow, a command.

Stone met fury. Brusk's tusks locked with the wolf's claws, and the cobbles beneath them broke under the force. The Bulwark lifted, levering the beast upward until its spine popped like tired knuckles. The wolf's body went slack before it hit the ground. Korvan would remember the sound. He was already moving, already seeking the next threat, the next scream.

Sera worked ahead of him, her movements swift and sure. Fennik's light threaded through torn skin, knitting ribs back together, sealing wounds with a gentle, relentless glow.

A call rose from the north. "More incoming! Harbor gate!"

Sera's face was streaked with soot, her focus honed to a razor's edge. They moved as one, Brusk shouldering aside carts like driftwood, Korvan cutting a path through the chaos. Dozens fled in their wake. Then hundreds. A boy tripped, his legs too small for the fear driving him. Korvan lifted him onto Brusk's back.

"Hold on tight."

The child's fingers latched onto the stone plates, his knuckles white.

The breach screamed, a sound that knotted muscles and set teeth on edge. Korvan's calves burned, his marks beating hollow and hot beneath his skin. Brusk rumbled once, a sound like distant thunder, then steadied.

Hold.

Korvan stood, lifting his glaive once more, facing the gate, the wound, the unknown.

His marks glowed faintly, hollowed but alive, a testament to the fight still left in him.

Initiates clustered around him, their armor dented, their faces streaked with blood and ash. Sera wiped a smear of ichor from her cheek, her hands steady despite the tremor in her limbs. Fennik curled at her feet, his light guttering but unbroken. Bren stood with his helm gone, one gauntlet lost, his brow split and bleeding. Thalen looked unmoored, his cloak torn, his gaze hunted. Midnight twitched beside him, her form a shadow given life, ready to strike.

Eris moved through the ruin, her armor scored and smoking, her spine unbowed. Kaelith wheeled above like a second dawn, her wings scattering the smoke. Talmar glimmered at her side, his presence soft. Coryn paced behind them, his eyes sharp and watchful.

"You held," Eris said, her voice cutting through the haze. "More than most would." She set the words like a stake, unyielding.

"This fight continues. The rift stands open, and something is holding it wide."

Korvan felt it too. The wrongness of it, the sense of a presence drawing near, watching, wanting.

"Our Champion and Knights are stabilizing the north piers," Eris continued, pointing east. "We hold this ground. No one moves alone." Her gaze swept over them all. They were filthy, terrified, but standing. "You took an oath. It begins here. You do not get to break."

Sera's hand found Korvan's, he squeezed her hand without thinking. Bren exhaled roughly, a crooked grin tugging at his lips despite the blood, the pain, the exhaustion. Korvan nodded once, a silent promise.

He would stand. They all would.

Kaelith's wings flared, scattering the smoke like chaff.

"Hold this ground," Eris said, her voice ringing clear above the chaos. "For Cael'Lumar. For the light we keep!"

A heartbeat.

Heat crept beneath Korvan's skin, a warning, a call. He turned to Brusk, his voice low. "Do you feel that?"

The Bulwark rumbled, a sound like shifting stone as the bound pulsed, *Here beside.*

The boards beneath their feet ticked.

The earth trembled. Amethyst light spilled from the breach, painting the harbor in hues of violet and shadow.

She stepped forward.

Catlike. Massive. Saber-fanged. Bands of violet fire wrapped in darkness coiled around its form. The roar that tore from its throat shattered windows, split stone, sent the wind howling through the streets.

Korvan hit the cobbles, clamping his hands over his skull as power ripped down his spine. Howlers swarmed the edges of the square, their mirror-scaled bodies feral, their movements a dance of controlled chaos.

Dozens.

Then more, slipping past Kaelith's blazing glare as if they'd learned the cost of that light, as if they'd adapted.

"Ranks!" Eris's voice cut through the storm. Kaelith dove, her wings a wall of flame, checking the pack by inches.

Korvan rose into the teeth of the chaos, Auryn's Edge flaring in his grip. The first beast came apart under his blade, ichor washing hot over his arm. Brusk crushed another into the stone, dragging his tusks free with a wet, grinding sound. The pack swelled, overrunning every gain, splitting for the flanks, for the healers. They were learning. Very mean. Too clever.

The saber-cat moved again, its presence a weight against Korvan's ribs, a name caught cold at the back of his tongue.

Vasha.

The thought came half-formed, more instinct than understanding. The creature pushed through the breach, its form flickering between presence and flesh. It roared, and the sound was a physical force, a blow that sent Korvan to his knees. A harbor wall crumbled, folding into seafoam and light. The ground shook, and Brusk took the brunt of a falling beam across his back, his plates locking like a mountain given legs. A hairline crack skittered along the ridge of one plate, but he didn't falter.

An initiate crawled past, his face pale. "What is that?"

Korvan's throat worked. "I don't know." His voice was raw, a rasp of sound. "But she wants through."

Farther down the line, Thalen shouted, his voice a blade against the chaos. Midnight hissed, her form little more than a fanged-shadow. Sera clutched her ribs, her breath coming in ragged gasps as Fennik's light flickered, thinning to a thread. Eris stepped forward, her three Veyrkin a seamless extension of her will.

"Do not break," she said, her voice steady beneath the storm. "We can hold together."

Another pulse hit the harbor, deeper this time, aimed. The ward-anchors along the quay chimed, their light dimming as if struck from the far side of the rift. It was learning. Adapting. Finding the weak points, the places where it could hurt them most.

Blood salted Korvan's tongue, the taste of iron and effort. His ankle burned where the poison had kissed his skin, his forearms shaking from the strain of overdraw. His left thumb was split at the nail, the skin raw and stinging. Brusk rasped once, a sound like stone grinding against stone, then steadied.

Hold.

Korvan stood, lifting his glaive once more, facing the gate, the wound, the unknown. "We stand."

He stepped to Sera's side, their shoulders brushing, a silent promise. Bren's hammer rose on his other flank, a counterweight to the glaive. Brusk pressed close, his bulk a reminder of the ground beneath their feet, the weight of their vow.

"On me," Korvan said, his voice low, certain. "Hold the line."

Chapter 8: The Breach

The breach tore open in a single scream of light and ruin. Air collapsed inward, warping like molten glass. Heat climbed Korvan's forearms; his Soulmark flared bright, as if his skin might split from the inside.

Then the saber-cat came through.

Amethyst stripes. A living storm. Its roar cracked Lantern Harbor's stone spine. Aethyrblight crawled over its hide in jagged pulses. Claws like knives. Eyes molten gold, hard with hurt. It looked at the world as if the world had earned this.

The formation wavered. A girl dropped her spear and ran. Bren held, shield shaking. Sera sank low, Fennik tight to her knee, the fox's light guttering to a thread.

Brusk surged beside Korvan, plates locking with the sound of falling rock. He made a wall. A low growl rumbled through the bond: Hold.

"Hold!" Eris's voice snapped the square taut. Kaelith burned behind her like a banner on fire. Talmar's Reservoir light trembled under the pressure that had come through.

The beast's second roar dragged a step from even Eris. The sound carried power and grief, stretched thin and mean.

Korvan's lungs forgot how to work. Lantern Harbor sagged like a chest after a blow. Stalls burning, fish oil and blood slicking the cobbles, welcome boiled down to smoke.

At the center stood the beast. Bigger than any Veyrkin he had seen, even Kaelith. Flanks scarred. Muscle like weather. Purpose in each step, war grown teeth and choosing to walk.

"Initiates, hold! Do not let it through!"

It lunged.

Lightning impact. Shields blew apart; bodies flew. An initiate hit a post; wood cracked, and something in his side answered with a dry snap. Another screamed as the wind of its passing tore him off his feet; he landed wrong, knee loose, boot turned the wrong way.

Their will cracked first.

The creature's gaze met Korvan's, and something shifted. Fear did not rise. Rage did not blind him. A rhythm formed under his skin that matched the pulse in her stride. It was warped, ancient, but deeply familiar.

She stepped closer.

Brusk coiled.

Korvan set a palm to his ribs.

"Hold the line," he whispered.

The words landed. Brusk stilled, watching.

Korvan stepped out.

"Korvan, what are you—" Bren's voice broke.

"Korvan!" Sera's cry cut the air. Even Eris paused, breath caught behind iron.

He did not stop. The name moved in his blood, older than fear and law. It sang along his marks.

He raised Auryn's Edge, not to challenge, only to steady his hands, and walked into the path no sane man chose.

The saber-cat roared.

Pressure swallowed sound. The harbor buckled. Korvan staggered; light flickered along the blade. Her eyes fixed on him and they were vast, forged by torment. Each step split stone. The air bent.

She leapt.

Korvan braced.

Death did not land.

Brusk hit first. His shoulder crushed into furred chest. Stone to sinew. Sparks blew across wreckage. He held, whole body shaking, tusks bared.

The bond thudded: *Go.*

Korvan went.

Noise and heat drew inward until the world narrowed to the span of his palm and the pound of his heart. He did not cast or command. He reached.

No circle. No glyph.

"See me."

The beast checked. In that flicker, he saw through her. A creature drowning. Fury for armor, pain for her chains.

Their eyes met, and memory tore through him.

Iron bars. Blood. The crack of a whip. The roar of a crowd that never meant kindness. A thousand wounds. Beneath it, sunlight and warm grass and salt wind. Freedom always a step beyond.

Her soul hit his. She was wild, broken, shaking.

Name me.

Her voice sounded petrified, a child's plea from the dark.

Korvan didn't hesitate. He let truth pass through unarmored. His marks seared open. Something in him recognized something in her and reached anyway.

"Vasha," he breathed. "You are Vasha."

The bond took.

Instinct sealed it, beyond sanction or rite.

Soul to soul.

Light broke through everything.

Korvan screamed.

His marks flared to a blaze no longer confined to his arms. Azure fire crawled down his ribs, wrapped his thigh, pulsed with each hammering beat. Agony, total and beautiful. For a breath, he felt everything. Her chains breaking, old scars tearing, hopes igniting.

Vasha changed.

Blighted fur fell to ash. In its place: silver and amethyst, sleek and radiant. Fangs shifted from rage to purpose. Claws tempered into protection. Her eyes, once wild, held a fierce clarity.

She roared, triumph pure enough to shake the stones.

She pressed her massive head to Korvan's chest. The purr that followed rumbled deep enough to stir cracked cobbles.

Thank you, little hunter. Your Fyrstrand called to me, even in my madness.

Even through the haze, Korvan knew what moved through her, her Aethyr was refined, precise, and oh so dangerous. An Obsidian Prestige.

His knees buckled and held. Vasha's gaze met his. A kindred force. A storm he could trust.

Brusk limped in, battered and steady, and touched his brow to Vasha's shoulder. A low, stone-sure sound. Three stood as one. Silence ringed them.

Weapons lowered. Initiates froze in a circle of ash and disbelief.

Eris strode forward. Kaelith landed behind her, feathers glowing in the ruin. Her helm tilted. "You bound a second one, and without a ritual." Her eyes fixed on the silver smilodon. "An Obsidian Howler."

Korvan nodded. The motion nearly broke him. His heart hammered like a siege drum. He stayed on his feet.

The breach still shimmered. The harbor still burned. Fear bent. Wonder stood where it had been.

Around him: shock, envy, awe, a different kind of fear. Two Veyrkin. Two bonds born of instinct and need.

She gave me her spark, he thought, and his mother's gift made a new kind of sense.

A breath. He didn't only taste salt and smoke. He tasted the weight of what had changed.

The Beyond pulsed, bleeding light into the haze. Blood and Aethyrburn thickened the air. Korvan stood at center, Soulmarks glowing, breath ragged. Brusk to one side. Vasha to the other.

Fighter. Shield. Blade.

The next wave screamed from the breach.

Vasha's bond surged. The predator's sight bloomed behind Korvan's eyes. Heat signatures. Motion trails. The stink of rust and rot. Every heartbeat matched her breath. For a moment, he staggered under the flood of sensation.

Then he saw it.

Harbor wards carved into the stone wall, half-hidden by smoke. Once bright, now blackened at the edges. Cracks radiating like veins. Deliberate. Sabotage.

Someone wanted this breach to open.

Vasha's hackles lifted. She felt it too. Fury sharpened between them.

Auryn's Edge kindled in Korvan's grasp. A howler leapt; he met it midair and split the chest. Behind him, Brusk broke another against the cobbles. The chip in the Bulwark's left tusk bled fresh.

To the east, silver cut the smoke. Ryn and Javek, the twin Veilwardens. Their falcon-like Pathcarvers flew dovetailed sweeps; light threaded from paired talons, scanning the breach's lip and laying a taut lattice.

"They're bracing the outer layer!" Ryn shouted.

Corrupted packs adapted, circling wide of Talmar's calm radius and testing the weak hinge at the wharf road. The line flexed, learned, set.

Korvan did not look. He moved, blade and instinct, bond, and purpose. Vasha danced beside him, a blur of claw and shadow light. Brusk anchored their flank with bone-rattling strikes. Together, they ripped through the pack.

"Storm's teeth, they're breaking!" Bren yelled.

Sera limped to the line, staff in hand, Fennik a thin glow. She worked what little she had left.

Midnight slashed down a final howler for Thalen.

Eris's voice cut through smoke like a blade: "Push them back! Seal the gate!"

Korvan roared and drove forward, Vasha and Brusk flanking like wings. For one breath, hope reclaimed the harbor.

Mages from the Third Ring descended. Dawnspire robes streaked with soot and blood, silver-threaded sleeves catching what light remained. They moved like surgeons. Chalk rings set with care. Powdered Aethyrglass in concentric arcs. A chant rose, soft at first, then clear.

The breach answered with anger.

It recoiled like a wound from needle and thread. Light stuttered. The nearest wall cracked. One mage flinched with scorched palms; another sank to a crouch as the ritual faltered.

The rift pulled at Korvan again.

His marks flared hot. Depth and distance unraveled at the edge of his vision, recognition sharp as pain. The Beyond saw him now.

"Korvan!" Eris called.

He looked up. Her iron face held an invitation. "You have the spark. You can reinforce it. Feel the flow."

Everything in him wanted to fight and force the wound shut. This power asked for something else.

Vasha stepped close, head lowered, watching. Brusk's low growl settled like bedrock.

"What do I do?" Korvan asked, throat tight.

Eris pointed through sigils. "Step in. Match the flow. Don't force it, guide it."

He nodded. Legs shaking. Breath short.

He stepped through fractured runes and crackling sparks. The breach reached for him, violet and sick with memory. It knew him. It wanted him.

He entered the heart of the lattice. Ground thrummed. Soulmarks found a rhythm older than breath.

"Breathe," Eris said, nearer now. "Don't let it master you."

He closed his eyes. One breath. Then another.

The chant rose like tide. Aethyr moved like thread on a broken loom.

Korvan did not push. He listened.

The current swirled, dense with loss and potential. He opened to it and let it pass the fractures in skin and will. He did not shape; he received.

The lattice flared.

Runes realigned, light stitching across the breach in gossamer arcs.

The Beyond fought. Echo and hunger clawed at the weave.

Korvan held.

Vasha's presence threaded through him, steady and proud. Brusk's rumble grounded the line.

He reached forward with trust.

The last thread caught. The seal locked.

A flash, brilliant and white. Silence.

The breach vanished, gone as fast as a breath.

Korvan dropped to one knee, strength stolen. Copper spread across his tongue; a line of blood slid from his bitten lip. His marks flickered once, then dimmed. Hands shook. A ringing set in his ears and would not quit. Vasha's flanks drew one shallow, shivering breath, then steadied.

Eris knelt beside him, armor singed. "Well done," she said, quiet. "Aethyrbound."

He tried to answer, to give back a smile. He noticed as gulls wheeled through smoke and cried over the water.

Darkness took him before he could speak.

Chapter 9: Awakened

The bells of Cael'Lumar rang in warning. Caelen heard them through glass, a distant, tolling heart.

From his Third Ring infirmary window, the city stepped down in cracked tiers. Black smoke climbed from Lantern Harbor in grasping spires, thick as tar. He pressed a trembling hand to the pane. Below, the harbor churned. A Breach gaped like a tear in the world, bleeding light in every direction. Figures moved like motes. Storm-blue cloaks. Silvered helms. Aethyr flashed. A roar rolled the cliffs so deep it shook his bones. The glass shivered under his palm.

More than sound, it was alive. Rage and memory braided until it felt personal. It reached through stone and ribs.

There, near the wound, a figure braced alone. Others scattered before Breach. But that one held. Tall. Hair whipping in the wind. A weapon of light gripped tight.

"Korvan," he whispered.

His brother's shape burned against the chaos, his figure cut by a force Caelen had no name for. A thread inside him went taut and stole his breath.

Another roar. A beast stepped through, massive and striped in violet fire, eyes like molten suns. The Veyrkin was as brutal as it was beautiful.

Light answered the thunderous roar. It flared so sudden and vast that Caelen reeled. Heat rose along his sternum. He clutched his mother's locket as if it were a lifeline.

When the glare eased, he leaned forward, forehead to glass. The harbor lay torn. The beast no longer raged. It knelt beside his brother. Korvan's hand rested in silver-striped fur.

Language failed but the feeling held. Caelen knew it, he'd always known it was possible. From the moment Korvan showed up with Brusk, that his older brother was special, that something about him was different. Caelen may have a mind for tinkering, for puzzles, and an uncanny ability to remember almost everything. Korvan had willpower greater than anyone Caelen had seen or read about. This confirmed it. Korvan had crossed a line, a line there was no coming back from. After this, the city would measure him differently.

Warmth lived under Caelen's fist. The locket's heat stood steady and alive. Pride surged hot and clean. Loneliness woke with quick teeth; he had not stood in that light, had not felt the bond take.

A whisper cut under the pride. *He's leaving you behind.*

He swallowed. The fog on the pane invited a small defiance. He drew a crooked glider, two stick figures on a bluff. Above them, he wrote: *You flew.*

The fog thinned, and the words blurred. He wiped the glass so none of Madam Ren's nurses would scold him, then tugged a scrap of paper from his nightstand. A few words, rough and plain:

Kor, I saw the light. I'm proud of you. Come back when you can. I can't wait to meet your new friend.

He folded it twice and slid it beneath the locket, palm resting on both for a long breath.

Far below, the Breach pulsed once more.

***

Korvan woke to the taste of burned herbs and sharp soap. The world smelled too clean, the sounds too loud. Each heartbeat rattled his Soulmarks which were raw and ragged. His Limbs ached as if he had shouldered stone through fire. Deeper, behind the sternum, something pulsed hollow and scorched, the afterimage of magic torn loose.

But he felt the most important, undeniable truth.

He was alive.

He opened his eyes to whitewashed stone. The medical ward's hush scraped against the battle still burning behind his eyes.

Everything was bright, the unforgiving smell of antiseptic ointments, rags and poultices pervaded his senses. His right forearm lay wrapped from wrist to elbow. The bandages hid branching paths of Aethyrburn. The marks beneath them answered, slower and stubborn shining through the bandages.

He shifted. Pain knifed under his ribs making his breath hitch.

Then he noticed the movement.

Brusk lay curled beside the cot, copper plates dulled with ash, a slow blink the only motion. Tail thudded once. *Hello sleeping Korvan.*

Relief hit so fast it left him shaking.

He blinked as he remembered and turned to the other side.

Vasha stretched along the stone like fallen moonlight. She was tall as a horse but quiet. Her silver coat was faintly gleaming, amethyst stripes apparent against the dim. Her massive head rested at his hip, taking up nearly as much of the bed as he did. A low rumble started deep in her chest, a warning to the world, a promise to him. She had kept the vigil and meant to keep it.

Welcome back to the realm of the waking. You are safe, little hunter. Warmth pressed through the bond. It was clear and steady. *Brusk and I are here.*

Here. Brusk's assent landed like a low drum.

Heat eased under Korvan's ribs. His throat burned; something in his chest cracked soft as old ice. He had a faint memory of being asleep and people trying to get Vasha and Brusk to move... she needed one growl to end that debate.

He tried to sit. Pain flared everywhere, but mostly in his arm and ribs. He fell back, teeth bared.

Footsteps drew his attention. Muffled voices overlapped outside the curtain, edged with awe and fear.

"He did it with no circle."

"No wardings. Nothing."

"Obsidian Howler. Dawnmother save us."

"Stronger than the Gilded Knight's pegasus?"

"Nothing's stronger than that flaming horse."

Their talk soured his mouth. Lantern Harbor had stood on a cliff's edge. Through fever, he had heard snatches of updates, but it didn't make much sense. Reserve companies were pulled from outer posts, Champions recalled, ward teams in alleys, contingencies stacked like a shield wall.

He fought because they would have died: Bren. Sera. And Caelen, who had not seen what he had become. Gods, he needed to see Caelen.

The curtain stirred.

Eris stepped through. Her armor shone again, mended clean; the shadows beneath her eyes did not. Kaelith stood in quiet blaze behind her, wings folded close.

"You're awake," she said.

"I think so, it's hard to tell," he rasped.

She crossed to the cot and drew the curtain. He started to rise; her hand found his shoulder, light and unyielding.

"Rest," she said. Not a suggestion.

"How close were we?"

A pause. Her eyes held his. "Closer than I like, but within reach. We layered contingencies. Ward teams in the alleys. Two Champions staged off the piers. Kaelith ready to break through if I called. Lantern Harbor is never left to chance." Her jaw set. "You faced a genuine surge, but the Aethyrguard stood with you."

His mind spun, he felt his heart begin to hammer in his chest and his mouth ran dry.

"It was a test," he said, flat.

"A proving," she said.

His wrapped hands shook.

"People died," he said. "Good ones."

"I know." Her voice thinned. "If we hadn't proved you and the others there, more die later. The Aethyrguard is forged where the world breaks, far from lecture halls." A beat. "And when the risk spiked, I was one breath from ending that cat myself." Her gaze slid to Vasha and back.

He turned his face to the wall. "It isn't fair, we let people get hurt for a test? People died."

"It wasn't planned for the harbor, we don't do it in the city, too much risk, and variables but we do plan for breaches to test our best and brightest. There are things I can't discuss here about how this happened... While we may prepare for such instances, this was real."

Silence rang.

"Flame take it, Eris," he said. "It cost too much."

Someone outside sucked a breath at his tone. Eris didn't blink. Her rank fell away as her head drooped.

"Believe me, it always does," she said.

He dragged his eyes back. "You wanted this to happen."

"We had a measure of your capabilities." Her gaze cut closer. "No one knew what you were until The Beyond reached back and we needed certainty." A thin exhale. "You did something impossible."

"I bonded like I bonded Brusk."

"Far more than that Korvan. You cleansed her." The words came soft, dropping even lower from the prying ears.

"A Veyrkin that far gone to Aethyrblight doesn't return. Protocol says kill or banish if you can't stop her. You had no Rite. No protective circle. No overseer. You didn't only bond. You burned the rot out of her and lived."

He met her gaze and the lights felt brighter as the small room shrank. "So, what are you saying, I broke the rules?"

"You didn't break them. You tore the pages out of the book."

She glanced at Vasha and back.

"Few understood what they saw through smoke and panic. A beast kneeling. An Initiate standing. Rumors will breed. For now," her voice lowered, "it isn't in my field report."

"You left it out?"

"I left out that you cleansed her. For now." Steel again. "The wrong eyes will drag you into chambers you don't walk out of. Nobles will hunger. The Temple will pry. Until I understand what happened, and whether you can survive it, you keep quiet."

A small nod.

"If asked, Vasha answered before the Aethyrblight settled. Say nothing about cleansing. Until today, there were only rumors that was theoretical, let alone possible. What you did is nothing short of miraculous and judging by the way you're looking at me, you don't even know how you did it."

Copper rose on his tongue. Eris was right. He had no idea, it felt just like when he bonded with Brusk.

"What if they won't take no for an answer? What If they push?"

"You send them to me."

Silence. Then he nodded.

"You're angry," she said.

"I'm tired."

"Both can be true."

She studied him, then set two fingers to his bandaged wrist where the mark beat. Her eyes went distant, as if listening to a far bell. "For the record: I don't need a Cadence Lens to read the Aethyr. It sings back to me, and loudly at Obsidian." A breath. "Whatever you are, Korvan Aric, you are far more than most."

Something loosened under his ribs. Shame, grief, doubt, each with duller teeth than before.

"Rest," she stood and turned, back "and for what its worth, I'm sorry."

He let the dark come and did not fight it.

***

The muster hall still smelled of blood and burned oil, though fresh banners hung from the pillars. Aethyrglass lanterns flared to push back yesterday's ghosts.

Korvan stood with the survivors. A new tunic chafed half-healed burns on his ribs. Brusk lay at his feet, tail thudding a slow, uneven count. Vasha paced behind, gold eyes on every shift of the room. Even at a prowl, she carried weight. Predator-sure steps set his balance to new heights. He found himself easing toward her shadow.

Initiates and senior ranks crowded the space, a battered wedge of storm-blue and dented steel. Bruised faces. Wrapped hands. Grief in the set of mouths. Pride in the way they stood.

Champion Korinar unrolled a scroll. Names of the dead cut the air. Each struck like iron. Fifty went into the Breach. Fewer than thirty stood.

A drawn heavy silence filled the room.

"Lantern Harbor stands because of you," Korinar said at last. "Because you held."

Another voice followed. A taller figure stepped forward, mantle marked by the sunburst crown.

High Warden Archion Dren. The leader of their order, the single most powerful human in Cael'Lumar, if not the world.

He moved the way winter comes, with unyielding strength and a certainty of purpose. His Silver hair pulled tight. Lines at the eyes that spoke of choice more than years.

"You proved what we must be," he said, low and resonant. "That we are Vigilant. We are Resilient. We are Unrelenting. Cael'Lumar will not forget the service you and the brave we lost have given to the defense of our city."

His gaze swept the hall and stopped. "Some revealed gifts beyond expectation."

Attention ebbed like the tide as eyes found Korvan.

Archion stepped close. The space between them went thin and cold. A pale Soulmark scar crossed his wrist too like Korvan's.

"Korvan, son of Varnrik," he said. "An Obsidian Howler. I've read the report of how you did it. You understand what that means I take it?"

"No, sir."

For a moment Korvan was sure he saw a glint in Archion's eye, but as quick as it was there the man's face remained impassive.

"It means you carry power. Power is a burden. Learn to bear it, or it will crush you. It also means, that you should make friends that can help you understand such burdens."

Nobles watched from the back, their cloaks catching the light at sharp angles. Several shifted and Korvan felt their eyes lingering.

Eris stepped to Korvan's side before that hunger could sharpen. "With respect, High Warden," she said, quiet and honed, "my Initiate remains under my command. I am happy to educate him about the burden of power."

Archion inclined his head. "So noted, Battlemage." He turned to the hall, hands lifted. "The Beyond does not rest. Neither shall we. Ready yourselves. Your trials are only beginning."

Applause began slow and uncertain, but quickly picked up as Archion's eyes drifted around the room.

Korvan held still. Surviving the Breach was one trial; the aftermath was another.

Outside the archway, the late sun silvered the ruined harbor. There were scars all over. Korvan could tell that healing would take time.

He sank to a bench, breath uneven. The air tasted of salt and a sweet note from high gardens. Some things were just as stubborn as weeds.

Brusk laid his head over Korvan's boots. Vasha pressed against his side and stilled. *Here. We stay.*

What does it mean to carry the spark she left me? What happens if I can't?

They gave no words, only the weight of their combined strength humming through his Fyrstrand.

Korvan drew the first breath since the fight that did not taste of blood. "I'll find the way," he said. "Somehow."

Across the cliffs, bells rang the evening watch. It was a vow to the city. A warning to their enemies. A hymn to what still stood.

He believed he could make his mother proud.

Chapter 10: Return to Training

The first bell still echoed through the mountain corridors when Korvan entered the training yard. Cold dew slicked the stone, and each flag bore scuffs and scorch marks from drills that never grew old. Mist hugged the ground, and the early sun threw a hard white sheen across the walls.

He moved without speaking, buckling the vambrace and setting the storm-blue half cloak at his shoulders which still felt too ceremonial for what they had endured. His breath rose in quiet puffs. The yard still had the dawn's chill, as if the stones remembered the ghosts of yesterday.

Brusk padded beside him, hooves soft under dulled plates. His tail swept the mist like a rudder. Vasha slid from the fog behind them, stretching tall. Her silver coat caught the light, and the amethyst bands along her flanks kindled.

A few Initiates shifted away at her approach, their wariness plain. She kept quiet, but her presence itself was enough to carve out extra space.

Korvan counted the heads. Fewer than yesterday. Fewer than last week. Lantern Harbor had taken more than the dead, some of the living lost their will.

Squads formed on reflex. Bond-pairs shoulder to shoulder. Check your partner. Brace for instruction. The weeks of discipline settled over them. Complaints long burnt out.

Champion Anders strode to the front, half-armored, half-shadowed by his Veyrkin which was an obsidian feathered hawk-like Pathcarver that perched on his shoulder. His signal horn hung unused. His voice was weapon enough.

"Form ranks. Bond-pairs only. Drill begins now." His voice remained iron-clad but a measure quieter than it had been in previous days.

A low groan rippled through the Initiates, but feet moved.

Late meant laps. Late meant punishment rounds without water. Late meant attention.

Korvan slid into line. Sera and Bren flanked him, their beasts matching their rhythm. Fennik trotted beneath Sera like a court fox on parade, and Rok lumbered at Bren's side, more boulder than beast.

Anders gave no preamble. "Footwork series, time to get you slugs moving. Bulwark variants. Five passes. Move."

They obeyed.

Low pivots, mirrored spins, switch-stance transitions with barely a breath between. Moving alone failed. Most of the group tried to move as one.

Despite all his efforts, Korvan moved as three. Tamer and Veyrkin had to pivot together, strike and withdraw on a single count. Hesitation meant injury, a misstep meant death.

The first pass immediately broke the old rhythm he was used to with just Brusk. His Soulmarks prickled hot under his skin. Brusk steadied his breath. Vasha pressed the edge of each feint, her hunger evident across their connection.

His legs had not yet learned her speed and his balance lagged behind Brusk's anchoring drag. He stumbled, slight but enough to make Anders's hawk cry and the Champion's voice crack the stone.

"You move like a caravan of beasts. Become one weapon. You are the Aethyrbound Aric, show me something special."

Korvan ground his teeth and forced the chaos into line.

Again. And again. And Again he moved. Until every Initiate gasped for breath and the yard smelled of sweat and strain.

Bren grunted mid-turn, barely catching his hammer before it tipped over. "This is what dying in style looks like."

Sera, somehow graceful even while panting, smirked. "You'd mistake style if it braided your hair."

"You're just mad I still have better footwork than you," Bren shot back, then almost ate stone as Rok clipped his boot on a pivot.

Korvan barked a short laugh despite himself. It cut off as Vasha surged to meet a swinging target dummy.

Her timing was perfect but there was far too much power. The padded arm snapped free with a crack, spun twice, and landed near Anders's boots.

A long pause.

Anders raised one brow at the saber-cat, whose shoulder topped his helm. "Control your Veyrkin...Initiate."

Korvan nodded, jaw tight. "Yes, sir."

Sera leaned close. "She wants to impress everyone."

"She'll win us double rounds," he muttered, fingers finding the spot between Vasha's ears. She rumbled, pleased with herself clearly careless of the thread of double rounds.

Anders carried the lesson forward. "Double time now Initiates. Blindside sweeps. Keep the same count."

Weighted poles sped from the Clockwork golems, not just faster but from worse angles.

Shield rotations next. Brusk proved immovable. Whatever angle the attackers took, he intercepted with precise focus. Korvan mirrored the line's Brusk made and redirected blows. Vasha learned too, eager to impress her new Tamer, but also the others around. She checked her first step and shaved power off the follow-through.

Korvan couldn't help it, they were moving as quick as anyone, maybe quicker and it felt easier than it had before. Clearly whatever he'd gained from this bond was more than just Vasha's strength, but it made him more too.

We move with easy grace now, little hunter, she sent, a clear note under the bruising pace.

Brusk's answer came low and sure. *Hold. Strong.*

The yard rang with the thud of wood, the grind of boots, and the sharp breath of pain mixed with the sounds of their clock-work golems cracking and fighting back. One Initiate collapsed mid-sequence, gasping on all fours while his Verdant howler paced in confusion.

Anders did not pause. Two attendants hauled the boy to the healer's bench. Drills continued.

Korvan's breath came back in inches as his sweat cooled in the wind. The sting along Korvan's forearms mapped where poles had kissed him. For all his speed his technique could still be improved. They were smart reminders.

Sera's foot slipped. Korvan caught her elbow without thinking. She steadied as Fennik threaded her ankles like a living glyph.

"You alright?" he whispered.

"Never better," she grimaced. Then softer, "You're faster now."

"It's Vasha... I don't really know how but, her strength and speed are shared with me. It's incredible... and a little frightening. I should be tired, but her bond blocks the feeling somehow," Korvan admitted.

When Anders finally called water, Korvan's hands trembled. His limbs obeyed on instinct alone, but his mind hovered just above the exhaustion. He crouched by the trough and sluiced his face. Breath steadied on a count of three.

Vasha pressed close, her fur warm against his back.

"I'm alright," Korvan said.

She sent a low assent. *I am here.*

Across the yard, Thalen stood composed, Midnight matching him. Thalen's gaze found Korvan's and held too long. Then it slipped away with the faintest curl of his lip.

Korvan's pulse climbed into his ears.

Boot-falls echoed before the order came.

"Form up," Knight Eless snapped. "Enough of you have reacquainted yourselves with the ground for one morning."

Korvan slid back into line, his chest still tight from the last sequence, but already he felt strength pour across the bond.

Vasha, her eyes met his and he felt her stare, and her Aethyr, pour into him. She shared her strength, and while it slowed her some, the gain it gave Korvan was immediate. He felt like he'd rested for a few hours in the span of a few deep breaths.

He sent a question to her across their connection.

She purred happily as her response.

Across the yard, Thalen snapped his glove straps and watched the arch.

A tall figure entered beneath it, dusk-colored armor moving like one piece. Bronze-gold skin. Eyes with a clarity that straightened spines on sight. But what caught all their attention, he wore no shoes.

"Champion Cristos of Vara'Lumar," Anders announced, flat and formal. "He will lead combat technique for Initiate advancement."

Murmurs rippled through the Initiates. Sera's brow ticked; Bren nodded once. Korvan did not know the name.

Cristos raised a hand and let the noise fall. His voice was a rich baritone with an accent that Korvan didn't recognize, it wrapped the words in a hug. "Thank you Anders for the warmest welcome. For those who have not bled on our stone: Vara'Lumar stands across the Sapphire Sea, a border citadel carved into far cliffs. If Cael'Lumar is the New Light, Vara'Lumar is where that light began. The original city of the Aethyrguard, where our institution began so many lifetimes ago. We train where the world breaks against a wilderness."

He paused, letting the words settle. "But I am not a history instructor. I am here to teach you a more practical set of skills. Shen'Drak is the Way of Closing. A body in harmony. Discipline becoming grace."

Whispers rose and died. Cristos walked to the center and let the yard come to him. His gaze measured every stance as if he were reading a script.

"Your stance speaks louder than your spells." His voice was a whisper.

He set one foot deep, the other angled, hands open. His body in contrast both relaxed and coiled. "This is Shen'Drak."

He stopped before a wide-eyed boy that flinched at the eye contact. Cristos only smiled.

"Fights rarely begin with honor. Most begin with pain."

He moved: knee, elbow, palm, sweep. Not an ounce of wasted movement, but each stroke had more power than it appeared. Korvan didn't know how he knew, but he was certain of it.

"Shen'Drak ends fights." Cristos continued.

Silence echoed in the courtyard. Korvan glanced and all the eyes were on Cristos. They'd done some light hand to hand work, but this was more advanced than anything shown.

"Partner up. Hands only. No Veyrkin, yet. We begin with breathing technique. Then balance. You will learn, power is in the breath."

Cristos took a deep breath and his skin flared with a mahogany glow, the soulmarks along his collarbones flared and when he exhaled a metallic sheen came across his body.

Wind moved through the yard, a sudden sea gale that brought a chill from the ocean.

Korvan lowered his stance. It felt wrong until he found Brusk's slow cadence at the edge of the bond and matched it. Vasha waited at the rail, still as a drawn bow.

Give this one your full attention, Little Hunter. He is a viper. I like him. she thrummed.

Edges, lines, even colors ran brighter with her near, her vision enhanced his, giving the world a saturation that took his eyes time to adjust to.

Cristos carried a different gravity, he was polished calm over coiled power. Breathing even, his weight placed with intention. The Knight's eyes always assessing.

Korvan felt it with Vasha, another wolf had stepped into their yard.

"Begin with your breath," Cristos said. "Lose it and you lose everything."

He drew long; the Initiates followed. Even Thalen.

"This isn't a dance or a show of strength. Certainty wins, intention wins. Every pause is a trap."

Korvan's weight found the balls of his feet. Hands loose. Heat along his Soulmark, but their pull was quiet.

"Strike," Cristos said. "Palm. Elbow. Knee. Heel."

Ryn and Javek flowed together, the perfect mirrors. Ryn went high. Cristos was there, a shadow inside her guard. "Lower," he murmured, turning her forearm a finger's width. "You don't need to fly to crush a throat."

Javek's return came thoughtful and late. Cristos caught it without looking. "Stop thinking, Act."

Pairs shifted. Korvan ran drills with Sera, light contact, their breath in constant focus. Fennik paced them like a stern tutor. Cristos passed by.

"You move like a river," he told Sera. "Remember, rivers drown if they lose their banks."

Color rose in her cheeks. "Understood."

A stocky boy with fast hands and too much proof in his eyes moved in front of Korvan next.

There was a knowing look in Cristos' eyes as he said. "Begin."

The boy rushed. Korvan pivoted, caught the arm, and cut the legs. Stone kissed hard. A gasp left the boy in a shocked bark.

Cristos nodded. "Excellent Korvan. Initiates this is what I mean. Use your attacker's strength against them. Place the power intentionally so you may spend less of your own. Balance and intention. Balance. Intention."

Across the yard, Thalen moved with scalpel-clean lines, all hard edges but no flow. Cristos set a palm to his shoulder. "You're too careful."

"I prefer precision."

"So does a scalpel. But you are not a scalpel, a scalpel is precise as it does not want to do unintended damage. You must be intentional. But you also cannot afford to spend too long analyzing. You are deadly with that blade young Ryst, but you cannot win every fight with the edge of a sword."

A few Initiates smiled. Thalen didn't.

"Redirection," Cristos called. "Palm to palm. Give and take." Every word showing the initiates what he expected of them.

He glanced across the circle. "I'll take the boy with the storm in his chest."

Korvan stepped forward. Brusk's attention deepened like an anchor. Vasha's presence brightened as all her focus turned to Cristos.

Cristos bowed. Korvan returned it.

"Breath," Cristos said. "Then balance."

They touched hands.

Cristos pressed with measured weight, no malice, probing Korvan's frame, hunting any drift in his balance.

Korvan yielded a hair, found the line, then felt pressure climb at his ribs, an urge to release. He held. Heat licked under his skin. Cristos shifted to steal the center.

Korvan moved before he thought, and his weight sank.

Hips turned. Feet where they had not been a blink before. Palm met forearm; elbow threatened the seam. Speed snapped through him like a plucked wire and Vasha's pulse brightened his tendons before he knew to ask.

Cristos gave a half step he had not offered. His eyes changed they brightened as he recalculated.

Then he adapted. Harder angle, quicker breath, still in balance. He bled Korvan's force past the ribs and returned a hooked palm that stopped a whisper from Korvan's throat.

"Again," Cristos said, quiet.

He's like lightning, Vasha thrummed. *But you are faster, Little Hunter. You have my reflexes now.*

Korvan didn't look at her, but her focus settled on Cristos like a drawn string.

They touched palms again. Cristos fed a sharper test, pressure, and feint. Time thinned.

Brusk steadied Korvan's feet. *Hold.*

Vasha slid a hotter line along his nerves. *Now.*

Korvan cut center faster than he had a right to. Cristos caught the second surge late and rolled the shoulder off the line. Enough to admit the truth Korvan was faster, but Cristos had the experience.

A third surge built, hot and bright.

Spend, from Vasha, silver prickle through the bond.

Place, from Brusk, stone under flood.

Korvan chose the stone. He set the force instead of spending it and clipped Cristos's balance without trying to break him.

Cristos smiled without showing teeth. "There it is."

He stepped back and let the air widen. "You feel the pressure to release. Good. Learn to place it. If power doesn't serve others, it consumes you. Your bonds listen to your instincts but you must listen to theirs too. You are fast Korvan, mind that Howler doesn't burn you both out though sharing her strength like that."

Cristos turned his eyes to Vasha, Korvan only noticed she was panting and for the first time since they'd bonded, looked fatigued.

Only then did Korvan notice his Soulmarks glowing, buzzing with power in his skin. He bowed, pulse drumming down to normal, unsure if the strength was his or theirs or the line between.

Cristos clapped once. "Enough. Let the body remember what it has been taught. Next time, we add some pressure."

A feral glint appeared in the Knight's eyes. "And it will hurt."

Korvan flexed stiff fingers. Wrists throbbed from catches. The half-healed burn along his ribs pulled each breath. Vasha's early excess had earned them extra rounds. Even after all of that, he still had laps to run.

***

Wind worried the high arches of the viewing ring, whispering along carved stone. From this height, Cael'Lumar sprawled below like a layered map. Sea-glint rooftops in the lower rings gave way to marble terraces, tiered gardens, and the gleam of Vaults above.

He stood near the rail, unmoving. His duskstone silhouette cut a stark figure against the cityscape. Robes hissed as the pale wind ran through the gold-trimmed hem. His gilded staff rested beside him, Aethyrglass under gold, the crystal tip pulsing faintly. A presence.

Eris came up the opposite stair, armor ringing soft. Though her hands were empty command followed like a shadow. Where the other drew reverence, she drew gravity.

They watched in silence.

Below, Cristos snapped a command. His voice cracked the yard like a banner whip. Initiates obeyed on the beat. Bare feet. Squared stances. A dance trained for violence.

"I had forgotten how beautiful Shen'Drak is," murmured, eyes on the ring. "A body in harmony, how discipline can become grace."

Eris gave a low hum. "You always did see poetry in bruises Maedryn."

"Of course." A faint smile. "A well-thrown strike is a verse. A parry, a stanza."

Bren dropped an opponent with a clean sweep. Cristos clapped once for rhythm.

"He's done well," Eris said. "Cristos. Vara'Lumar's blend impresses me. Pressure stances and bone-locks, its efficient, and brutal."

"And needed." Maedryn tracked a formation shift. "You can see it in their shoulders. They begin to trust their bodies already, even the smaller ones. But that's not the only thing that impresses you is it Eris."

His gaze slid to her. "Your call, replacing Vael with Cristos?"

"The others voted," Eris said. "I insisted. We needed a fresh perspective. My feelings aren't relevant to the matter, my duty is."

"Duty again. It is always duty with you Battlemage." The phrase edged delicate as a stiletto.

"We cannot all afford to idle away the hours in noble banquets, Archmage."

Maedryn of the Quiet Flame, the Archmage and second in command, of the Aethyrguard by rank, but one many believed held at least as much power as the High Warden, put a hand to his chest feigning injury.

"Touché Eris, touché." His eyes sparkled at her.

She let it pass. Her eyes found Korvan, rolling up from gravel into a counter that landed with finality. Vasha stalked behind, bobbed tail low, gold eyes always watchful.

"That one," Maedryn said. "He channels as if the Aethyr seeks him, its undeniably drawn."

"He's green, impulsive, dangerous," Eris said, voice cooled. "He even made Cristos move, but he still fails to see how much that Howler lends him."

Maedryn listened to the yard, "He holds two currents in one. He's trying to ride the seam rather than blending them together.

Yet another rare gift young Aric seems to have, And costly if untaught." He turned to her. "I see the danger, but I think given time, young Korvan could become something special."

"Training won't save him when nobles start carving futures for all of them."

"It might if he learns to place power instead of spend it." Maedryn's tone stayed soft and a glint appeared in his eye. "You forget, old friend. Often the dangerous ones burn brightest. Our work is to keep them from burning out."

Eris couldn't help but roll her eyes.

"Then teach him to hear what you hear."

"I intend to. And I expect I won't be the only teacher."

She said nothing. He meant her, and they both knew it.

They had come through the Guard together once, both young and stubborn, wearing their faith in the institution as if it were armor. She flexed her fingers behind her back.

"He's bonded to two already," Eris said. "One an Obsidian Howler. That pull seldom happens by accident. You said he carried two Disciplines easily?"

"He did." No awe in Maedryn's voice, just a matter of fact tone. "The work nearly tore him open. His raw potential. I don't recall the last time I saw that much. Not since you that's for certain."

Bells pulsed slow and distant. Below, the ring breathed: impact, exhale, the scrape of skin on grit.

"The nobles are watching him," Eris said, low. "Too closely."

Warmth dimmed in Maedryn's eyes; steel showed. "They always do and as you've requested I've done everything within my power to push them away or misdirect them. But you know how they are as much as I do. They place all their hope and wrap it up in bloodlines. They keep fear wrapped in power. An exhausting dance. It is agonizing. I am mired by agendas, supply lines, and dignitaries asking inane questions."

"I am grateful Maedryn, I know I haven't said that enough. So thank you." She gave him a smile that he returned. It didn't last.

"They see a weapon and refuse the protector. If he draws too much light too fast, he'll drown before he learns to swim." Eris said.

"Then teach him to float." His smile lingered.

Her breath cut short, half laugh and half curse. "You always make it sound easy."

"Because I still love what we do."

Their eyes met, hers weathered by command, his bright with something close to wonder.

"I'll watch him," Maedryn said. "Not as Noble or Council. Not even as the Archmage. As teacher. A flame needs tending."

Eris nodded. "'Maedryn of the Quiet Flame. Gods how did you even get that name," She let out a peel of laughter, "As will I. For good or ill, this troop is the strongest in a decade. Korvan, Thalen, Sera and Bren are the best of them."

She hesitated, gaze fixed on Korvan. "Do you think he could be hers?"

Maedryn's brow furrowed. "Any of them could be. If it is any, him. Should we say something to him?"

Eris shook her head. They both knew it wouldn't do any good. They thought it wouldn't. They both knew the truth.

They hoped he wasn't because he'd never forgive them.

They left the thought unpinned. Old memory moved between them. Below, the yard echoed with breath and bruises. Young warriors learned the city's rhythm. Limbs forged by pressure. Hearts still deciding what it meant to stand, what it meant to pursue your duty, what honor truly meant.

***

The garden nested behind a veil of ivy-clad stone, half-hidden under a Third Ring spire. Sera's favorite: part wild, part tended. Sun-warmed loam and lavender. Moss softening cracked paths.

Drills stayed outside. Bells stayed with orders. Air went green and quiet, dappled with birdsong and far chimes.

Korvan sank into the grass with a low groan, legs still angry from terrain sprints. Bren collapsed beside him in the boneless sprawl of the truly spent, half a loaf of seed bread crammed into his cheek. Sera sat cross-legged by the fountain, flicking petals from an orange bloom at anyone who looked too serious.

"I think my spine's broken," Bren mumbled around crumbs.

"Don't worry, Fennik and I will fix you if you ask politely," Sera said, flicking a petal onto his nose.

Korvan let a smile loosen his jaw and draped an arm over his eyes. Sun filtered through leaves and old runeglass panes high in the wall. For once, the light soothed instead of scalded.

"You've barely spoken since the lesson," Sera said. "Though we do love your dramatic brooding."

"I'm fine," Korvan said. Then lower, "Just tired. I meant to visit Caelen on Restday. Again."

"How long has it been?" Sera asked, blade-gentle.

He counted and flinched. "Three weeks. Almost four. I keep meaning to go, but…"

"But the minute the horn stops, you drop like a stone," Bren offered, gentler than usual.

"Exactly."

Sera tucked a blade of grass behind her ear like a flower. "Next Restday, we drag you out of bed. Deal?"

"Deal. I'll go," Korvan said. "I want to. It's just hard."

"You haven't failed him you know," Bren said, sitting up. "You're surviving. That's what he wants too, yeah?"

"Maybe." He stared past the fountain's lip. "Feels like I'm losing him a little more each day."

They let that settle. The kind of silence that asks for no words.

"You're blocking the walkway," a dry voice said.

Thalen stood a few paces off, arms crossed, flanked by three noble youths in cadet sashes and fine-cut cloaks. They looked unsettled, by the dirt or by Thalen's pause.

Bren grinned. "We're in the garden, not the street. Come sit with us unless you're afraid of grass stains."

Thalen blinked. The others murmured. He lifted a hand. "Go on. I'll find you later."

A pale girl with inked temple markings started to protest. Thalen's look closed her mouth. He lowered himself to the grass with care, brushing an invisible speck from his uniform. "I suppose even weeds have their charm."

Sera flicked a petal at his chest. "Call this garden a weed again and I'll hex your pillow."

His lips twitched. "Noted."

They passed what remained of the seed bread and a pouch of dried citrus Sera had tucked into her satchel. For a few minutes, peace held. Even Thalen, posture perfect and spine too straight, seemed to relax.

"Didn't expect to see you out here," Korvan said.

"My father requested I observe noble-led drills," Thalen replied, clipped, and practiced. "Performance assessments, mostly accounting, logistics and other mundane drivel related to the family businesses. Then he insisted I deliver the notes myself."

Sera lifted a brow. "And you said yes?"

A hitch and the perfect mask cracked. His voice dropped quieter: "Choice rarely belongs to me. Legacy expectations being what they are and all."

Silence shifted. Sera's family were minor nobility, Bren's family legacy smiths and artisans of some renown, all but Korvan had some indication of the expectations of the legacy a Ryst had and the pressure under it. But it didn't take an expert in nobility to see it, something cracked beneath the precision mask in Thalen, a strain worn into bone.

"Heavy name to carry," Sera said, gentler now.

Thalen watched the fountain's rim. "My family has served the Aethyrguard for ten generations. The nobility longer. Tradition matters to them. Our duty, our bloodline, our fucking image. I'm expected to uphold it. All of it."

Korvan watched him. He was all pride and tension, a spring ready to snap like one of the little machines Caelen tinkered with.

The breeze turned. Petals spiraled. For a breath, they sat in uneasy unity. They all were from diverse backgrounds and on slightly different paths. But they were still together.

Bren reached for the last honeyed slice and held it out. "Peace offering. Mam's sweetbread. Best in the city. Maybe the world. Probably the world."

Thalen eyed it like it might detonate, then accepted with a wary nod. "Thank you."

He took a bite, "By the gods... Is there more?" He snatched the paper and licked it clean, the veneer of nobility now truly broken.

Sera, Bren, and Korvan laughed, thin and incomplete, but more than enough for now.

Chapter 11: Bonds

A month carved new habits into his bones.

Korvan felt it in the burn of muscle, the thin scars on his knuckles, the second skin across his palms. Days blurred to one drumbeat: drills, lectures, drills. The work hollowed even the strongest of them. A relentless workload after horns rousing them at dawn.

Thankfully, the food kept them upright, rich stews and honeyed bread, fruit bright and fresh made the narrow cots at night bearable. The cycle felt endless, wake, work, eat, repeat.

For most their privacy was respected, but never fully their own, all part of making them a unified force. Their rest was never complete, minds were always full of added information, fatigue, and thoughts of the future. But what rest they did find was just enough to recover for the next day, but not enough to forget what the work made of them.

Korvan stopped counting hours, instead he counted breaths like Cristos taught them. Breaths on the obstacle lines, carrying their packs and armor, with and without their Veyrkin. Every end of the day his Soulmarks throbbed until the ache became a metronome.

Brusk thrived on all the ambient Aethyr in the Arc-Tower Barracks, and the regular feedings that the Veyrkin saw. Plates shone on well-fed Aethyr. Every motion trimmed to purpose. He took every charge head on and gave no ground. A Bulwark was meant to keep the line.

Vasha burned at the edge of him, their connection felt like a second pulse. She sharpened everything: the attack angles exact when threats were near. With her he moved faster and hit harder, he was more aggressive. With her, the cost came due. He bled for the aggression she lent him, a predator didn't care as much about getting hit back, they only cared about the attack. His instructors worked to get that in line.

Eris drove them past exhaustion and past each failure, sanding them to the truest parts of them, that most foundational part that would not break, the keel of their ship. She measured will more than strength. She listened for the click when a body wanted to quit and didn't.

Vasha put him there often. He took her momentum wrong and the mat took his breath. Speed tore timing from his hands. His marks blistered when he overreached, then peeled and healed thin leaving pink skin behind. New scars brightened along his forearms and collar where magic burned through his Soulmarks and left a map. Some days he hated the mirror Vasha held up, the wild that she displayed showed where he was slow, where he was small, where he broke the easiest.

But every day Korvan stood back up. Despite the pain, despite the fatigue, despite all the pressure his instructors could muster, he stood back up.

He couldn't quit. He wouldn't quit.

He had made a promise.

***

Korvan sat on the low step behind the Vaults and worked some salve into a fresh patch of raw skin. The stench of pine pitch and bitter metal bit his nose. The balm found the Aethyrburn at his wrist and he hissed.

Brusk nosed his knee once and stilled. *Place, not spend.*

Vasha settled behind him with a huff that lifted the fabric of his collar.

Breath deep, the pain will ease, she sent, a clear note under the ache.

He rubbed the last of the balm across knuckles.

"That's gonna leave a scar." He said to his Veyrkin.

The sting that followed proved him right.

Eris never praised him. She didn't stop him either. Most of her feedback was in silent looks. But he'd caught a few smiles, even though they were brief.

Wind slid off the cliffs and cooled the sweat on his back. Above, Cael'Lumar's towers kept lanterns like small constellations against the Aethyrglass backdrop, they flickered with the echoes of the days efforts.

He let his guard ease a fraction. Breath went out ragged but came back smooth.

He was still standing.

Bootsteps crossed stone drawing his attention.

"You look half dead," Bren said, voice rough with a laugh. He clapped Korvan's shoulder and almost sent him into the wall.

"Feel half dead." Korvan said. "How many tower runs they make you do today?"

"Six," Bren said, proud. "Two more because I crushed someone's foot during formations."

Korvan smirked. "You have both the strength and grace of an ox Bren."

"That's what they tell me."

Sera's voice joined, soft and wry. "You haven't seen Bren sleepwalk into the washroom door, that is the pinnacle of his grace.."

She stepped from the arch, staff slung across her shoulders, Fennik curled in her arms like a loaf of warmth. Damp hair clung at her temple, but her smile held.

"I can't believe it, tomorrow is all ours," she said.

Korvan nodded. "Eris confirmed it. Three days, three days of rest."

Sera bounced on her toes. "Good. I'm seeing my sister. And I want one night without this one hogging the foot space." She nudged Fennik.

The fox grumbled and burrowed deeper into her arms.

Bren chuckled. "Heard that, though Rok doesn't hog the foot space as much as the food."

The bear-kin chuffed hungrily in response.

Ryn and Javek drifted in, their hair wind-chapped, and eyes wide with excitement. Her spear bumping against Ryn's shoulder, Javek still taming gauntlet straps.

"Three days off," Ryn sighed, sliding into the circle. "Dawn-mother's mercy."

"I'm going to the Night Bazaar," Javek said, eyes huge. "Ale till I fall over. Who's coming?"

"Only if you're buying," Bren said.

"For you? I'd need to take out a loan." Javek replied with a wide smile.

Laughter loosened the courtyard. After weeks of ache and barked orders, laughter was a balm for the soul.

Thalen arrived.

He moved with careful grace, storm-blue cloak immaculate, breastplate polished like he had never sweated. Midnight shadowed his heel, obsidian fur like poured ink.

"You're all too relaxed," Thalen said. "This is leave for restoration and to assess what we need to improve, not indulgence."

Bren elbowed Korvan. "Guess the Noble is allergic to fun."

"Let him be," Korvan said. "Some can't shut it off."

Thalen's eyes held him too long. It didn't feel like hate, but it was tension, two blades that had not yet crossed. He turned and left his boot leaving a spark on the stone.

The dismissal bell rolled through the Keep with finality and the group fell quiet.

Crickets filled the silence. A forge sang far off. Korvan rolled his shoulders until a rib clicked and the bright pain dulled to something he could carry.

He breathed once for the names the Breach had taken and once for those who had learned how to stand.

***

The sun rose clean on the thirty-second day. Eris waited at the gate in plain linen instead of steel. Her dark braid hung loose. She carried no weapons. She didn't need one. Her command ran deeper than any armor or blade.

Korvan joined the formation, his cloak still damp from the wash, Brusk and Vasha sentinel at his side.

Restless grins tugged the line. Heels bounced. Tension wound tight and ready to spring.

"You have earned your leave," she said. "Two days, as promised. And you are fortunate as tomorrow is Atheris' Light. The city's sacred rest day "

Cheers rose. Her smile brightened as she listened.

"Three days in total. Enjoy them. Rest. Eat. See the city. Remember why you wear that emblem." Her gaze warned and steadied.

"Kael'Thir's Vigil closes the month. At dusk on that day, the city renews its wards. If you are not inside the Fourth Ring by the second bell..." A tired smile touched her mouth. "I will find you."

"Remember conduct matters. You are sworn to the defense of this city and the principles and conduct of the Aethyrguard. While you will be recognized for your skills and rank among us you are not celebrities. This is your warning. No tavern brawls. No wagers. No cloaks traded for kisses. If the city honors your name, it will be because you stood when others ran."

"But enough protocol. You have three days," she said, softer. "Don't waste them."

Ward locks hissed. Ancient clockwork gears hummed. Light ran carved runes. The barracks gates unsealed with a thunder-soft groan. Storm cloaks stepped into sunlight snapping in the wind the way the sails in Lantern Harbor do. Korvan lingered one breath at the threshold. Salt wind tugged his cloak. He smelt a fresh wave along the breeze. The sea, steam, herbs, stone-baked bread and the ever-present sent of metal being worked. The city wrapped him with its smell.

For the first time in weeks no one required him to stand at attention, but he still did.

He turned to the Battlemage, permission on his face.

At Eris's nod he stepped into the light.

***

Cael'Lumar sprawled like a living map its walls terraced, tiered, and glistening with the morning dew. The stones retained a faint Aethyrglow. Not enough to dazzle. Enough to remind of their strength.

Korvan moved through the hum of workers, shoppers and more. Pipefitters swaddled a steam line with cloth and curses. Jugglers sent glass orbs skipping rainbows along the stones. Children chased a hoop downhill, laughter skittering like pebbles over water. A beggar traced a ward in soot on his bowl. Hands touched luck and left coin behind with dismayed shouts.

He walked without Brusk or Vasha. He felt naked without them, he could still feel them across the bond, but they'd not been this far apart in over a month. It wasn't policy, Aethyrguard were allowed to walk with their Veyrkin unlike most citizens. But it was his choice. They drew eyes, especially Vasha.

Today he just wanted some quiet, and to be Korvan again.

Acolytes painted prayer glyphs on some of the Third Ring stairs. A baker sang lemon-glazed and mint-seeded loaves and customers streamed in. A steam cart hissed toward the Crown Keep laden with food and other supplies.

People stepped aside when they saw his Soulmarks. No one was afraid of him, which came as a relief. But the recognition was different. The storm-blue meant something now, it marked all who wore it as dangerous just by being part of the Aethyrguard. It also meant they were the city's elite protectors.

For Korvan it was still too new. Before he had crawled under dock carts to hide, he took odd jobs to keep a room over their head, he stole bread when hunger gnawed so hard it split him in two. But now He was Aethyrguard. He had survived.

Pride did not fill the hollow, not yet. Despite what they all said about the Breach, he hadn't earned it yet.

His hand brushed the coin pouch at his hip a leather bag heavy with Silverbrands.

Fifty a month.

A fortune for a boy who once counted Ashers for every bite. The Quartermaster's pouch had stunned him. The weight still did.

He turned down hospice row.

Hanging planters rocked and long grown vines threaded shutters. Bells chimed soft at each door. A familiar green-ringed lantern marked the clinic beneath the emblem of the Twin Flame.

He set his jaw and went in.

Warmth met him and the smell of simmered herbs, boiled linen, the clean bite of salve rose with the warmth. High windows spilled light inside with motes of slowly spiraling dust. A matron sat behind a well-loved wooden desk writing notes in a leather-bound tome. Her hair hung in silver rings at her collar. Her face was wrinkled with years of lines. Her eyes had always been kind. Various potions and linens lined the walls around her and the room itself was immaculately clean. It was comfortable as it could be for a clinic.

"Korvan, is that really you? My you've really filled into a young man. And in an Aethyrguard cloak? No wonder it has been a while." Madam Ren said, looking up from a ledger. Her voice was what he thought his grandmother's might have been and in the moment she saw him he could see her putting together a great many things they'd talked about before.

"He's awake. Third alcove on the left, I'm sure you know he had to be brought here full time…" She hesitated and then added, "I am sorry to say but, your father is quite behind on payments."

Korvan shook his head, "Thank you Madam Ren for taking care of Caelen even without Varnrik's help. I don't feel too different, still just me. Better fed though," He forced a chuckle, "How behind are we this time?"

She nodded solemnly, "Five Silverbrands, four Ashers, nineteen split-crowns."

He counted ten Silverbrands into her palm as he silently cursed their father, nearly 2 months behind, and an insurmountable sum if Korvan didn't have the coin of his new post. "Gods, I am sorry… I owe you so much more than just the coin. Here this is more than enough and additional payment to cover the next month. Is it possible to get Caelen a private room upstairs? He deserves his own space and a door."

Surprise flickered across her face as her eyes flitted between the coins and Korvan's face. It settled into approval. "More than enough. He'll have the garden view by sundown. Now go, enough of this business. See your brother I will take care of moving him."

A breath eased the knot in his chest and he turned to go behind the counter.

"And Korvan," she called causing him to pause.

"You're a good man. Don't let anyone tell you otherwise." She nodded once and set to work leaving him with her words.

Korvan felt his eyes mist and an old ache spring in his chest, with a sniffle he pushed through doorway.

The Ground-floor alcoves were beds behind thin curtains. A girl coughed. Two old men slept. A child wheezed under wool.

"Kor?" A voice came thin and clear.

He stopped. His heart stumbled.

Caelen sat upright against pillows, curtain drawn back. Hair long past his shoulders and some of it curling at his ears. His frame too slight and his skin paler than the last time. But his eyes remained the same, identical to Korvan's, the same as their mother's. Silver, and bright with an internal fire.

"You finally came," Caelen said.

Korvan crossed the space in three strides and went to his knees. "I'm sorry," he managed. "I should have come sooner."

Cool fingers pressed his scraped knuckles. "Shut up, Korvan. You came back. That's more than enough."

His breath finally shook loose.

"The training is brutal," he said. "I didn't know how to stop. I didn't mean to leave you alone."

"You did leave me alone and that's ok because you promised me you'd come back," Caelen said, a small smile rising. "You held on. Just from farther away."

He squeezed Korvan's hand once.

"Oh, I heard the bells when the Breach opened weeks ago," he said, low. "I saw the lights. I knew you were there."

Korvan looked up.

"A flash," Caelen said miming in the air, "Silver in the sky. A roar that shook the glass. That was you wasn't it?"

"It was my new bond," Korvan said. "Her name is Vasha."

Awe and relief crossed Caelen's face. "You did it. You're becoming what he said you never would be. Strong."

"I did it for you."

"No," Caelen said, frowning. "You did it for us. That's the difference between you and him."

That truth rocked Korvan onto his heels. He blinked rapidly to clear his eyes.

Korvan set the pouch on the shelf. "You're covered now. No more ration lines. No guessing if the healer comes back. No coin for him to drink. I paid for a private room. Ren will move you today."

Caelen watched his face instead of the pouch. "You've changed brother."

"In a good way I hope?"

"I think so, you feel more confident," Caelen said. "I've been here, held together by poultices, patience, and Ren's kindness."

"You've been here holding me together."

A companionable silence settled between them, so many things to say, so many old wounds that needed healing from their parents, but their focus for so long had just been on getting to tomorrow. Now it was here and they didn't know what came next.

"Tell me everything," Caelen said, tired but bright.

Korvan told him. How The Beyond opened his eyes. How Vasha came through the Breach and chose him. How training sanded him down to the bone but made him strong.

He showed Caelen the shape of all of it. He set stance with a cushion for a target. "Shen'Drak steals the center line. Palm to forearm. Heel to hinge. You don't shove," he shifted a hair, "you place."

The cushion sighed. Caelen snorted. "Terror of pillows. The city is saved."

Korvan laughed. Then, gentler, "You'll love this, an item called the Cadence Lens is kind of like a shallow bowl of Aethyrglass. When a bond flares over it, bright rings form. Verdant shows one band. Ironmarked shows two with a faint element thread. Yours would look like a star if you were well." He caught the slip. "When you get well."

Caelen's fingers found the locket at his chest and steadied. "Tell me how it felt when she answered. The feeling."

"Like the world remembered my name," Korvan said. "Like thunder tried to make me whole. Like home. I can't wait for you to meet her."

He didn't recognize the look in Caelen's eyes but it was gone just as quick as it appeared.

His brother peppered him, questions tumbled out in rapid succession, reminding Korvan out of the two of them Caelen would've been the one to excel in his educational instruction. He answered everything. Details about Shen'Drak lock holds. How the Cadence Lens works. Whether he knew Vasha's name before he spoke it. The voice in The Beyond and seeing the Dragon.

He loved every one of the questions. He had not spoken this freely to anyone. He spoke on Bren's heart. Sera's laugh. Thalen's edges. Ryn and Javek from the fields who were much tougher than they looked. Days on Disciplines until his hands shook; moments when Auryn's Edge sang true; drills that showed where strength ends and will begins.

Caelen's answers thinned. Sleep took him mid-smile, lashes damp, breath shallow and even.

Korvan tucked the blankets close and slid a few more coins into the drawer. He found a note that Caelen had left. The note from when he bound Vasha. His eyes watered and drops fell.

He left his own note beneath the locket.

Get what you want. Write if you need more. I'll come back soon.

"We'll find a way, little hawk," he whispered. "I don't know how yet. But We will fix this sickness."

He stepped into the foyer and found Madam Ren trading healer's robes for temple blues. Her Laugh lines shown through with a sugar-warm smile.

"I've instructed my attendants," she said. "If your father comes, he won't be admitted. If you want that."

"Of course I don't, but Caelen should make his own decision," Korvan said. "He's nearly sixteen. If he asks, let Varnrik in. If he threatens him or tries to take him," his knuckles clicked, "send word. I'll handle it."

"This is a house of healing," she said. "I hope he won't dare."

"I'll keep coin on Caelen's account. Any books or mechanical parts, he really likes to build. Whatever he asks for, would you get it?"

"Of course, hon," she said, warm hand on his forearm. "I'll see to it."

She lifted a small satchel from a hook. A calico cat spilled from a shelf to her arms, then waddled ahead of her after as she locked the door. Lantern light slid over rain-worn stone. Salt and herbs rode the air.

Korvan waited until the ward sigil dimmed, drew his cloak close, and climbed toward the Rings.

At the bend above Lantern Harbor he found the memorial wall. A section nearly as old as the city itself. Countless names etched into duskstone. Old scorches adorned the base. Fresh chalk circled three lines near the bottom from an unsteady hand. He set two fingers to the stone and read until the letters steadied. They were his fellow Initiates. They might've been friends one day.

He let the ache rise, a burden he'd carry for them.

At a corner shrine to the Twin Flame he paused. Candles guttered in colored glass throwing ghastly shadows along the ground. Soot blackened the niche above Atheris' open hand. He pressed two Ashers beneath the lip of the shrine and touched stone with three fingers. One for his mother, one for Caelen, one for names he didn't know. Heat soaked his fingertips and wiped his brow.

A ritual for the believers, Korvan wasn't sure if the gods were watching or if they cared. But the water was warm and the belief felt good, even if he wasn't devout.

It wasn't perfect, though it didn't need to be.

It was enough.

***

The holding pens stank of straw, oil, and old rain. Iron gates clicked and chains whispered. Light fell in slats and turned dust to silver flakes.

Brusk stood like quarried stone inside his stall. Plates warmed under the lamps; copper veins throbbed a slow count. He watched the lane and let other beasts measure themselves against his stillness.

A Bulwark didn't posture. He endured. When an unfamiliar Taurhorn rolled a shoulder to press his space, Brusk shifted one hoof and placed his weight loudly. The sound carried. The elk-kin turned and gave him space.

Brusk snorted happily.

Across the aisle Vasha paced, her large pads quiet as snowfall. Silver fur took the light and gave it back in thin knives. Amethyst banding smoldered along her ribs. The pens held a dozen Howlers at least. Most Verdant, some Ironmarked, only two Obsidian besides her.

She read their scent and posture: fear under one breath; old blood in another's mane; a third who wore his scars like a crown and watched the exits more than the aisle.

None held her eyes for long.

Fennik trotted up with clean paws and a combed tail. He lifted his nose, chuffed once, and accepted a low head from Brusk. Rok followed heavy and sure, hide clean, and claws oiled. Rok and Brusk touched skull to skull and held, plates humming with a comfort only Bulwarks shared.

Handlers moved a crate past. Metal squealed in response. Vasha stilled mid-step, a familiar sound that reminded her of her chains.

Further down, Midnight watched from shadow. When Vasha's gaze slid over toward her they held their gaze. Neither postured. They didn't have to. While Midnight may have the advantage of some Spellcraft, she was a fraction of the size, strength, and speed of Vasha. Both knew how their fight ended.

Brusk listened past the surrounding clatter for the sound of a familiar gait.

Too many boots on stone. The rhythm of a heart he knew through another chest. Not here yet. He set his jaw and grounded his weight until the wood quit creaking.

Vasha tasted the air again. Salt. Sweat. Ink. A thread of helm smoke from the city below. Beneath it, the echo that made her skin tighten, the heat of a Soulmark that matched her spirit now. Korvan was near and coming closer. Pens felt smaller when he was not within reach; the world tilted a degree off center and waited to be corrected.

She lay down and set her head on her paws as if sleep had found her. It hadn't. Her whiskers tracked footfalls in the yard. Her ears gathered the soft sounds walls tried to keep. Brusk lowered himself beside the rail, his breath synchronizing to a count that belonged to a different body.

Around them, beasts dozed, chewed, and gamed their handlers for extra feed. Chains clicked. Buckets thumped. Lamps hissed.

Two hearts held the same rhythm and saved their hunger for when it mattered.

Korvan would step through the arch any moment.

***

The climb back felt different. Carts rattled. Laughter spilled from a covered alley. Steam and salt stayed on the wind. He had shifted. Steadier now. Anchored in a way he had not felt in moons.

He stopped for kettle tea poured from a copper urn etched with river birds. One cup for his hands and one he didn't need. A boy counted Split-Crowns twice and came up shy. Korvan slid an Asher across the counter and left before thanks could catch him.

He bought sweet rolls in waxed paper. One Silverbrand gone without a flinch.

By the time he reached the barracks, sun slid behind the cliffs and painted rooftops gold. Dice clicked on a stairwell. He passed unseen and chose the hush.

The dormitory held the quiet between sunset and supper.

Korvan sat on his cot and tore the pastry in half. He set a piece on the stone between them.

Vasha's whiskers twitched. She didn't take it.

We hunt first, feast after, she sent, amused.

Brusk's answer rumbled the bunk post, as he shifted to eat the pastry with the sound of contended chewing.

Gold eyes watched in the dim. Plates shifted. Warmth breathed steady.

He leaned into the stone and let the day finally relax. The coin pouch rode lighter from small gifts and a promise to Madam Ren: monthly coin for books, diagrams, parts. A room that could be Caelen's.

"Thank you, both," he whispered. "For staying here. For waiting on me."

His mark thrummed. Their warmth steadied his vow.

Coin mattered less than this. Caelen lived. They were safe. They would not be hungry again.

Korvan drew one deep breath and felt it settle in that place behind his heart where vows keep warm.

Chapter 12: The Echoes of Freedom

The morning bell of Kael'Thir's Vigil rang through Cael'Lumar echoing down its many archways. The city stirred beneath their call: shutters thumped open, banner-cloth trembled, apprentices, messengers and runners of all kinds sprinted uphill to claim perches before the crowd thickened.

Today was a day of revelry and rest and under it an older tradition of protection. A promise of renewal.

Korvan blinked into the light spilling through the narrow window above his cot. He moved slow, body marked by the previous months' work. The bone-deep ache in the shoulders, a seam of pain along the ribs, but the tenderness felt well earned. His Soul-marks answered his passing hands with a faint shimmer, silent fire threading under skin. The magic was no longer foreign but not wholly his either.

Vasha's heat burned quick. Brusk's steadiness thrummed beneath it. Korvan breathed through both and found the center. He'd not mastered the differences in their bonds but knew they complimented each other. Vasha's pull was stronger, her Prestige of course was higher. But Brusk's was older and more familiar. In the brief time he'd been bonded with Vasha he'd already felt it improve, soon enough he knew he'd have better control.

The barracks gates sighed open on released wards as they had the previous day.

An assortment of color met him in the streets.

The Second Ring had bloomed overnight. Silk swayed from balconies and watchtowers, brilliant against pale stone. Dozens of crests and guild sigils, twin-temple blessings, luck-charms. Even the oldest corners wore lanterns, Aethyrglass hearts glowing in hues that shifted with every gust.

He drifted along with the crowd having never gotten to participate before, always looking for more coin. He looked for nothing, sought nothing specific, just got to focus on one thing.

Being.

For the first time in countless moons: no barked name, no bout waiting to lay him flat. Just this, his city, alive.

A vendor hawked violet-dyed braids. Another turned finger-length fish over coals the perfume of chili and citrus sharp in the air. Children ran in circles with wrist-streamers; a tangle became laughter, no one scolded them not on this good day.

By mid-morning, the square swelled with people. Stages rose beneath Aethyr-fed trees. Skyship riggers sang a frost-eel ballad; masked players pantomimed the Eight Aspects, one a Howler so wild the crowd howled back.

Korvan let a quiet smile come.

His old habits kept him on the edge of things. The storm-blue earned nods and long glances, yet his body moved like a boy used to being passed over.

That's when he noticed Bren.

The big Initiate towered near a food stall, wrestling a meat skewer and a sugared pastry in the same hand like. Fennik watched from a bench with priestly judgment. Sera haggled over a shell-and-glass bracelet, green ribbon in her braid, and an easy laugh. Even Thalen had left whatever shadow he favored, dressed sharp for the Vigil. Midnight circled him her obsidian fur glistened like drying ink.

Bren spotted him first. "Korvan! Try this. It's weird as blight, but I love it."

Korvan cut through the crowd. "It's half gone already!"

"Doesn't matter. Still worth it, trust me and take a bite."

Sera glanced up. "At this rate, he'll need Rok to roll him home."

The bear chuffed on cue.

Korvan bit the pastry. A unique mix of honey and heat, and then a twist of citrus. He couldn't remember eating anything this good.

"Ok I need one of those," Korvan said.

Bren's smile became infectious; he turned immediately to the vendor to get another one.

"This is what we're fighting for," Sera said, coming up quietly at his shoulder. "Not just stone, our oaths or even each other. This." She gestured to the festival and the thousands of smiling faces that poured into Artisan's Row.

He nodded and let the layers of sound and light settle. His chest filled with a content breath. On the exhale he felt an odd tug, something just at the periphery of his awareness. A thread along his marks asking to be followed. He dismissed it and focused on his friends.

No one counted down the hours today. Drums and lute notes rang all morning and into the afternoon. Acrobats danced through their warmups. The square buzzed with celebration.

The group found shade by a hawk-fountain whose bronze feathers spilled water in fans of light. Sera folded a parchment into a fan. "If we survive another month, I'm opening a shop. Potions and pie. That's it."

"Terrible business model," Thalen drawled, "You'd poison someone within a week."

She shot him a feral grin, "Maybe I would, but only if they deserved it."

He rolled his eyes at her.

"You could call it Sera's Sweet Remedies," Korvan said. "Or Fatal Flavors."

Bren barked and nearly choked on one of his many snacks. "Don't Die Deliciously. I'd eat there."

They all stared at the crumbs that fell down Bren's tunic. Laugher echoed in their small corner.

They ate their fill and let stories drift between them the way embers bounce around a fire: Bren once slept in full armor and woke face-first in a trough. Sera turned her mentor's eyebrows violet for two weeks with the wrong ingredient in an elixir.

After a long quiet, Thalen admitted, "I released an illusion in my father's manor. Out of boredom. Forgot to dispel it."

"You, how scandalous," Sera said.

"The staff hunted a phantom bear for two days, I even made it leave random *accidents* throughout the house. But you can't tell anyone, my family was mortified at my *uncouth and rebellious* behavior," Thalen rolled his eyes as he said it.

"Too late," Sera said. "Fennik heard everything, by morning the whole Initiate class will know."

They were interrupted as minstrels threaded the crowd, their lutes and flutes sounding clear even against the wind. Many couples turned as ribbons flashed. For a moment, the square became a whirl of skirts and boots.

"Dance with me?" Sera nudged.

"With these boots?" Korvan said as his cheeks flushed.

"He's the noble," Bren proclaimed jutting a thumb at Thalen. "He must dance. It's law."

Thalen groaned. "Fine. One dance, but don't get upset when you can't keep up, Midnight has more grace than all of you combined."

Sera gave Korvan a coy smile and stepped out with Thalen.

Korvan knocked the pastry out of Bren's hand.

"Hey! What was that for?" Bren asked.

Korvan gave him a look and then gestured toward Sera and Thalen dancing.

"Oh... I... didn't think that through." Bren's face fell.

Sera's laugh echoed out and she was looking at Korvan over Thalen's shoulder. He didn't know how, but she heard them.

Sugary snacks abounded, spiced drinks warmed their bellies, and the sounds of a festival gave them all joy.

He let himself laugh even as Bren looked mortified. He focused on Sera as she danced. He thought that she was the most beautiful woman he'd ever seen.

***

By afternoon, the revel shifted as golden sunlight deepened to copper, then rust, then violet as the sun fell; shadows lengthened between rings. That strange tug along his marks returned, this time it was steady, insistent.

He drifted from the group while the others argued about which wine to have with fried dumplings.

"Back in a minute," he said, though none of them seemed to hear.

The crowd thinned on a spiraling ramp toward the quiet edges of the Second Ring. Lanterns leaned as he passed. The smells of the wind changed. It was paper, crushed herb, and a floral note he couldn't name. At a three-street junction, a sudden silence filled the area.

To the right, an alley opened like a seam too narrow and dark. Rune-lights weakened down its spine to a single pale glow. A wooden sign creaked on a chain: a spiral inside a rising sun.

His marks thudded once, urgent.

He stepped toward the dark.

"Korvan."

Thalen stood a few paces back, arms folded, Midnight moved in his shadow. "What are you doing? You've been gone twenty minutes. Bren's about to buy a whole boar and Sera is trying to talk him out of it."

"There's something here," Korvan said. "It's been calling to me all day."

"Metaphysical? Magical? Or some other idle curiosity?"

"I don't know. It just feels like I'm supposed to be here."

Thalen sighed, "Fine, but I swear, if you get us hexed, I will never forgive you."

They entered the alley.

Sound dulled down to a memory. The bell above the door didn't ring; it swung once and stilled without a note

Inside, the air felt ancient and revered. Aethyrglass lanterns along the walls shifted between violet and sea-green as the pair moved deeper. Shelves bowed under strange things: a compass whose needle spiraled without end; an obsidian serpent devouring its tail; a jar of dust that glimmered like starlight at a well's bottom.

Nothing labeled, or even priced.

"I've lived here my entire life and I've never seen this store before, it shouldn't be here." Thalen murmured.

Korvan followed the pull. Past wall mounted blades and other reliquaries.

There.

Ashwood. Smooth and clean. A single spiral carved into the grip. Opaline inlay... Gods there was true Aethyrglass, clear as the frozen dawn.

He reached for it.

Something unlocked in him at the touch.

His mother's hands felt steady, warm, and threaded light through air in that same spiral.

"Strength only for yourself is dangerous," her voice called, and the sound felt like being home.

"Strength for others," the spiral brightened ",that becomes more."

Heat blossomed under his palm.

"Ah," a voice said.

An old man stood behind the counter. He hadn't been there before. Dark-green robes stitched with silver. Lined face. Eyes without bottom.

"Most overlook that one," he said.

"Who are you?" Thalen asked.

The man didn't answer. He watched Korvan. "That staff knows you," he said. "Or it remembers someone you loved." The old man's eyes grew distant.

Softer he said: "Steady hands, little Echoborn. Even when you were small, you reached for light you could not name."

Korvan froze.

His mother had sung that name to him. Little Echoborn. It was part of his lullaby.

"What did you say?" he asked.

The old man had already turned away.

Korvan looked down. The spiral shone as the moon does on water. Memory pressed harder into him. His mother leaning over a cradle, drawing light in spirals to his infant brother's chest.

"This staff," he whispered, he felt ice run his back, gooseflesh pop on his arms and legs, his mouth ran dry. "My mother had one like this. No... not like it. This was hers. How did you get this?"

"Some things find their way to me, they often are waiting for someone to find them again. If you recognize it then it waited well."

"How much?"

"One Silverbrand."

Thalen choked. "Storm break me; if that's a true mage's staff, it's worth a thousand Glimmers, more with the actual Aethyr-glass. It's a one-of-a-kind item. Either it's cursed or it's a walking stick. No way Korvan, don't trust this charlatan."

"I assure you there is no curse. No trap," the man said, eyes still on Korvan. "This shop does not trade in coin alone."

"What, then?"

"I often find the things most valuable to a person are stories. The best stories are priceless. But other times some things simply want to be found. Some things choose their keeper, and this staff has chosen you."

"That's not how the world works," Thalen interjected.

"And yet," the man said, "here it is. And here he stands."

Korvan set a Silverbrand on the counter. Warm from his hand. Another soft impact, another memory.

His mother's voice again, 'My little Echoborn', the lanterns flickered.

The merchant was gone.

The shelves stood empty and the shop was silent, the light from the lanterns gone, all that remained was dust and silence.

They listened to the new quiet until their heartbeats steadied. The staff's hum matched Korvan's pulse, then eased.

Thalen came to his side and shook his shoulder. "Korvan, you're talking to yourself... what was that?"

"What? No I wasn't. I don't know what that was." He tightened his grip. "But this was hers."

They stepped into the alley. The sign hung still. The breeze had died.

Behind them, where the door had been, a solid blank wall stood that was as aged as the stone around it.

Thalen turned a slow circle. "What the... It was right here," he said. "I walked through the Dawn-cursed door."

Korvan said nothing. Soulmarks glowed faint under the sleeves. The staff held a low note.

"Back there," Thalen said, lower. "You kept muttering. You spoke about a your mom, something about your brother, and the very strange part. A dragon..."

Korvan blanched, his throat snapped shut and he felt ice run down his back. Thalen's brows both arched.

"I... saw something in The Beyond during my Trial. He was massive Thalen, wings wide as a ship's sails, and a presence, a power you wouldn't believe. He didn't give me a name, but he knew me somehow."

"You bonded with it?" Thalen's voice was barely a whisper.

"No. He said I wasn't ready, or he wasn't ready. Bonded or not he's part of me now. I feel him watching me sometimes, like he's testing me."

"That's impossible. Dragons are supposed to be extinct."

He let the impossibility stand between them.

"Korvan." His voice hardened. "Not a Wyvern, not a Drake. A Dragon. You know what that means."

"I think so."

"The first of the Veyrkin. The strongest. The Aethyrguard teaches they were wiped out, maybe by Aethyrblight."

A colder breath walked the alley. Gooseflesh rose. Thalen's stance shifted and his hand slid to where his sword normally hung and his fingers twitched when no hilt was found.

"I don't think they're gone," Korvan said. "I think they're hiding. Besides if they were that strong, what could have wiped them out, really?"

Midnight's tail flicked, agitated. Thalen's voice came back thin. "I don't know, this is all exhausting and has made my head hurt... Why you?"

"Maybe because of my mother, what she did to me."

He looked at the spiral.

"She was more than she seemed. Maybe she was protecting us from this."

"You need to tell someone," Thalen said. "This could change everything, everything we think we know about the Beyond. Shit it could change the way we look at Veyrkin."

"They'll call me mad, try to lock me away."

"Or they'll believe you; then you'll be hunted by every noble family in the city, maybe the world."

The words landed heavy.

"Thalen, why did you follow me really?" Korvan asked.

Thalen's eyes narrowed, and an unfamiliar expression crossed his face. Korvan had grown used to his arrogance, the pride that was always there and the general air of superiority that he always attempted to convey. Whatever this was, it was nowhere near any of those expressions. Korvan thought it was almost sorrow.

"Because if you vanished too," Thalen said, "I'd be the one explaining it to Eris." His voice dropped low, the next words a secret he didn't want to admit but couldn't hold back. "I've failed enough for one lifetime."

They stared at each other for several breaths.

The Vigil's music thrummed against the stone. Lantern glows licked the mouth of the alley; the wall at their backs stayed blank.

"So what do I do?" Korvan finally asked.

"Whatever this is," Thalen said, sure, "keep it close. Learn everything you can. Tell no one. Not Eris. Not the Arcanists. Not yet, too many risks for no reward."

"You just told me to tell someone."

He exhaled. "The Guard protects the order first. If they think you're something they didn't design, something they don't control, they'll break you to fit in, or they'll just break you."

"Why are you helping me?"

His mask cracked again, but practiced grace put it back, Thalen was a noble's son after all. "Because if this spirals, I don't want to be surprised. I've had enough surprises lately."

"You know, Thalen, I don't think you're as much of an ass as you pretend to be." Korvan smirked.

"Don't get sentimental." Thalen turned toward the light. "Come on, before Bren buys the whole bakery and starts begging us for coin."

Korvan followed. The staff pulsed once, warm along his spine.
***

Lanterns bobbed low in a soft wind. The city eased to murmurs. He stepped beneath the iron arch near the barracks and breathed the hush. His marks warmed along the arms in a familiar measure.

Come back.

The whisper moved through him like breath. Air rippled in a slow spiral; the veil thinned.

Brusk arrived first, a small landslide with hooves. He huffed and thudded his tail in excitement. Vasha slid out a heartbeat later, her fur glistening in various shades of amethyst and gold in the lamps.

Korvan scratched behind Brusk's ear-plate. "Sorry for leaving you again. The square was too tight, you'd have knocked every cart sideways."

Brusk head-butted him square in the chest and nearly sent him stumbling.

Vasha circled and nipped his sleeve, a mild rebuke but with play in it.

"I know." He grinned. "Next time we'll find a wider street. I don't like leaving you behind."

They settled at his sides. For the first time all day he felt a stillness in his heart.

"Korvan."

Eris stood at the square's edge, braid down, midnight-blue tunic softening her usual severity. Captain Darien loomed beside her, scarred and smirking, a flask balanced in his hand.

He rose. "Battlemage."

"Not tonight," she said. "Tonight I'm just Eris."

Darien tipped the flask. "I'm Darien. Just ran out or I'd offer to share."

"That's ok, I've had plenty today."

Eris studied him. "How are you Korvan? Truly."

He brushed Brusk's plate and the staff's spiral. "Much better, I spent some time with my brother and friends, ate entirely too many sweet treats, Bren has a nose for finding every cart with something covered in honey."

He glanced at the them both pulling his eyes from Vasha's fur. Darien's arm was around her waist and Eris was resting her head against his shoulder. Korvan couldn't help but find it cute as Eris was head and shoulders taller than Damien, even with Damien wearing boots.

"And I guess, I'm still tired, training is brutal, but I'm loving it."

"That's good enough," she said. "For now."

Darien grinned. "You're already a legend in the Fourth Ring. Tales of hero gossip for our young prodigy."

"I'm not—"

"You are," Eris said, quiet. "Even if you don't want it, you can't pretend as if you don't stand at the head of your group."

Her gaze flicked to the staff. "New?"

"Found it," he said. "It called to me and I had to have it."

"Keep it close," she said. "Sometimes the Aethyr gives a gift before it gives a reason. That is Aethyrglass, that is a genuine tool of the Disciples... Did you steal it? An Initiate couldn't afford such a thing."

He went blank searching for something to say; old guilt erupted within him.

She lifted a hand, amused.

"I'm teasing, Aric. Yes, I know, even I can manage to jest from time to time."

Darien snorted and caught an elbow to the ribs.

"I'd love to find more jokes that you can tell Eris. Good night, Korvan."

They left on soft feet in twinkling lamplight.

Korvan knelt between Brusk and Vasha and set his hands on their shoulders. Let their weight tether him. For once he did not feel like a boy pretending to be something else.

***

The next morning broke sharp and cast silver across the world. Sea wind threaded the garrison. Second bell rang clean across glass and stone.

Korvan moved with renewed vigor, every movement felt sharp and precise. A sailor sure legged in a squall.

He buckled his harness and called Vasha and Brusk with a thought.

Eris stood at the square's head.

"I trust you all managed to enjoy your rest. I hope so, because now it is time to act with renewed purpose. This is where your will is forged," she called. "The Beyond tested your resolve, many of you stumbled. I will test your skills and now your heart to continue even after a failure. Because in the end magic runs out. Strength fades. But mastery of yourself, that endures."

Drills stormed their ranks, relentless and unyielding. Bladed forms until sandstone darkened with sweat. Rotations pivoting around the Bulwark anchors. Sparring with summoned beasts under senior eyes that gave nothing away.

Korvan pushed. Auryn's Edge cut cleaner. Brusk's blocks rose faster, less drag. Vasha pressed angles earlier, slips tighter, more controlled, and less feral.

Days blurred in a tide of History, Discipline, Combat, Breathing and pain.

Thalen and Midnight met him often, a subtle tension coiled under the restraint. They adapted each other often distance would be stolen and stolen back the next day. Korvan realized that while he had a clear advantage over Thalen in the Disciplines, and was physically stronger and faster because of Vasha, Thalen was undoubtedly the better Duelist.

Sera's skills lied mostly in disruption with Fennik, using her Mender's variation of Lightweaving to stun or surprise opponents leaving them exposed for her to follow up with rapid thumps of her quarterstaff.

Bren's hammer sounded with thunder on every blow, the man only knew one way to swing and that was with everything he had. Rok placed paws like boulders and snorted a kind warning a breath before every strike.

Eris corrected them all when needed. The occasional step too wide. A grip too soft. A hesitation too long.

Sometimes one word: "Better."

Night after night he wrapped raw palms, rubbed bruised ribs, and told himself:

You are not the boy who crossed that gate.

Weeks fell like embers. Each scar earned a new line. Each ache told a cost.

At dusk one night Eris climbed the steps and let her voice carry. "Four more weeks," she said. "None of you broke. Two months in, and my aren't you stronger."

A murmur moved through them. A tired disbelief mixed with a glint of pride.

"When, not if, the next call comes," she said, "you'll be ready."

Korvan glanced left, Brusk, stone steady. Right, Vasha, eyes bright with a hunger that had finally tempered.

The square emptied as Initiates ran to their rest.

He sat and unwound linen from a bleeding palm. The staff lay beside him, warm with a steady hum.

"You're stubborn."

Sera stood at the edge with a towel over one shoulder, braid loose at her collar. Fennik yawned and blinked.

Korvan smiled. "Tell me something I don't know."

She sat. Quiet gathered, the kind that gives something.

"You're pushing too hard," she said.

"I'm supposed to be the best, you've heard the way Eris, Maedryn, Cristos all talk to me. The twice bonded, the double Disciplines... I can't afford not to push hard."

"I've heard that before. You mean you won't stop, not that you can't."

He didn't answer, he didn't know how to.

Vasha nosed his shoulder. Sera brushed the Howler's flank with reverence that landed like a benediction. "She's grown," Sera said. "She's much less wild now."

"We've all grown, I hardly recognize myself in the mirror some days."

"Then breathe. Enjoy what we're training to protect. I want to see you happy."

I want you to be happy Kor. Caelen's words rushed into his mind as she said it.

"I don't know when to do that. I don't know how, but I know I want to. I want you to be happy too."

She rested her head on his shoulder. He held still and let the moment be.

"I don't know if I'll ever stop worrying," he said. "About Caelen. About what's coming."

"You don't have to stop worrying, but you also don't have to face it all alone. Because you're not. But you also need to learn that's how you know you're alive," she whispered. "Because you still care."

Her hand found his knee. She turned her palm over.

He slid his hand into hers. It was warm, steady, and slightly damp from the work of the day. She squeezed once. He exhaled.

Silence settled between them.

***

Thalen sat two tables away, his supper cooling.

The hall hummed, dishes clinked, low laughter rolled, the good noises of spent bodies. Fire cast warm shapes along stone.

Korvan leaned to catch Sera's soft words; she laughed, head tipped back, braid brushing his shoulder, their hands always near. Bren roared at his own jokes; Rok thudded paws like a drum. Fennik stole bites with priestly impunity.

A pack. Messy and loud. Whole.

Thalen drank and tasted nothing.

His gaze returned to Korvan. No bloodline, no crest, and they still moved with him. Even Midnight watched the other boy when she thought he wasn't looking.

His fingers curled under the table.

You were born to lead, his father had said. *But only if you remain above them.*

He had tried to believe in bond over birthright, loyalty without title. The last time he stepped down from above, he hadn't saved the one who mattered.

He rose with practiced grace, left the tray untouched. No one called after him. Midnight padded at heel and looked back once at the fire.

Thalen didn't.

He couldn't sleep.

He sat in the upper alcove above the training square, arms crossed tight against cold stone. Midnight dozed beside him, ears twitching. She was ever listening, ever there.

In his palm, a ring caught thin light.

Silver and black. A falcon crowned in flame.

Lareth's.

The last time he'd seen his brother was the garden wall at House Ryst: servants pretending not to listen. Thalen's voice cracking on the edge of boyhood. Lareth crouching to meet his eyes full of bronze and brilliance, laughter that made fear feel optional.

"I'm sorry but there are no send-offs," Lareth had said. "Not for failures."

"But you didn't fail!"

The smile hadn't held. Lareth pressed the ring into Thalen's fist; the tremor in his hand betrayed him. "They say a bond can survive anything. Mine didn't." A thinner breath. "I felt him vanish, a door closed inside me."

"What happens now?"

"I don't know," Lareth whispered. "The Guard says I'm unfit. No one says it aloud, but... They mean to erase me."

"You're a Knight. You're my brother, no one can make you go."

"That second one matters more, don't forget that." He stood. Cloak flared. "Don't follow me, Thalen."

"I—"

"I mean it, little Panther. Stay here. Make them remember our name for the right reasons." He turned. "I love you; I'll be back one day."

He left that night under the darkness with no escort and no ceremony.

Three days later: a sealed missive bearing news. Lareth Ryst, deceased. Killed in Action.

They never found his body. They didn't even have a memorial. Silence stacked on expectations for Thalen. They tailored Thalen a new uniform and taught him how to bow. He bowed. How to Duel, he dueled. How to be a perfect noble and smile. He tried to smile.

He petitioned once. The docket came back with the High Warden's crest. The matter is closed.

He obeyed.

He hadn't followed.

Now the city called him noble, and he saw the shadow of the one who had worn the ring first.

Midnight lifted her head and brushed his thoughts, a cool steadiness, her balm. He let it pass. He didn't deserve the comfort.

The ring didn't quite fit. He wore it anyway.

Because someone had to remember.

If another door ever tried to close in his chest, he would do something. Next time, he would not stay silent.

Chapter 13: The First Mission

The month of Stonefall drew a hard line. Five months since Korvan first dove into an Aethyrgate. Five months of bruises, Soulmark burns, and nights that smelled of linen and powdered salve. Five months of late dinners. Dreams he told only to Caelen, Sera, Bren, and as of late, to Thalen. Gone was the heat of summer as old leaves bronzed along the cliff roads. The rhythm of the world had shifted.

Birthdays had punched light through the grind. Thalen's 20th was stiff and quiet; Bren's 21st was frying-pan catastrophe of spice cakes and worse dancing. Even Eris had allowed a smile when Bren dared her to arm-wrestle him. His face was stunned when he lost with a thud.

Caelen's sixteenth, normally a massive affair, came and went without grandeur. He'd been having a fit with his sickness. It was little more than Korvan, Ren and Caelen with a few gifts, sweet treats, and stories. Caelen should've had dancing, music, endless food and to pick his trade. Still, for what it was, Caelen insisted it was the best birthday he'd ever had.

For precious moments basking in the light of the Arc-Tower lanterns, they'd felt like a family.

The month's colors painted everything. Aethyrglass along the barracks pulsed a cooler blue. Crews strung sigils for Kael'Thir's Vigil. Whispers of the Mid-Year Trial coiled in their bunks. Training changed, no longer about theory, now it focused on endurance. The instructor's also contained far less mercy and everything had more cost.

Korvan felt the turn in his marrow. He was nineteen now, he'd not said anything about his birthday, he hated it. A constant reminder that he grew stronger and older, while Caelen withered away.

He hunkered in his bunk, a bandaged ankle and reading the most recent letter from Caelen, though they saw each other every rest day, Caelen still sent him letters almost every day. This letter spoke about his newest design, a telescope, but not for the stars, for Aethyr, he still hadn't gotten it to work yet, but Korvan knew he'd figure it out. Caelen was always the smart one of the two.

"He's hanging in there, we'll hang in there too."

Vasha and Brusk sprawled at either side of his too small cot. They didn't move, but their mutual support rolled over him like the tide.

Almost Caelen, we're almost there. I've not figured it out yet, but I swear I will.

Hold the line, Vasha's golden eye looked at Korvan as her rumbling purr began.

"That's right girl."

Sleep claimed him as he scratched the massive cats head.

***

The briefing chamber smelled of oiled parchment and old sea. Lanterns throbbed blue making the room feel cooler than it was. Korvan stood with Sera, Fennik asleep at her boots. Bren cracked his knuckles; Ryn and Javek jostled their pack. Thalen folded his arms and narrowed his gaze.

They had trained, they had been bruised, beaten and bloodied. They were prepared.

The summons finally came.

Champion Varos stood at the far end of the room. He bore a missive bearing the High Warden's seal.

"Initiates," he said. "You've been given a priority assignment."

He didn't pause.

"A shipment of unrefined Aethyrglass left Lantern Harbor for Drakoth Forge in Vel'Drakos. It vanished somewhere along the road to Riverpost."

Eyes widened, but they remained silent.

Aethyrglass. The living metal, bright as a star. It powers ward-lines and lanterns, feeds skyships and storm-forges, runs the mirrored conduits beneath Cael'Lumar. Without it the city loses its primary export, Cael'Lumar had found a way to work it and harness the Aethyr within it. Capable of nearly anything, an entire shipment was worth a fortune. Korvan didn't know how much exactly, but it was enough that the city requested the Aethyrguard directly intervene.

"Vel'Drakos, or the Emberkeep as you've likely heard it referred to, sits on the Ashen Chain," Varos said. "Drakoth Forge is their capitol. We send our raw Aethyrglass which feeds their Ember Crucible; their smith-priests forge it and send bac ward-anchors and blades marked with Ember Sigils. Those sigils steady flame Disciplines and keep our ward lines from eating themselves."

He let that land but went on. "The Ember Circle governs there. They are not part of our direct oversight, but their oath binds them to the Aethyrguard and us to them. If we strain that oath, it frays one of the oldest contracts we have. They are our partners, and it is not clear which of us needs each other more."

He turned. Eris stepped forward. Her posture firm as steel and there was dusk in her voice.

"This is no drill. You'll operate beyond the city without reinforcements. Only training, each other, and the bonds you've forged. Trust each other. Guard each other. Bring the shipment home."

Bren half-lifted a hand. "And if we don't?"

Varos didn't blink. "If you wish to remain in the Aethyrguard. You will."

Sera gasped, Bren's jaw fell, Korvan felt his fists ball. Thalen smirked.

Eris gave a single nod. "You have tonight, prepare as best you can, but recover your strength. This is a no small test, and failure means you will no longer be welcome in the Aethyrguard. But you are ready, you don't have a choice."

Softer she added on: "I believe in you. Dismissed."

Boots scraped. Cloaks breathed. The line dissolved into thought.

Korvan lingered. Eris met him at the corner of the table.

"You were born for more than surviving," she said and the iron in her shoulders eased. "Remember it. Tomorrow's the first step."

"I won't let you down." Korvan responded.

"I'm sure you won't Aric."

***

The second bell rang low. Korvan stood over the staff on his chest at the foot of his bunk. The Ashwood length, spiral of opaline adorning the top, Aethyrglass insert drinking the light.

All this time later and yet... it still didn't feel right.

He left it.

Instead, he put his gear on. Leather straps over chainmail with bracers to match, his Initiate sunburst marking the clasp of his cloak. It was comfortable now, a welcome weight adorning his shoulders.

He checked his travel satchel with familiar rhythm. Rations, water, and a compact survival kit.

Some recent additions he was encouraged to get. A short-sword, three balanced throwing knives, poultice laced bandages, a vial of silver-flecked ward ink, an emergency way to conjure a protective circle.

Lastly, his resonance chime.

It had a mirrored steel, the outer ring of his Soulmark etched in it to match. If panic snapped your concentration, the note would call your Veyrkin from the beyond.

His hand hovered for a breath too long, and he saw a brief tremble. He clipped it to his belt and stepped into gray light.

Everyone was waiting in the yard.

Bren wore his crooked grin, hammer slung over his shoulder. Sera adjusted her clasp, Fennik looped warm around her shoulders. Thalen stood stoic, cloak folded perfectly, Midnight shifted slightly to remain in shadows. Ryn and Javek slid in together, both lanky and wind-bitten, but still sharp-eyed.

The twins continued bickering about gauntlet straps and balance points, still finishing each other's jokes. Above them, their Pathcarvers circled once and vanished into the clouds.

Eris waited beneath the arch with Kaelith. The pegasus was dawnfire gold, her wings half-folded. She was only here to see them out.

"Ready?" Her voice was loud in the grey mornings calm.

"Ready," Korvan said.

Her gaze held a heartbeat, then she turned toward the gate.

They crossed under Cael'Lumar's out walls as the mist burned off. Sun stitched golden rays through stone ribs. The city crowned the cliffs in ascending spirals, each ring humming with contained light. Only the road remained.

The trade route wound west through orchards and barley. Ward-totems watched, charms flickering passively. Farther out, a still green tide of forest lifted, stitched with forgotten shrines and old boundary stones.

Korvan breathed new smells, loam, and pine. The air tasted fresh.

"That hill over there," Bren pointed. "They say a giant fought there."

Thalen arched the cleanest brow Korvan had ever seen. "A giant, or a large drunk?"

Ryn snorted, her drawl growing more prominent the further from the city they made it. "Bein' that drunk sounds like a right good day."

Javek raised a hand, in homage to a priest. "Listen well you lot, respect the legends of the happily shitfaced."

Even Thalen's mouth ticked at that and for a mile laughter rode with them.

They descended into farms where irrigation lines wore a gloss of dew and stone fruit hung heavy as lanterns. The farmers Veyrkin trotted the ditch lines in a protective patrol, little cranes with rune-inked legs, a badger in harness hauling a weed-sled like a king. Beyond, dense woods sprawled like a veridian sea.

They made camp at a stone bridge over black water that was cold enough to bite bone.

Vasha prowled through the tree line, only sign of her was the glint of her eyes between trunks. Brusk settled to Korvan's right, tail curled close. Overhead the stars burned bright.

Here, Brusk settled under his ribs.

Vasha cut a slow circle and pressed her shoulder to his back. *It is good to be beyond the walls, the fields are freeing.*

The camp was quiet, the nerves of what was ahead of them evident on everyone's face, or in the silence that moved between them. Tomorrow they'd pass the warded farms and step into thin places where the road no longer had a name. If the shipment were truly lost, they would find whatever had taken it and learn what wanted the two great partners of Cael'Lumar and Vel'Drakos weakened..

A grueling day of riding meant that old costs tallied up in the quiet: ribs that still ached from Shen'Drak pressure drills, Soul-marks tender where Vasha's speed outpaced his grip, and sleep debt like silt in the blood. His mind also raced, thoughts moving between battle plans, old instructions and how to get everyone back.

Sleep found a way to claim him anyway.

Dawn took them farther from the familiar. The ward-totems thinned leaving them longing for the familiar comfort of their ambient Aethyr, and what the safety they represented. Half a day beyond the last farm, they found the first sign of a struggle. A splintered mile-post sunk into ditch water, its runes hacked, then smeared with clay.

Sera knelt. "This was deliberate, someone tried to hide it and get folks lost and not point the way back to Cael'Lumar."

Thalen crouched opposite. "Or didn't want it to point *any-where*." He glanced at Korvan.

By late afternoon they reached a narrow pass where the road bent around a low ridge. A wagon had turned here, heavy wheels chewing the soft shoulder. Bren swung down and traced the gouges with two fingers.

"Loaded heavy, must've been at its breaking point. Then the tracks get lighter," he said, frowning. "See? The depth changes."

"Unhitched here," Javek added, pointing to crushed scrub. "They shifted weight around, at worst or more'n likely moved cargo to a second wagon."

Ryn shaded her eyes and whistled low. Her crow-like Verykin slipped from the thermals and dropped on to her glove. She murmured to them something Korvan missed and loosed him again. Light threaded from his talons as he skimmed the ridge. A glare painting a thin lattice where dust hung in the air appeared tracing something.

Footprints. Too many to count, Human, mostly. A few clawed, they didn't have many Veyrkin. At least on foot.

Sera's mouth tightened. "No beast left those tracks."

"People adapt faster than beasts," Thalen said, "Especially when coin is heavy."

They pushed on. The road stepped down into scrubland and old thorn. Evening appeared as a new scent grabbed their attention, something alkali and the copper of old blood. They found the ward-post in a shallow gully: fallen, wheel shattered, conduit glass blackened at the edges. Someone had packed the seams with ash to make it look like time had passed.

Korvan brushed the rim. A hum of lingering Aethyr that felt wrong in his bones. He flinched and hissed as the magic burnt his fingertips.

Vasha stiffened.

"This was deliberate," he said. "They overloaded the conduit out and tried to cover it up like it burnt out on its own."

Sera unfolded her kit. "I can mend it, at least partially. The conduit looks salvageable. It'll offer more protection than nothing anyway."

"Do it," Korvan said. He caught himself giving orders and looked to Thalen.

Thalen didn't bristle. He nodded once. Eris had placed Thalen in charge after all.

"Bren, get some food going. Ryn, Javek, keep your eyes everywhere, I do not want us caught unaware. I'll pick a direction once Sera's finished her work. Korvan, use Vasha and Brusk to keep a close perimeter, anything gets by the twins, its up to you to slow it down. I'll help Sera."

They worked without wasted words. Fennik's light found the clean fractures—Sera set new sigils but worked slow. The damage was worse than they thought, but she and Thalen could manage. Bren set to work, forgoing a fire in favor of small hot plates, to prepare a simple meal. The twins vanished upslope.

Korvan stood watch. He felt exposed and vulnerable. His skin crawled and he could not shake the feeling of being watched even though Vasha smelt nothing of concern.

With Korvan. Korvan strong. Many friends. Brusk nudged his hip and gave him as close to a smile as his crag-like face could muster.

Korvan scratched his head.

He exhaled and stayed in the now.

It only took an hour to repair so they decided to cover a bit more ground. With the ward-totem repaired at least for now it gave the group renewed determination.

By dusk the road had widened into a shallow basin ringed by thorns and breaking shale. Ryn signaled from the ridge: two fingers, then a fist. Two targets. Stop.

They eased into the basin's lee and flattened to the ground. Below, in a spill of shadow, fresh ruts scored the hardpan. A smear of mirror-bright dust glinted in a track where something heavy had bounced and cracked.

Javek's whisper barely moved the air. "They stripped a crate on the move, that's Aethyrglass dust."

Thalen traced a sigil in dust and opened a faint, false shimmer, a mirage of empty road to anyone looking in appeared behind them. He didn't look at Korvan, but he didn't have to. "We're not the only ones hunting out here."

Night came too quickly. They made a dry camp and ate in a ring of quiet: hard bread, dried meat, water that tasted like tin. Korvan took second watch. The sky turned to frost. Somewhere a vixen barked once.

Footsteps padded to his right. Thalen sat without asking, Midnight right behind.

"Can't help but notice you didn't bring all your gear, as the squad leader its my job to make sure the group is adequately prepared. Why did you leave the staff?" Thalen said.

Korvan didn't look over. "I'm not ready, it doesn't feel like it belongs to me yet."

"Good, bringing a tool you're not comfortable with is asking for trouble, it unnecessarily risks your squad's safety on an untested tool." Thalen's mouth twitched. "It's easier to drown when your pockets are full of stones." A beat. "I meant the metaphor, not your ability to swim."

Korvan huffed. "I can swim."

"I assumed. You are a dock rat after all." The words should have landed like a slap. Thalen pitched them like a fact.

"I was wondering when you'd choose to wield the fancy stick,"

"When it feels like it belongs to me and doesn't leave me with more questions. Then I can use it."

"That's not how it works, Aric; questions *are* weapons. You'll never get more comfortable with it if you are afraid to even pick it up."

Silence softened between them. Midnight's tail thumped once. Brusk's slow breath did what it always did, made Korvan's own breath steady.

"Why Riverpost?" Korvan asked. "If you were going to strip a shipment, why not nearer the harbor?"

"Closer to the city means faster response times, far more risks and heavier wards." Thalen's eyes tracked the ridge line and he had a surprising heat in his voice, "Out here the Crown Guard pretends to watch while the trade corridor rots, they haven't had a true threat in almost fifty years, not worth truly patrolling it like they should. When the law isn't here to keep the peace the only real law becomes price." He flicked two pebbles into the dark. "Someone's adapting to the complacency of the city. They want the city hungry *and* blind to what's going on beyond our grand walls."

"You think nobles are behind this, the way you're talking feels personal," Korvan said.

Thalen didn't answer. Which was an answer.

Ryn relieved them near dawn, her Veyrkin already awake.

She squinted at Korvan's wrapped hand. "You're squeezing that hilt like it owes ya a glimmer."

"It owes me something." He flexed his fingers and felt the old Shen'Drak bruises complain. "Too many hard days of training, not enough sleep."

They moved at first light.

Tracks turned toward the river that named the town. The water braided through flats and willow-choked bends, slow and brown with silt. In the distance, a low haze hinted at Riverpost. Closer, they found a ferry landing, but the ropes were cut, planks scattered, anchor-stone rolled away.

A sign that should have read TARIFFS AND INSPECTION lay face-down in mud.

Sera knelt by the waterline where swirls of pale dust had taken the current like pollen. "They ferried at night. Didn't want the wards tight on the bridge."

Bren sniffed the air and grimaced. "Smoke, not a cooking fire, a Kiln or smelter."

"Glassworks?" Javek whispered.

Thalen's mouth went thin. "Or someone is trying to learn how to refine our Aethyrglass."

They ghosted along the bank until the river took a tight turn and the trail opened to a shallow bluff. Below it, a longhouse hunched among tamarisk and rusted anchors, roof patched with old sail and pride. Light leaked at the seams and low voices, moved within. Outside, six horses stood with tack on, not tethered but ready to go.

Korvan counted bodies, doors, windows. He felt Vasha coil under his skin like a kept flame. *It is time to hunt.*

Thalen's hand ghosted a stop in the air. He met Korvan's eyes. No time to argue, he had a plan.

Ryn and Javek slipped off along the bluff with their birds. Bren rolled his shoulders until bone popped. Sera's fingers hovered over Fennik's ruff, a pulse of quiet medicine moving into the ready.

Eris wasn't here to set the pieces, or give them the orders. Korvan would.

Korvan whispered, "On my mark."

Thalen's mouth curved, somewhere between contempt and respect. "Don't make me regret this."

"Wouldn't dream of it."

Boots scraped on rock ahead. Two shapes lingered at the signal brazier, river-wind rustling their cloaks. Dressed in town-watch garb, posted by the Crown Guard. One older, jaw bristled; one young, eyes too bright.

Thalen angled off, his Discipline letting him blend with the background. Korvan came center, sunburst clasp catching gray light. Vasha slid from shadow and stalked behind Korvan; Brusk's plates ticked once, a not-so-subtle warning.

"Afternoon," Korvan said. Not a question.

The older watcher swallowed. "You're far from the ring-road they're lad."

"A shipment went missing," Thalen said appearing like a specter. "Raw Aethyrglass bound for Drakoth Forge. We're tracking it on behalf of the Aethyrguard. We'll have your names." He pointed to their cloaks as they did.

Even as Initiates they were empowered by the Crown Guard and the Crown Council to carry out investigations and enforce the law. The unspoken truth was that they were more politically influential than the Crown Guard. They had Veyrkin after all.

The men stiffened. The younger glanced at the brazier like it might answer for him, the older of the two drifted subtly toward his spear.

Vasha padded three steps closer and fixed them with molten gold. Her head crested over Korvan's, an impressive sight considering how tall he was, but she was still the size of a draft horse.

The older man's hand rose from his spear by inches.

Korvan didn't raise his voice. "Judging by the tracks we found, you met a crew last night. Two wagons riding under a heavy load. You gave them a way past the weigh-house and passed the check-in."

The crackle of the signal brazier and the heavy exhales of the Saber-cat behind Korvan was the only answer. He focused his attention between the two men and settled on the one closer to his edge. Vasha's focus shifted in an instant to match Korvan's.

The younger broke. "Halsen Pit," he blurted, words tripping. "I'm Halsen. He's Brann Rook." A breath. "They said they were a river-cart from Vale Hallow, something about grain overstock, on a back-haul to the Stonewatch quarry, it sounded right."

Brann shot him a sharp look silencing Halsen. "We didn't open the gate."

"No," Thalen said, precise, "you told them how to move around it and avoid the main roads."

Halsen flinched. "We pointed them to the Silt Cut and told 'em to skirt the old mill culvert. That's all. Just... directions."

"And they paid for those directions?" Korvan asked.

Brann's jaw worked. "A few Ashers. Nothing worth trouble."

"It will be worth trouble, they bribed officials of the Crown Council and sworn guardians of the realm. And you accepted," Thalen said. "Write your full names and ranks." He offered a slate. "You'll present to the Crown Guard house at the south gate of Riverpost no later than a fortnight from now. Its a long walk, but you'll make it."

Brann bristled. "We've got families to feed, you can't do this."

"We can and we have," Korvan said. "Or we come back with a squad and haul you away. Run and my Howler gets to hunt you down."

Vasha's tail drew a slow S in the dust. Brusk set his weight and the stone remembered.

Halsen reached for the slate with shaking fingers. "Halsen Pit. Watch turn three."

Brann hesitated, then scrawled: "Brann Rook. Watch sergeant." His voice sanded down. "We didn't know it was Aethyrglass."

"You knew it wasn't grain," Thalen said. "Your dereliction of your duty has put the entire farming basin at risk."

Korvan tucked the slate. "You point anyone else toward the Silt Cut?"

Brann shook his head. Halsen flushed. "One, one more crew. Red scarf at the wrist. They asked after the marsh road. We said it was flooded. They went anyway."

"Thank you for telling us the truth," Korvan said.

Vasha's gaze held them a beat longer, then eased. Brusk thudded his tail once.

Hold the line, Korvan sent through his bonds.

Korvan turned away and felt the hunt lean forward in his bones. "Back to work," he murmured.

Thalen's mouth curved, barely. "If you don't show up the consequences for abandoning your post is being labeled as a traitor. I don't need to remind you of the consequence of that. Be sure you arrive at Riverpost and report, they'll be expecting you. Don't make me regret not hauling you to Cael'Lumar now."

"We wouldn't dream of it, sirs." Brann said.

The wind exhaled for them.

***

They reached the crossroads by midday, where the stone-paved trade road split toward Riverpost and a string of smaller villages between. A mossed milestone marked the divide, its old runes worn soft by salt wind and rain.

The scent of pine and freshly tilled earth swirled in the breeze, but there was a note under it, something he couldn't place.

Korvan felt it first. The hairs along his arms lifted; Vasha's restlessness picked up.

They passed the blackened shell of a waystation. It must have been gutted years ago and left to collapse under vine and rot. Completely empty. No wagons. No carts. No trail-hands. Only the wind and leaves listening.

Thalen frowned. "Where is everyone? This is a primary artery. Even on a slow day, we should have crossed half a dozen caravans."

Ryn slid her spear to rest across her palms. "This road feeds the whole basin. We should'a seen a wagon or three."

Javek's fingers tightened on his satchel strap. "Ain't heard a bird in a while. That ain't right either"

Bren dropped to a crouch at the verge and traced a churned rut. "No more than a day old. Something heavy rolled through. Then more tracks. These were smaller, lighter, sharp edges, must be people taking turns riding in it. I've not seen any discarded gear. Good news is, we're gaining on them."

Thalen knelt beside him. "You've got a good eye."

"Da was a hunter. Taught me to track before I could walk straight."

Sera scanned the tree line; Fennik bristled against her shoulder. A howl pierced the sky around them. She let out a startled, "Wolves?"

Ryn and Javek glanced at each other and their eyes flashed white as they looked through their Veyrkin's eyes.

Javek hesitated, then shook his head. "Nah, look at this groove." He followed a long scar in the ruts. "Claws. Deep ones. Ain't no wolf I know that makes a mark like that."

Vasha slid ahead, low, and silent, hackles up.

The wind is wrong. Thin and sharp.

Korvan crouched. Stone under his palm felt leeched of warmth. His Soulmarks prickled.

"This was chosen as a trail," he said. "Something wanted this path, Vasha smells something on the wind."

Brusk planted in the road's center, broad and immovable. *Brusk guard.*

Tension climbed the line like a spark catching dry reed.

"Close order, defensive positions" Korvan said. "No one breaks."

They moved toward the bend. The road narrowed. The woods kept their counsel.

They veered onto a cattle track barely wide enough for two. Brush clawed forward clearing it. Branches slapped against him and weeds choked old ruts. Vasha paused and looked back. Warning lived in her eyes and along the bond, *Little Hunter, there is something that smells wrong ahead.*

"Vasha smells something off ahead, Ryn, Javek, can your bonds check it as we go?"

They replied "Aye" in unison.

They topped a low rise. The path broke into a clearing.

Wreckage.

A merchant's wagon lay on its side, axle snapped, a wheel flung into scrub. Aethyrglass crates scattered like bones; a few were cracked, runes coughing dim pulses.

Korvan's gut pulled tight.

The air stank of blood sweetening in heat, wood char, and a bitter tang like burned copper and the sulfur of Spellcraft.

"Storms take it," Ryn said, spear lowering. "A simple bandit don't do that."

Fennik whimpered.

Javek edged closer, voice low. "Smells like a ritual went real wrong."

Sera touched a gouge in lacquered frame. "This isn't panic clawing at the boxes. Something picked through this deliberately."

Thalen's jaw firmed. "So it took what it came for, or it got driven off by something else."

"Whatever did it, it was sent with a purpose," Korvan said.

Brush stirred.

Vasha dropped, a growl rolling up from chest to teeth, all the warning they received.

Two shapes burst from the green. Duskwraith Vulpar's, lean-fox-shaped Veyrkin. Verdant Prestige, Shadebound Aspect, like Midnight but not as dangerous or they wouldn't have been except they were covered in Aethyrblight.

Fur hung in patches; black ichor pulsed under skin like tar. White eyes without pupils fixed like blame.

One lunged.

Auryn's Edge answered Korvan in a bright line. He swept it across the beasts flank catching its ankle. A tendon twanged and its foreleg folded wrong. Black hiss steamed against the grass.

Brusk thundered through the second before it reached Sera. Sera pivoted, staff low; Fennik leapt and locked its back ankle. A cracking retort where wood met bone.

Thalen moved sharp, custom longsword already at hand. He split shallow down the assailants spine and his voice snapped, "Eyes up, two on the ridge."

Above, the Pathcarvers wheeled their rune-marked wings cutting patterns into the light piercing the illusion and revealing the trap. Ryn's falcon screamed and knifed to tree line like a warning flare.

"Cover the flank," Ryn called. Fear lived in her eyes; but her grip held steady.

Javek fed sight through his bird, palm a dim glow. "Two watchin, they ain't moved."

"Focus here first," Korvan said. "Keep formation."

The nearest beast shrieked and hurled itself at them on its wounded leg. Brusk blocked again. The hit hammered ribs through the shared brace, but the Bulwark would not be moved.

Bren crashed in, his hammer whistled through the air. Ribs folded with a wet crunch; breath wheezed out like punctured bellows, and it went still.

Sera streaked through with crackling staff. "They aren't knitting themselves," her voice confused between breaths. "The blight is eating the Aethyr out of them."

Vasha flowed low. She found Korvan's line and tore wide, the newest beats ribs gave in a series of pops.

Korvan stepped through the lane and drove the glaive into its throat. A brief shudder followed, then its body went slack.

The second twisted to run.

Ryn's spear arced and buried deep, pinning it to the loam. Thalen arrived in three clean steps, blade straight and quiet to the heart.

Ash sloughed. Violet threads winked and died.

A breath.

Bren wiped sweat and filth from his face. "Simple milk-run my ass."

Korvan flicked ichor from the edge and faced the crates. Faint runes wavered over the fractured Aethyrglass.

This was no accident.

"Thalen... how much?" Korvan asked

"Not sure exactly, not my expertise, but four crates, its counted in Flamecoins."

Bren interjected, "If this was refined Aethyrglass, it'd be priceless. My Da liked to hunt, but he was a Smith by trade, he worked on darksteel and built ship ribs and spines for some of the trade ships." Bren knelt beside inspecting it. "This is raw, unrefined, not nearly as valuable as the worked material because its so damn challenging to refine. Thalen's right it's probably ten to twenty Flamecoin for the lot, but this is only half of it or so."

Flamecoin, Korvan thought. He'd never seen a Glimmer in person let alone a Flamecoin. Flamecoin was worth at least ten times a Glimmer and Korvan's Silverbrands only made five Glimmers a month. It was hard for him to fathom.

"More's the pity, its a kings ransom that," Javek said.

"Come on. Let's find who left a fortune behind, and where these Veyrkin came from." Korvan said.

The trail ran deeper, a game path tight with thistle. More churned earth, snapped brush, and iron-capped boot scrapes wrote the route for them to follow.

Korvan led. Vasha ghosted at his knee, muscles taut, ears pinned. Each step set heavier in his chest.

It was far too quiet and too clean. He could feel it on the edge of his awareness. Something waited.

Sera floated close, Fennik's nose flicked anxious huffs; his tail tapped her collarbone. Bren took the rear, Rok lumbered beside. Ryn and Javek held their center. Ryn's spear half-lifted, jaw locked; her Pathcarver floated above while Javek flitted from shadow to shadow keeping watch.

Thalen watched the other edge, leaving the front to Korvan. "The trail's scrubbed, it's obvious they want us to follow, we're walking headlong into a trap."

They all shared a brief glance and nodded.

No turning back now.

The Forest thickened. Sun broke into gold shards through the branches, the breeze shifted wafting a new scent, moss, ash, the ghost-scent of a fire put out too late.

A clearing opened.

Trees ringed a dead tower, roof partially caved, ivy growing through. Aethyrglass glittered along the path like dying stars.

"Hold," Korvan breathed.

He crouched. Vasha went still.

Thalen narrowed his eyes. "No sign of sentries. Either sure of their strength or foolish enough to think no one is on their trail."

"Hopefully not the strength one," Korvan said, standing.

Thalen put them in motion. Brusk to the arch; Thalen and Bren holding the flanks; Sera and Ryn in the rear; Korvan with Javek watching the center and the sky.

Brusk filled the doorway. Korvan followed, Auryn's Edge warm, mark humming low under his sleeve.

Air hit like a slap, dense smoke, old meat, sweat, and the undeniable smell of liquor. A makeshift camp ringed a dying fire. Six men lounged amid the wreckage. They wore patchwork armor and dust-colored cloaks. The inner wall stacked with cracked Aethyrglass, unstable, but still glimmering.

One looked up.

"Aethyrguard!" he jerked, scrambling for his feet and a weapon.

Steel flashed, ugly and poorly kept. Two crossbows came up shaky.

Korvan stepped forward. "Listen, we don't want any trouble. We're here on the authority of the High Warden and the Aethyrguard. You don't have to fight for the stolen glass," he said, even. "Stand down and no one gets hurt."

A heartbeat of maybe.

Greed and fear turned the moment foul.

A thick-necked man with a brand-scar spat. "We bled for it already, means it's ours. Hand it t'city brats? I've got mouths to feed."

His blade rose. Hate lit behind the eyes.

Korvan's grip set.

"Please don't do this." He tried.

Motion cracked the clearing.

The thickset man lunged, hook-swing for Korvan's chest. Auryn's Edge met it; cheap iron screamed and chipped. Korvan slipped inside and drove a knee to ribs. Air blasted and the man's body folded.

A hatchet came from the left. Bren snarled; his hammer smashed the blow wide. Bone gave in a crack. The man skidded into stone and stayed down a silent scream as he clutched what remained.

Bolts hissed past the hearth.

Thalen's cloak tore as he spun. Two steps, two cuts and bow-strings parted, tillers split. Crossbows fell in neat, useless halves. Hands flew up in instant surrender.

Sera danced, and a wardline snapped from her staff in a razor crescent. A dagger clattered away as nerves jolted. Fennik dropped from her and clamped a shin. The man screamed and folded. Sera spoke three crisp syllables; light rebounded and pinned another to stone without blood.

A plank club hammered Brusk's plates. He didn't flinch. His tail arced in response; the striker hurdled into the wall going slack.

"Left," Javek warned, and flicked a mirrored blade. It bit a wrist. Steel rang on flagstone. The thief grabbed a wet, useless hand.

Ryn's spear whirled. The haft punched mace wielder's gut; the return spiral cracked shoulder and jaw. Above, her Pathcarver stooped and scored a face bloody, blinding him in a fan of red and talon.

But cornered things still bite. A pitch pouch burst at Korvan's boots. Smoke billowed and a tongue of fire licked his trousers. Heat bit his calf. He cut through the veil on instinct; Vasha's pressure kept his lines true. A chain swept for Sera's ankles; she stepped past center and flicked her staff sending it off course.

A runner sprinted for the Aethyrglass stack, desperation on his face.

"No."

He reached for the coiled heat under his ribs and shaped it with both hands. Exhale down the forearms, he let light take the line.

"Radiant Binding."

Bands whipped from his marks in spiraled rings and snapped shut mid-stride. Arms, chest, legs all bound in shimmering light.

The runner gawped, frozen.

Sera was there; her staff kissed his elbow. Bren's low kick took the knees out. The body thumped and stilled.

Silence drew tight. Smoke mixed with sweat and hot iron.

Groans. A few crawling shapes. Others very still.

Korvan let out a breath. The world tipped once and steadied.

"We should secure them," he said.

Thalen nodded once. "Already on it."

"That went well everyone, you all did splendid. Bren, help me with the wounded," Sera called out already moving toward the thief with a mangled hand.

Ryn and Javek moved with practiced speed, checking pulses and tying wrists. Their Pathcarvers circled above for any others

Korvan turned and laid a palm to the nearest crate. Runes pulsed under skin and wood.

They did it. They found Aethyrglass, and managed to take all of them prisoner.

But he couldn't shake the feeling of being watched and as he turned toward the fallen tower he knew. Something else waited.

It was beyond the arch. Behind ivy and collapsed stone.

Vasha edged the doorway, hackles lifting; a low rumble unfurled. *Be careful Little Hunter.*

"I will girl, stay, keep the others safe." Korvan said.

Sera started to answer. He waved her off to keep at the wounded and slipped through the gap.

The side chamber was colder than it should've been. Dust spun like ghost-motes on his breath. Cracked mortar framed a space that had been forgotten.

The pull came from a cage within. Strong but delicate, it appeared entirely crystal-wrought. Korvan blanched as he realized what it was. A cage of mirrored Aethyrglass, each bar etched with dense glyphs that pulsed in a slow, living rhythm.

Inside—

Something moved.

Feathers shimmered across a sleek, raptor-like frame, near Sera's shoulder at the withers. Powerful legs and a thick tail, but light-bodied. Every motion suggested speed, rippling muscle under downy plumes that shifted hue: sapphire to gold to silver-pale. A being of grace, of stillness. Of mind.

Its eyes met his. He forgot how to breathe.

A Reservoir.

He didn't know how he knew, but he could read it on her.

How? Why here?

The cage alone demanded high-tier glyph work, a knowledge hoarded by Arcanists.

Vasha's presence warmed the threshold. The creature turned toward her clearly unafraid.

Then it touched his mind.

You are burdened, Initiate and you carry many wounds beyond the physical. You are brave to persist.

He staggered.

I have waited for you, Echoborn.

His Soulmarks flared as pale Aethyr unspooled down his arms.

"Who are you?" he whispered.

Feathers shimmered violet and gold.

You already know it. Name me.

His knees nearly buckled.

Caelen's small hands, clasping his.

Auryn's Edge, the light he harnessed for more than killing.

The fire in his mother's eyes the day she vanished.

He wasn't just changing.

He was remembering.

Three bonds.

He wasn't supposed to have three.

But no matter the argument that came, he knew, deep in his core he knew.

This was right.

The creature turned and cast dawn light across stone in prismatic threads. His Fyrstrand stirred with purpose. A melody returned.

Name me.

Korvan's throat tightened. He thought of Caelen's dreams. His mother's lullabies. Hands wrapping wounds in the dark.

A name that could carry that weight.

"Solace," he said.

Light lanced the cage in a brilliant burst. Wards shattered. Aethyr flared through the chamber in radiant arcs, and Korvan's Soulmarks ignited. Ribbons of light spiraled down his arm.

Solace stepped free and pressed a luminous brow to his chest.

The bond unfurled like rain after drought soaking into cracks the world had left. It steadied. A current that smoothed breath and hushed the wild beat of his heart.

Souls met with a resonance unlike either of his previous bonds.

His Fyrstrand opened wider than it ever had, more than he thought it ever could. The raw Aethyr that flowed through him was startling, it felt endless. Within that flow there were three threads now, Brusk, Vasha, Solace, braiding in luminous sync.

Within the braid a faint tension lingered. A quiet space between notes, as if the pattern had shifted to make room. He felt it the way you notice a missing weight only once you move, something not yet settled.

His breath caught. Shoulders sagged. Hands trembled.

He didn't stop the tears.

Mother... I knew you'd be proud.

Solace tilted her head and shimmered from pale violet to sunrise gold.

Her thoughts moved through him with the gentleness of a promise: *We are whole, spark-carrier. Let us protect what you love. Together.*

He exhaled a breath he'd held since the Trial.

He stepped back, chest thudding, arms pulsing faint with new light. The tower no longer felt like a cage.

Solace followed quiet as snowfall.

There would be questions. There would be consequences.

He would learn who had caged her. Who had tried to use her. Who had failed.

But that didn't matter right now.

Now, he stood unafraid.

Three bonds.

Back in Cael'Lumar they would whisper that this was reckless, that he was not supposed to be able to acquire such strength yet. That it made him a threat.

He looked through smoke at the men they had folded like thin tin and understood why a city feared its own guardians. A single weaving of a Discipline and he had bound a body mid-stride; a single step and Bren had folded a ribcage; a single line of light and Sera had turned a blade-hand into a trembling fist. Against those without it, Aethyrcraft was... a beautiful and terrible power.

But he knew, he would keep using it for the right reasons. To continue to protect those he cared for the most.

Brusk had stood for him. Vasha had chosen him. Solace had heard him.

They were his and so was Caelen.

He would carry them forward.

Not only as an Initiate. Not only as a survivor.

As something that finally began to have a name.

Chapter 14: Threads of Power

Korvan stepped from the ruin's side chamber. Solace drifted at his flank, feathered forelimbs shifting through impossible hues in the newborn light. The Reservoir moved with grace, her sleek-limbed, long-tailed, frame composed to the bone. Where Vasha prowled with restless readiness, Solace carried snowfall's hush and deep water's stillness.

The others stared, mouths open, eyes fixed on the unfamiliar Veyrkin, then on Korvan.

Thalen's gaze pinned Korvan's wrists, then traced the distinct glow of a new bond.

"Three," he said, voice brittle. "Three Veyrkin, Korvan?"

His voice roughened. "Do you know how many people break trying to bond a second time, let alone a fucking third? Do you know what it costs to wield that kind of magic, that much power?"

He didn't wait.

"I had a second bond lined up," Thalen said, eyes glass-bright. "A Wyrmkin. I mapped her cadence for months. She burned through my Soulmark in an instant. My training, my pedigree all for naught. I wasn't strong enough. I woke three days later in the infirmary. My father didn't even visit. 'Undignified to condone a failure.'"

The words struck the ruin like dropped iron.

"And you?" Softer now but far more dangerous. "No ritual. No anchor sigils. No godsdamned struggle."

"Thalen—"

"Shut up, Korvan. Just shut the hell up. I am done with your quiet woe-is-me act." His laugh cracked.

"Your brother is sick? Mine died. Your 'mommy' left? I haven't seen mine in years. Your dad's a drunk? Get in line. But here's the part that really rots my teeth: you'll say you didn't ask for it, that you didn't secretly crave all this power and attention, but I know the truth, that you relish it."

He leaned in, blade finally turned. "You're not the only one with family problems, you insufferable prick."

No one moved.

Bren glanced to Sera. Tears pooled in her eyes. Korvan's mouth stayed open. Ryn and Javek edged back, heads down, the ruin holding the echo of Thalen's voice.

A thought edged in to Korvan's mind: Thalen was right.

Thalen dragged a breath. His head shook. "You keep shattering guardrails, and the world makes room for you. It leaves the rest of us behind like we don't matter, like we don't work just as hard, like we don't sacrifice for people we love…"

His head hung and a crystal drop splashed off his boot.

Sera stepped closer, steady, and low. "Thalen, he's our friend."

Thalen's look cut colder than steel. "Is he? Or the next tyrant looking for a crown?"

Korvan's jaw set.

"You're walking into something none of us can follow," Thalen said. "And nobody's asking what happens when you fall."

He turned. "Keep your beasts. Keep your shining Soulmarks. Keep your humble act."

A beat.

"I'm done pretending this is fucking fair. I'm done being part of it."

He walked away. Boots ground stone. His cloak snapped. Midnight hesitated, looked back once, then slipped after him.

A thin breath returned to the ruin.

Silence pooled. Even the wind kept its distance.

Bren exhaled. "Damn. He went for the jugular."

Sera came close, eyes rimmed red, voice low. "Korvan, are you safe to stand with us right now? With the bond, I mean."

Korvan's jaw clicked before he answered. His hands had balled so tight the knuckles popped. "I am." Anger rode the word.

He took another breath. "I am."

Solace inclined her head. A quiet assent.

"He crossed a line," Korvan said. Flat.

Ryn scratched her jaw and didn't look away. "Did he? Make no mistake, he said it like a right arsehole." She shifted her spear. "Yet he ain't wrong. You're not like the rest of us, Korvan."

Javek nodded, uneasy and honest. "Folk do break tryin' what you just did. I seen a mill lad shake hisself clean out of his skin. Thalen's wrong in how he swung. Not in what he swung at."

Bren cinched a strap until it creaked. "Doesn't give him leave to be a bastard."

Korvan's hands curled. "No. It doesn't." Heat rose under his marks. He let it crest and pass. "But I heard the part I needed."

Sera searched his face. "Which part?"

"That this gets bigger than me if I'm careless." He swallowed. "That I owe you all more than quiet. That you deserve more than quiet."

Fennik flicked an ear. Sera's thumb pressed his forearm and grounded him. "Good. We'll be ready to talk when you are. He'll come back, he's just as stubborn as you are."

She offered a weak smile.

Korvan just shook his head.

They moved because they had to. Work steadied the air. Bren snugged bindings with square knots. Vasha traced a slow ring at the clearing's edge, eyes hard as river glass as she inspected the captives. Brusk watched the rear. The prisoners tucked chins and flinched when Solace slid past.

Korvan set his palm to moss-dark stone and counted.

In, two three four. Hold, two, three, four. Out, two, three, four. The breathing rhythm Cristos had taught, to center yourself.

The wrap under his glove tugged where earlier skin had split. A quiet ledger line.

Three bonds now, but he still stood, and he felt strong.

He ran a hand down Solace's flank. "You're something else."

Solace blinked once. *I am just me. I am happy to be here with you.*

Bren finished the last knot and glanced over. "You're not going to quit on us, are you?"

Korvan arched a brow, "What do you mean, of course not. Sera just told you I'm stubborn." He tried for the joke but it didn't quit land.

"Good. Didn't think so, but it felt right to say it," Bren said, grin pulling back to life. "Couldn't leave you behind anyway, what with the code and all."

Ryn shouldered her spear and jerked her chin toward the trees. "We still have to get home 'fore we worry about that."

"Ryn's right. Let's get home."

No one argued.

***

After some slow travel pulling their captives along, the city's high walls rose from mist as if the cliffs had grown a crown. The Crown Keep's Aethyrglass towers aglow in the new sun.

Korvan eased the pace turning back to those in tow.

"Ok now that we're back, time to get the specifics sorted. We'll start with names," he said.

The thick-necked one from the fight kept his eyes on the ruts. "Yask," he muttered. "Dock-hand."

"Daggan," said the bowman with the cut wrist, voice gone small. "Used to run grain."

A third cleared his throat. "Syle. Farm hand."

"Good," Korvan said. "Now tell me where you found a cage like that." He pointed at the broken remains on top of the wagon.

Blank looks cracked. Fear did the rest.

"We bought it," Yask said at last. "From men... not from here."

"Describe them," Ryn said.

Syle swallowed. "Didn't see any house crests or Soulmarks. Had clean wrists but scarred like they wore iron once. Spoke soft. Never gave names."

"Where?" Korvan asked.

"Two nights downriver from Riverpost, old limestone quarry," Daggan said. "They had carts. Showed us the lattice, said it would 'hold any Veyrkin.' Said if we broke it, we owed double."

Solace's attention settled on the men.

Do not give in to rage, she sent, warmth smoothing the spike in Korvan's chest. *It is not them you're furious with.*

"That's all fine, but how'd you lift the Aethyrglass?" Bren asked, easy as a neighbor over a fence.

Daggan looked at the ground. "We didn't lift it alone."

"Who helped?"

"Some of the hired crew," Yask said. "The original haulers. We waved them off their ward-post with coin and drink. Two drivers and a forward-rider. We staged a rockfall, swore the wards would shatter if they kept the seals hot through the bend. They dimmed the sigils for 'safety.'" Shame soured the word. "Made it easy."

"Give me their names," Korvan said.

"Kes Brennor. Mael Pike. The forward was called Talla or Tallen, thin girl, scar under the eye." Daggan winced. "They said it was a one-time favor."

Ryn's mouth thinned. "One-time favor. Out the goodness o' their hearts, I reckon."

"Who told you where to take it?" Sera asked, voice like cool water.

"The men at the kilns," Syle said. "Said we weren't to know more than we had to. 'No questions if you want to breathe easy,' is what they said."

"Where were you supposed to take it," Korvan pressed.

"The Iltherean Wilds," Yask answered. "Said there was a drop-point past the old survey stones. Said there'd be a sign, a black ribbon on a thorn-post. Supposed to leave the crate and the cage by sundown, walk away, don't look back."

"Which trail into the Wilds?" Ryn asked.

"Any," Syle said, helpless. "They said the Wilds would 'open if you were meant to find it.'"

Korvan breathed once and let the anger move through muscle and bone.

Place the anger, don't spend it, Vasha reminded him, Cristos' lesson beneath the ribs.

"So, you met people in an old Limestone pit, bought a cage that they said could hold any Veyrkin, bribed the guards of an Aethyr-glass Caravan that are known to be paid so well they're all but immune to bribery. You are dockhands, grain runners, and a farm hand, and you don't have any bonds. I don't believe you had the coin to do this on your own. So, who hired you first, who is your backer?" he asked.

Yask stared ahead. "A broker at the Harbor. Never gave his true name. Called himself the Listener."

"What did he look like?" Bren said.

"He had on a long coat, and kept his face covered. But his voice sounded like he'd swallowed soot. He had a worker's hands, too well used for a boy's. Wire around his neck with a shard at the end, had the look of gemstone, but cloudy."

Sera stepped closer, low enough only Korvan heard. "Houseless men with manacle scars. Brokers with false names, coin to bribe caravans and buy mystic cages. This is more than a simple wagon hit. This is organized."

"They use a phrase?" Korvan asked the line. "Any sign, I need something to identify them"

His voice came hot, the anger at all of it was bubbling up.

Vasha let out a growl in response and Solace's feathers started to rise.

Daggan nodded, swallowed his tongue and a miserable expression appeared. "When the deal's done, they tap their wrist twice. Like they're breaking something that isn't there."

"They said they were moving 'memory' out of the city's reach," Syle added, too fast. "That's what they called that beast. Memory. Said it would 'wake the old ways' if freed. Swore we'd never see it again."

"You've broken more laws than I can count, given up good lives. How much did it cost to give up your honor, how much did it cost to conspire against your home?" Korvan asked.

"Half up front in, the second half when the ribbon was cut," Yask said. "Fifty Glimmers, for each of us."

Korvan's mouth fell open. A Glimmer, one of the gold-veined coins, was worth ten Silverbrands. It was nearly what he made in a year as an Initiate, but for a Farmhand or dockworker it was nearly a decades worth of wages. Cael'Lumar was designed that any could survive there, but the more coin one had, the easier things always tended to be.

Korvan's stomach growled absently, he couldn't help but think of the times he scrounged for an Asher to buy day old bread. Fifty Glimmers? That would change your world.

Yask continued, "It was enough to feed my family, keep me from working so I could take care of my niece."

"She sick?" Bren asked.

Yask flinched. "Aye."

They walked a dozen paces with only rope and boot-wood talking. Wind moved in the pines. The road felt longer.

The Initiates all exchanged some glances. Korvan saw it in their eyes, they didn't understand, why someone would risk so much for coin. Korvan did, and he reminded himself, none of them had ever gone to bed hungry.

Korvan kept his tone level. "Here's what happens. You give this statement again to the Crown Guard when we return you to the city. You tell them everything, mark every location. If you lie, the Aethyrguard will find out and the sentence will be worse. If you hold to it, you may live to work off what you've done."

Daggan glanced at Solace, then at Korvan. "Fair enough young master. Since I've ruined my life for her... What is she?"

"Not your business," Bren said.

Korvan let silence answer. The men kept walking.

Hold the line, Brusk sent, warm and heavy.

We will, Vasha added, pleased.

We do, Solace echoed, and the three notes met and settled in him.

***

No one hurried the conversation.

"Still no Thalen?" Sera asked, matching Korvan's stride.

"No." He worked his jaw. "I'll send word to the barracks after our debrief. Maybe he checked in."

"Don't sweat it," Ryn called from the middle. "We know where he broods. We'll poke the shadow till it meows."

"Mm," Javek added. "Rooftop garden, starin' out, thinkin' on fate. He'll be fine."

Bren snorted. "Or maybe he'll be loud again and we'll find him quick."

Sera allowed a small smile. "He's proud and arrogant, and he proved what I think a few of us are thinking. He's jealous of Korvan's strength and your gift for bonding Veyrkin. But I don't think he means to be cruel."

Korvan stopped in his tracks, he felt his face twist into a knot, "Jealous?"

Bren's head tilted to the side and he stared blankly at Korvan, "You're serious Korvan? You didn't realize? Of course we're jealous of you. You have a gift."

"I... I didn't mean..."

Sera put her hand on his, "We know Korvan, you aren't trying to show off, but Aside from Eris, you're the only person we've seen with three Veyrkin. Sure some Champions and of course the High Warden have several bonds but they've got decades of experience. You're supposed to be like us."

He looked at his friends and saw them all nodding with Sera's words.

"I'm sorry, I never realized you all felt that way."

Bren slapped his shoulder, and chuckled, "Talk to us more you lug, you are our friend but you're quiet as a wall somedays."

"He sure is," Javek.

"I find the brooding handsome," Ryn said giving Sera a wink.

Sera rolled her eyes and added, "Thalen will come back. He just needs some time to calm down."

"I know," Korvan said, too fast.

A breath. "I hope so."

He let anger open a door instead of closing one. He focused on old lessons, taming his emotions, finding balance. He didn't know about Thalen's brother, but he knew how he would feel if he lost Caelen. He would give Thalen the grace he deserved and do what he should have months ago. Ask Thalen about himself.

Ask all of them.

"I'll make space for him when he does," Korvan said. "I'll be ready if he doesn't."

Solace tilted her head. A low trill radiated, more felt than heard, and his marks answered with a layered beat. *We are with you.*

Vasha pressed a thought like a hand at his back. *Hold fast, little hunter.*

Brusk rumbled, steady as ground. *Still here. Always.*

He nodded once to all three. "Still here."

The prisoners stumbled on the grade as they climbed the stairs, too many for one of the lifts. Bren steadied one by the collar. Sera eased another's binding when it bit his flesh. Ryn and Javek kept the pace clean.

"Listen," Sera said, voice for him alone. "People will use that crack Thalen opened. Nobles. Priests. Cowards who want your light without. Don't let them widen it. Don't let them use your heart against you."

"I won't."

"Good," Bren added over a shoulder. "Because if they try, I'll introduce their jaw to my hammer."

Ryn barked a laugh. "Save a swing for me."

Javek lifted a tied wrist to scratch his cheek. "Aye. Perhaps a drink first though."

"Am I really that bad at whispering?" Sera groaned. Color climbed her cheeks.

"Not really. We jus' got good ears," Javek said, and barked a laugh.

The line breathed easier. The hurt found a place to sit.

Korvan looked at the city and let a promise form. He would speak to Caelen. He would speak to Eris. He would name what the Beyond had put in his path, not as a boast, but as a burden he chose to carry in the open.

For now, he led them forward.

The wall grew closer and the crown towers caught light.

He kept breathing.

***

At the gate, Crown Guards waved caravans through. They were full of smoked fish, dyed linen, ore for the cliff forges. One guard hardly older than Korvan, froze as Solace passed in a hush of light. He forgot to salute.

"Sir, are those three Veyrkin yours?" he blurted.

"Yes," Korvan said, neutral. "And no, you can't pet them."

The boy laughed, jittery, and fumbled the ledger. The Aethyrguard seal did the rest.

Inside the gates they turned toward the First Ring Crown Guard house, nestled between the Docks and a Skyship tower. The barracks rose as a stockade of discipline and order, all sharp angles, and clean lines, built to convey control.

"Let's get these through intake first," Korvan said. "Then we go to command."

They turned into the Inner Mustering Court where custody changed hands. Wardwrights in gray had chalked a bright circle on the stone. An Arcanist team waited with damp cloths and grounding rods to cool the cracked Aethyrglass. A Crown Guard lieutenant stepped up with two scribes.

"Identify," he said.

"Initiate Korvan Aric, Aethyrguard. I have six prisoners and the lost shipment. Nine Aethyrglass crates. Four fractured, five sound." He kept his tone even.

The lieutenant's brows rose at the Veyrkin and dropped at sound. "We'll stabilize the broken first."

Arcanists moved. Wet cloth hissed on hot runes.

Korvan handed over a stained packet. "Written statements from these three, Yask, Daggan, Syle." He nodded down the rope line. "the rest is in there."

The lieutenant's jaw set. "Destination?"

"The Iltherean Wilds." He kept going. "Intent was more than theft of Aethyrglass. They were contracted to deliver a Reservoir."

A scribe's pen stuttered. Arcanists glanced up. The lieutenant's eyes cut to Solace. "And that…"

"Is under Aethyrguard protection," Korvan said.

The lieutenant worked his mouth once, then nodded. "Prisoners to the Crown Guard cells, ledger-stamped under my seal. The glass to Custody Ring Two. You'll receive the receipt. The Crown

Guard thanks you for your service and for the Aethyrguard's continued support."

Scribes wrote faster. One pressed a wax sunburst and passed the duplicate. Korvan folded it into his pouch.

The breath he'd been holding eased a fraction.

Some time later and they had returned their own Barracks. Ironbound doors swallowed them. Twin statues flanked the entry, Aethyrguard cast glass and granite, weapons raised. POWER HAS PRICE read the motto.

At the council stairs, Eris waited.

Arms folded. White braid coiled like a blade on her shoulder. Her eyes counted everything.

When she saw Solace, her posture shifted a fraction.

"Report," she said.

"Prisoners transferred to Crown Guard custody. Shipment stabilized and logged." Korvan met her gaze. "It wasn't only Aethyrglass. They were sent to cage a Reservoir. Also, Thalen is..."

"A Reservoir," Eris repeated, gaze returning to Solace. The creature dipped her head in acknowledgement.

"Yes, Battlemage."

Her attention moved to Korvan's arms, The third light running under skin.

"And you bonded it," she said. A fact.

"I did," he said.

Eris exhaled. "We'll discuss it later."

She signaled him up the stair and stepped close, voice low. "You've drawn attention you don't yet fathom, Korvan Aric. Three bonds. Do you understand what that means?"

"It means I have to keep getting better."

Her mouth tilted something between regret and resolve. "Obviously. Beyond that it means you won't move unseen by the nobility again. You've entered a game I hoped to spare you from."

"Up," Eris said. "Command wants every detail. After that, you and I speak alone about the path you've chosen."

Korvan followed.

The council chamber was a stone amphitheater it held seven concentric rings, cold and exact. Aethyrglass veins laced the floor in living arcs, pulsing with the city's wards. Seven chairs sat at the highest ring. A high window framed whitecaps marching the horizon.

Korvan stood on the central disk. Spine straight.

Solace sat left-heel, still as starlight. Vasha paced right in a slow storm. Brusk kept behind him.

Eris took the edge and let the echo of their entrance fade.

"Initiate Korvan Aric and squad returning from a field mission to recover stolen Aethyrglass shipment" she said. "Shipment recovered. Prisoners secured. No fatalities. "

An elder councilor leaned forward, his black hair was shot with silver, eyes like flint. His voice snapped taut.

"Initiate, do you understand what you protected today?"

Korvan's gut tightened.

"I know it is vital to the city, sir—"

"Vital?" He cut in.

"Aethyrglass powers the wards that keep rot off our walls. It holds the city to these cliffs. Without it, Cael'Lumar doesn't bend, or weaken. It breaks. We'd tumble into the sea."

Cold climbed his spine.

"I understand," he said.

"Do you?" The gaze sharpened as others continued reading the report. His eyes read until they widened. His voice was thin, "You bonded a third Veyrkin, a Reservoir, without sanction, without a protective circle, without an overseer? That isn't valor. It's hubris."

"It was the only way," Korvan said, even.

Silence pulled tight.

Eris stepped in, cool and exact. "His Soulmarks are stable. The Reservoir is attuned. No trace resonance backlash. I stand by the bond."

Flint eyes turned. "Then you own it, Battlemage. You are his direct overseer. Effective immediately."

Her shoulders tightened by a hair. "Understood Sir."

"Your report, Initiate," the councilor said.

Korvan kept to the bones, but recounted the entire journey. He didn't mention Thalen, rather leave him out entirely than risk labeling him a deserter.

Pens scratched. The elder nodded once.

"Dismissed," he said. "Remember, Initiate, power this great is never free."

Korvan stepped back, heartbeat loud. The instant his heel touched the stair, Eris caught his sleeve and drew him into column-shadow.

"Do you know how close that was?" she hissed.

He started. Her hand cut the air.

"No. Listen. I just staked my rank for you, my entire career. They were a breath from stripping your marks, your name, your place."

His head fell to his chest, arms went limp.

"Meet me in the practice yard before first bell."

Her voice fell. "You do not understand what you've done. But we will fix this. Together."

"Thank you, Battlemage, I understand," he said.

She released his sleeve.

"Good. Go. Rest. And hear me, Korvan Aric, hear me well. After tomorrow, you are afforded no mistakes."

She turned back into the room's hush.

He stood a moment longer. Marble too polished. Sun through colored glass too soft. None of it matched the storm under his ribs.

POWER HAS PRICE.

The mantra embossed on every surface.

"Maybe I should have listened to that more." He said to no one.

The doors closed with a deep, patient boom.

He stood in the corridor, the only sounds his boot-clicks and Solace's soft tread. Vasha ghosted the hall mouth, ears flicking at each echo. The wrap under his glove tugged where his palm had split in the skirmish.

That close. They had almost taken everything from him because he bonded Solace without thinking. He knew it was the right choice at the time, but maybe... maybe he didn't have to do it right then. Everything he'd been taught so far was that Veyrkin pick their tamers just as much as the Tamers decide. If Solace were truly meant for him, she'd have waited for an investigation to be completed.

He exhaled heavy, it came out with a shake, "Maybe I was a little too rash. I've been so focused on getting stronger and getting better for Caelen I've not paid attention to everything else. Thalen was right, I do want to be stronger. I just want to do it to help Caelen."

Brusk thudded into his thigh and the sureness of the boar-like Veyrkin was wrought in the stone, *Korvan good, Brusk know.*

Korvan let that answer hold.

He did not turn toward the barracks, his own rest could come later.

He needed Caelen.

***

Bren's voice had made Caelen known among the Initiates long before the Guard formalized anything. In the end, Command offered what few received: a private room in the lower infirmary. Madam Ren, who had never once failed the boys Kingfisher Street forgot, made the trek to him, determined to help as much as she could.

The chamber was small, but clean, and more importantly quiet. A narrow window caught mild sun and gave a view out to the Harbor and the Sapphire Sea. A woven blanket lay folded over a cot. A shelf held well-loved books. Air carried alcohol's bite and crushed mint.

Korvan knocked once and stepped in.

Caelen looked up from a chair, blanket around his legs, a bowl of fruit at hand. He smiled, the kind that broke frost without asking permission. "Korvan!"

Korvan dropped to one knee and drew him into a careful embrace. Bone and warmth. Heat had returned to Caelen's skin; yet the tremor under it had not improved.

"You're back early," Caelen said. "I heard something happened?"

"How you heard already is astounding, but we made it through."

His gaze drifted to the faint glow under Korvan's sleeves. "That's... a new one?"

"Her name is Solace."

Solace stepped in at the cue, feathers blooming in the light. She bowed her head with poise and the room's quiet changed around her; the air warmed and felt tranquil.

"She doesn't look real, she's like a memory of something," Caelen whispered.

Korvan's brows shut up, Caelen was not the first one to call her that. He'd file it for later.

"Can I—?"

Solace moved first. She lowered her head and waited.

Caelen's fingers brushed feathers and reptile skin.

"She's warm," he said, surprised.

"She isn't like anything I've ever seen, or that we've studied," Korvan murmured.

Something passed between Caelen and the Veyrkin, Solace leaned a fraction into Caelen's hand, and her colors slipped to silver and soft blue, Kael'Thir's hues. Kael'Thir, The Keeper of Threads, the god of memory, protection, and boundaries. In a blink the colors were gone. Korvan thought he might have imagined it.

Heat surged under Korvan's marks. Vertigo tugged the floor a finger's width to the side. He did his breathing cycle from Cristos. The room steadied.

"You okay?" Caelen asked.

"Not really," Korvan said. "But I'm here. A lot on my mind."

They let the quiet stand. Solace curled beside Caelen's chair and rested her head near his feet. Feather-edges chimed faintly when Caelen's breath evened. When it hitched, the chime dulled.

"I'm glad you came," Caelen said. "We don't get to see each other that much anymore.

Korvan blinked. "I know... When I'm a Knight, I'll get to have much more free time and be able to spend more time with you, and I'm here now."

A grin, but it didn't reach his eyes. "But you'll be gone again. I'm sure."

"I just got back, I'm sure I won't have to leave again so soon."

"You're always working, Korvan. Long before the Aethyrguard." The words were true, not cruel.

"I mean it this time."

"I know, you always mean it," Caelen said, and the steadiness in it mattered more than anything the council had thrown at him.

Three bonded Veyrkin, one brother that needed him most.

Being back here was a relief, for the first time in days, Korvan felt level.

But he'd made a promise. To talk more.

"Thalen called me a tyrant," he said at last.

Caelen's head snapped up. "He what?"

"Said no one should hold this much power. That I didn't earn it. That I'm dangerous."

Caelen's fingers tightened in the blanket. "Do you believe him?"

"I'd be a fool to think I'm not dangerous, but I don't think I'm a tyrant." Korvan stared at his hands. "I didn't ask for any of this. But when Solace reached for me, I didn't hesitate. I broke her out of the cage they locked her in. I should've waited. Veyrkin chose their Tamer just as much as we chose them."

"That's not tyranny," Caelen said. "Tyrants devour, only seeking power for themselves. You are strong and so you try to shield everyone, even at your own expense."

His voice sank, dark and true. "You carried me when he broke my ribs. When he locked me in the crawlspace. When he said I was weak and a curse and shouldn't have been born. You stood between us. So many times you stood between us and took the brunt of his anger."

Boots on stairs. Firelight. Caelen's scream of pain. Korvan's breath thinned at the memory.

A cough sounded, small at first. Caelen pressed fingers to his lips to hide it. The cough deepened, tore loose, and refused to stop. The bowl tipped. Fruit rolled. The blanket slid and showed a wrist too sharp for comfort.

"Cael—"

Korvan reached for him and the fit racked harder. His brother folded over his ribs, sound gone to a raw scrape.

The door banged. Madam Ren swept in, "Hands under his shoulders," she said, already moving. "Head forward. Good. Don't pat his back. Let it pass."

Korvan did as told. Caelen's breath fought him, seized, lost cadence.

"Eyes on me," Ren said. She pried open a tin, lifted a vial. "Tongue." A drop of dark tincture kissed Caelen's mouth. "Again."

She pressed her palm to his sternum and counted under her breath.

The fit crested. It broke in ragged shivers. Caelen sagged against Korvan, his whole body spent. Ren kept her hand where it was until the rhythm returned. Only then did she cut Korvan a look.

"He's worse today," she said. "He hid the morning spell from me." She smoothed sweat from Caelen's hair with fingers that trembled only after danger passed. "Storms follow you, boy. He's not built to stand in them long."

"I didn't know," Korvan said.

"You didn't want to." It was a sad truth, A breath later: "Now you do."

Caelen blinked, eyes glass-bright. "Still glad you came," he whispered, voice rasped raw. He tried to sit straighter and failed. Ren adjusted the blanket and slid a folded cloth beneath his wrists.

Solace hadn't moved during the fit. She had gone very still, feathers dulled to a soft gray. As Caelen's breath found a kinder rhythm, a faint shimmer returned, silver first, then that patient blue.

I'm with you, her eyes flitted to Korvan then turned back to Caelen.

"Keep it quiet now," Ren murmured. "If he talks, it will start again." She set the vial on the shelf and placed three more beside it. "One drop if it returns within the hour. Two if his lips go pale. If his hands shake uncontrollably, send a runner for me or a Mender. Sera if she's near, she knows what to do."

Korvan nodded. "Yes, thank you Madam Ren."

Madam Ren's look softened a fraction. "You're not the only one holding him up. He's the bravest young man I've ever met." She touched Caelen's temple, checked the pulse at the throat, and left as fast as she came, the door easing closed.

The hush gathered again. Korvan eased back and kept a hand on Caelen's shoulder. He counted the rise and fall. Solace lowered her head to the floorboards and breathed with him.

His eyes blinked opened when Caelen shifted.

"I'm here," Korvan said.

"I know," Caelen whispered.

He wanted to shout his rage and make vows and thunder like a storm. It was so unfair that as he got stronger Caelen withered.

He chose steadier ground. "If tyrants devour, I won't qualify. I've been full of looking after you for years."

That pulled a breath that might one day be a laugh. It faded quick.

Caelen's gaze drifted to Solace. "She's... different," he said, thin. "Different close to me."

Korvan felt it too. Something in the way the light along Solace's throat answered Caelen's breath, how the field around her settled.

"You should rest," Korvan said.

"If I do, you'll leave." The words tried for jest and missed by an inch.

"No. Not tonight. Tonight I'll stay with you." He tucked the blanket the way Madam Ren had taught him.

The worst had passed yet the cost remained.

Caelen's eyes slipped closed, opened, closed again. Solace watched him, unblinking. The glow along her flight-feathers counted his breaths.

Korvan's throat worked. "Thalen said I didn't earn this," he whispered. "That I'm dangerous."

Eyes still shut, Caelen found the words. "You took Solace, and maybe that does make you selfish, but it doesn't make you a monster, not for the reasons you did it. You want to be strong for me, but I know you also want to be strong for you. You've always put me first. You didn't run from power brother," he murmured. "You ran from our father's kind."

Korvan bowed his head. He stroked Solace's feathers. Warmth pulsed through his palm, and a second warmth, something fainter, echoing, rose where Caelen's wrist brushed the raptor's neck. Not exactly another bond, but the idea of one. A first lantern lit somewhere deep.

He looked at his brother, fading but still bright and fierce. Then at his Veyrkin his steadfast sentries. At the life they were building with bruised hands.

He said the line their father mocked and made it honest.

"I love you, little hawk. Thank you for believing in me."

Caelen smiled, fragile and bright, though his eyes remained closed. "I love you too, Kor. Thanks for taking care of me. Now hush, I'm so tired."

Solace's eyes never left Caelen. Though his brother didn't feel it, Korvan did. A pattern had begun under the surface, slow and sure. Lanterns kindled outside one by one until the dark had to make room.

Hold the line.

Chapter 15: Battlemage's Station

First light made the yard hard. Polished stone still wet with ocean mist. Smell of salt on the air. A faint thread of rose oil from guttering ward lanterns.

Eris waited in silence, arms folded across the bracers of her Battlemage kit. Her staff rested against the wall; inlaid sigils cast a pale blue. Cristos stood barefoot on the slick stone, hands loose at his sides. He inclined his head as Korvan entered, then went still again.

Korvan crossed the floor with Vasha at his knee and Brusk a half step behind. Solace came last. The air tightened around the Reservoir; she was a fulcrum of Aethyr and hummed with energy.

"Today," Eris said, voice like a blade slid free in the dark, "you learn what it means to wield three."

His mouth dried. "Yes, ma'am."

Scorched dummies waited in the yard's center. Eris gestured toward them. "This training isn't standard. It isn't recorded. We don't write down how to teach it, because almost no one survives getting here." A breath of quiet. "How many living Aethyrguard bear three bonds or more?"

He shook his head.

"A few dozen, perhaps fewer. The High Warden bears five. Archmage, six. I have three." She let that land. "Most manage one. Some make two. Three is rare. Those fives and sixes often include mostly Verdant bonds. The true rarity is a Fyrstrand carrying three Obsidian-prestige bonds without collapse. I am one of the exceptions."

"The Archmage has six?" It slipped before he could catch it.

"You'll catch flies like that, Initiate." Not unkind. "Don't be grateful yet. What comes next has no mercy."

She turned to the field. "Begin."

Korvan closed his eyes and reached.

Brusk: stone and steadiness. Vasha: quicksilver. Solace—

His knees kissed stone.

An ocean pressed through his marks.

Cold.

Endless.

Pressure climbed. Deep water, formless and alive, beautiful enough to drown a man who stared too long. Sweat prickled his neck.

"Focus," Eris snapped.

He shaped channels. He set walls to guide the Aethyr, but the flow slipped past every shape he made.

He hit the stone with his palms.

Eris knelt beside him, voice low and edged. "Don't fight it. Guide it. Think of the harbor. Think of when Vasha came to you, let your instincts take over."

"I can't." The words scraped. "It's... too much."

"You can." Steel through softness. "A Reservoir isn't like a Howler or a Bulwark, they are pools of strength, unlike anything you've ever known. Try to own it and it will drown you."

A shadow fell over them. Cristos didn't touch him; he didn't have to. "Have you learned nothing from my instructions young Aric. Your breath sets the floor," Cristos said, quiet as rain. "Four in. Hold for four. Out for four. Repeat. Place the weight on your heels. Keep your head light. On the exhale, soften your ribs. Don't hold power in the throat. Place it in the hips. Again."

Korvan matched the cadence.

Four.

Hold.

Exhale.

Repeat.

The tremor in his hands eased a fraction. Vasha's ear tipped to him. Brusk's nerves settled into a slow thrum through the bond.

"Good," Cristos murmured. "Widen your stance a thumb-width. Unlock your knees. The breath rides the spine; you don't shove it. Place. Don't spend."

Korvan stopped trying to pour the sea into a cup.

He opened himself.

Aethyr surged again and moved through carved places. The channels along his body flared to life, the Soulmark that normally adorned his arms only flooded across both arms and one of his legs. It felt cool along the forearms. Steady at the wrist bones. The ocean rushed through stone, accepted but not yet mastered.

The world steadied.

Brusk. Vasha. Solace. All stood ready.

Another breath and his chest loosened as his pulse dropped. Mist condensed on his lashes. The taste of salt thinned to clean air.

Eris's tone eased a degree. "That feeling is why we bond and train by rite and with oversight. If that happened in the field..." She let the rest hang.

He blew breath out until the shake left his hands.

Eris rose and planted her staff. Korvan wiped salt from his lip and tasted copper. His tongue was swollen, he didn't remember biting it. Heat along his Soulmarks fell to a tolerable glow. The ring she traced into the mist was small and clear.

"Stand aside," she said. "Watch."

He obeyed.

Light climbed the staff. Eris's voice dropped into a language he didn't know. Old. Weighty. Syllables with weather in them. Pressure changed in the yard. The hair on his arms rose.

Three shapes took the yard.

Kaelith first: Pegasus body lit with dawnfire, wings furled, hooves sparking gold with each step. Talmar next: the Reservoir Owl, high on the ledge, feather-layers inked with runes, gaze deep as the still places in a storm. Coryn last: dusk-coated Howler, low and sinewed, a wolf cut from mist.

They moved the instant they formed.

Kaelith launched and broke the front rank with a radiant shock that rippled the puddles into perfect rings. Talmar swept a wing, and the yard thinned as a flood of energy sank into Eris. Coryn flowed through the ruin with precise, tearing fury. Every strike a period to his partners notes.

Eris barely moved.

A glance toward Kaelith's turn. Two fingers shaped Coryn's angle. A breath let Talmar release the held sound as muffled thunder that finished the row. Command gave way to certainty.

The clockwork golems adapted. Stands flexed. Spacing reformed. Target plates rotated to guard the next pass. Eris shifted the rhythm without warning. Kaelith banked late. Coryn checked mid-lunge. Talmar changed altitude to cut a new lane. When the last target sagged to ash, she whispered a word and Talmar and Coryn turned to light.

Korvan realized he had been holding his breath.

Eris lowered the staff. "That is three," she said. "Harmony. Precision. If you can't guide them like your own hands, they will rip you apart."

At the yard's edge, Kaelith's head turned just enough for one gilded eye to catch him. A voice like calm wind through rigging touched the air, only a shard of sound. "Breathe."

Eris's mouth twitched. "She is fond of obvious truths."

"Obvious keeps you alive," Cristos said.

Korvan counted four in and four out. Shoulders lowered a notch. Heartbeat dropped from a rapid drum to a calm metronome. Mist chilled the back of his neck.

Eris stepped closer. The cost showed only at the corners of her eyes, a fine strain she did not hide. "Few walk this path and there is no forgiveness in it. Only consequence for failure, but if you do master it…"

A beat.

"Are you willing to keep going?"

His chest tightened. A thought loosened where he had pinned it:

"You didn't run from power… You ran from his kind…"

He met her gaze. "Yes."

She let out a fierce smile and any fatigue in her eyes vanished, "I had hoped so."

She lifted the staff and a clap of thunder answered, "Again. I want to see Solace. No holding back."

Cristos slid a thumb along his jaw, then spoke without looking away from Korvan's stance. "Keep the breath. Four in. Four out. On release, put your weight into the boards. Let the ground help carry the cost."

Korvan set his feet and found the cadence Cristos reinforced.

Brusk, shield. Vasha, edge. Solace, he reached.

Light slammed the yard open. Sight went white. His marks burned to the bone, as more energy than he could fathom roared through his body. The world became a glistening brilliance and smothering weight. He stumbled.

Vasha snarled. Brusk set and groaned under the pressure bearing through the bond. Solace poured cold and unchecked.

Eris struck the staff to stone. A ripple rolled out, bending the flood around him instead of through. Somehow it helped.

"Focus," she called across the roar. "You don't dictate, you invite, you guide."

"Anchor," Cristos added, calm in the gale. "Heels. Hips. Crown. Place the exhale. Place it."

He clung to their voices. To breath. To stillness. The torrent slowed. He offered and It listened.

With a smile, He moved.

Brusk set the lane. Vasha cut it clean. Korvan opened only a thread of Solace, two fingers' worth, riding the exhale through his hands.

A lance of white tore three targets. No flame. No crack. Only a whisper of power. Ash fell in response.

The array re-formed on the far side, plates angled to deflect a repeat. New targets rolled out to close his best lanes. Cristos toed a bucket, sloshing water across the stone to slick his footing.

He hit his knees, lungs clawing. A pale haze edged his sight. The afterimage of that white lance burned across it like a scar. Breath stuttered, then found count. Four in, hold, four out, repeat.

The marks dimmed by degrees. The yard returned.

Eris crouched beside him. "Do you see it now?"

He nodded, breath rough. "It's the ocean, no one could control that much power, we only partner with it."

Her mouth tilted, almost a smile. "You're beginning to learn."

Cristos tapped Korvan's wrist once with two fingers, then set them gently against his lower ribs, not quite touching. "Again," he said, softer. "When the sea rises, you rise wider, never higher. Balance is your key."

Eris turned her face to the wind. For an instant, the ward lantern flames along the wall leaned toward her, as if the whole yard breathed in the same direction. "Once more," she said, without looking back. "Then we stop. You're not here to impress us, Initiate. You're here to survive this power you've gained."

Chapter 16: The Path Ahead

The courtyard's hush carried the aftertaste of magic. Korvan knelt, breath rough, scorched air ash-sour at the back of his tongue. Sweat cooled fast in the sea breeze and left a salt crust along his hairline.

Brusk rumbled beside him, a low, steady note that settled into bone. Vasha held a poised line, claws barely kissing stone. Solace lingered behind his shoulder, feathers giving off a faint gleam.

It felt calm after the surge, a shoreline after a storm.

Eris let the quiet stand. Ward lanterns guttered and steadied.

A hand anchored his shoulder.

"You survived," she said, voice level as still water. "That alone means you're worth the work."

A raw laugh scratched his throat. "Worth the work? I almost destroyed the yard."

"Yet you didn't. You pulled back. You trusted Cristos and I to see you through. The yard remains stone. That willingness is why you are worth the work."

The heat eased under ribs and his pulse found a slower count.

"How do you do it?" he asked. "Three Veyrkin, and unless I'm wrong they're all at least Obsidian tier. How do you keep control?"

A slow exhale aged her. "Control is a myth," she said. "Discipline and Practice have given me a bond with my partners that few people understand. I walk with them, fight beside them, bleed with them until command becomes instinct, I'm no more their leader, than I am their friend. I love them, and I would do anything to protect them. So I master myself, so I can be the best. For them." Her hand left his shoulder but he felt her resolve linger.

Down by the arch, Champion Cristos dismissed a pair of curious Initiates with a flick of his wrist and a few quiet words to a watching Knight about the ward lanterns. His steps faded toward the gate, then returned in an easy, barefoot cadence that ignored the slick.

Korvan hesitated for an instant.

"One more thing. Since the Initiate's Trial when I reach for them, I feel something else beside their bonds. Massive eyes, wings in the darkness, and scales that look harder than any metal. Its attention is always around me like its waiting. It's appeared in a few dreams, and sometimes I've felt it even when I'm awake."

A flicker crossed Eris's face. Her pupils narrowed and her jaw set. She gave the briefest tilt skyward before iron returned. "Some dreams warn some are merely a test. But what you've described is not something that I've heard of in my lifetime, but something about it sounds familiar. For now, keep that between us. And Korvan, thank you for trusting me enough to share."

He nodded and took a belly breath. "Yes, Battlemage, you're welcome. I trust you with my life."

Bare feet scuffed stone. Cristos stepped from shadow, dusk-leather sleeves rolled, expression unreadable. The sea wind tugged a strand of hair across his brow; he didn't bother to move it.

"Instinct," he said. "And breath." He dropped to one knee opposite Eris, angling himself so Korvan caught them both. "Shen'Drak doesn't meet power with power. It places power. You do not need to be stronger than your opponent if you can use their strength against them." Two fingers tapped below Korvan's sternum. "Place it here."

Eris's mouth tilted, a ghost of agreement. She stepped back so Cristos could work. Korvan nodded. "Yes, Battlemage. Yes, Champion."

"Up," Cristos said.

Korvan rose on unsteady legs. Cristos set his stance, rear foot a fraction deeper, front knee soft, hips stacked. A nudge settled weight along the balls of his feet.

"Show me the cadence Initiate."

Korvan did and centered his stance mirroring Cristos.

One Cycle.

Again.

On the third cycle, the tremor in his hands eased.

"Good, we'll make a fine Tamer out of you yet." Cristos said. He lifted Korvan's forearms a finger's width and let them fall into line. "The surge will want out. Let it pass through you if you must. You are a man, strong, durable, tough, and set in some of your ways. But still, you are young. Do not try to outrun our wisdom because you believe you are wiser."

Eris's staff thrummed pulling Korvan's attention. "Every day," she said, "you will train. You face that ocean and let it move through you, not against you. When you think you're finished, when you have nothing left, you continue."

He nodded. Shoulders shook once, then steadied. Something rooted under the fatigue.

We are with you, all his Veyrkin lent him their own strength.

Eris paused. "You're a pain in the ass, Aric. But I see the shape of the man you could become."

Not praise, exactly, but for Eris it was as close as he'd ever heard.

"Master this," Cristos added, glancing to Solace, "and perhaps I'll salute you one day."

Solace chimed, a quick, bright tone.

Korvan's laugh came easier. "So, no pressure then."

Eris's own laugh landed light as rain. "No pressure at all."

Cristos offered a waterskin. Cool water cut smoke from Korvan's tongue.

Eris helped him up and nodded toward the gates. "Report to your squad. Formal drills, continue even for you. Show them what bonding with three means. Show them you are not a threat. Do not hide your strength. You, like me, are Aethyrbound, and we will not hide our gifts for fear of what others may think of us."

He gasped but caught himself. "Yes, Battlemage."

Her hand caught his arm "One more thing," she said.

Cristos folded his arms, already knowing.

"I'm assigning you extra hours under Champion Cristos."

Cristos dipped his chin. "There is no better way to learn to balance such gifts than by mastering your body. You'll curse me by sundown, and thank me by the new moon."

"It is a lot to take in, but I'll do it."

A foreign expression touched her face that Korvan couldn't place. Her next words were softer than he'd ever heard her utter, "One day... you'll understand the cost more."

"And before that day," Cristos said, dry as salt air, "you'll think I'm trying to drown you. I'm teaching you to float where the water runs deepest."

Korvan squared his shoulders. "Then let's begin."
***

Korvan cleared the arch.

Eris braced her palms behind her on the cool wall. Cristos stood beside her, head cocked as if he could still hear Korvan's breath fading down the corridor.

"Well, what is your opinion of our new star pupil?" he asked.

"Raw," she said. "Enough potential to drown himself and all of us. He learns fast. Much faster than I like."

Cristos's mouth tugged. "You don't like much."

"I don't like being assigned babysitting duty." Her jaw worked once. "Council made it formal. Direct oversight. They know I take such orders poorly."

"You? Begrudge an order?"

Eris heard the sarcasm drip from Cristos, "But you took this one."

"I did." Leather creaked as she rolled her shoulders. "If there's a leash, better a hand that wants him protected than paraded through the streets."

"You want him protected?" Cristos asked.

"Of course I do, He's a blade that wants to be a shield. The world loves turning people like that into weapons of war."

She gave him a side-eyed stare. "You of all people should know."

Gulls cut the sky beyond the parapet; the sea threw back dull silver. Far below, the city stirred. Market calls, a cart wheel ticking over a seam in stone, the faint clack of a practice staff.

Cristos toed at a loose rock. "He's taken to all the advice well. Surprised how quickly he's been able to center his focus."

"You were right about the ledge drill." A breath that almost became a laugh. "Not that I'll admit it in front of him."

"Battlemage Vale, are you teasing me?," Cristos said.

Eris watched the gate where Korvan had vanished, a pointed non-answer. "Solace widened his Fyrstrand on contact. I'm surprised she's only Obsidian Prestige. It felt like she has as much raw Aethyr as Talmar."

Cristos nodded. "Felt it from the arch. Felt like got pulled out."

Two fingers tapped his sternum. "His center is a house mid-build, it's impressive to see someone continue to grow at the pace he does. Explains why he feels the need to force control over things, he can feel how tumultuous his Fyrstrand is and believes raw willpower will set it right."

"I told him the truth, Discipline in place of control" Eris said.

Cristos tipped his chin. "Plus, consequence."

"Plus, consequence," she echoed.

"How do you feel about the rest? The politics; the eyes?"

"I hate it," she said, and then added, "But I'm grateful you're in it with me."

"Always, Eris." He halted, his hand twitched toward hers, then tried, "We haven't spoken about—"

"Don't." Her voice stayed iron. The weight behind it did not. She steadied her breath and looked past him to the sea. "I don't speak of it. I can't bear it, Cristos."

Cristos bowed his head a fraction. "Forgive me, Battlemage. I forget my place."

"At ease, Champion Vale," she said, softer than the words would mean on their own.

"I was surprised when I got your letter to come... you hadn't changed your name."

She looked up and met his eyes; she felt the mist in your own and found it mirrored in his.

"I don't blame you for what happened Cristos, I never did. I know it was unfair of me to end things... Well, I suppose in truth I never did end things, I left. That was cruel of me."

"Grief makes all of us do things we would not normally do in our right mind."

This time he did not hesitate and grabbed her hand.

"Eris, I know you are my superior now and I will always respect that and your order. I do not blame you either, both of us needed to grieve in our own way. I have loved you since the day we met, when you were just a young girl with a bird perched on your shoulder. You were covered in sap and mud, having run through the woods. For now I will remain Champion Cristos, our past is for us to know and us alone. If and only if, you decide to tell any-one, I will be there to support you. I love you Eris, no distance has changed my heart."

She felt the tears stream freely down her cheeks and her chest begged to release the pressure within and sunder the sky with her voice. But she is the Battlemage. She is the face of their order.

She is composure.

"You are a better man than I deserve Cristos. I am not ready, and I cannot tell you when I will be…"

She turned, and met his gaze, her hand touched the side of his face.

He leaned into it, "I love you too."

He nodded and let his hand slide from hers, though he she noticed he kept his frame angled towards hers.

They stood a while longer watching a yard still scuffed with ash.

"He will be a force for us, we just have to shape him right," Eris said at last.

"He could, or a storm we spend ourselves stopping," Cristos said.

"If it comes to that?"

Cristos's gaze slid to the far corner where shadow clung thicker than it should. Two fingers rose, a lazy flick.

Darkness stirred. Scales like night-sky glass uncoiled and took the faint dawn. It was starlight trapped in obsidian. One head lifted, then another, then another; three sleek jaws breathed mist pricked with cold fire. The bodies braided back into a single thick trunk. Claws set to stone without sound.

"Tenebrix," Cristos said. "A proper rival for your Kaelith I'd wager." The central head dipped to Eris; the others watched the exits with patient malice.

Eris held her ground and floated a hand a finger's breadth from the nearest muzzle. Cold radiance rolled over skin. Immense to be sure, the strongest Veyrkin she'd ever felt another person have, yet not deeper than Kaelith. She gazed into the eyes of the Hydra and let her Aethyr fill her to display her in power in challenge.

Six eyes blinked.

"You've been holding that card all this time? The Fist of Vara'Lumar keeps good partners. I've heard whispers you found a new partner, but I've never seen a Hydra outside The Beyond."" she said.

"Vara'Lumar teaches us to play long games," he said, lip thin.

"If we had to do it. If he fell?"

Cristos weighed it with the body as well as the mind. "You alone *could* do it, at least as he stands today. The true issue is... would you?"

He touched two fingers to his heart and let them fall. Tenebrix sank back into shadow; stars along his scales winked out, one by one.

"A year from now, if he keeps climbing at this rate, the calculus changes. Let us hope it never comes to that."

Eris blew a breath that felt half blessing, half curse. "Then we give the Council nothing. We forge him into the shield he wants to be."

"I'll keep his breath centered; you keep him out of the viper's den." Cristos said.

"Thank you, Cristos."

"You do not need to thank me Eris," Cristos said, his voice low, nearly horse. His shoulders drooped, not from fatigue but from the thing neither are speaking about now. His eyes fell and looked on the floor. His hand moved to hers. It was warm, strong, and gentle despite the callouses.

"I'm here for you. Always." His voice was little more than a whisper.

Cristos' hand dropped back, and he turned. The Fist of Vara'Lumar remembering his strength.

They started toward the arch. Behind them, the yard kept its silence like a vow. Below, the sea beat the cliff, the city's oldest metronome counting down the work ahead.

Eris wiped the drops that had formed on her cheek. She didn't want Cristos to see.

She turned Korvan's words again: *wings in the dark.*

High above, her Soulmark warmed. Kaelith rode the upper currents, cloud-spray in her mane, eyes on her city.

Is this what I think it is? Eris sent, tight and controlled.

Warmth answered. *There is something about him. Korvan Aric is no simple Initiate.*

Cristos noted the minor change in her breathing. She met his look. "Later," she said, and kept walking.

Later, she sent to Kaelith and let the tether hum.

***

By the time Korvan reached the yard again, his arms burned, and his legs ached. Drill-dust clung to sweat like salt. The leather at his palms pulled against split skin where the glaive haft had chewed earlier in the week. Morning blurred into a storm of orders, weapon strikes, relentless forms. Brusk took blow after blow. Vasha moved like a living blade, coil to cut. Solace kept a quiet rhythm at the back of his mind. She was present, steady, waiting to be guided. Eris's warning threaded every motion: discipline over control; instinct over panic. A trainer barked orders on the far lane, the sound bouncing off the stone.

The bell rang for midday meal. Relief moved across the yard.

Korvan drifted toward the long tables, drawn by bread, roasted lemon cod, honeyed stew. Steam curled from bowls; a tang of ferment rode the air from the casks. Bren and Sera held their usual seats. Ryn and Javek were already there, tongues held tight. Thalen's bench stayed empty. It had stayed empty for days.

Korvan glanced that way and swallowed against the twist in his gut.

Ryn picked at bread with a small knife. "Checked the top stables again this mornin'," she said. "Still nothin'."

Javek nodded. "And the towers 'bove the Fourth Ring. No one's seen'em."

Sera frowned. "He'll come back. He just needs time." She slid Korvan a slice without comment. She knew he liked the heels of the bread the best.

He gave her a soft smile as thanks. She beamed back at him.

Korvan nodded, the ache unchanged. "I know. I just...Wish I'd said more. Said anything."

Bren set his tray down with a soft grunt and leaned his elbows to the bench. "He'll come when he's ready. Patience is princely or something." He pushed the water jug toward Ryn with a knuckle.

Ryn took it, jaw tight, and drank.

Silence settled between them as the kitchen clatter softened to a heartbeat under it.

Korvan broke it. "So, what's the newest rumor?"

Sera leaned in. "Local trade town suffered a big hit. It was well organized."

"Organized how?" Korvan asked.

Javek stabbed a carrot and stared at the table. "Word runs fast here. Folks spook quick-like after the Harbor."

"The Crown Guard sent a dispatch," Sera said her tone sharpening. "This is well beyond a rumor, but there's not much detail yet."

Bren's brow furrowed. "Overheard Champion Varos talking with some of the Knights. They may reinforce the southern roads."

Korvan took a slow bite and worked his breath. Pressure gathered under his ribs. Another town. Another theft, or something worse?

"If they're preparing to deploy," Sera said, "we could be sent."

He didn't answer.

He straightened. Will answered where certainty could not. He passed Ryn his last slice of bread; she took it without looking, jaw still set but shoulders lowering a finger's width.

***

Later, sun slanted low between courtyard pillars. The final bell rang from the watchtower calling three sharp chimes.

Korvan froze mid-step. So did everyone around him.

"A mission summons now?" Sera said, tying her hair back with quick hands.

Bren's jaw set. "They don't ring that for drills."

Instructors swept from the arches and spaced themselves like markers on a map. Initiates moved fast, forming tight ranks, shoulder to shoulder, backs straight, boots set. Armor creaked. A gull cried once.

Crown Guard Commander Sael took the fore. Black cuirass; twin insignias. The tower of Cael'Lumar and the sunburst-and-shield of the Aethyrguard. Many had questioned how she could be in such ranking positions within both institutions, but none did so to her.

Her gloved hand rose.

Silence.

"You've trained. You've bled. You've bonded," she said, voice sharp as frost. "You crossed into The Beyond and returned. Now the real work begins."

Korvan's pulse thudded. Vasha's tail stilled. Brusk's plates clicked once and quieted. Solace's feathers hushed along a single cooling breath.

"There was an attack near the Myriath River," Sael said. "A town called Feldmar. Hit fast. Wards shattered. Blood left behind."

The name hit harder than the quiet.

Ryn flinched; Javek went pale as drift-ash.

"Feldmar?" Javek rasped.

"Our home," Ryn said, fists white at her sides.

Gasps rippled and died. Ryn's voice held Korvan's ear more than the crowd. Her jaw set like stone; her stare fixed on the Commander and burned low.

Sael went on, "We tracked them, though they changed tactics once the ward-lines began to activate. Runners report broken glyphs rewired as traps for those doing repair, too familiar to the damage found at Lantern Harbor." She let the weight sink. Wind curled the flag at her back and fell flat again.

"This is short of open war today. Yet make no mistake war walks toward us. The work at Feldmar was clean and precise, an organized enemy."

A pause long enough for banners to settle.

"Five squads will reinforce key routes and investigate. Feldmar is among them. From this point forward, your mistakes will cost lives. Prepare accordingly."

Aides stepped forward with scrolls. Names rolled like thunder.

"Squad Twelve," came the call. "Korvan. Sera. Bren. Javek. Ryn. Thalen. Route: Main trade road, Cael'Lumar to Riverpost. You'll depart at first light. Feldmar is your priority. It is a lengthy ride. Prepare yourselves accordingly."

Korvan's breath caught.

Sera's eyes widened.

Ryn's exhale hit like a gut punch.

Bren's knuckles cracked once.

They all knew why this squad would take the main road. Out of all the initiate groups they had risen to the top. While none of them were officially Knight rank, their raw strength was higher than some Knights in the order. Korvan with three bonds; Sera with a Mender's craft; Ryn and Javek not heavy on spell work but unmatched in finding things they shouldn't; Bren a bruiser with Rok to anchor them; Thalen the scalpel.

Thinking of Thalen hurt.

The aides moved down the ranks with wax-sealed packets and slate tokens for gate clearance. Ink still shone wet on some of the orders. A narrow map-board came out behind them. Their routes chalked in white, danger-marks in rust.

Commander Sael's gaze cut across the rows and stopped on Squad Twelve. "You carry two obligations. First, stabilize the trade road. Second, bring back truth. If you must decide which to prioritize, you choose the road."

Ryn never looked away from the board. "We'll follow the west rise," she said under her breath, already mapping distances. "Scree shelf's quicker if it ain't flooded."

"Too exposed if the wind kicks up though, winters on us, it'll get mighty cold," Javek answered.

Sera rested her hand on Ryn's shoulder. "You two know the area best, and Feldmar is your home. You'll ask people what they know, the right questions matter."

Bren nodded. "I'll float between Anchor and Flank Position since we're down a man. Kor, you, and Brusk stay in the middle."

We hold, Brusk answered.

We'll find them, Vasha whispered.

We are with you, Solace breathed.

Sael lowered her hand. "Dismissed. Depart at first light."

Orders were passed out, benches scraped, two gulls fought over a strip of cod skin near the drain. Korvan's world narrowed to his squad's faces and the line of the map stitching itself into his head.

He let one breath go long, then another. Readiness did not feel calm. It felt like a door set on its hinges.

He touched the edge of the orders packet and felt the wax warm under his thumb.

The yard swallowed their voices. Below, the sea kept its count.

No matter what, training was behind them now.

This was the path ahead.

Chapter 17: On the road again

Korvan sat on the edge of his bunk, new boots black as wet stone under low Aethyrlight. Gear waited in quiet order: hardened leather light enough to move, honest about what it could stop. Brusk would take the worst of it. That was their pact. No need to speak it; always kept. The short sword gleamed. It was standard issue, but untested. The remainder was rope, small tent, tinderbox, waterskins, rations, spare clothes.

Everything he needed, little of what he wanted.

The staff lay apart. Months ago It had called; he had answered, but the rest of him lagged.

At his feet, Solace stirred. Moonstone plumage caught in the light. Her eyes found his.

You fear the power it offers. The thought moved slowly like the rising tide.

He nodded.

You would not harm me; you freed me. You fear harming others. You joined for Caelen to keep him safe, to give him a better life. Now I feel that purpose has widened. It is now them. The city. Your friends.

Her presence folded over his thoughts, snow softening coals around his heart. *Is that all, spark-carrier? Did you join only for him?*

Truth hollowed a space under his ribs. Words stalled.

"No," he said at last. "That isn't the only reason."

Name the truth you buried. There is such power in the truth.

Brusk settled close, a furnace at his thigh. *Here.*

Vasha ghosted in, brushing his knee. *You keep tenderness hidden like a claw, little hunter.*

He bowed his head between them.

"I didn't want to be alone anymore," he admitted.

"Caelen leans on me. I can't show weakness to him, he has enough. I carry everything. The absence of our mother. Our father's drinking. Caelen's sickness. The nights of being hungry, being cold, being bruised and bloodied. It's all too much, just too light-damned much. I saved him from Varnrik, I moved him from being out on the streets, but I can't fix him, I can't save him no matter how strong I get. I just wanted someone to... no one ever came to save me. I'm so tired of needing to be the strong one all the time and I'm afraid Caelen will leave too."

His breath shuddered, his lips trembled, and he tried to press them together. There was a lump in his throat he swallowed until he couldn't.

Tears came clean then.

You wanted rest, you wanted a life, not only survival. You love your brother. You must love yourself, too. Solace murmured.

Brusk pressed closer. *Here. With. Always.*

Vasha's purr thrummed through him. *Nothing will part me from you, my Korvan.*

"Thank you," he whispered into the bond. "You're all so precious to me."

A gentle chime, and he let them slip to The Beyond.

He held still. Counted one breath, then another. Pulse eased under his thumb.

"Korvan... I'm so sorry. It's time." Sera's voice was soft, but steady where he wavered.

He wiped his face and stood. The staff felt right in his hand.

She stepped closer. "Is there anything I can do, are you ok?"

Her gaze took in his cloak, gear, staff, then settled on him.

He drew a breath, then kissed her cheek. "I love you, I should've said it before, and I should have shown you better, but I won't pretend I don't. I was very recently reminded that I deserve to be happy too." he said.

Heat rushed his neck.

She blinked, then smiled, it was the sun breaking through a morning fog. She fisted his collar, pulling him in for a proper kiss

It was warm and certain. His breath caught; heat climbed his spine; the hum spilled to his forearms until his fingers trembled at her waist.

A heartbeat beat loud in his ears. Chest to chest. Breath to breath. The world narrowed to skin, air, and steadiness.

She eased back, laughter low and rich, and tapped his sternum where the marks still glowed.

"I agree with everything you've said. Take me on a real date first," she said, eyes bright. "Then we'll talk about loving each other."

He swallowed, overheated and a little dizzy. "Deal."

"Good." She smoothed his collar.

"Right behind you," he managed.

He shouldered his gear and followed her toward the gate. Obligation had carried him for years.

This felt like walking toward hope.

***

Bren hadn't meant to spy. He'd come to knock, crack a joke, herd them toward muster. Instead, he'd boot-scuffed like a farm-hand in a temple and watched Sera's hand curl in Korvan's collar while their mouths found what they both needed.

His ears went hot. Two steps back, palms raised to no one. He retreated to the corridor and leaned a shoulder to cool stone until embarrassment passed. What rose after was pleasant.

Good. About damned time. He sent to Rok. The bear chuffed in agreement.

He'd called Sera kid sister since week one. She was all sharp elbows, and a kinder heart than he'd ever met. Seeing her laugh into a kiss set something right. And Korvan, stoic as a tomb and twisted into knots. Maybe this would pry the lid a finger's width. Finally let some air in him

Rok's heavy head nudged his hip. Warm breath rolled through leather and wool.

"We're fine," Bren murmured, scratching between plated ridges.

Rok rumbled like shifting barrels. Agreement.

"Hope he lets us in, big fella," Bren added, half to Rok, half to the hall. "Keep carryin' all that alone, he'll snap in half."

Lantern Harbor pressed in, Korvan's weight over Bren's shoulder, straps biting, the fool too proud to complain. Bren hooked the memory with a promise. *We're your family too, whether you notice or not.*

Bootsteps. He straightened, rolled his shoulders, hung his grin.

Korvan and Sera stepped out lighter. The grin stayed.

"If you two are done inventin' new warm-ups," he said, easy, "we've got a road to beat, and I am not lettin' Rok carry all the romance."

Sera's eyes danced. Korvan flushed to the ears.

Good, Let the world be hard. Bren thought.

They'd be harder and kinder. They'd be together.

***

Nearly two weeks' worth of quiet days and roadside camps carried them west. Korvan rode Vasha now. She outmatched a horse in size and had the endurance to carry Korvan and his gear. She preferred his weight; the bond steadied her, and her presence sharpened him.

At the ridgeline, the path pinched through thicket, then spilled them into a valley cupped by forest and low hills. Midday gilded the river, its waters refracting the sunlight.

Above the flood-line hung a sign: Riverpost.

Riverpost, or as the locals call it, The Lifegate Hamlet, is a hub of a few thousand souls. It is a trade lifeline that is home to Granary Row, cold-stone warehouses, and the famous Wagon-Circle

Market. Riverpost serves as the midway point of agriculture inspection and a redistribution hub.

Korvan took it all in, it looked nothing like he imagined from the books. Weathered timbers, steep roofs, bright shutters. Walkways veined the terraces. A brass spire crowned the square, ringed in mirrored plates that turned slow in the breeze.

"Smells like boiled beets and fresh catch," Bren muttered. "Gods, I missed real towns."

"It smells alive," Sera said, adjusting the strap of a bracer.

The hum of hammers falling, and market calls road the wind. Beyond the docks, a faint ward shimmered, but strong as any they'd felt.

"That's what keeps this place standing."

"I thought only the capital used full wards," Sera said.

"Most towns don't need 'em. This is an older style, more like a scent marker. It's a deterrent," Javek said.

Bren squinted at a pylon. "Looks nearly worn out. How long do they last?"

"Depends on the seal. Decades if set right, but they need a recharge every few months." Korvan added remembering a lesson from Archmage Maedryn.

"The local guard should be able to handle that," Sera said.

"Thalen would've had five theories and a lecture by now," Ryn said.

"He'd have talked our ears off before we crossed the wall line," Javek muttered.

Neither smiled.

Korvan tightened his chest strap. "We need to meet the outpost commander."

"Then what?" Bren asked, settling a coil of rope.

"We make a plan from there."

The road bent through tall grain bowed by its own weight. River water crawled beside them, bridged by a timber trestle.

Squat boats nosed the banks, tied to iron rings polished by years of rope.

Riverpost opened in full.

A shallow wall, two men high, timber-braced and banded in rust. Two carved obelisks flanked the open gate, runes faint in sun, dormant and waiting.

Boots clicked on cobble. The town exhaled.

Children stilled mid-game. Mothers drew them close. A blacksmith paused with hammer raised. Merchants traded glances. Veterans in the crowd gave quiet nods.

"Y'all ain't in the capital no more," Javek said, hand taking in weathered fronts.

River silt rode every breath. No Aethyrglass glow just flaked paint, brick ovens, iron hinges blackened by hands. The garrison squatted at the far end made of stone and iron, more warehouse than stronghold. Ranged spears and drying mail told another story under the plain face.

They passed the gate. A tall figure stepped from shadow.

She moved like a whetted blade all long-limbed and deliberate. A Crimson colored pin in the shape of a rearing beast clung to her cloak showing her rank: Champion. A pale scar climbed from temple and vanished into tight braids. Her eyes weighed each of them like tools she meant to use.

"Squad from Cael'Lumar," she said. Fact. "About time." Her gaze checked them all and returned to Korvan. "I'm Commander Ilvara. The side barracks are for your bunking. Speak plainly when questioned." Her voice hardened. "I have no patience for green-blood dramatics. There's a problem here. I need fighters, not dreamers. Understood?"

Korvan straightened. "Understood."

A single nod. "We'll hold the briefing at dusk, go settle in. Welcome to Riverpost. Dismissed."

They peeled off. Tension pooled behind them. Heads turned. Whispers followed. Riverpost felt like a scab ready to split.

The sounds of work reclaimed the street, a mallet on a fence peg, the hiss of a tea kettle, arguing over fish heads. Salt and smoke threaded the wind.

Squad Twelve answered the war-room call. A wide circular table held a map with the region's topography. Other hand-drawn maps and ink-stained ledgers were stacked in ordered piles, edges curled from use. Charcoal marked danger, absence, and guesses. There were two guards at the back wall, armor plain but with sharp posture. Ilvara at the head, arms folded, cloak like a second skin.

"Riverpost isn't a farming dot on the map," Ilvara said. "Three thousand live on these stones. In an ordinary year, that many hands push smart trouble to softer roads," Tap on the garrison mark.

"I hold two bonds, a pair of Howlers. Two Knights ride from this post to Cael'Lumar keeping the roads clear. Stationed with me are fifty Crown Guard who can shut the gates in under a minute."

Ryn nodded once. "This place keeps the inland corridor fed. Folks know better than to test it."

Javek traced the board's edge. "If y'all still asked for help, means something's braver than it ought to be… or it thinks it can't be stopped."

Ilvara's mouth didn't argue. "That's why you're here."

"This is the last reliable stop before trade heads into the wilds," she went on, clipped and certain. "Everything we hunt, fish, harvest, or cure passes through here. That makes Riverpost a target."

"Two weeks ago, three farms on the southern bend fell silent, one of them Feldmar. No fire. No raiders. No blood. Not a soul-scoured clue. Just gone."

Sera leaned in. "Gone?"

"Gone. Tools left mid-use. Beds still made."

Korvan's gut pulled tight. Beside him, Ryn's jaw set; Javek's hands stilled over a stray map weight.

"Last night a fishing boat drifted into harbor. Nets showed a full catch. Nobody was on the boat."

"Could be Veyrkin," Bren offered.

"One theory," she allowed. "Yet the ward pylons remain intact. No claw scoring. No corruption residue. No field disruption. Whatever hunts here knows how to walk between our lines."

She flipped a ledger. "After we increased pylon checks in the immediate area and farms around us, the disappearances shifted further north beyond the lake and into the northern branches of the river. More of the same results."

Ryn crossed her arms.

"You're here because we need reinforcements, I can't be everywhere, and I no longer feel comfortable leaving this city without someone with Veyrkin to defend it. The Aethyrguard sent you. You must be the best of your year if they sent you."

Javek snorted. "Aye, we've seen a thing or two."

A twitch at Ilvara's mouth. "I suppose we shall see, tell me, what do you think of this."

She drew a small bundle from beneath the table and unwrapped it.

A curl of skin. Tanned from the sun with blackened edges. Scarred with the remnant of a Soulmark that looked twisted.

Sera looked away, hand leapt to her mouth. Fennik pressed to her throat. Bren swore under his breath. Ryn didn't move. That stillness unnerved Korvan more than fury.

"The owner of this skin wasn't ripped apart," Ilvara said, quieter. "This mark was the only injury we found."

"Why?" Ryn asked, voice scraped flat.

"We don't know. It has happened twice since."

The cloth closed.

No one moved.

"There are whispers, only things I've heard out here. They say that the Aethyrguard chain the world. That power should be free. That bonds shackle rather than gift. A small faction is behind this, I think they're sending a message."

Korvan clenched his fists. "What's the message then?"

"That they're former Aethyrguard, they know how to beat us with our own tricks. That its time for a fight."

She pointed to the southeastern trail. "Tomorrow you scout the old Witherfield farms between here and Feldmar. If it's quiet, good. If it isn't, return here, do not risk yourselves."

The silence that followed was brittle.

Korvan looked to his people. Sera was already ordering triage in her head. Ryn's brow pulled tight. Bren ground down the urge to volunteer for every hard piece. Even Javek had stopped joking. Thalen should have been here. He would have had contingencies. But this was the squad they had.

He drew a breath, it tasted like sweat, fireplace smoke and warm leather.

***

The barracks ran colder than he expected. Two lanterns flickered by the door. A long row of cots adorned one wall. The smell of oil and damp wool hung in the air.

Korvan sat at the edge of his bunk, elbows to knees, eyes on stone beneath his boots. Pack half-unrolled at his feet. Food untouched.

Across the room, Bren polished his hammer in slow, practiced arcs; leather rasped steel. Ryn leaned into the doorframe, fletching a new arrow with rhythmic focus, tongue caught between teeth as she trimmed a stubborn vane. Javek hovered at the narrow hearth, poking a dented kettle, eyes flicking to the door. Sera sat beside Korvan in a comfortable but watchful quiet. Fennik's tail ticked her shoulder.

Silence held until Ryn cut it. "So, what's the plan for t'morrow?"

Korvan glanced up. "We follow the southeastern trail. Scout the Witherfield farms. We keep together and stay sharp."

"That ain't a plan, that's a route," Javek said, still worrying the kettle.

Korvan straightened. "It's recon. We don't know what waits out there."

"Exactly. So we need more'n 'stay sharp.' If we find somethin', who's on point? Who draws eyes? Who calls fallback?" Ryn cut in.

"We improvise," Korvan said. He couldn't deny how thin it sounded.

Bren looked up. "Korv... I'm with you. But this isn't Cael'Lumar drills. People are vanishing. Soulmarks burned out. You don't improvise against a thing that knows how to unmake a person."

Sera stirred. "We're all tired. This isn't only on Korvan."

"No, but Ilvara set the weight on him. We felt it." Ryn said.

Javek turned, voice lower. "Thalen would'a had a plan. A Signal. Fallback spots. Some kind of idea."

Korvan's jaw tightened.

Sera stood. "Thalen isn't here. That isn't his fault or Korvan's."

"No. You're not wrong, Javek. I'm not Thalen," Korvan said, voice steady.

Eyes found him.

"I'm not Thalen, I don't pretend to be. I don't have a full plan. I haven't led outside the walls, the Aethyrglass mission was his I haven't tracked a group before. I have instincts and I have a lot of power. I only hope it's enough."

Brusk shifted in the corner, plates clicking soft. *Here. With.*

Solace lifted her head from shadow, eyes steady.

Vasha padded to his side, fur warm against the chill. *You have more than instinct, little hunter.*

Korvan went on, "But I do know this. Whatever hunts out there wants us broken before we fight back, it wants us fighting amongst ourselves. It feeds on our fear and doubt. I know that way better than most, and we beat it by giving it neither. We move together. If anything feels wrong, we fall back. Anyone calls the retreat we listen. No lone plays. We stay smart. We hold the line together."

The stillness after held.

Javek exhaled. "That's most of a'plan."

Ryn nodded. "We're with ya, but just own it, Korvan. Not because you're the smartest; because you're bonded three times over. Like it or not, you're different."

Korvan blinked.

Bren snorted, softer now. "Hard to play humble with a feathered miracle curled at your feet."

Korvan looked at Solace. She didn't look away.

He nodded once. "Then we start by walking. If the trail turns dark," His voice settled. "I'll lead us through."

Sera's mouth softened. She took his hand and squeezed. Fennik burrowed into her neck with a determined chuff.

Javek turned back to the kettle. "Right then. But if I die, I'm hauntin' you."

Korvan felt his mouth twitch into a smile.

"Deal."

***

Torches along Riverpost's outer wall burned low. Shadows jittered across grain stores and pillars. The town held its breath: windows shuttered, doors sealed, silence threaded through mortar.

Korvan stood at the overlook behind the barracks, arms folded, eyes on the southern tree line.

Solace paced nearby, moonlight given feathers, a traveling sheen like starlight in motion. He didn't turn as the barracks door creaked.

"Couldn't sleep?" Sera's voice came soft, low against the chill. Fennik padded beside her, runes banked to a modest warmth.

Korvan kept his gaze on the dark. "Didn't try. My mind won't stop."

Another voice, rough and steady as stone, came from the arch. "Figured I'd find you two out here. Stars are too damn quiet."

Bren stretched until joints popped. Rok lumbered behind, massive and unhurried. Vasha lay by Korvan's boot, a dark hill of breath and fur. He hadn't noticed her return.

Bren rubbed his neck, sheepish. "Just so it's said. I wasn't trying to spy when I saw you two. Walked in on the kiss because I'm a menace with doors. Gave it some time, so you wouldn't think I thought it was weird."

Sera's mouth quirked. "You are a menace with doors."

"Point is, I'm happy. For both of you." He angled a look at Korvan. "Sera's like my baby sister. Annoying, smarter than me, somehow always right. And you, big man, you gotta let people in. A squad can only carry what you set on us, but we're your friends. Don't want to just here orders or the easy stuff."

Sera bumped into Korvan's shoulder. "He's right. We don't shatter easy. We're tough."

Heat climbed Korvan's neck. "I'm... trying."

"Try harder," Bren's voice was soft as he could make it.

Sera's eyes warmed. "Also learn the difference between a battle plan and a date plan."

Bren snorted. "If someone's gotta walk you through your first real one, I'll draw a map."

"He does not need a map," Sera said.

Korvan found a small, honest smile. "Maybe a legend and a north arrow."

"That's a map," Bren said, grinning.

Sera eased onto the wall's lip. "The waiting is the worst. I hate just standing here not knowing what's coming."

They held there. Three bodies. Three Initiates. Six eyes on the dark.

The Veyrkin weren't asleep, and all moved to something. Fennik's ears stood up alert, Rok went stone-still, Solace's hackles lifting once, then smoothing. Brusk came last and settled like a wall at Korvan's back.

Korvan let out a breath he hadn't meant to keep. "I hate not knowing what to do. I can bleed, train, take orders. Waiting gnaws at my thoughts. Wondering if the next scream belongs to someone you know, someone you love."

His voice frayed.

"I just..." He swallowed. "I wish Thalen were here. For all his smugness, he always had a plan. Now we don't even know if he's alive."

Bren butted in. "You're doin' better than I did."

Sera's smile came soft and real. "He's alive. I can feel it. But it's okay to worry about your friend. I'm worried about him too."

Warmth worked under Korvan's sternum.

"Thanks, both of you."

Sera stepped close, fingers warm on his sleeve. "I know you care deeply, and for all his flaws, you miss Thalen. Hope weighs on you. I'll help shoulder it before I let you fall over. He's important to me too."

Korvan met her eyes. Twin stars, quiet and unshaken. He let himself study her: strength sharpened by softness; a tender gentleness threaded every move. What held him most was the small crinkle at the corners of her eyes when she smiled, that near-blind squint that carried more light than sight.

Finally he said, "Are we ready?"

"I never feel like it, but yes." Sera said, steady.

Bren huffed. "Ain't that the Aethyrguard way?"

You are not alone in the dark, Korvan. You never were. Solace pressed his leg, the thought curling like low tide around a wounded reef.

He closed his eyes and let it settle into the hollow.

"Let's make sure we all wake up tomorrow. If the trail turns dark..." He looked to each of them. "We walk it together."

"Together," Sera echoed, bumping his shoulder.

He caught her arm and pulled it into his. He swore her cheeks got went rosy in the dark.

"So long as there's coffee at the end," Bren added, rolling his neck.

A wind stirred the fields, something slow and heavy. Deliberate.

Every Veyrkin stilled.

Sera's fingers slid toward the stone wall. "Did you hear..."

Korvan raised a hand, eyes on the tree line.

Silence answered. Only air moving where it shouldn't.

"Just wind," Bren muttered, though his hand had found his hammer.

The quiet thickened, dense with watching.

They stood as sentries under a nervous sky. Waiting together made the next thing survivable.

A patrol crossed the inner lane with lanterns hooded. Metal buckles whispered. Somewhere a shutter clicked, then settled. The nearest pylon answered with a thin hum, ward-lines rippling like heat above a kiln. Sera watched the shimmer with suspicion and said nothing. Bren spread a palm on the parapet until grit pressed crescents into skin; he needed something solid to measure against the air.

Korvan flexed sore fingers and felt old drill-splits pulling under their wraps. Salt lived in the seams of his knuckles. He rolled his shoulders; the leather answered with a tired creak. When the wind shifted from the river, fish brine and smoke carried a second message. Boats still moved even if there were fewer than there should've been.

"First light comes fast," Sera said, barely above the ward's thrum.

She didn't move to go.

None of them did.

***

Cliffs closed around the trail. Wind knifed the broken road, threading jagged stone with a drop yawning to his right. Each step rang hollow.

Midnight followed, her silent, bright eyes unblinking.

"Don't look at me like that," Thalen muttered, fingers flexing on the hilt at his hip. "Pity won't help."

She didn't answer.

He had walked so long he'd lost track. It had to have been a couple of weeks since he'd left, weeks since Korvan had once again defied every rule of the Aethyrguard.

His rage had cooled long ago, and had been replaced by an icy grip that hung behind his heart.

Time blurred when the race ran inward. Korvan had bonded a third, the same impossible way he'd taken Vasha. The world seeming to bend for him.

Thalen had been raised on earned bonds: discipline, House sanction, rank oversight. Korvan kept breaking the lesson.

Fairness soured in Thalen's mouth.

His boot clipped granite. A chip skittered over the lip and vanished. No sound climbed back.

"I should've been the one," he whispered. His Soulmark stayed cold.

He turned from the edge to face the memories behind him. Lareth's ring cooling in his palm the night House Ryst got the missive. His father's hand on his shoulder at the memorial-that-wasn't, duty preached above grief. Eris's eyes sliding past on selection day. Something in him folded.

The air changed. Wind died and a weight settled. A presence older than truth pressed down until the stone felt tight across the bones of the world.

Midnight froze and the sky trembled and shifted.

Mist lifted above the ledge as the wyvern descended. Wings like banked coals, membranes veined with dull fire. Smoke-dark scales caught the last light like storm-glass. Talons kissed granite and carved furrows with a glass-torn sound. He arrived in a single decision of wing and weight.

The name rose to Thalen unbidden, as if the cliff taught his blood to speak. Ashwing.

Judgment given scales, larger than any creature Thalen had ever seen. A long head lowered, horned and terrible. One step and the world made room.

Midnight slid back, ears flat, a ripple of shadow.

Thalen's legs quivered but they held.

His lungs locked. His Soulmark flared, silver-blue cracking along skin.

You wear your lies like armor, son of Ryst.

The voice folded behind his ribs and rattled his soul.

It was thunder given shape.

Thalen staggered a step. Salt dragged off the sea and burned his eyes.

Ashwing advanced, obsidian eyes shot with molten thread.

The Noble Son. The Polished Blade. The Heir Who Deserves. Smoke slipped from his nostrils, almost amused.

You wrapped yourself in the legacy so tightly you forgot how to feel. You forgot how to bleed.

"I've bled," Thalen rasped, anger striking flint.

"I bled for my family's name."

Ashwing tilted his head, vast and intent. Heat climbed. *Then bleed for yourself.*

The Soulcall lanced the places he'd hidden the boy he was. His knees hit stone, with a crack. Midnight made a sound he had never heard from her, a torn whimper, but she stayed. Thalen gripped the rock as something in him tore. His Soulmark seared bright along his forearms as his Fyrstrand expanded. Glyph-lines widened, split. A second shape kindled beside the first. Heat drove tears without shame.

"I didn't want their fear, I wanted to be seen. I wanted someone to stay and to choose me," he said, truth ripping free.

Lareth's laugh in the garden. The ring pressed to his fist. 'Don't follow me'. His father's voice at his shoulder, always legacy above doubt. Korvan in the council chamber, light on his skin, chosen by the world. The beautiful bastard.

Ashwing lowered, inevitable. The smallest of his horns touched Thalen's brow. Stone shivered under his palms.

The wyvern's voice came out as gentle thunder. *Ah such pain and grief... that is truth. You both love and hate Korvan, you wish him to see you not for the noble's son, but for the one that kept following him... I see you, Thalen of House Ryst. You are arrogant because you fear being forgotten. You are brave because you think it hides your fear. And you are good because you attempt to atone for sins that were never yours. You are not perfect. Yet you persist. You are what I need. Headstrong by choice, noble by intention, not by blood. One of the sky-lords must carry purpose. Purpose for we have no need for titles.*

Thalen gave way. Posture, drilled breath, each Ryst-perfect answer sloughed like a husk.

He screamed, raw and living, until the sound emptied and only breath and salt remained.

A breath. He found a rhythm in the wreckage. four in, four out. Cristos' lesson. Pulse settled against stone. The wind returned as a thin thread along his neck.

He had nothing left. Only the boy who had waited too long to be chosen for anything that didn't want performance. Only his truth.

His Fyrstrand flowed strong, more robust now than it had ever been. It ran his lungs, threaded his blood, touched the small place he never let anyone near. He let it happen.

Light appeared and cooled within a breath. His Soulmark settled. Two glyphs now, twin silver-blue sigils etched over bone, cooling to a steady glow.

Ashwing breathed out, quiet and true. Mist thinned. The cliff stood bare beneath a new sky.

Midnight edged in and pressed her shoulder to his. Thalen's hand found her fur. No circle. No chalk. No stabilizing sigils. No handler's hand. He had done it. He had broken law and training and the Guard's quiet preferences and he still stood.

"We bonded... Without a ritual, how is that possible?" he whispered, shock braided to grief.

Since Lantern Harbor, the world's balance had shifted. Bonds drew close. Everything pulled tight. He had blamed Korvan for bending order to his will. Maybe Korvan had only found a new door and walked through it.

"This is how he did it," Thalen said, hoarse, reverent, and resentful at once. "How he took Vasha. How that Reservoir came. They chose him and he accepted... You chose me, you didn't even ask me to name you. That's not supposed to happen."

He swore Ashwing was smiling. The wyvern's wings folded, a cathedral of shadow drawn tightly behind him.

Thalen touched the new edge of his mark. The ache remained, changed in weight. He saw Lareth's as a child and while his memory isn't perfect he recognized elements of it here. No secret that all the Draconids were Starlit bloodlines and his bond with Ashwing felt immense, more Aethyr than anything Thalen had known or felt.

"Stay," he said. Neither command nor plea.

I will not be parted from you now Thalen. We are bound. But you must breathe. Let go the noble and become more.

Thalen closed his eyes and obeyed for the first time in years. He breathed, not like during training, but like he could finally let go. Midnight leaned in like a promise, and a second bond hummed quiet and wild beneath his skin, a new note braided to the old.

He didn't know how any of it was possible.

He stood, then swayed. Midnight shouldered his thigh until his stance remembered how to stack bones. Ashwing's chest rose and fell with him. One breath, then another, until his ribs learned a new rhythm against scale and sky. Far below, a wave threw itself against black rock and sheared to white. The hiss climbed as proof the sea kept time.

A sliver of iron glinted near his boot, the shard he'd kicked from the cliff. He picked it up and set it on the path's inward edge. A small promise: remember where the fall begins. He looked at his hands and did not see a prince's polish. He saw scraped knuckles and the faint tremor from a chord still ringing.

"Eris will kill me," he said to no one, then huffed something like a laugh. "Or she'll run me ragged." The thought steadied him. Consequence gave shape to wonder.

Ashwing's pupils narrowed, then widened, mirroring the slow dilation of stars as cloud thinned.

Learn the weight of quiet, you rush to fill it when it asks to teach, the wyvern murmured.

Thalen gazed at his new companion and rubbed his hands along the great spines of his neck and the horns that formed a crown on his head. He found a small patch of soft scales behind Ashwing's ear and gave it a scratch.

The wyvern rumbled. Thunder rolled in his chest.

Thalen laughed. The laugh of a carefree boy.

The Wyvern was purring.

He knew the world waited when he finally lifted his head and looked to the dawn.

"Come on you two. Let's find our friends."

Thalen mounted Ashwing and felt what it meant to truly be free.

Chapter 18: Witherfield

The road to Witherfield Farms was quiet in the wrong ways. Dust clung to their boots. No birds in the hedges. No frog-call from the reed beds. Even the wind dragged its heels.

Korvan led, staff strapped across his back. His eyes worked the crooked fences and sagging silos, all of it jutting like broken teeth. Two crows perched on a dead limb. Black. Watchful. Silent.

Sera kept his right. "I don't like this," she said. "Not just the quiet. The air feels thin. Like it's been pulled away."

Bren shifted behind, pack clinking. "Storm weather. Back of my neck's been pricklin' since we cleared the wall."

Javek grunted. "Storm's coming, or we're walkin' into a grave-yard."

Ryn's voice softened. "Still... good hearin' folk that sounded like home again. Smell of it too, even with the rot."

Javek pointed with his chin. "That cottage was Miss Krelle's. Pears for gossip. Jam if she liked you."

Korvan kept his thoughts to Ilvara's warning. They'd found Soulmarks gutted and destroyed. The way she'd looked at him implied he should already know why.

They topped a low rise. A splinter fence marked the fields. Late harvest should have stood thick. The soil lay bare, of all vegetation.

Korvan slowed. "This... this is wrong."

Ryn's gaze sharpened. "These plots were active last year. Root veg, corn, maybe beans. This ain't fallow. It's just empty."

Bren pressed a leaning post. It powdered under his glove. "This was scrubbed clean."

Korvan's pulse climbed. "Spread out. Keep in shouting distance."

They moved through empty squat cottages. Stone bases. Tired roofs. The locks weren't broken or windows smashed in they were simply vacant..

Half an hour passed, and the weight of the emptiness pressed on them.

Korvan stopped under a wind chime. It swayed on dead air. The tone too clean.

"They didn't all leave... they couldn't have just vanished," he said.

Sera went pale. "Then where are they?"

He didn't answer. His fingers brushed his Soulmark seeking comfort.

Sera saw it. "What?"

"Listen."

At first, nothing. Then a low pulse under the world, a hum in the dirt.

He crouched. Palm to ground and at the edge of his senses he felt it.

"There's something under us."

Bren stepped back. "Nope. That's the 'we're-about-to-get-ruined' tone."

Sera skimmed a well rim. "This well's dry."

Javek frowned. "Can't be true. These are ran year-round. Wells don't vanish without leaving at least some mud behind."

Korvan pointed. "Cellars, that's it. Check all of the cellars.."

He drew the short sword, untested but better in tight quarters.

First house. The hearth was cold and the dust was thick. A crescent scuff where heels turned in haste. The rug was turned, revealing a trap door.

"Here."

Sera and Bren slipped in. Korvan lifted the hatch. A slight creak preceded a draft of bone-dry air.

He dropped first. Stairs cut narrow into earth. Empty shelves. Cloudy jars. A chair with a snapped leg propped back.

At the center: a black ring burned into packed dirt.

Bren swore. "Storms break me…"

Sera came down slow. "No ambient Aethyr left, its at least a week old, next to impossible to tell now, for me anyway."

Korvan crouched. Ash glittered with pale blue flecks, crystalline like frost.

Sera's breath caught. "Aethyrglass residue, it was powdered to make the ring."

"You sure?"

"Before Fennik I was an apprentice to an apothecary, I would it into powder. This is the residue when you burn it."

Korvan rose. "So they did it here, and then burned the evidence."

Bren shifted. "Why a root cellar?"

No answer. Above, the wind chime gave a single careful note.

The wind hadn't blown.

***

The third house sagged like the rest. Stone footings. Bowed roof. Garden gone to dry hands. The warped door groaned.

"Another."

Sera followed. Light opened in her palm. The same seen of a house left used, but clean greeted them.

At the back, a trapdoor cracked ajar.

Korvan knelt. Root-smell. Damp wood. Under it, a living thread at the back of the throat.

"There's someone down there."

Her light brightened.

He lifted the hatch. Stone steps fell away.

"Bren, Javek, Ryn get over here."

Steel came quick. Ryn and Javek held the door and watched behind them.

Korvan descended, staff forward, if they were going to fight other Discipline wielders, he'd have every bit of strength he could. The cellar was lined with shelves of dried herb and preserves. Dust curled in corners.

Movement under a frayed blanket caught their eye.

Sera gasped. "By the Light."

A boy in his late teens shivered on a makeshift straw bed. His lips were split, chapped and his skin was thin as glass.

"Hey," Korvan said, kneeling. "You're safe, now. We've got you."

Eyes opened. Voice rasped. "Don't... touch the mark."

Korvan's gut turned. "What mark?"

The boy trembled. Collar torn. Flesh below the shoulder burned smooth. A circle erased. Edges cracked white. Hollowed out, just like the others.

"They made me watch," he whispered. "Said if I wouldn't take the brand... they'd take it all instead."

Sera set warmth over ruined skin. Hands steady. "He's in shock. Hold him steady, I'll do what I can."

Korvan met her eyes. "This is evil."

She nodded. "And it walks among us."

"Who did this?" Korvan asked. The boy's breath slipped. Silence folded him.

They carried him up. Wrapped him in a bedroll. Sera set a glow at his chest, and poured light into him. His breathing eased.

The got a small fire in going in the hearth and made his home as safe as they could. Dusk bled violet over the hills.

Javek cracked. "What in the gods' names is this?"

Bren sat rigid. "He said 'brand or purge.'"

His throat worked. "What kind of magic..."

Sera spoke low. "Old rites. They don't sever your connection they collapse it on itself. It pull's Aethyr at both ends. Crushes whatever is between it."

Korvan's jaw set. "Which, is almost always fatal."

"Unless someone has some kind of Discipline I've never heard of," Sera answered.

Ryn's voice shook. "Korv... I know him."

Javek leaned closer, color gone. "Davrin. He was a farmhand, had a knack for mending fences. We used to throw stones behind Maela's for sport. Gave his winnings to the littles."

Ryn nodded. "Always did."

Javek's mouth worked. "What the fuck happened to our home?"

Again, no one could answer.

***

They tried for Riverpost but gave it up an hour in. The boy wouldn't last the road.

They laid him close. Every blanket on him. Cheeks gone to bone. Breath in thin shivers.

Sera crouched. "Water."

Korvan passed the canteen. Drops to cracked lips. He swallowed and let a rasping breath.

"...they came... from the field..."

"Who?" Sera asked.

"People. Eyes like fire. One with a staff that sang. Wards didn't care. Walked past." A blink, his eyes lost focus.

Korvan's chest tightened. "Hang in there Davrin, we're almost to safety. You mean the ward was up?"

A nod. "Watched from the trapdoor. They didn't see me. Or didn't care. They burned my brother's mark right in the field. He didn't scream. He just... got thinner 'til he broke."

Ryn whispered. "Ash and Silence... poor Brenen."

Javek turned away, shoulders locked.

Sera's hands stayed steady. "They're trained, they're methodical, and clearly are no longer afraid of witnesses."

The boy's fingers closed on Korvan's sleeve. "Said... if we won't swear... we don't deserve it. Called it a gift. A chain. Said we had to break—"

His hand slid away. His chest caught once. Stilled.

Sera touched his throat. Shook her head. "He's gone."

Air cracked.

No one moved.

Korvan's arms hung. His boots furrowed shallow lines. He ground earth like it might answer. Too long before he straightened. One more breath before he stepped back from the corpse that was no longer a boy.

Soot and iron clung to his teeth. Davrin's eyes refused to close. Whatever light had lived there was gone.

His mark beat wrong. A dull skip every third. His palm found it. A fire raged within him.

He turned so they wouldn't see his face. His eyes were wet, but his hands kept clenching and unclenching. His neck was flushed and he felt every fiber of his forearms ache as he fought to keep them still.

A life cut mid-sentence, all their strength, all their power. They couldn't save him.

He wasn't strong then.

He folded behind a crumbling wall.

His hand shook once on his knee. He closed it. Sat inside the tremor. Not here. Not now.

Something fine cracked in him.

"I'm fine," he'd once told Sera. He wasn't.

Bren called soft from the fire. Korvan didn't answer. Watched a bead of blood slip from his glove. Fall. Sink to dust.

Seconds. Hours. He didn't know.

He rose at last. Slow. Jaw set like thin iron still meant to hold.

"We take him back, and we'll bury him in the customs of his people. He deserves that much." He kept his eyes on the fire.

"Then we find who did this."

Javek's voice shook. "And if they find us first?"

Korvan let heat and pressure forge the words.

"Then the sons of bitches will find that it isn't farmhands waiting for them. It's the Aethyrguard."

***

The sun bled low behind Cael'Lumar's arches. Shadows ran long across the sparring ground.

Eris stood on the platform, arms folded, eyes on the dust and noise below. Wooden blades cracked. Breath came harsh. Discipline was better. Not enough.

Cristos leaned the rail, ankles crossed. The breeze tugged his sleeve. He watched like he always did, with a lazy look that missed nothing.

"That one leads with her shoulder," he said, nodding at a redhead. "Telegraphs the strike. She'll break her collarbone."

Eris grunted. "She'll learn. Or she won't."

"Always this forgiving?"

"I'm tired of children dying before they have a chance to live."

His face remained passive, but it was forced.

"You've been watching the horizon more than the pit."

Below, two Initiates collided. One fell. The other helped him up. Dust hung like ash.

"They're not ready, this group is miles behind where they should be. Our enemies are ahead of us and there are too few Knights and Champions to protect the city." she said.

"War always changes, usually long before the orders do," Cristos said.

"The Riverpost squad is overdue for a report."

"Sera will write. Bren too. And Korvan—"

"Burns too bright, too fast, too loud for his own good" she said.

"Fire tempers steel. Or shatters it. That all depends on the smith," Cristos said.

"And if the blade tries to forge itself?"

"We make sure the hammer lands true."

She snorted without venom. "Oh Cristos, it is always riddles, parables and pragmatic lessons with you."

"Very well I shall speak plainly. We are their instructors. Their mentors and their protectors. We guide them to survive their first mistakes."

"Think they're making one now?" Eris asked, turning to look at him.

"I think they're learning what to hold when the world cuts pieces away."

"They follow him, of that I have no doubt. Even Ryst's son did." Eris said.

"That kind of easy companionship is rare," Cristos said. "Korvan will need to stay grounded or he'll fly apart."

"He won't admit he's near breaking. None of them will."

"They're young, and all have had hard lives in their own way. We give the advice we wish we'd had when we were their age."

She slid a look at him. A small smile found her mouth. "Do you miss the field?"

"Of course. I'd miss them more if I failed them from here though."

"I miss it every godsdamned day," she whispered.

The bell rang. Initiates stances dropped. Bows to their partners. Drills ended. War hadn't started.

Not here.

"Push them. Remind them who they are when war tries to make them something else," Cristos said.

"If they live long enough to be anything."

"When they do Eris, they'll remember who stood in their corner when the cost came due."

They left in silence.

But not in peace.

***

Morning haze clung to Riverpost's roofs. From the tower, a handbell struck three sharp chimes. Formal Summons.

The gate creaked.

A guard stepped forward. His gaze hit the pale shape bound in their cloaks. He lifted the edge and flinched.

"That's Davrin Donner," he said. "By the Twin gods."

No one answered.

Korvan walked ahead. Stretcher weight in his hands. Sun gilded thatch and stone. No warmth reached him.

Commander Ilvara waited in the square. Her gaze went straight to the body.

Korvan spoke first. "Davrin Donner. Hid in a root cellar and saw what happened. He held on long enough to tell us some."

Ilvara's mouth tightened. "By Light and Memory."

Her eyes read each of their faces. "The rest?"

"Gone, nothing left," Korvan said, his shoulders sagged and a hand came up to his face.

She turned to one of the Crown Guard. "Record his name, see that he's buried with honor."

As the stretcher passed, Korvan stayed rooted. Eyes on the southern trail.

"We need to find who did this, and we need to move," he said.

"Walk with me," Ilvara said.

They stepped aside. Wagon wheels ground stone. Hooves tapped cobble.

"Anger's a hell of a motivator Initiate Aric. But you'll lose your reason if you let it guide you." Ilvara said, low

Korvan felt his voice get hot and gain venom, "He was a boy... he was terrified, alone in the darkness, dying. No one saved him."

"But you did, he held on to a hope that he could tell anyone what happened. He told you. That matters," she said.

"We were too late. They're not kidnapping people Commander, they're unmaking them" His hand closed.

Ilvara halted. "You're sure."

He nodded. "Davrin's mark wasn't just wounded. It was gone."

"The Council won't act on words, we'll need proof," she said.

"We have proof," he said, pointing to the shrouded body being taken away.

"Magic that deep unravels. We need a name. A sign. Something carved or stamped. Something that won't fade," She met his eyes and he saw a kindred expression to the fire within him. She was furious, but knew they needed more than a body.

Korvan's eyes hardened. "Then we bring one back. Dead or alive."

Something flickered across her eyes, "You've got fire, Initiate. Make sure it burns for the right reason."

He nodded and rejoined the others. The ache in his chest hadn't eased but It at least had a direction.

***

The fire cracked low. Riverpost's watch lights flickered like tired stars. Squad Twelve sat outside the gates, not ready to go back. Dirt still under their nails from the grave.

Korvan hunched. Sera curled to her knees. Bren picked at rations with a dagger tip.

"Think he had a good life?" Korvan asked.

"He mended fences and worked with goats, always wore a smile, and played with the youngins. He was good people," Ryn said.

"Just a kid, didn't get to fight back," Bren muttered.

"No tracks, no broken doors, not a damn blade of grass out of position," Korvan said. He flexed his fingers, his hand had gotten stiff from the constant tension, he felt a throb in the back of his neck, a headache was forming from the tension.

"Worse than ghosts," Bren said. "Ghosts leave cold spots."

Korvan looked at him. "Thank you, Bren."

"For what?"

"For being here."

A tired half-smile tugged.

Sera nudged his arm. "You alright?"

He weighed it.

"No. No I'm not ok. None of this should be happening."

Stars burned. The hush held.

"You care more than you let on, but this isn't just about Davrin or the missing farmers is it," Sera said.

"You think?" it came out sharp.

Sera recoiled.

Korvan inhaled. Two, three, four. Out, two, three, four.

"I'm sorry Sera... I shouldn't have snapped at you. That wasn't fair. I won't do that again."

She slid her arm back into his, "We're all on edge, I know you aren't mad at me. But thank you for the apology. I forgive you."

He put his forehead against hers and mouthed a silent 'thank you'.

"You're right though, I do care a lot, and no, it isn't just about the farmers."

"We all do, You don't have to carry it alone, Kor," Bren said.

Korvan huffed a small laugh. "No one calls me that but my brother."

"Oh, sorry—"

"No, no, it's good. I like it. It reminds me of him. You and Ryn have both done it recently."

He fell silent. He started to chew the inside of his cheek, and felt his foot start to rock.

They keep asking me to let them in, that they can take it, that I don't have to carry it alone. But...

The strength of the earth thrummed into him, his oldest bond, his living shield, and steadfast protector broke into his thoughts that were starting to run wild.

Korvan. Bren good. Sera Kind. Ryn, Javek, funny. They help Korvan, like Korvan help all. Korvan talk now.

A smile spread wide, and he looked over at the Bulwark to his side. That was the most he'd ever said at once. Clearly he thought it was important.

"You're right buddy. Thank you."

He scratched Brusk in his favorite spot, that point where his lower tusk rubbed his bottom lip.

He looked back at the group who had waited, various expressions of confusion on their faces.

"Caelen's sick. Really sick and he's getting worse all the time. He's lived longer than all the healer's thought he would. We don't know what it is exactly, but His body won't hold Aethyr. He can't bond. Even just a walk drains him. Bad days outnumber the good anymore. So I joined for him, well for us. I joined to get strong enough to find out what's happening with him, to try to find a way to save him. To get us out of the life we came from. My parents are... not around."

Some truth's he wasn't ready to share.

Silence rippled.

"I'm the youngest of six," Bren said, low. "I know what being invisible feels like. If he sees half the man you are, he's lucky to have you."

A knot formed in Korvan's chest. He tried to say thank you, but the words wouldn't come. Bren grabbed his shoulder and pulled him into a hug. Sera squeezed them both.

Ryn stirred. "If it's all the same, I'm stayin' here."

Javek nodded. "Me too. Folks here need faces they trust. If that fire-eyed bastard comes back, I'm not lettin' another Davrin die in the dark."

Korvan studied them. "I want him caught as much as any of us. You sure you want to wait here?"

The twins shared a glance before Ryn said, "Aye. We ain't simple soldiers. We're the line. 'Tween us and the commander, we'll hold."

"They'll sleep easier with you here," Sera said.

"Not sure we will," Javek said going for jest.

The fire popped.

Bren stood. "I'll check our gear, rats love salt and I intend to have rations on the road."

"Come sis, let's leave these two be." Javek pulled Ryn up.

They whistled off into dark.

Sera stayed, her expression bland. Her eyes shined in the fire.

"You wear that hurt like armor, I've never seen you put it down."

"I don't have a choice."

"You do," she said, moving closer. Their legs touched and she huddled against him stealing some of his warmth.

"Even warhorses rest. Even blades need cared for. I'm not counting on you to be strong all the time."

"If I rest, I fall apart, I'm terrified of what happens if I stop."

"Then fall where someone will catch you."

The hush stretched.

"I wish I could take some of it. I know I can't, but I want to," she whispered.

"You already do, every day," he said.

He shifted his hand. Her knee found it. Her thumb rested under his eye.

"You don't have to be strong for me, just be you. That's enough," she said.

His breath caught. He leaned. She met him.

Their lips brushed.

It was like coming home.

They rested brow to brow.

"Still scared?" she asked.

"Not the same kind as before."

"Good. I'm here, Korvan. Let me help."

He kissed her forehead and drew her in. Fennik protested and resettled. Her braid slid between them. He caught the faint smell of orange and honey.

They sat wrapped in each other until only embers lit the night.

***

He stood on an obsidian plain under storm-silver sky.

Air shimmered with an ancient weight.

Stone stretched endless as if it had waited eons for this footfall.

Movement on the horizon. A beast vast enough to blot the stars. Each stride shook air without sound.

Moonlight took midnight scales. Slate-smooth. Streaked in drifting blues and dawn gray.

A dragon. No, the dragon.

Its head lowered. Eyes met his, ancient against anxious.

You are not yet ready.

Korvan's throat tightened. "You found me again?"

You called to me, I thought you were ready.

"I didn't mean to. I don't even know how I did it"

Your mind did it for you. Your fear that you are not strong enough, that you need more. Fear carried your call through the Veyrth'Kael.

"The what?"

Smoke curled from the dragon's nostrils.

The true name of what you call the Beyond.

"Am I just dreaming this, are did you pull me to you somehow?"

Does it matter?

His marks glowed with his heartbeat. "It does. I need to know if I'm losing myself. Or if you are more than a dream."

The dragon's shadow covered him.

You are not losing yourself, Korvan, protector of Caelen, son of Varnrik. You are remembering.

"Remembering what?"

What your blood forgot but what your soul still holds. What the Aethyr longs to reclaim. A heritage that was kept from you.

Stars rippled like water.

"What does that mean? What are you?"

I am an echo of what once was and the hope of what must come again. But I am not yours. Not yet.

"But you will be?"

When your purpose outweighs your fear. When strength grows not only for others, but for you.

"I want to be ready."

Wings unfurled. Wind smelled of stone and starlight.

Then prove it. Name me when you've earned it. Want is not ready, need is not requirement. 'Ready' is a decision.

The dream frayed.

Leaving only a voice behind.

I'll be waiting, little brother.

***

Korvan woke with a gasp. Sweat at his neck though the air was cool. His hands trembled.

No way it was a dream. It was too vivid.

Details flashed by, slate scales. Deep-water voice. Eyes that read his soul.

He wrapped his blanket around him but the weight was inside already. His staff pulsed faint in the dark, the way it answered near Aethyr sources. The Dragon had visited him, or he had summonsed him somehow.

He was certain of it now, that the Dragon was real, but he had no idea what he meant about heritage, or what was in his blood.

He looked up, the stars had shifted. The horizon was still black but the deep of the night had passed.

He padded to the river. The calm water mirrored the stars.

He splashed his face. The cold bit deep and refreshing.

The immense voice lingered.

Something that saw him. Peeled away the layers of his armor. It truly beheld him.

"I didn't imagine you," he whispered.

The current rippled.

Couldn't be an answer, just an old river. Right?

He knelt until his breath steadied. Unsure if what he felt was honor or fear. Probably both.

One truth settled clear as the frost on the grass.

This was far from over.

Chapter 19: The Second Disappearance

It had been three days since Korvan dreamt of the Dragon.

Mist clung low across the hillocks east of Riverpost, a hush so complete even the birds kept quiet. Ryn and Javek had stayed behind bracing for the threat to rise again.

The Initiates moved single-file through haze, boots whispering in dew. The trade road pinched to a game path through sparse trees toward the next outpost. Bren took point. He was the best tracker among them.

Bren's frame moved with care; gauntlets wrapped in leather to soften scrape. His eyes swept left, right, keeping the rhythm of search. Readiness rode every step. "Two bodies passed here," he said, crouching by a snapped branch. "Heavy boots, packs were laden with gear. They pushed hard."

"Could it have been a patrol?" Korvan asked.

"Not likely, not the pace they were keeping. Look, one stumbled." Bren rose, grit dusting his palms. "Wounded. We need to keep moving, we're catching them."

Sera ghosted their flank, hooded eyes narrowed, Fennik tight to her boot.

They crested a rise and found ruins.

A watchtower sagged like a burnt rib. The barracks had collapsed inward. Tiles lay around black beams. Smoke had finished its work, but the air kept its taste, ash, spent oil, and a metal bite that thinned along the tongue.

"This wasn't wildfire, this whole area would've burned." Korvan said.

"Here," Bren called, stepping onto scorched soil.

A ring scarred the ground, lines and spirals cut deep, a dark hollow centered like a socket where a tooth had been.

Sera knelt, hand hovering as her Lightweaving traced its edges, "It's a ritual circle..."

Fennik shimmered, glow dimmed to green-gold dusk, and let out a small whimper.

Sera's face set. "It was for purging…"

Korvan's heart slammed twice. Sweat cooled along his spine despite the damp air.

The memory came to him…

A vault dense with Aethyr, copper and chalk sharp on the tongue. Archmage Maedryn's staff caught light and shattered a rune-stone in a single flare.

"Overdraw," his voice carried. "Overdraw occurs when you grab for too much power and your body cannot hold it. Staves help serve as a guide, not just flashy ornamentation."

A chuckle passed amongst the initiates.

The Archmage continued, "You use grounding circles to bleed excess Aethyr before your fyrstrands tear themselves apart. But be warned: inverted anchors become siphons. They consume the source of the Aethyr. Drains opened to the heart of the world."

Maedryn paused letting his worders linger.

"If you see an inversion circle, you leave it alone. You get help. You do not attempt to destroy it on your own," Maedryn said. His tone brooked no argument.

Korvan blinked back to the now.

He crouched at the ring's rim. "This is our proof. Sera, this is it, what Maedryn taught us."

Sera nodded.

Bren's hand hovered on his hammer haft.

A voice rasped from the broken barracks. "I wouldn't stand there if I were you."

Korvan moved first. Auryn's Edge woke clean and white; light cut the smoke. "Positions."

Bren slid left with Rok, hammer half-raised. Sera drifted right, Fennik tucked to her calf. Solace uncoiled from the wind, Brusk rumbled into the center and Vasha took to the opposite flank.

Only a fool or a brave man reveals his position to his prey. But perhaps he is not a predator, Vasha breathed along the bond, her voice was surprised. Few things got the drop on her.

"Hands high, palms open. Step toward my voice. Stay outside the ring," Korvan called.

A figure eased from the shadow. He lifted his hands, fingers spread. A spear lay across his back; two knives rode his hips. He kept his boots clear of the scorched lines. Mist beaded on worn leather and ran off the edges.

"Stop, put down your weapons," Sera ordered.

The stranger complied without argument. He unhooked the spear and set it where they could see the point. He laid the knives beside it, blades outward. He toed a third knife from his boot and slid it forward. Then he lifted his hands again and did not blink at the light.

"What's your name?" Korvan asked.

"Lareth," the man rasped.

"I said it because I meant it. If you stand in there, that circle will drink your Aethyr."

Bren's gaze never left the centerline of the man's chest. "How would you know?"

"Because they used a similar one on me."

He loosened his scarf and let it fall. A Soulmark spiraled the side of his throat and cracked through the heart, edges seared to a pale rim. It wasn't broken like the others they'd seen, not entirely, but it was undoubtedly damaged.

"Hold there," Sera said.

She flicked two fingers; Fennik's light thinned to a ring tracing the dirt at Lareth's toes. "Step into the light. Not beyond it."

Lareth stepped.

"Tell me why your hands aren't shaking," Bren said.

"They used to when I was younger. I learned to stop after what was done to me, I have nothing to fear. Not anymore."

"Why show yourself to us?" Korvan asked.

"Because I tracked a cell west," Lareth said, eyes flicking to the circle but never crossing the edge. "I lost them at a village that doesn't exist anymore. Because I saw the same lines burned into a schoolyard. Because if you step in there, you give them what they want."

Sera's chin tipped toward the scar. "You're still marked."

"Barely. I thought it was, but I was wrong. But my partner is fading away," His mouth tightened.

Bren pointed to the ritual. "You know an awful lot for someone who they attacked. Explain this as simple as you can."

"It rips the Fyrstrand out of you through the Soulmarks. It severs your bond, but they believe it allows you to work all the Disciplines. It resets your connection to the Aethyr. They want what they want," Lareth said.

"That doesn't make sense, we need the bonds to use the Disciplines. Who taught them?" Korvan kept his blade level.

"I didn't say it made sense, you asked what it was. But I don't know specific names. Only that they were once Aethyrguard, and they'd grown bitter with the order," Lareth's voice had grown softer.

Even Fennik gave a soft, mournful chuff.

With you, Brusk thudded through the bond.

"You said 'they want what they want'," Bren pressed. "What's the want?"

"To be unbound to work the Disciplines without a Veyrkin, to lift the oaths from their skin and call it freedom. They don't want the Aethyrguard gone, not yet anyway, they people afraid and to see it to see what it's become."

"What it's become?" Korvan asked.

Lareth sighed, "The Aethyrguard rules unilaterally and without any real opposition. The High Warden has unrivaled power. Sure the Crown Council handles most of the cities daily obligations and infrastructure, but the big decisions? The *laws* that govern people, it's all approved to ensure that the Aethyrguard stays in control, no matter the cost to the people."

Sera, Bren, and Korvan all exchanged a glance. Korvan felt his eyebrows threaten to climb off his head.

"That... is a lot to take in. Say we believe you, could you prove it?" Sera asked.

"If I could prove it, I wouldn't be out here alone."

"Walk with us, help us uncover more of this plot and maybe we can help with that," Korvan pointed to the wounded Soulmark. He didn't believe everything that Lareth said, but enough was true to interest him, growing up poor, he'd seen enough cruelty from the nobility to give it a chance.

"You don't trust me."

"No. I definitely don't." He didn't try to soften it.

"But you know more about this than we do, and I can't pretend we don't need the information. And if you were able to sneak up on Vasha, you've got skills we could use."

Vasha let a low rumble out. The ring vibrated in response to her power.

"I'd get out of that circle, like right now." Lareth's eyes widened and he stepped back a few paces.

Bren didn't blink. "Try to touch a blade and you won't finish the reach."

"I mean it, move," Lareth said, and proved he'd been watching by taking the long route around the ring, matching Korvan's earlier steps print for print.

Korvan moved first, Bren and Sera moved quickly behind him.

The ring had begun to slowly pulse and faded as Fennik's last paw stepped out of it. A wave of Vertigo washed over Korvan but passed just as quick. His eyes flicked to his marks and saw some of his strength had been spent. He hadn't felt the pull, none of them had.

He glanced at Lareth who must've noticed their worried expressions, "I did try to warn you, that is how insidious it is. You couldn't even feel it happening, I wasn't sure it was until the big one started to sweat." He gestured toward Bren.

"Why leave a trail?" Sera asked, her breath shook as she eyed the sigils.

"I remember when I was younger, some travelers from the Ravaryn Dominion came, I remember listening as they spoke of their machines and how they used them for everything. That they no longer needed Veyrkin because their engineers could build anything they wanted. They sounded like zealots. But it was just faith, that's what this is. Whoever they are, they have faith that they are right, and they'll kill for it." Korvan's hands had gone cold.

Bren crouched again and touched a char line with one knuckle. "Circle's done now. Scent's old smoke and oil. We're too exposed."

He stood and pointed through the trees.

"Let's get to the high ground northeast. Should have good sightlines. We can set up camp and plan."

"You're calling the shots?" Lareth sounded surprised.

"Until someone proves I shouldn't," Bren answered.

Sera nodded. Korvan gave Bren a brief, tired smile. "Bren's the best tracker. Follow his lead."

They peeled off the kill-ground in order. Mist folded behind them and took the sound with it. Lareth's fingers drifted to his ruined mark and fell away. He kept the distance he'd been given.

Bren didn't look back. "If they want to be seen, they're watching and setting a trap," he said.

"Stay on your toes."

***

"You're holding it too tight," Sera said gently.

Lareth sat with one knee drawn up, his spear resting across it. He stared down at his Soulmark. It was cracked along the curve, pale skin around it laced with thin red veins.

"How else am I supposed to hold it," he muttered,

"You can still hold it," she replied.

"But if you want Fennik's magic to flow through," she motioned to the mark, "you must stop bracing against it. You're not stemming a wound. You're choking a tether, the Fyrstrand isn't something you force. Have you been to a beach, and know that when you pick up sand, you can only grab so much because it runs through your fingers and the harder you squeeze the quicker you push the sand out."

Across the camp, Fennik sat upright. His runes pulsed soft green-gold, tail brushing air in slow, even sweeps.

"I'm not a Mender," Lareth said flatly.

"No, you aren't. But he is," she admitted.

The runelight flickered brighter. Fennik chuffed once. A subtle ripple swept through the space between them, brushing the edges of skin and thought. Lareth winced. His hand snapped to his side and white knuckled his pants.

"Pain means it's working," Sera murmured.

They all looked on as breath by breath the red veins began to recede, the puffiness calmed and the surrounding skin gained a bit of color.

Lareth exhaled through gritted teeth, then glanced up, with the faintest glimmer of respect. "You're unlike any healer I've ever seen."

She smirked. "That's because I don't carry bandages. I carry miracles."

A quiet laugh broke from the trees.

Bren crouched near the edge of camp, driving bone stakes with the butt of his palm. Each was etched with dull black sigils, linked by near-invisible cords threaded between rocks and roots.

"You say that like it's not terrifying, she's got a glowing fox that hums when people lie and hands that knit bone without stitching. That's not healing. That's cheating death with flair," he called over.

Korvan gave a faint smile from where he sat wrapped around his staff, eyes half-lidded. "And you're what Bren, honest labor?"

Bren stood, dusting grit from his gauntlets.

"Nah, I'm the anchor, I make sure you don't need her miracles," he said simply.

He crossed into the firelight's edge, expression unreadable, and drew a small disk from his belt. A compass that was threaded with Aethyrglass, its needle weaving in a pattern that pulsed rather than pointed.

"Westward now. If there's another trail, we'll catch it before dawn," he muttered.

Korvan cocked his head. "You're sure?"

Bren tapped the compass gently. "This isn't a regular compass. It's for detecting Aethyr. Skirmish scouts use 'em out near the Thalos Waste."

Sera raised a brow. "Those aren't issued to Initiates."

"No they're not, I earned mine before I joined, before I had Rok," Bren said.

Korvan studied him a beat. "Thanks. For watching over the group."

Bren's eyes flicked to Fennik, now curled beside Sera's foot, rune-glow matched to her breath.

"You're not the only one who cares what happens to them," he said quietly.

Lareth shifted. "Must be nice. Having people like that."

Sera turned her gaze toward him, softer now. "Can you still feel your bond, even with the wound?"

"Barely. What you did seemed to help my physical wound, but I'm not sure about my bond" he answered and looked past the fire.

"His name was Blaze. Wyrdkin. He's a Drake."

The fire popped and wind whistled through the branches.

Sera inhaled sharply. "You're a Drake Tamer?"

Lareth nodded once. "Born of fire and fury. Blaze didn't just wield Fire, he understood it. It's hard to describe, but he could see the heat of the world. But in battle..." He hesitated.

His voice was quieter now, "He didn't burn. He consumed. Left nothing but glass and char."

Korvan's knuckles whitened on his staff. They'd let a predator into their camp.

"How did you find him?" Sera asked.

"That's a story I don't tell anymore, it just, hurts to think about," Lareth said.

Sera reached across and rested a hand over his Soulmark. It wasn't for a spell this time, just to be a companion.

The fire cracked. Bren stirred it with a stick; a spiral of sparks climbed the dark.

"We sleep in turns, I'll take first watch," he said.

Korvan nodded. "Wake me second."

The wind shifted again, faint, and dry, brushing the ward threads like fingers drumming glass. Lareth turned from the fire, one arm curled over his ribs. Fennik's ears twitched, but he didn't rise. Korvan rested his staff across his knees. Sera lay back slowly against him.

***

The fire fell to a low cradle of embers. Sera leaned against Korvan, her head tucked beneath his chin, where his breath rose and fell with a steadiness that belied the weight he carried. His arms were loose around her, protective even in sleep, his fingers curled near the base of his staff.

She closed her eyes. Not to sleep. Not yet. Just to listen.

His heartbeat had slowed. Strong and steady if quieter from a day spent working.

Her mind drifted. Back to the barracks, to his voice frayed and eyes filled with tears.

I love you.

She hadn't said it back. Not yet.

She watched his face in the emberlight. His forehead sleep-creased, jaw slack, the lines at his mouth deeper than most his age should bear. Not blocky like Bren's or refined like Thalen's. Sharper, hawkish, all hard edges. But it was his eyes she kept returning to. Two pale gray orbs, the color of the sky before the dawn.

He always carried too much. Wore strength like a shield and silence like armor. She saw the cost. He didn't have to be perfect for her. When the moment came, soon, maybe too soon, she'd tell him that.

Her fingers brushed the edge of his bracer. Soft. Reverent.

"I see you," she whispered.

He stirred and didn't wake. His grip tightened pulling her in.

Sera let herself sink into his warmth. Even as she rested her cheek to his shoulder, her gaze drifted past the fire to where Lareth lay, half-shadowed against the ridge. There was something about him. Not just the voice, or the scars, or the coiled stillness.

It was familiar.

She couldn't place it. But she would.

For now, she let sleep come.

One hand on Korvan's chest, the other curled near Fennik's fur.

The fire burned low.

Chapter 20: Reckoning

Dawn bled thin over the eastern ridge. Wind shouldered mist into torn gauze that dragged along the forest floor. Too cold for insects. Too early for birds. Pine sap on the air.

Bren froze mid-step, hammer slung one-shouldered. "Stop."

They stopped. Fennik's ruff lifted. Vasha's ears snapped.

Bren crouched and brushed the soil. A thin groove crossed the trail.

He rose.

"Trap."

The word hadn't finished leaving his mouth when the woods split.

Limbs. Steel. Runes. Morning ripped open. Mist burned away in jagged lines of power.

"Down!" Bren shoved Korvan aside as a bolt of white Aethyr scythed the space his head had filled.

Sound hit without mercy. Steel rang. Beasts snarled. Magic clawed the quiet to pieces.

Korvan rolled and came up on a knee, staff held high. Vasha launched with a blaring snarl and met the first attacker mid-swing. Red fire ran along his blade; her claws took his shoulder seam and the metal screamed. She bore him down and ripped with massive canines, his hamstring popped, loud as a canon, his leg folded under him like wet wood.

Brusk shouldered through one attacker and jumped. He took two bodies together. One hit a pine and shook down a green rain. The other rode Brusk's tusks, left a ribbon of gut on bark, and slid down to a sit.

Sera stepped back with Fennik tight to her shin. A word left her mouth as much reflex as practice. Runes woke across vulpine fur. Heat rippled out as a shield sprung up, crossbow bolts turned to slag before they reached her.

Bren met the press without romance. The hammer drew ugly arcs. Each step measured. Each strike a decision. Rok took spell-heat with small groans and threw men like sacks. One skull popped against a root with a hollow crack.

Lareth arrived out of mist like a banshee. His spear turned tight circles. It bit wrists, peeled guards, pried plates open, bodies fell with each contact. A throat collapsed under the butt-end with a wet click. A knee split sideways under a short hook. He wasted no motion and spent his strength wisely. He spent men without remorse.

"Eyes up, they're moving in pairs," Lareth said, voice like stone.

They did. A crossbow cracked from brush. A hook-net skimmed for Sera's legs. Lareth's spear butt caught cord, flipped it over her shoulder, pinned the thrower's palm on the return. "Netters! Cut the knots."

Korvan surged upright. Solace feathers flared as the air closed around her prismatic shimmer. Their combined Aethyr thickened.

His Spell ran down the haft of the Staff, "Hammerpulse."

The staff kicked a cone of force. The front rank left its feet. Ribs snapped when they landed, metal plates buckled, and for that instant silence claimed the clearing.

They reeled.

But their attackers did not break.

A mask peeled back with a grin. Blood painted his teeth.

A cracked Soulmark gleamed wrong under his collar.

"Yes," he hissed. "That's what we wanted."

Cold slid under Korvan's sternum.

Shapes came from deeper trees, more masks, most without Veyrkin.

"We're being boxed." Bren's warning came loud.

A human howl tore thin on fervor. Cloaks snapped like cut banners. A dozen at least. Lines neat despite the chaos.

"Form up!" Bren lifted his hammer.

Korvan moved before the order finished. Aethyr climbed his bones.

"Kinetic Lance."

A line of force hit a leaper mid-air and folded his breastplate into his lungs. Blood responded, in a thin mist, as he fell like a stone.

Another came too fast for a second cast.

Rok appeared and pinned him to a trunk. The bark split. Something inside the assailant did too. Rok turned and covered Sera's flank without waiting.

Three knifemen broke left for Sera under a rag of smoke. Fennik flared, mystic light cracked the air and staggered all three. Sera took the nearest on his blind side and folded limbs to sleep with clean cracks. Her heel took the second's knee. The joint gave with a dry pop. He screamed into her gauntlet. The third ran at Rok, then thought better when the Bulwark's shoulder shattered some of his teeth.

Lareth carved water-lines through steel. A pole-axe hooked for his ankle. He lifted, let it miss, and punched the ferrule into the wielder's larynx. Another blade slashed. His spear shaft rode the swords edge. He pinned the sleeve pinned to tree bark.

"Flanks. Tighten up." he clipped, catching a short sword on the quillon and shoving its owner into Brusk's waiting tusks.

Korvan felt Vasha hunt.

The bond pulled his hearing wider. Angles mapped in a heartbeat. Footfalls split into weight and intent. He kept up because she let him. He kept up because the world slowed to her speed.

"South." Sera's voice cut clean. "They're pressing Bren."

"On it."

Protect Sera, he sent towards Vasha.

Hunger answered in his bones. Vasha blurred through brush and hit a man high, her jaws closed on his clavicle. She shook once and tore an arm free in a spray that peppered ferns black-red. Another swung at her shoulder. She rolled under the blade and unstitched his inner thigh with a foreclaws. He dropped screaming, hands on what would never close.

Korvan ran for the ridge edge with Vasha a streak of dusk and silver at his side. A sigil covered glaive rose. He slid low and smashed his staff into knees. The joint parted. Vasha took the opening, teeth shearing the mask and cheek until bone showed.

Another charged. Korvan flung a Kinetic Lance and staggered him. His heel slipped on blood. The counterstroke flashed for his ribs—

Bren's hammer took the choice away. Two bodies flew like dolls.

They fought back-to-back. Bren anchored. Korvan wove. Hammer. Staff. Light. Bone. Steel. The line held because Rok and Brusk became a wall and because Sera kept them from bleeding from dozens of cuts.

It wasn't enough.

The enemy adjusted.

Spiked wedges slammed into earth. Chalk-lines woke between them and began to drink light. Air thinned. Aethyr drew tight like a belt cinched one hole too far.

"Inverters! Break the steaks!" Lareth's snarl carried.

Vasha's growl guttered. Brusk's plates clicked. Solace cooled against Korvan's ribs. He felt them weaken all at once.

Korvan sprinted for the nearest stake. A masked caster rode his line, black sigil rolled between fingers. Lareth crossed shallow and cut low. The hand dropped at the wrist. The sigil died in mud.

"Stake," he said, already turning.

Korvan smashed it. The circle faltered. Air came back in a rush that tasted like rain.

The press surged again.

He didn't see the sickle until it had already opened his arm. Vasha bit down hard, the man's head came free and his body slumped without a twitch.

Sera tucked tight and let out a shout. Fennik's aura sent heat in waves that steadied breath and sealed the worst leaks. A hooded man broke for her with a hook-blade. Fennik flashed hot and the hook went dumb midair. Sera snatched the shaft, twisted, threw him over her hip into bracken.

"Rok, hold them!" she ordered, dragging Korvan into her radius.

Light hissed needle-fine into the gash along his thigh. "Do not move."

He did not. Relief took a slice off the world's noise.

His Pulse steadied. His mind became clear.

"Go," she said.

He went for Solace hard. Power shouldered back. Rhythm slipped. White crawled along his sight. His forearm locked around the staff and would not obey.

The weave came apart.

"Don't overchannel!" Lareth's warning cut.

Too late.

Feedback speared him. Heat climbed his arm and bit once before Solace shouldered it aside. The staff clattered from numb fingers.

"On me!" Bren's shout cracked the ridge.

They answered. Bren stepped into a shieldman's centerline and reversed the hammer, he hooked the rim, yanked the shieldman into Brusk's shoulder. Ribs broke. His breath left and didn't return.

Korvan scooped the staff and swept an Aethyr Push, knocking ankles apart. Lareth slipped their line and punched through. Three strikes, Three bodies. Before a fourth appeared, revealing their plan.

Above, a jaguar of smoke and iron dove for Rok. Sickle-teeth raked plates and found meat. Rok bellowed and staggered. It kicked free with a mouthful of skin.

It got through.

It hit Korvan.

Red heat, then a numb that scared him more. Blood ran off his thigh in a quick rhythm and pattered leaves. His knee found dirt. Brusk roared, took the thing on his tusks, and hammered it into a trunk. Its spine broke first. Legs kicked twice and went slack.

Sera slid. "Bren... I need space."

Her palm set to Fennik's spine. Light sank into Korvan's torn muscle. Threads drew. Skin closed, but the blood poured.

The world spun, where was this blood from.

His blood?

His leg felt cold.

There was so much red on the ground.

Vasha roared.

It wasn't sound. It was violence given a voice. The field stuttered. Masks turned. Blades slowed. For one ragged heartbeat every eye fixed on her.

She towered in the mist. A harbinger of fury her silver-dusk coat matted with ribbons of blood. Some hers, most stolen. Scores across her flanks. A steady drip off her haunch. Fury burned hot in her eyes. She wasn't close to done.

She lunged.

Her sabers clamped across a brute's chest. His scream cut short with a wet pop as ribs gave and spine folded. She shook once, like any dog with a toy, and the man tore in two. His upper half landed face-down. His legs twitched three paces off.

A canid Veyrkin slid for her blind side. Too slow. Her paw snapped forward, claws like hooked scythes. She caught it midstride and opened it from belly to shoulder. The back half hit dirt in a rain of organs. Its ichor steamed and stank like burnt copper.

She kept moving. Low. Rolling shoulders. She'd seen her partner be wounded, she'd make them suffer as he suffered. Her second roar hit harder. Trees shivered. The ground felt like it chose a side.

Her bond raked Korvan's chest.

I will not leave you, little hunter. Pain threaded her words, but her voice remained iron.

He staggered under it. Her heart hammered against his own. Rage sharpened him. Heat ran his veins. Faster. Stronger. Awake.

For the first time since she named him, she felt fully herself in him.

She stopped in front of him, steam lifting off blood slicking her coat. She stood over Korvan and Sera both. The remaining masks didn't rush. Even through iron and cloth, he saw fear.

Her roar came once more, a terrifying cacophony that shook the trees and rattled the foundation of the world.

The sky answered.

A gale tore down. Trees bent. Branches snapped. Roots shuddered. The canopy peeled.

Something fell like a comet.

A wyvern cut from a storm cloud, wings wide as sails, smoke-gray hide veined with pale lightning scars. Eyes cold. Knife-bright under starlight. The world made room when he landed.

On his back, armor scored lightly, cloak torn, longsword bright...

Thalen.

Korvan's breath missed a step.

The Draconid roared. Wind detonated outward, a ring of pressure that flung enemy Veyrkin like toys. One hit a pine and went boneless around it.

Vasha answered with a roar of her own, the defiance reforged into elation.

Her thrill surged down the bond. *At last, a worthy hunter for the pack.* She prowled at the wyvern's flank like she'd been waiting her whole life for that sound.

Thalen vaulted free. He didn't speak. He killed. The blade worked fast and clean. He ripped three off Korvan and Sera before they could reset. His hand smashed a throat, edge burst a thigh, edge slid through a visor seam and took teeth and tongue with it.

"Get up." Winter-steel voice.

"Thalen—"

His sword dropped the last flanker. The space he left was one breath wide.

Sera filled it. "Hold still. This is going to sting."

Fennik's glow speared Korvan's thigh.

It stung, but He held still.

"Go," Thalen said.

He went.

Korvan shoved upright. Staff snapped into his palm as Solace pulsed. Soulmarks thrummed like a drum. Power waited.

He raised the staff and let the Aethyr carry his words, "Force rend."

Air collapsed and blew sideways. Five charging men left their feet. Armor folded like tin. One's shadow burned to a trunk before he slid into himself. Another landed wrong and his shin split like kindling.

Silence held a heartbeat.

"Null-salt!" Lareth barked. Six vials arced. Gray fog burst. Color drained. Aethyr went dull. Sound flattened.

"Don't breathe it in!" His spear flicked and one vial shattered back into its thrower's face. The man screamed and dug for his own eyes.

Bren barreled through the veil with hammer high. Shoulder. Knee. Skull. He made a door and stood in it. Rok planted beside him, one eye swelling shut, plates painted red. He laughed once, a raw sound, and swallowed it.

Korvan swept low through the haze, staff spitting arcs of Radiant Flare. Vasha streaked slashing as she did, every swipe meant tendons were gone.

Vasha's roar met the wyvern's thunder. Recognition. Pack-blood. She surged with the storm. Silver and dusk with gray hide. Korvan's pulse stumbled under the thrum.

The line felt it. Something in them set. No longer Initiates scrambling under slaughter. They became Teeth. Wall. Light, Force and Storm.

Bren and Rok braced center. Hammer and bear. Immovable. Brusk planted behind buying them spaced. Sera pressed the seam between them and Korvan, hands steady, Fennik bright at her shin. Lareth moved like the thought of a blade, faster than Korvan could keep up with.

"Right gap, two," he clipped. "Bren, break. Korvan, now."

Korvan answered.

"Kinetic Lance." The line tore.

Bren filled it with hammer strokes.

Thalen moved like a man on fire. Ashwing's gales kept lanes clean. The sword made punctuation of the attackers.

For a breath, Korvan stood inside it and felt the set. Vasha's hunt surging, Solace humming marrow-deep, Sera sealing wounds as fast as they opened, Bren holding ground and breaking each advance, Thalen cutting paths to keep them clean. No longer moving as lone.

They moved like a squad.

The enemy felt it. The little army faltered. Masks that had thrown themselves forward with glee edged back. Eyes searched for exits.

For that pulse, Korvan knew the truth: they were not prey anymore.

"Hammerpulse!" His voice detonated and raw force boomed from his staff in a shockwave.

The line of attackers shattered.

Bren's hammer fell with Korvan's staff. More men folded. Rok crashed the flank and came back bloody but unbowed, bellowing defiance. Brusk bulldozed the wounded and denied retreat.

Sera's voice stayed low. "Steady. Step left. Now." Her hands marked light into wounds before blood finished leaving. Fennik carried that strength outward.

Korvan covered her. His eyes sharp with Vasha's senses he noticed a few make their way around in the confusion and aim for Sera.

"Radiant Shards," His voice rang, and Spears of light pinned shoulders and thighs whistling past Sera's head.

Korvan snarled as more came through, he stepped in front of Sera blocking them from her.

"Force rend."

Again a wave of pressure surged, the ground bucked and split under the power. Three more collapsed as their formation did.

Lareth punctuated each break, ensuring no attacks from behind could come.

Vasha was a whirlwind. She tore an arm free and hurled it. She turned and split a wolf-Veyrkin, sinew snapping, spine cracking. She loved the work. Korvan felt it in his teeth.

For all her fury, she was not the only one that their attackers feared.

Ashwing was a hurricane. One wingbeat scythed a gale through the canopy and shook archers loose like rotten fruit. His roar rattled molars and flung three Veyrkin into trunks where they burst and went still. Thalen moved with a speed he'd never had before, he cut whatever the wind exposed.

They stepped forward together driving them back. The first to break was a shield-man with a cracked visor who dropped his weapon and ran. Vasha reached him in two bounds. What came back wasn't whole.

That was enough.

Spells went wild into trees. Veyrkin limped away. Some screamed. Some didn't. The rout spilled in every direction, masks scattering like leaves under storm.

Bren lifted the hammer and let them see his teeth through blood. "That's right, you run back to your masters," He spat red.

The forest swallowed the last of them.

Silence returned.

The ground was thick with iron and ash.

***

Korvan stood in the ruin of it, chest heaving, staff slick with blood. Vasha padded back, flank cut open, eyes bright, muzzle painted.

Little hunter. Did you feel it? Did you feel what we are? The thought rumbled.

He did.

Sera knelt, hands trembling as she pushed light through Bren's gouged shoulder. Bren grunted and held still. Rok leaned on a shattered tree, breath ragged, grin feral. Brusk lowered his tusks and set himself between them and the trees, sentinel in the hush. Lareth cleaned his spear with mechanical care, gaze far.

Thalen stood at the clearing's edge, Ashwing's shadow vast behind him, sword on his shoulder, eyes on the horizon. He didn't speak. He didn't need to yet. For the first time Korvan felt the shape of them.

They were a pack.

The clearing fell still. Blood thickened the air. Fennik curled at Sera's feet, glow dim to a flicker. Her hands hovered, steady but shaking. Bren's gauntlets were black to the knuckles. The hammer lay across his knees.

Lareth leaned against a tree. Split open at the brow. Knuckles white on the shaft. He glanced once at Thalen and away.

Around Korvan, the Veyrkin fanned a loose guard. Vasha paced, ears hunting each sound. Brusk rested beside him, chest heaving slow. Solace drifted, her reservoir just as full as when they began.

And then there was Thalen.

He stood beside the wyvern. Smoke-hued scale caught light. Ashwing's breath pulled the air taut. Thalen's armor was dented. Mud and blood striped the filigree. His sword arm trembled once. The rest of him held.

"You left us," Korvan said.

"I did." Flat. Even. Too still.

"Didn't plan on coming back." His voice was uneven, too many emotions barely held in check.

"Then Ashwing found me. He nearly killed me, but instead, He chose me. Not for my name. Not for the House. For me. Kind of like how they chose you."

Korvan nodded, "Why did you come back?"

The mask shattered.

"Because I had to," Thalen said, voice fraying.

"Because I had to show you aren't better than me. Because every whisper turned into a prayer with your name in it." The look he gave wasn't hate. It was pain.

"They called you a prodigy. The one who might matter. All I saw was everything I spent my life becoming, the legacy I was sup-posed to have, slipping through my fists." His tone cracked.

"It was supposed to be mine. I just wanted people to want me for me, not because of a Light-damned name."

He turned sharp and paced. Boots ground soil to mud.

"I wasn't going to be a footnote. Not anymore."

From the trees:

"You were never a footnote, little panther."

The words cut the quiet. Even the fire snapped once and stilled.

Thalen froze. His head turned slow. "...Lareth?"

The name tore out a second wound.

"You shouldn't be here, you... how are you..." Thalen whispered.

"I'm not here to be forgiven."

Korvan saw it, something in Thalen snapped.

"Forgiven? Forgiven? Of course you aren't. Because you don't deserve it. You vanished. You left me to it, to all of it. You died Lareth, and I had to carry what you left behind"

His stance unraveled.

"Three days after you left, a letter came. Said you fell near the Ember Reach. I believed it. Gods help me, I believed it."

"I didn't write that letter," Lareth said.

"Of course not," Thalen spat, tears in the voice now, "but you didn't stop it either. You never came back. Never wrote. Never checked on me. Not once."

"I died," Lareth said, quieter.

His grip tightened on his spear. "Not in body. What I was. It broke. I left so you'd hate me and never follow me into it."

"You were my brother!" Thalen shouted. The shout broke hoarse. "I needed you. You left me with them. You were supposed to stay—"

His voice splintered.

"I waited. Every godsdamned day. For a letter from you. For a sign. Anything. I never wanted to believe that my brother was dead. You were always too strong, I just knew it couldn't be true that you died. Instead, I watched our father erase you like a mistake. And I let him. Because I thought, if you pretended, I wasn't alive... maybe he was right to pretend you hadn't existed either."

Lareth flinched. Just once.

Korvan moved.

Like a brother.

"That's enough Thalen," he said.

Thalen spun. "Stay out of this."

"No." Korvan's voice didn't rise.

"You don't get to blame him for what your parents did. I know that better than anyone."

Thalen's breath hooked.

Korvan stepped close. His tone trembled with a heavy truth, "I know what it is to be broken by a parent who should have loved you. To scream into the void and wonder if it was your fault. But you don't get to use that pain as a weapon."

He held out a hand, "I don't want you to become what broke you. You're not alone, Thalen. Not unless you choose to be."

Thalen stared. Jaw tight. Words failed him. His knees bent a fraction. He turned aside and covered his face. His armor rattled. Steel couldn't hold everything.

Lareth didn't move.

Korvan kept his hand out.

Ashwing shifted, wings rustled. Solace stepped beside Korvan and stood. Sera covered her mouth, tears bright. Bren said nothing, but his grip eased on the hammer.

***

The sky cleared but no one relaxed. The fire crackled low. Iron and ichor stung the air.

They drifted to their corners. Sera whispered to Fennik and smoothed scorched fur. Bren rasped the hammerhead and watched the tree line. Lareth sat with his back to a trunk, posture slack but watchful, spear across his knees. Ashwing coiled behind Thalen like a hill, wings folded, tail ticking the ground.

Korvan sat apart, arms folded over bent knees, Soulmarks dim to old light. He stared into flame and still found Thalen in the edges.

Thalen broke the silence.

"When I left, I thought I'd come back to your corpse. I thought your luck would run out long before your arrogance did," he said, low, eyes on coals.

"You're not wrong."

Thalen cut him a look. "About which part?"

"Bren's been leading the scouting. Ryn and Javek held Riverpost. We were out here in the dark. If you hadn't shown up? My luck's a dry well, so take your pick."

That got a scoff. Dry. Almost humor. Thalen stepped closer and crouched by the fire.

"You're too raw, you let rage and fury take control. You've got more Aethyr than me, even with Ashwing, but you lose focus," he said.

"And you don't?"

His eyes stayed on the flame. "I've trained my entire life for this. I was basically born Aethyrguard. My people built the Vaults. One of my grandsires set Cael'Lumar's stones. We don't chase excellence. We're supposed to be the proof of it." His mouth thinned.

"Then you walk in with a boar, a saber cat, and a Reservoir no one has a name for, and you're proclaimed the chosen one. You think that doesn't rattle people?"

"It rattled you. I never realized how bad."

Silence. One, two, three beats.

"I was supposed to be the best," he said, softer.

"You are the best, you're smarter than me, you're better at logistics and tactics than I am. Solace gives me a bigger power source, but before you showed up I almost blew myself up, ignored all the lessons I've been taught. Because you're right, I got mad and let it rule me. I'm not better than you Thalen, I've been jealous of you since the day we met." Korvan said.

That caught him.

"I don't think whatever is going on cares who trained harder," Korvan went on. "It doesn't care about lineage. So I didn't earn it the right way, maybe the right way needs to change."

"And you're fine with that? With being the exception? With tearing the system instead of proving you deserve your place in it?" Thalen asked.

"I didn't ask to be outside it and I'm done apologizing for surviving. I didn't chose to be whatever I am. The wrong I did was not letting the people I care about in. Not letting you in," Korvan said.

Thalen rocked back on his heels, eyebrows up and mouth slack. He rose slowly. Shoulders tight.

"Ashwing nearly killed me, I tried to force the bond like I was taught. Make him submit. He didn't choose me until I broke. Until I asked."

Korvan glanced at the wyvern.

"I understand, all three were like that for me. Just need. Just… connection." He paused.

"Did it make you feel better, having something like him pick you?"

"No, it made me be honest," Thalen said.

Ashwing's eyes opened, and the pair settled into a delicate silence.

***

Korvan didn't hear Sera until she was beside him. She eased down. Firelight traced the line of her cheek. Fennik's runes still glowed faint where he lay against her.

"Thalen's still awake, if you wanted to talk to him more," she offered.

Korvan shook his head.

"No, not tonight. I think I overstepped with him and Lareth, I don't want to push. But yeah he's always alert. Even when he acts like he isn't."

"I'm glad he came back."

"Me too. I missed him," A beat.

She chuckled. Eyes squinted in that way he'd come to love.

"Are you going to tell him?" Her voice was nearly silent.

Korvan blushed, he'd confessed to her he may have liked Thalen, saw him as more than just a rival.

Thankfully, she spared him from speaking on it.

"How did we miss that Lareth is his brother? Side by side it's obvious."

He exhaled hard, somehow it sounded grateful.

"He's older than us. We were also rattled when we met Lareth. Thalen never spoke of a brother. Well, I never asked."

She watched the coals. "You two... you're both so stubborn. But he came back when it mattered."

"He did. Still, I don't think he likes me."

"Korvan, tell me you don't really think that. Of course he does. He was devasted when he left. I don't think He just likes you, He clearly respects you too. I saw it when Ashwing landed. He looked at you like he'd found his way back where he belonged."

The warmth of it moved through his chest.

"Maybe, but it still feels like we're missing each other, like we keep shouting over the storm, but it doesn't land. It feels like we hate each other more than we like each other," Korvan said.

"He's proud and you press on everything he was raised to value. You don't mean to but you make him question himself and things he thought were facts. That's hard. Hate isn't the opposite of love. Indifference is. If you hate something, it means you care enough to feel that passionate about it. When you're ready, ask him to talk. That's all you can do."

Something in him unclenched. He leaned and set a slow kiss to her brow. A thank-you given skin. She blushed, fingers finding the loose end of her braid.

"What did I do to deserve you. Thank you. Please don't let me forget," he said.

"I promise. Don't lose yourself trying to prove what you already are." Her fingers brushed his.

"The rest will come, or it won't. Either way, we'll handle it."

The fire cracked. Coals talked to themselves.

"Bren was a wall today," she said.

Korvan followed her gaze. Bren at the ridge, chest rising in gentle rhythm, Rok beside him.

"And Lareth, I've never seen someone move so fast. No wonder Thalen is how he is. They must have trained as boys."

"He's been alone a long time now, necessity made him lethal," Korvan said.

Sera looked back at him.

"I still can't believe the Aethyr you threw around. Champions train for decades to wield the Disciplines like that. You did it wounded."

"I wasn't trying to impress anyone."

"You didn't impress me, you saved me, you saved all of us. Thalen turned the tide with Ashwing, but you got us through," she said.

He looked away and back. "Thank you."

"For what?"

"For reminding me I'm not alone."

She leaned into his shoulder.

"You never were."

Above them, the stars wheeled. Below, companions shifted and settled, wounded but alive. The sea was far away, but its old count beat under Korvan's ribs.

***

Ashwing opened one eye, it was a combination of fire and moonlight.

Thalen sat beyond the fire with a hand on scales, eyes low.

The bond pulsed. A benediction that needed no words.

Shame wound tight with a want he didn't have language for. He'd left because Korvan did what he could not. He stepped beyond the rules and requirements.

Then Ashwing happened.

Ashwing didn't care for titles. He tested His soul and shattered it.

Now, Thalen sat at the rim of firelight and watched the rival he was raised to surpass lead without apology. Korvan wielded magic like he was born to it. Led without trying. Fought like someone the world had already decided on.

He should hate him. Hate was easy.

What he felt now was harder.

The longing for something more than friendship mixed with the pain of a rival being left behind. But still Korvan reached back, determined to not leave.

"You don't get to become what broke you."

Korvan's words echoed within him.

Thalen looked at them. Korvan, Sera, Bren. Lareth.

What would he do about Lareth?

A decision for another day.

For now, Thalen knew he didn't belong. He'd shattered their trust and left them when they needed him. Abandoned them when it got hard.

Sounds familiar does it not. A behavior you learned from your brother perhaps. Ashwing's voice cut Thalen's spiraling thoughts.

"Smart-ass Wyvern, still not used to you being in my head like that."

It will become second nature in time, or at least that is what my blood tells me. You belong, as much as any of them. But you should speak with him when you are ready.

Belong.

Gods help him, he wanted to.

Ashwing exhaled. Heat settled along Thalen's spine.

He didn't lean forward. He didn't pull away.

If they'd have him, he'd stand inside that ring. Not outside of it.

Never again.

Chapter 21: The Weight of Return

Bren walked ahead of the group, boots sinking into cold, soft earth, jaw clamped so tight it ached. The trees leaned close over the path, their crowns blotting the thin dawn, sap, and wet bark sour on the air. He stared at the trail. At the bend. At anywhere that wasn't the last place Korvan fell.

Korvan had gone down.

They'd all bled, but Korvan had dropped like a cut marionette. For a breath that felt like a minute, Bren had believed the fire in him had gone out. The emptiness that followed was worse than fear. Shame pooled behind Bren's ribs; he should have been there, he's the Bladesworn.

The others kept pace behind him. Sera walked near the center, her steps measured to the tremor in Fennik's legs. The fox's runes smoldered low. Thalen haunted the column's edge. Lareth followed further back. Vasha and Solace flanked Sera and Korvan. Brusk and Rok moved heavy but determined, the Bulwarks anchoring Bren's lead.

"You alright?" Sera asked, voice quiet, catching up to Bren's stride.

Bren didn't answer at once. His fingers flexed on the hammer strap until the leather bit his palm. When he found words, they came low, sanded raw.

"He shouldn't've gone down. I was supposed to cover it."

"It wasn't your fault," Sera said.

"It wasn't his either." The snap came fast; he swallowed it and tried again.

"Sorry. I was too far left. Guarding the flank when the front broke. Then it was noise, all steel and screaming mouths and him in the dirt."

Her hand warmed his forearm. "You kept us alive."

Bren stared ahead. "Feels like I barely held my end. Like mam's stiches, one pull and the whole thing tears." His voice thinned.

"I was supposed to be the wall."

Silence took a few steps with them. Dew tapped down from the pines like slow rain. The forest smelled of ash that had learned to hide.

"Now Thalen's back," Bren said. "On a fucking dragon."

"A wyvern," Sera murmured.

"Call it what you want, it's a bruiser, and I thought Vasha was ferocious," He dragged a hand over his face, smearing soot he'd missed.

"And Lareth? The brother back from the dead? I'm a man with a hammer Sera, I don't know what to do with this."

"None of us knew about Lareth, Thalen never said," Sera said.

"That's worse. Grieved his own brother, just for him to appear." He let out a breath that felt too big for his chest.

He stopped walking. The hammer head bumped his boot; pain flashed against a bruise he hadn't noticed.

"It's too much. I'm not built for this."

"What do you mean?"

"I'm not a leader." The words cracked.

"I hit things. I stand where it's hardest and I refuse to move. But this, whatever Korvan is carrying, is bigger than my back. I'm a smith's son with a good swing and hands that don't shake when under pressure."

Sera opened her mouth, then closed it. She tried again.

"You're more than that. You've got a strong swing, but you're a kinder friend, you're let people in. That steadies them."

"Maybe." He started forward.

"But I can feel the hairline cracks like its iron that's been worked too much. One more day like that..."

Her hand stayed at his arm a moment longer than comfort demanded.

She didn't argue. He didn't ask her to.

***

The sun lifted as they reached Riverpost. Fog threaded the riverbank like gauze, laced through rooftops and plowed furrows. Battle's fingerprints remained where scrubbing hands had missed soot in timber seams, stone gone a shade darker than it should.

Riverpost had endured.

Javek waited at the lane's center with four town guards. His Aethyrguard cloak hung askew. He was mud-splashed, a clasp gone. Relief outshone the sag in his shoulders.

Ryn was not with him.

"Y'all'r alive," he said, letting a grin break.

"Color me impressed."

Korvan offered his arm; Javek clasped it and pulled him into a shoulder-bruise of a welcome. Korvan didn't hide the flinch. The mark at his thigh leaked heat more than pain, Sera had healed the worst of it, but he needed to rest.

"We had help," Korvan said, stepping aside as the squad filed by.

"Thalen found us."

At his name, Thalen angled a glance over battered steel, offered Javek half a nod then a smile.

"And this is Lareth."

Javek's gaze shifted. He took in the cracked Soulmark that laddered down Lareth's neck, the careful economy of the man's stance, the spear that looked more like a verdict than a weapon. "Another Initiate?"

"No," Lareth said.

Javek squinted. "Same jawline 'tween y'all, could pass for kin."

Lareth looked away. His grip on the spear eased a fraction, shame and anger wrestling behind his eyes even when his face refused the tell.

Bren stepped forward before the moment could sour. "He stood with us. Bled with us. That's enough."

Javek let out a breath and nodded. "Good enough for me. Ryn's hurt. Come on."

***

They gave the report in pieces, picking at stale loaves between sentences. When Korvan described the ritual circle the room went still enough that the stove's tick carried.

"They were trained, and extremely dangerous. They knew what we could do, but they didn't expect us to be as strong as we are," Sera said.

Javek leaned back, arms folded.

"Matches what happened here. Coordinated. Tested the ward first, then pressed. If Ryn and I hadn't dug in, Crown Guard would've crumpled."

"How many?" Thalen asked.

"Hard to say."

"Forty," rasped a voice from the doorway.

Ryn braced in the frame, skin sallow, arm bound tight. Her eyes burned clear. "I counted. Forty bodies. Only a handful with Aethyr on the tongue, but that's all they needed in a town without bonded protectors ."

"Ryn," Javek pushed off the wall.

Sera was already there.

"Sit."

The word brooked no debate. She guided Ryn to a chair by the banked fire, Fennik slipping in close with his head low and his runes a soft river light.

Ryn bit down on a laugh that wanted to be a groan.

Sera's palms hovered. Light gathered along skin, thin and steady, then seeped with a hiss into bruised flesh. Fennik's glow braided to hers; the room warmed.

Ryn's breath left on a harsh exhale, then returned smoother.

"Ah, hell." She blinked, "That's... better."

"This is what a Mender does," Sera said softly. Sweat stood along her hairline; her fingers trembled.

Korvan saw it, Sera was spent.

Javek watched like a man afraid to hope. Even Thalen leaned a fraction, calculation set aside by something he didn't have a name for. Ashwing's shadow fell past the threshold and lingered, the wyvern's slow exhale brushing dust in lazy spirals across the floorboards. Shame tightened Thalen's jaw; the breath sounded like judgment.

Ryn assessed her rib with a careful breath. Relief made her eyes glassy.

"Thank you."

Bren cleared his throat.

"You kept them steady, you kept Riverpost safe," he told Javek.

Javek shrugged like the praise didn't fit.

His gaze slid to Lareth. "And what about you?"

"I've tracked them for a long time, fought many of them one at a time. But I've also lost enough to stop caring who gets credit." Lareth said.

Korvan studied the man. Guilt lived in the set of Lareth's shoulders.

"We're not finished," Korvan said.

"No, there needs to be an accounting," Lareth agreed.

Fog thinned as smoke rose from kitchen chimneys in thin lines. People moved around them with respectful silence.

Javek adjusted his pack and fell in beside Korvan.

"You know this ain't what we were sent to do."

"I know."

"We're real late, I reckon somebody is gonna want explanations."

"I hope they will, it's about damned time they listened. From everything we've seen this has been happening for years right under their noses." Korvan's mouth drew in a tired line.

***

They stayed long enough to see Ryn's color come back, to check Brusk's plates and Rok's stitched flank, to walk the ward's and feel for any new thin places. Every small task carried weight. Every thanks from a villager weighed heavy because of the people they hadn't saved.

Bren found himself on the outpost steps with the hammer across his knees, staring at his hands. The knuckles were split under dried blood, skin feathered where the handle had chewed. He flexed and felt each cut wake. The image wouldn't leave: Korvan on the ground, the way the light had stuttered, Sera's voice steady while her hands shook, Thalen falling like a verdict, Lareth's spear speaking in joints. Bren's shame sat where breath should. He should've been there sooner. He should've stopped the blade before it bit.

Sera came out a while later and folded onto the step beside him, breath shallow. She drank, grimaced, and passed the canteen. "Taste like old coins to you?"

He drank. The water was all metal and river flavored.

"Sure does. You look worn out. No offense."

"I am exhausted." A small smile.

"You shouldn't have to be."

"We all did what we had to do."

She bumped his shoulder with hers.

"We would've lost without you."

Sera gave him a tired smile.

"I don't think so, but thank you, I did my best."

He breathed once, deeper. The shame didn't leave.

***

Inside, Korvan stood with hands braced on a table scabbed with knife marks. His Soulmarks had cooled, but his forearms still shook if he let them. He hated that anyone could see it. His pride nagged him, but the shame bit deeper. He had overreached once and nearly paid with all their lives. The thing Eris, Cristos, Maedryn... all his instructors had warned against, and he still did it.

Thalen leaned on the opposite side, helm at his side, gaze level.

"You're burning yourself out," he said, voice low.

Korvan's jaw set.

"You think I don't know the cost?"

"I think you keep pretending you're the only one who has to pay it." Thalen didn't move.

Korvan swallowed.

"I can't leave room for failure."

"Keep trying to do everything on your own and you will fail. Make room for help."

A beat.

"Asking for help isn't failure, I learned that the hard way. If I hadn't shown up, maybe you all could have held. Maybe you'd all be dead. You're strong, you were the strongest of us, but we're not your brother. We don't need you to protect us."

Shame flickered again. The shame that came from the people he cared about truly seeing him. The shame that said he'd ruin them all if he didn't let them in.

He nodded once, small, and real.

Ashwing's shadow crossed the windows again. Thalen's eyes slid that way, guilt tightened his mouth, then eased.

"Ashwing sees me for who I am, not who I was pretending to be," Thalen said quietly.

"He accepts that I'm growing. There's a difference."

Korvan looked up.

"What difference?"

"Between us and what we say we serve." Thalen said.

"You keep trying to earn what already chose you."

Korvan leaned back from the table, breath shuddering once.

"I hear you."

"Good." Thalen lifted the helm.

"I'm not saying it again, and for what it's worth..."

Thalen's voice dropped to a whisper, Ashwing's eyes flitted toward him an unknown expression on his face. Korvan's eyebrow rose.

"I missed you. We... we should talk, once all this calms down," Thalen turned before Korvan had the chance to respond.

Lareth's reflection hung in the glass of the door, a dark shape framed by fog. He hadn't come in. Shame and longing sat on him like twin mantles. Korvan watched him for a moment then stepped to the threshold.

"How long did you try to fight them?"

"Long enough to lose count, long enough that I've forgotten how to stop," Lareth's tone didn't shift.

"You don't have to keep paying this debt by yourself."

Lareth's smile didn't make it far.

"Debts like this don't settle from someone else's coin. Or blood in this case."

He looked past Korvan to the others.

"But I can walk a more dangerous road with a unit at my back."

"Then walk it with us."

A breath.

"For now, I will, but I don't know how long I can stay."

By noon, the mist lifted to a high, pale sky. Riverpost breathed with brittle relief. Good bread appeared out of nowhere. A child brought Vasha a strip of smoked fish and fled when she lowered her great head to take it. Brusk let two boys count his tusk scars. Rok endured a girl's careful pat with a patience that belonged to older beings. Solace stood in the shade, eyes half-lidded.

Sera slept sitting up for a span, mouth parted, Fennik a warm crescent along her ribs. Bren threw a cloak over them without waking her. He stood a while, guarding her sleep.

Thalen cleaned his blade with slow, precise strokes. Ashwing set his jaw against the earth and watched, curiosity evident in the Wyvern's eyes.

Lareth adjusted the wrap on his palm, retying a strip of cloth that had gone dark. The blood smell rose but he didn't flinch. When he glanced up, Javek was already looking. They exchanged a knowing nod.

Korvan watched all of it. The ache in his thigh pulsed with each heartbeat. The ache in his chest did too, but for an entirely different reason.

"Let's move out at in the morning, give Riverpost one more night of watch, give us another day to rest," he said at last.

No one argued.

Morning scraped at the edges of the town when they climbed to Riverpost's lane and turned their backs to it. Breath smoked. Boots sucked at damp earth. The squad wore exhaustion like it was another layer of their uniforms.

They left without a word to spare. Six Initiates and one broken Soulmark. West, toward the Skyborn Jewel, west toward Cael'Lumar.

***

Days later, they hadn't yet reached the outer gate before the summons found them.

A white-robed runner hit the causeway at a clip, breath fogging. He handed Korvan a pale seal and couldn't hide his stare.

They all knew the state they were in.

Korvan broke wax. Read the hand.

"Report to Tower Meridian. Archmage present."

—Eris

Bren's grunt said the meal could wait. Lareth muttered about courtyards and eyes from windows.

The compound bustled. Yards rang with steel. Mews clanged with feed buckets. Scribes scissored across bridges with bundles of paper.

Inside the Tower, all that noise fell away.

At the summit, guards opened tall doors. A wide blackstone table held maps and reports and quiet authority.

Eris stood at the head, but not in the center, her arms folded. Her gaze pierced them.

A man rose beside her.

Silver-thread robes moved like water around a wire frame. A golden staff touched the floor like punctuation. Hair white but not from age. But it was his eyes that locked them in place. Violet eyes flickered, but their were no torches present.

The Archmage.

Maedryn of the Quiet Flame. Right hand to the High Warden.

"Enter," Eris said.

They did.

Eris didn't sit. "You were sent to investigate. You vanished for days, engaged with unknown assailants, returned with a civilian and no report, save what the Commander of Riverpost sent me."

She cut her stare to Korvan.

"Speak."

"Feldmar was misdirection," Korvan said.

"Their true target are Bonds. Ours or anyone they can catch. They're not stealing. They're severing bonds, making people afraid."

Eris didn't blink. Her fingers tightened on the sword-hilt beside her hand.

Korvan tipped his chin toward Lareth.

"He's tracked them for years; he knows it better than any of us."

Lareth stepped forward.

"Lareth Ryst. Knight of the Aethyrguard. Hello again, Battlemage."

For the first time, they saw Eris lose color. Her eyes hit the scar in his throat and the spear he wouldn't lean away from.

"You were killed," she said.

"Not killed, not that there aren't plenty who wish I were. Just wounded," Lareth said.

He pulled his collar and showed what remained: a Soulmark torn down the neck, light gone to dark vein, lines half-severed.

"Eight years ago, Vel'Drakos mines went dark. I was nearest. A Drake-Tamer walks alone, so I investigated. Who better to investigate in a volcano than one born of fire," he said.

He touched the break as if memory still burned.

"They promised clarity. Power. Freedom. Said my bond would deepen, that I'd hear Blaze in an entirely new way."

His voice hit stone and cracked once.

"I wish any of it had been true. I fear he is now lost to me forever."

Silence took the circle.

Maedryn stepped up, voice smooth.

"Do you know who they are?"

"Not by name or by a house banner, but by their actions. They call bonds chains. They cut what makes us whole and call it mercy when the Veyrkin die."

Maedryn's eyes narrowed.

"The lost son of House Ryst comes home," he said, soft as an incision.

The words opened an old wound in the middle of the room. Lareth didn't blink. Thalen went stone and did not breathe for a heartbeat.

Bren's hands closed to fists.

Sera stepped up, voice steady.

"It was designed like our rituals. Sharp geometric lines. They ripped a boy's Soulmark out. It wasn't accident. It was deliberate."

"Describe it," Maedryn said.

They did. In as much detail as they could muster. Lareth added details in broken sentences.

When they finished, Maedryn was quiet for long enough that everyone grew tense.

Then he turned to Eris, and she gave a slow shake of her head.

"We must prepare the missive."

Eris inclined her head.

"Missive?" Korvan asked.

Maedryn's gaze held the weight of too many campaigns.

"Effective immediately: any bonding outside sanctioned rite will be deemed reckless insubordination; such bonds must be reviewed, registered, or relinquished."

Sera stiffened.

"What of the ones beyond our walls? The ones who don't know your lines?"

"They will learn," Maedryn said; a gate closed in his tone. "We tolerated improvisation. That lenience ends."

His eyes shifted to Korvan.

"Consider what happens if a Starlit, or worse, a Mythborn Veyrkin manifests beyond... oversight."

He let the last word cut. His gaze locked with Korvan's.

Korvan held it. Every nerve drew taut.

They didn't suspect, they knew. They knew he'd been hiding something.

Thalen watched and said nothing. Ashwing breathed heavily behind him.

"You'll have two days' reprieve. Then training will resume. Debriefs will happen separately," Eris cut in.

Maedryn turned away to the border-maps.

"We will find these heretics. We will end the blasphemy. Aethyr is duty. Discipline. Our oaths must hold, because if they fail…"

He left them to imagine.

Korvan's fingers brushed cooled light under his sleeves. He found Thalen across the table and saw his own understanding mirrored back.

They were marked, Thalen with Ashwing and the Dragon that had marked him in the Beyond had left fingerprints others could read.

***

Eris stood with her back to the table; arms folded like a barricade she meant to hold alone. Ward-light pulsed in the stone ribs overhead.

Maedryn paced the far arc. Staff idle. Hands clasped behind his back.

"You said the missive would be strong," Eris said. Her voice cut like steel in sheath. "You did not say absolute."

"The wording belongs to the High Warden. I edited where I could," Maedryn replied.

"You agreed."

He turned. Slow.

"I obeyed."

The distinction cracked the air.

"This is foul Maedryn, it is rank with fear of the unknown. How are we—"

His hand going up in a plea cut her off.

"Eris, please," Maedryn said quietly.

"I know it is cowardice; the High Warden does not listen on this matter. He is determined to see our legacy continue as it has for nigh on twenty generations. Our law lags reality. But we aren't gods who can unmake decrees with a whim. He decides. We enforce it."

"You taught me that line," Eris said.

Her eyes did not move.

"I know the shape of enforcement. I also know that this edict is going to punish people for doing nothing wrong. Flame take it Maedryn this is asinine."

"It buys time."

"Time to interrogate children for surviving?" Her voice snapped like a whip.

He didn't answer.

He didn't have to.

She pressed, stepping forward.

"Look at Aric. Three bonds. No rite. And still he holds. Solace answers him. The cat guards him. The boar follows. And what do we hand him? A threat wrapped in parchment. And now Thalen has returned from gods know where and he was with a Wyvern. One of the Skylords has bonded an Initiate. He should be celebrated; it is an achievement we thought lost to our order."

"Thalen is of Noble blood, and a legacy to having a Dragon-kin bond with him. If memory serves Lareth has a Drake. As for Korvan, the Reservoir made him a question. You should know better than anyone, that the council, *despises*, things they cannot control," Maedryn's voice had grown pointed.

"And the boy he saved?"

Eris shot back.

"The Breach he helped close? The Aethyrglass his squad recovered. Do we ignore those because naming the true enemy costs too much courage?"

Maedryn looked away, his voice fell to a whisper.

"Be careful Eris. You are getting dangerously close to insubordination, and you know I am bound to act... You know this is not what I want either."

She took a breath; she let her shoulders drop and unclenched her hands.

"Forgive me Maedryn, it is not you I am mad at."

She turned and gave her a smile.

"A poor friend I would be if I could not suffer your anger occasionally. There is nothing to forgive Eris. I know you think this is as poor a decision as I do."

She nodded and added, "If he keeps snuffing out lights, we'll be blind when the night finally shows up."

Maedryn's next words came measured and tired.

"Do you know how many Initiates I've buried? How many lies I've had to cover up to keep the gears of this city spinning. To keep the Crown Council from ripping itself apart. While you fight the threats of Monsters and villains in the wild, I fight those who would rip us apart from within. This is a poor decision. But it is the decision."

He tapped the staff once. The sound was clean.

"And yes," he admitted. "The Council is wrong...."

Eris's jaw locked. "What do we do now, Maedryn?"

"We walk the edge," Maedryn said.

His voice sagged. "And pray the ones worth saving don't fall before we're allowed to catch them."

***

The decree hit before dawn.

It didn't arrive with trumpets. It came the way laws preferred, quiet and inevitable.

Korvan was half into a bunk when the tether sang. He sat up sharp.

Across the dorm, Sera rubbed her forearm; Fennik nosed her boot.

Bren groaned and rolled to sitting, a curse chewed in half.

They weren't the only ones. Knights and Initiates crowded the center room until breath made weather of its own.

A courier set a sealed scroll on the table. Deep-red wax. Tower Meridian's sigil. No words. Just a quick bow.

Champion Varos arrived with two Champions and a face like a verdict.

Eris followed, cloak whispering. She did not nod.

She broke the seal. Unrolled law.

A breath of binding rose off parchment.

Her voice rang clear.

"Henceforth, by order of the High Warden: all unsanctioned bonds with Veyrkin, wild or otherwise, are forbidden. Any such bonds formed without ritual oversight or certified Arcanist approval are null. Those who persist shall be stripped of rank and expelled. No exceptions. The Rite preserves balance; it is not convenience.

This is for your protection."

—High Warden Archion Dren

The last word hung, and the walls went still.

Sera's mouth opened and found no sound.

Bren's hand found his hammer and stayed until the knuckles went colorless.

Korvan didn't breathe.

He didn't need air to understand.

This wasn't protection. This was control veiled in pretty words.

He looked at the cooled light under his skin. He thought of Caelen.

Sera's fingers brushed his elbow. Something real.

Eris's voice cut the hush. "This will not be debated. Spread the word. The Rite is law."

Bren ground through the silence.

"They're scared."

"Someone pushed the lines too far," Sera said.

Korvan kept the answer behind his teeth. They all suspected who this was about.

The courtyard fire cracked, throwing clawed shadows over stone. Most left with stiff backs or dead eyes. A few stayed and pretended it hadn't happened until their hands stopped shaking.

Korvan sat cross-legged, staff cold beside him. Thalen leaned on a crate, arms folded. Sera stroked Fennik's fur without thinking. Bren paced holes in the grit. Lareth stood just outside the light.

"So that's it," Thalen said.

"'The Rite is law.' Convenient."

"Outlawing everything outside their reach doesn't make us safer. It makes us brittle," Korvan said.

"They want us alive," Bren said.

"Do they?" Korvan snapped.

"If I'd done it their way, Solace wouldn't be here. Lareth would be dead. And you," he looked to Thalen, "you said Ashwing nearly killed you. Would you rather be right and dead?"

"I don't regret it," Thalen said.

He tipped his head toward the wyvern. "I'd rather die than be cut from him."

Korvan turned to Sera and Bren. "The enemy severs Soulmarks using our own rituals and we're arguing about protocol."

"It isn't only Protocol," Sera said.

"The Rite exists for a reason. You don't know what a failed bond feels like. We can't all bond like you, Korvan. Trust me...."

Bren went red and stared at his boots.

Korvan sank to the stone and braced his forearms on his thighs.

"Fear isn't wrong here," Sera said.

"Wild bonds are volatile. You hold one because you're... you. If someone tries to follow your footprints and isn't like you someone dies."

Lareth answered from the dark. "Or worse, the Tamer survives, and the beast doesn't. The mark stays, but hollow."

"I didn't die," Thalen interjected.

They all turned to him.

"Did you think I made a circle, went through the right, found an overseer? No, Ashwing found me in the wild. I bonded with him like Korvan did to Vasha. Don't ask me how, I still don't know.

The fire popped.

"It still feels like they locked the door after the building caught fire," Korvan said.

"Welcome to nobility, blame someone else long enough and people will start to forget the truth. It's a bull-shit tactic, but it is effective," Thalen said.

"I'm not saying you're wrong Korvan, but Thalen aside, Bren and I, Ryn and Javek, we're not like you. The Rite matters. But for what it's worth, we stepped off the safe path near Riverpost, when we followed you into the wild," Sera said. She looked up at him, her eyes wide. He saw a teary sheen there.

He met her eyes and found his footing.

"I'm not here to burn the Guard down, I just want us ready for whatever is coming," he said.

She smiled at him and squeezed his forearm.

"Then we stay sharp, because next time, I imagine the law will arrive with something a little more like handcuffs," Bren said.

"And if they come for our bonds?" Thalen asked.

Lareth stepped into the light. Still as a grave that had already been dug.

"Then we remind them what lives in the woods outside River-post."

***

Fog clung to the Third Ring. The hospice tower kept night even after sunrise; the chill in its stones got into joints.

They'd moved Caelen again. After the decree, no one risked more attention. Madam Ren took him into her home instead of the clinic.

Sera walked beside Korvan. It was long overdue that they went together.

Madam Ren opened the door herself. Sleeves rolled tight from work. Her eyes slid over Sera and settled on Korvan.

"He's awake," she said.

"That's good," Korvan answered.

"It isn't enough. I fear I've run out of things to try," she said.

Korvan lowered his eyes.

"May I see him, not that I'm sure you haven't done everything, but maybe a little magic can do the trick?" Sera asked.

Madam Ren studied her, then stepped aside. "He'll like you."

The upper room was bathed in sunlight from its long windows. Stacks of books with worn in spines. Thyme and warm stone eased the air.

Caelen sat propped, a book on one thigh, the other leg tucked under. His hair looked freshly combed. Skin thinned to paper light. His face lit like a lamp finally given oil.

"Korvan!" he beamed, then wheezed and pressed a knuckle to his lips. "And... about time. You finally bring the girl you won't shut up about."

Heat climbed Korvan's neck.

Sera's mouth tipped toward Caelen, "That bad?"

"Relentless, almost embarrassingly so I'd say," Caelen said, bright with mischief and fever both.

Sera laughed, a rich, warm thing. She unwrapped a small bundle and took something out.

"Candied ginger. Warm from the Market. Don't tell Madam Ren," she said with a wink.

"Oh, a rule breaker. No wonder he likes you," Caelen's grin was infectious.

Korvan let the light sit on his brother's face before he looked for shadows. He saw them anyway. Caelen's hands trembled. He made a wince on a small lean. Effort glazed every motion he made.

He drew a chair close. "How are you?"

"Like a prince. My court is dust mites and birdsong," Caelen said between chews.

The joke broke on a dry hitch. The hitch became a cough. One became a string. It tore him open. His shoulders curled; the book slid; bright specks spattered linen. The sound scraped the room raw.

"Caelen." Korvan was already halfway up.

Sera moved faster. Fennik pressed to her shin, runes waking up.

She set her fingers to Caelen's sternum and throat, gaze gone strict.

"Breathe with me," she said, low.

"Short in, two, three, hold, two, three, four, Out, two..."

Caelen tried to follow. But he couldn't. His chest seized again, harder. Red threaded the spit at his lips, his eyes bulged and went wild, and his hands gripped the sheets.

"Fennik," Sera clipped. "Now." The fox's glow steadied, a warm pulse synchronizing to her breath.

"Soothing Thread," she whispered, and the weave of Aethyr bloomed. Thin bands of light crossing under her palms, widening the stuck places. Her light poured into Caelen.

He gagged once, twice. The convulsion eased. His hands uncurled from blankets.

Sera held until the tremor wore down. Then loosened her touch a finger's width at a time.

"There," she murmured.

"Stay with me."

Caelen blinked tears. Shame flickered, Korvan caught it.

He tried a joke and failed.

"New trick," he rasped.

"Didn't mean to perform and ruin your visit."

"Don't fret, I'm not so easily scared off," Sera said.

Korvan heard a board creak and looked behind him. Madam Ren stood in the doorway, jaw tight, a cloth in hand. She did not interrupt.

Korvan's hands had gone white on the chair. He forced them open.

"Thank you, Sera," he said. Even he thought his voice sounded rough.

Sera nodded without looking away.

"You're all right," she told Caelen.

"Eat the ginger, it will help your throat."

He obeyed.

"May I examine you?" Sera asked.

Caelen glanced at Korvan. Got a nod. Gave one back.

"Please. Before my brother starts hovering any closer."

Her fingers found his wrist. Light pooled under his skin. Fennik lent his strength, in short pulses of light. Sera closed her eyes. Runes unwound from her hands and laid themselves over him in careful rings. Caelen watched the circles spin, wonder and worry twinned on his face.

"His Fyrstrand is bending back on itself," she said after some time.

"It's not shattered. It is twisted. The current wants to run, but a piece inside keeps folding it the wrong way. I can't find any hex, or disease causing it, it's something in his Fyrstrand, I just, can't see what the cause is."

Korvan stared. His palms slicked. His exhale stopped.

"Can... can you fix it?"

She opened her eyes slowly. They were wet at the corners.

"I'm sorry, but no. I can ease your pain, help you breathe, help you sleep. But this needs deeper reach. If I had more strength or a

Mender with higher standing. If Solace could share some power..." her words failed, and she closed her eyes.

"But, that's not how it works, we can't share Reservoirs," Korvan finished.

"No, we can't," she said.

Fennik wasn't offended, by the implication of not being strong enough to help. He hopped into Caelen's lap and curled. Caelen's hand sank into bright fur. His breathing evened by degrees.

"Well, at least he is warm and is this his magic I'm feeling?" Caelen asked, his eyes were red, his cheeks were wet, but somehow his voice was strong.

Sera wiped her tears and nodded, "Yes. Being close to Fennik grants some healing of its own. A special gift of a Mender Aspect. The 'Mendtouch' they call it, it'll heal minor wounds all on its own. Only downside, it makes him hot to sleep with. That and he likes to hog the foot space."

Fennik chuffed at her and spun on Caelen once, using his tail to block her.

Caelen let out a laugh and scratched his head.

Madam Ren entered with a folded cloth.

"There aren't many left with the old depth," she said.

"Menders are so rare. How many in your order? A handful? That's why I still have a place."

Sera cupped Caelen's hand. No fake smile. "I'm sorry, Caelen. I wish I were stronger."

"You don't have to be sorry. You tried, that's more than most," he said, but his eyes stayed on their hands.

He chased the tremor from his mouth with bravado.

"Kor, I made you something."

He brought up a small brass boar-like creature. It was polished, gears tucked tight.

"I made a miniature Brusk," Caelen said, pride flaring behind fatigue.

"Madam Ren bought parts with the Silverbrands you sent. Watch."

He wound the dial. The miniature charged, turned, did a little hop that looked like the real thing. It chuffed and wagged its tail. Caelen laughed from a place that didn't hurt for a heartbeat.

"Do you like it?" His eyes shot to Korvan's.

Korvan's throat closed. His eyes flooded, and he ached so hard he thought it would split.

"I love it, little hawk. You have always been amazing at making things."

Korvan lifted the clockwork Brusk with both hands as if it were alive and easy to startle.

Sera's hand settled on his shoulder. Steady weight.

"Caelen..." Korvan began, but sleep took his brother mid-smile.

Korvan looked away. Tears soaked his cuffs. He didn't hide them.

"Madam Ren," he said, low.

"Whatever you can do, please do it. I'll pay, I don't care what it costs, I'll pay it. We'll get stronger but just keep him stable until we are. How... how long until..."

Madam Ren's face settled into something next door to heartbreak.

"I don't know, hon. If nothing changes, a few months. Less than that. He's already lasted longer than he should have. It isn't what you want to hear, but it is the truth."

Sera's fingers slid into Korvan's and locked. Her hand shook. Maybe it was his. He nodded. Madam Ren bowed a little and left them to the sun.

They stayed until the rhythm of Caelen's breath wrote itself into Korvan's bones. At last, he reached for the Fyrstrand and called Brusk. Copper light shuddered and stood. The copper forged boar filled the foot of the bed.

"Stay with him my friend," Korvan said.

"He needs you more than I do."

Brusk dipped his head. His voice sounded like gravel. *Brusk keep little hawk safe.*

He pressed his head into Korvan's hip, then went and became a wall.

"Thank you, Brusk," Korvan whispered.

***

They didn't speak until the hospice steps.

"Now I understand," Sera said.

Korvan looked at her but felt hollow. She didn't explain. She didn't need to.

"He's why I can't quit," he said.

Sera didn't move on. Not yet. She touched his arm.

"You've carried him alone long enough. You thought no one else could lift the good weight or the bad."

He swallowed hard.

"Thank you for bringing me, for letting me in. I'm sorry I couldn't help him like I wanted to, but you don't have to carry the burden alone anymore," she said.

"I don't know how to ask for help, not with this, not for me," he said.

"I'll be there; you don't have to ask for the things like this. Not the things that truly matter," she said.

"I can't lose him, Sera... I'm not strong enough to—"

The rest drowned in tears.

She didn't answer with words. She wrapped him tight in her arms, stepped onto her toes, tucked under his chin, and squeezed until his ribs ached. They cried together.

Korvan wasn't sure how long they stood there but when Sera finally let go, she looked as tired as he felt.

"My sister bakes better than anyone in the south rings. My father also thinks no one deserves me. I'd love for you to meet them, it would be nothing if not entertaining to see you have to listen to my father," she said.

Korvan let out a quiet laugh he didn't expect. "I'll think about it."

"I'll count that as yes."

They walked on. Her hand found his.

He didn't let go.

***

Cael'Lumar tightened after the decree. Whispers hunted markets, temples, and training yards. Not everyone accepted this new law.

Some argued behind doors. Some didn't sleep in their bunks again. Soulmarks still bright. Floor-spots left clean. Veyrkin gone with them.

Eris appeared more. Champions at her shoulder. Lists in hand. Each name read, cost them all something. Those who refused inspection didn't get a trial. They got excommunicated.

One evening a Knight of the Third Ring stood in the courtyard, she was broad-shouldered and known for dragging survivors from the Thalos Wastes. Her Reservoir circled above, a purple-colored hawk wreathed in gray flame.

Lower your arm," a Champion said.

"I bonded to him before this mark," she said.

Her voice carried.

"You did not give him to me. You will not take him."

Eris didn't move. Her voice cracked once.

"Then you forfeit your place among us."

The Knight unpinned her sigil and let it ring on stone. She walked out without looking back. The hawk circled until she vanished down the stairs.

Those who remained spoke in corners.

"They're protecting us."

"They're dividing us."

"They're afraid."

"Fear makes people do awful things."

Lareth stood on the Outer Wall at dusk and watched bronze and violet break apart over the cliffs like a bruise healing backward. The wind snapped at Korvan's cloak as he stepped beside him.

You're leaving," Korvan said.

"I've stayed longer than I meant. They don't have any intention of taking it seriously. I won't wait around for it to all fall apart," Lareth said.

"We need you."

"They need the truth, and I need, to go back to where I lost Blaze." he said.

"I'm not sure what Sera did, but ever since, I've felt him again, well, felt him more than I have in years. Something about it feels... better. Like I can find him again. I've got to and just like the first time, I've got to go alone."

"I hope you succeed; we'll need all the help we can get," Korvan said, offering a smile.

Footfalls found them.

Thalen came slow. His armor was off. Bracers on. Hands shoved into his belt. His spine held too straight.

Lareth looked over his shoulder. Said nothing.

"You're leaving?" Thalen asked.

Lareth didn't answer.

"I don't know how to ask you to stay, but I know that I should," Thalen said.

Lareth turned then, softer than Korvan had seen.

"You don't have to ask," he said.

"I'll come back."

"You said that last—"

Thalen stopped himself. The old wound still bit.

"This time I mean it," Lareth said.

His arms twitched. Half extended toward his younger brother.

Thalen's hands came out from his belt and hung there. Unguarded.

It was enough.

"Next time, little panther. I hope I get to be your brother again."

Lareth looked at Korvan. "If you call, I'll come."

"I will," Korvan said.

They clasped wrists. The kind of promise men keep because they need it true.

Lareth stepped into the shadows of Cael'Lumar. His eyes on Thalen.

The younger brother of house Ryst spun a ring on his fingers.

***

Beneath the Crown Keep, where stone keeps secrets, a second ledger scratched itself onto parchment. Suspicion. Names of those who bonded beyond the Rite. Watched. Measured. Mapped.

Veyrkin noted. Movements tracked. No one said the word in daylight.

It echoed anyway.

Doubt.

Doubt had come to Cael'Lumar.

Doubt had come for the Aethyrguard.

Chapter 22: Echoes and Consequences

The sun tipped beyond the cliffs and poured amber light down the spires. From the Artisan's Row, a bell rose in three bright chimes, then one lower note. Rest, and a little joy. Atheris' Light.

Korvan tugged at the collar of his new tunic. His Soulmarks itched under linen, unshown, unhappy. He had lived in leather and mail since the Initiate's Trial. Tonight wasn't for that. Tonight was for her.

After all, he had promised her a date.

He waited by the ivy-laced fountain where elder glassblowers set their wares on old boards. Families bargained. Someone sugared citrus on a brass pan.

She arrived without calling his name. She smiled; the same half-lidded confidence she wore after a clean spar and slid her hand into his.

"You wore the tunic," she murmured, nudging his elbow.

"I did," he said, aiming for easy and landing near stiff.

"It's wrinkled."

"I don't know how to fold it."

"I didn't expect you to. You look very handsome," Her fingers tugged.

"Come on."

They moved through the small music of the square: a three-string dulcimer, a child spinning a ribbon of light, two retired soldiers arm-wrestling on a crate to balcony cheers. The night softened the city and left the edges kind.

"You always walk this fast?" Korvan asked, smiling but almost winded.

"No. Besides didn't Vasha make you faster," she gave him a wink.

She stopped at a narrow cart wedged between spice stalls. The vendor's hair shone like silver thread; her eyes held motes hazel. She handed them cones of chilled mango drizzled in honey and dusted in powdered violet root.

Korvan blinked. "What is this?"

"My favorite treat and old memories," Sera said, biting once.

"I was twelve the first time. Stole three Ashers from my tutor, bought a cone, and ate it under that arch, felt like a thief and a queen."

She tilted her chin at a low marble arch where lamplight pooled like wine.

"You get caught?"

"No, but I went back the next day and confessed." A small shrug.

"I've stolen food before, for me and Caelen when dad hadn't left any coin. I tried not to feel guilty about it. How do you always know what's right?"

"I don't, I just listen to my conscience and try to accept what I can control."

The answer came without flourish.

"That's why I asked you out here, so we could not just be initiates but Korvan and Sera. Talk about things that aren't missions, or battle tactics, or Disciplines."

They sat beneath the arch with their legs thrown long. Her head rested on his shoulder. The square kept laughing behind them while a hush coned around their bench, in a shared quiet. Eventually drips of sticky sweet clung to their fingers as they listlessly enjoyed their treats and watched the crowd. Fennik happily cleaned their fingers.

"I had the dream again," Korvan said.

"The dragon?"

"Yes." He weighed the next words.

"I don't really think it's a dream, but I don't know what else to call it. It's like he pulls my soul into the Beyond and other times I can always feel him watching, like he's waiting for something."

Sera finished her cone and folded the paper into neat quarters.

"It's starting to make sense. The more time I spend around you I'm starting to realize it. The Aethyr feels... bigger around you. Like its more alive, no, no more alive, just more, but different. But I get why a creature like that would want a partner like you, you're special."

"You don't know that."

"I do." She laced their fingers. They were still sticky.

"I knew it when you stood your ground terrified and didn't pretend you weren't. You have more power than anyone I know, but you only want to use it to protect people. I don't care what any-one says, that is special."

A group of not-quite-teens ran through and splashed in the fountain; Sera sent a dazzle of lights at them. They cheered and laughed at the small firework display and kept running down the street, laughter echoing along the stone walls.

The clamor blurred to a hum as she led him through lamp-lit alleys and ivy-stone steps. They climbed toward thinner noise and salt air.

"This way," she said, turning through an iron gate furred with windflowers.

He followed. Her hand stayed light in his.

A small terrace opened between two rooflines. A low wall held the world back. Beyond it, Cael'Lumar fell to black ocean punc-tured by ship lights.

Then the stars opened, thousands, blooming slow.

"Wow, I've never been here, its beautiful," Korvan said.

"This is my favorite place in the whole city," She set her palms on weathered stone.

"When I was little I came to this spot and tried to learn all the names of the stars. I thought names would make the world make sense."

"Did it work?"

"Not even once, but it was fun," A soft laugh.

The wind tugged their collars. Far below, a Skyship's Aethyr-charged sails glowed dull and patient, painting light across roofs like slow clouds.

"I didn't plan on joining the Aethyrguard," she said.

"I wanted charts, lenses, and scopes. I wanted to see all the stars I could. Study what makes them shine and move. How they affect everything. Then the Beyond tore near my home. I watched the horrors that came through, and I watched people stand. It wasn't perfect, but it was purpose, and they helped people. I like helping people."

He studied her instead of the constellations. Stillness lived in her face, rare, earned.

"Do you ever wish you'd have become a scholar instead, spent your life studying the stars?"

"No. Most days, I wish it were a little quieter sometimes, and the workouts are brutal. But we've saved lives, and our careers with are just starting, imagine what we can do as we get stronger," she said.

Korvan hesitated. The words stuck, but he forced them forward anyway.

"Caelen and I used to build things when we were boys. Once we tried to make a glider out of scrap canvas and cedar slats. Hauled it up the ridge by our cottage. He swore it would carry us clear across the valley if I built it right."

Sera's lips curved. "Did it?"

"It carried him into a blackberry thicket."

He huffed out something between a laugh and a wince.

"He had scrapes everywhere. Caelen still says it almost worked. He made me promise we'd try again someday when we were stronger. When we could really fly. I think that's my favorite memory of us. Of those few seconds when he got to fly and forgot about being sick, about being hungry, about our dad..."

Her smile softened into something quieter.

"That's what you want, isn't it? Not the power. Not the soul-marks. Just... to fly."

He swallowed. "Maybe. I don't know if it's wanting or needing. But I've never stopped dreaming about it. What I really want, I'm too scared to say."

"You can tell me if you'd like," her voice was scantly more than a murmur.

He turned and gulped again; he felt sweat bead at his nape and his hands started to tremble. His eyes locked on her, and she grabbed his arm. Her hand was warm and strong, but gentle in a way he still wasn't used to.

It helped.

"I want to save my brother, I don't want him to be sick. He's dying Sera, and I don't know how to help him."

Sera's gaze lingered on him, steady as the sky.

"Then we'll find a way."

"I don't deserve you, you are so sweet to me."

"Korvan, I've been courted by princes, been sought by noble dignitaries from Selin'Dae to the Dominion. Do you know why I like you?"

He shook his head.

"Because you don't treat me like a prize to earn. You don't try to bribe me for my affection or woo me with your riches. You treat me like a woman, like a friend. Like I'm real."

She stood on her toes and kissed him. She wrapped her arms around his neck and pulled him in tight. A fire lit in him that he'd not felt before. The world spun and his body flushed, gooseflesh rippled along his body and he felt alive.

She turned. Starlight doubled in her eyes. Just a lean, a shared breath, the press of mouths that asked nothing but the moment. She pulled him back and leaned against the wall, shielding them in a dark, private corner, so they could kiss some more.

Below, the city smoldered like scattered flame. Above, stars held their vigil.

***

The yard carried the sound of metal thumping against wood.

Korvan stood at the rail and watched Bren break the spar-pillar down one measured inch at a time. The post had long since splintered. He kept swinging with relentless endurance.

The moons looked pale over it.

Sera sat near the chalk line with Fennik tucked against her hip.

"Over an hour," she murmured.

Korvan nodded. Soldiers cracked like this where war couldn't see. Bren hadn't cracked. He's Bren.

They had spoken less since the debrief. Bren kept his own counsel most of the time, but this felt different.

Korvan stepped forward. "Bren."

The hammer hovered in midair. Bren didn't turn.

"You'll wear through the handle," Korvan said, sliding to the edge of the arc.

Bren lowered the weight. Breath came harsh. Sweat striped his face. His eyes only held fatigue.

"Good," he said.

"Then it's working."

"Want to talk?" Korvan asked.

"What's there to say?"

Sera rose, careful, not crowding.

"You've been far away."

"No, I've been focused."

"If this is about Riverpost," Korvan began.

"It isn't." Bren cut him off.

He set the hammer's head to the dirt and leaned into the haft. "I need to be ready. I'm not you."

Korvan's brow furrowed, "What does that mean?"

"It means you have Brusk. Vasha. Solace. Sera. You even got to have Thalen come back with a Dragon. Power pours off you like the gods set a crown on your head," His voice roughened from somewhere deep.

"People look at you and see change. Destiny. Eris sees it. The Archmage sees it. Hell, the High Warden saw it months ago too."

He let air go slow, bitter.

"I have a hammer. A bear who needs a larger door. I'm the youngest son of a smith, no prophecies, or pedigrees for me. Just grit. I don't know if grit will hold."

"You have us," Sera said.

Bren's chest rose and his knuckles tightened around his hammer.

"I don't need your light-damned pity."

"It isn't pity," Korvan said.

"It's respect. You stood in front when the spellfire started. You held the line when I was bleeding. But upset or not Bren, don't cuss at Sera."

"Apologies milady," Bren said, it had a mocking quality to it.

"Bren, this isn't like you. What's wrong," Sera asked, ignoring everything else.

Korvan started to interject but her look stopped him.

"I held, I was the wall. Good Bren, tough Bren. But I didn't win, I didn't save anyone. That was Korvan and Thalen, I just kept fucking swinging a hammer," Bren stated it like he was ordering lunch.

Korvan blinked.

"I'm scared," Bren said, knuckles whitening.

"I'm the one that won't keep up. I'm not fast enough. Not strong enough. Not blessed enough."

"You won't be left behind Bren," Korvan said.

"You can't swear that."

"Maybe I can't, but I can damn-well try."

He set a hand on Bren's shoulder. The hand stayed there long enough for the ache to crest.

Bren stepped away. "I've got to get back to my training."

"I'll be here every morning," Korvan said.

"No, I... just, no thanks Korvan."

Bren shook his head.

"We're not leaving you," Sera said.

He turned, lifted the hammer, and swung. The strike rang the yard. Conversation over.

Korvan fell back to the bench beside Sera. She folded her arms like she might come apart if she didn't.

"Do you think he'll be alright?" she whispered.

The next strike fell.

"No, and I don't know how to help," Korvan said.

The moons drifted. One by one, the yard emptied, save for a man under stars who refused to stop, and the two who refused to stop watching.

***

The practice kiln lay empty. Not the main smithy, Initiates were kept from that fire, but the old room in the lower barracks where stone hummed and iron heat smelled like home. Bren liked the quiet here. No marks glowing. No Champions counting. No pace to keep up with but his own.

He lit the bed with flint and tinder. The way his Da had showed him. The flame came slower that way but He preferred the old way.

The smithing hammer wasn't his usual weight. The grip's leather had gone slick from overuse. He set a bent buckle on the anvil and brought steel down repeatedly.

It didn't matter what he made. It mattered that he made.

His arms burned. He kept going.

Korvan meant well, voice low, brow knotted like he could hold all the pain himself. Like he was the only one bleeding. Bren ground his teeth and tried to explain to a post, because iron didn't try to answer back.

Hammer. Shield. Repeat.

A star called Solace had stepped out of fog and everyone nodded. Vasha carved more meat than a butcher. Thalen returned with his thunder-wing and it counted as proof of something.

What was Bren? A good swing and a thick wall. He had stopped dreaming of more. That was the worst part. None of them noticed, none of them asked about how he tried and failed to bond more. They just saw Korvan and Thalen keep climbing higher than no one questioned if they'd get left behind.

The buckle popped under a bad strike, brittle and wrong.

"Damn it," he muttered.

Rok rumbled behind him, low, companionable.

"I know," Bren said softly.

"I'm being stupid."

Rok didn't argue. He never did.

Bren set the hammer down. His hands shook, not from the forge. From the fear under it. He wiped sweat with his shirt and leaned into warm stone. Shadows from the coals crawled the ceiling.

"They think I'm strong," he said to the empty room.

"But I'm scared. Scared I won't keep up. Scared I'll watch them fall and not be fast enough to stop it."

Rok nosed his shoulder. Bren didn't smile.

"I miss when it was simple," he whispered.

"Before the missive. Before Solace. Before—"

He stopped.

He stood.

He dragged his palm along the stone as he left. The shadows went on moving without him.

***

The courtyard stood near-empty. Wind sighed through the spar posts; lanternlight poured long and soft across stone. Indigo rose; first stars pressed through the thinning veil of dusk.

Korvan sat on a low bench, elbows braced on knees, Soulmarks dim under cloth. He wasn't meditating. He was thinking.

Brusk snored nearby. Their bond felt thin and stretched. Spending time that far from Korvan had drained them both, but it was worth the cost. Korvan wanted Caelen to always have someone with him and who better than a living shield.

Solace perched higher on the wall. Vasha lay in the pillar's shadow, ears forward, breath slow. Korvan noticed her ears flick up but she didn't move. Clearly it wasn't a threat.

Stone shifted beside him.

Thalen dropped into the seat without ceremony. No armor; only a light cloak and ash along his sleeves. Windswept hair. He had been flying.

"I thought you'd be in bed already," Korvan said.

Thalen shrugged. "Figured I'd give you the yard before Bren tore it apart."

Korvan's half-smile did not last. "He's not wrong about feeling left behind."

"No, we've left them all behind in a way," Thalen said.

Silence held, full but usable.

"I used to think I was the best," Thalen said at last.

"Not only from pride, but before you, I was the best. From practice. If I trained hard enough, no one could question why I belonged."

Korvan didn't answer.

"I see you," Thalen went on, gaze set somewhere past the dark.

"You carry things differently. People lean toward you. Maybe it's the Veyrkin. But I think it's you. There's something different in the air when you're near. It's hard to explain."

Korvan's throat tightened.

"Different maybe? That's what Sera said anyway. She told me the same thing you just said. Did you rehearse it with each other," Korvan joked.

"That is... interesting."

That was all Thalen could manage.

Korvan turned to look at him. Thalen had always been felt taller, older somehow. But looking at him now he didn't see it.

Maybe Korvan had just grown but, he was a bit taller and more filled in. Thalen was undoubtedly nobility, his features made him look molded. Aside from his windswept blond mane, he was the pinnacle of nobility. And yet... he was blushing.

"Are you ok?" Korvan asked.

Thalen let out a cough,

"Yes, I'm fine, just got lost in thought. No Sera and I didn't rehearse anything. Just find it interesting that we've both noticed it. But like I said, whatever it is, it's something about you."

"I don't always know how to lead."

"No," Thalen said, turning to meet Korvan's gaze.

"You know how to shield. You take hits for others. That's why they trust you, why I trust you. It's also why we don't reach for you. You wall up, even with us."

Korvan looked down.

"I try not to."

"You do try," Thalen allowed.

"But you make us pull things out of you like we're pulling a rotted tooth. Sera coaxes things. Bren cracks jokes to ease the tension. I've spotted the pattern and still let it slide because you're easy to be around. You think if you stay quiet long enough, we'll just understand. That isn't leadership, Korvan. That's fear."

Korvan's shoulders set. "You think I'm afraid?"

"I know you are, and if you aren't you should be," Thalen said.

"Fear is useful when you understand it. Leave it nameless and it shapes you in silence."

He leaned forward slightly.

"Bren feels like he's fading behind you. Not only because you're better, because you never reach back. You offer drills and pointers, not belief in him. You train beside him, but you don't see him."

A salt breath moved up from the lower rings; the faint tang of seafoam reached even here.

Korvan exhaled hard.

"Then tell me how to fix it."

"Damn it. That is the entire point Korvan," Thalen said, his eyes rolled, and his breath came out in a huff.

"You think everything has a fix, that if you just take on more it'll work out. If you grow strong enough, fast enough, people will know your heart without you opening it. People are not problems to be solved by holding all our issues for us."

Korvan's voice dropped. "I would bleed for any of you."

"Again, that is not what I'm saying. You'll bleed and die for people, great. You'll let your body get bruised and broken and utterly spent. But you need to live for people too," Thalen said.

"You have enough strength for ten lifetimes, and none of us knows how to reach you unless you speak."

The yard answered with small sounds: leather creaks; flag-rope ticking against a pole; the wet thud from the far pit where someone had forgotten to empty the rain barrel. Lanterns popped as gnats found heat and died.

Thalen scraped his thumb along a nick in the bench.

"On patrol today, Ashwing took a crosswind over the harbor," he said, idly.

"He folded a wing to descend, then rolled into it. I held his scales so tight, I was terrified of falling. But the point is, he didn't need me for any of it."

He huffed once. "That's what I keep learning. Things I thought were mine to force will fly better when I stop clenching so hard."

Korvan swallowed. "I don't know how to unclench."

"Start small," Thalen said.

"Tell Bren you need him. Not him guarding the line. Him. Tell Sera when you're frightened instead of showing her the aftermath. Tell me when you think I'm about to do something foolish. Be our friend, not our protector. I know you're used to being a Bulwark for your brother... but we aren't sick like him."

Korvan's mouth fell open and his shoulders tensed.

A corner of Thalen's mouth tipped. "You can start tonight."

"I am frightened of letting you all down. Of letting you leave again without trying to stop you. Of failing him," Korvan said, the words landing like stones set in place.

"Caelen," Thalen said, gentle for once.

Korvan nodded.

Silence refilled the yard.

"I'm not trying to leave anyone behind," Korvan murmured.

"I know," Thalen replied.

"But if you keep walking forward without looking back, we'll still be gone."

Thalen's tone softened. "I don't know where I fit in with the group now. I thought I was built for this. Now I wonder if I'm just hanging on because I don't know what else to be. There are things I haven't shared either."

"You're part of this, whether you like it or not," Korvan said.

Thalen smirked.

"Sounds dangerously close to friendship."

Korvan rolled his eyes.

"Do not make me take it back. Prick."

Thalen rose a soft smile at the corners of his eyes.

"Get some rest Aric, the world isn't done with us yet."

Korvan watched him go. Only the old ache between what he meant and what he knew how to say. Vasha slid against his side, heat, fur, and steadiness.

"I'm trying girl," Korvan whispered as he grabbed handfuls of the big cat's fur.

"I don't want to be like dad. I'm afraid I'm not enough for them."

The only sound was the gentle snap of flaps in the sea's breeze and the sound of a big cat purring.

Fear robs you of your power. Fear can never harm you, it only gives you the strength you let it take. Do not be afraid you are not enough, simply be more.

He chuckled, "You sound like Sera."

Vasha's purr turned into a deep rumble; *The Huntress is incredibly wise.*

"Huntress? Sera is the huntress and I'm little hunter?" He asked, stunned.

Though he couldn't see Vasha's face, he swore he could feel her smiling.

***

Thalen didn't go far.

He stopped under the outer arch where the garden met the yard, one hand on cool stone. Midnight padded beside him, eyes bright in shadow. Through his bond he could feel Ashwing soaring overhead, always present but far too big for the City's streets.

From here he could still see Korvan. His faint outline haloed by Vasha's soft glow. A man curled like a question.

Then the words reached him. "I'm trying girl... I'm afraid I'm not enough for them."

Thalen's breath hitched. He had braced for deflection, not honesty.

Midnight's tail flicked against his boot.

"I feel the same," he said to the dark.

Not always. Not when watched. But in the sluice between demands and the expectations wore off, doubt rose within Thalen.

He crouched, one knee to stone, fingers combing Midnight's fur.

"He thinks leading means holding the problems alone," Thalen murmured.

"If he stumbles, everything breaks. I believed that once."

A pause. "Lareth was the brave one. I measured myself against him even after he was gone."

His voice thinned.

"I'm still trying to become someone he'd be proud of."

He looked again at Korvan. stubborn silhouette anchored by guilt and care both.

"He almost caught me. Sera and I said the same thing... Who knows what the means. Damn it. Of course it means that he affects us. I'm going to have to tell him. Gods, why am I like this Midnight? Its like a school-boy crush when I was twelve all over again."

Thalen, you know why it affects you so. Because you are conflicted on if you should act upon the feelings or not. You of all people know that desire alone is not a good enough reason. But for too long you have listened to what your house demands from you. What do you want?

Thalen cocked his head at Midnight, his jaw hung open. "That is the most you have ever said to me. Sage advice as always, my feline friend. Right now, I know I want him in my life, what shape that takes is not only up to me."

See, you too can learn.

He swatted for her but she shifted through the shadow easily avoiding him. She licked her a paw content with herself.

"He reminds me of Lareth, or what Lareth stood for I guess."

She moved back and pressed her head to his shoulder. *He's kind, if foolish, he doesn't see how much you all care.*

He nodded.

"I wanted to hate him," Thalen said.

"Some days I know that would be easier than this. But he, he isn't the enemy. He's another burden I didn't ask for," he said.

"But maybe the one I need."

He rose; cloak whispered. "If I start quoting poetry, drag me off the ledge," he told Midnight.

They slipped into shadow, quiet as smoke. Thalen knew he wasn't close with Korvan yet, but A crack in the wall had started to show.

***

Sera stood barefoot in the chapel garden. Stone paths held the day's warmth; the night smelled of cypress and rosemary. Fennik curled at her feet, light dim and steady. She had come to pray. No words arrived. Tonight, the stars hung sharp and indifferent.

Her hands trembled as she rinsed them in the basin beneath the Twin Flame. Korvan was fraying, even if he couldn't see it. Bren burned from within. Thalen had become fragile as glass. There were edges everywhere.

And Sera? The healer. The one who soothed burns, bound wounds, whispered hope into those who carried too much. For all her magic, she could not fix this. Not the cracks between them. Not the pressure building under the Guard, the city, the Beyond.

Not Caelen.

Her fingers curled. She had felt the twist in him. The Fyrstrand folding against itself, a river turned back by its own banks. No curse to cut away. No invader to name. Just a life unwinding on its own.

The chapel's statues stood with their faces rubbed smooth by thousands of different hands. Prayer cords hung in loops from hooks, wool gone shiny where fingers worried them bare. Beeswax clung to the lip of old sconces like amber teeth. She had sat here as an apprentice, palms nicked and raw after her first triage day, and taught herself how to breathe without crying. Her mother would have told her to rest. Her father would have told her to hold fast. Ashlyn would have pressed bread in her hands and made her eat first, talk after.

Sera smiled at the phantom of it and let it go.

I am here, Fennik's presence brushed against her.

"I know," she whispered. "Help me keep them safe, my sweet fox."

Fennik yipped and trotted next to her. She traced a prayer cut into stone by some other hand. Not a formal verse; just three words: Remember the light.

She repeated them until they stopped sounding like command and started sounding like choice.

She looked over the low wall. The Fourth Ring stretched in silver rooftops and torch trails. Somewhere out there, Korvan sat alone with his marks. Somewhere, Bren paced by the forge, jaw set. Somewhere, Thalen walked between two worlds and claimed he didn't have to choose. They were all thinning. She chose to be the thread. Because of Korvan. For his mercy. For his heart.

She had seen it the first day of training. In a quiet hand offered to a fallen Initiate. The kindness of someone who refused to dim even though darkness swirled around him.

He already looked tired then. Someone who had carried too much before anyone thought to help. He still offered help freely. Mercy like that dies fast in places like this. So, she would stay. To remind him his heart mattered as much as his strength. That he did not have to bear it alone. Even if he did not yet know how to let her in.

He had said, I love you, so soft, startled by the shape of it. She had smiled and let it pass. Because he didn't know what he meant yet. Love that lets someone see the vulnerable parts. Love that asks for help. Love that doesn't always wear armor. She loved him. Gods, she did. But silence is a poor house for love. She could not always be the one pulling him back from the dark. Even if one day he broke and didn't return. Some part of her hoped he would come back sooner than that. Because she wanted more than his strength. She wanted him.

And part of her knew, another truth, one that made her heart sing for Korvan.

That someone else wanted him too.

How could Thalen not want Korvan. It was so obvious looking back on it. Thalen couldn't keep his eyes off Korvan when he came back, and the fear in his eyes when Korvan bled on the ground... She understood, she was that afraid too.

"I can't say I blame him, huh Fennik. Korvan deserves all our love. And, with arms like those who could resist. The real question, which one of them will say something first. Silly boys," she said, rustling his fur.

She would be there for all of them, asked or not, thanked or not. The stillness in the center. That was her vow to herself. Be what steadies. Heal what you can. Carry what they cannot say.

She knelt and pressed her brow to Fennik's.

"We can do this a little longer," she whispered.

"They'll need all the light we can give."

His tail brushed her knee.

Above them, one star winked out.

A simple fact.

Even light can vanish.

So carry it while you can.

Chapter 23: Cracks in Stone

Morning drew thin gold across Cael'Lumar's rings. Salt rode the wind. Korvan stood in the sparring circle, staff loose in hand. Brusk took his right, stone steady. Vasha prowled left, ears pricking at sounds the city swallowed. Solace shimmered behind, feathers dancing in the breeze.

Three Veyrkin. Three rhythms. One intention.

He breathed. He moved. No flourish. Just will. His Fyrstrand drew tight between their bodies.

"Radiant Binding."

Gold chains flew and caught two rushing golems mid step.

Brusk hit hard, shoulder first. Gears cracked.

Vasha slid through the seam, slipping through the blinding light and reappeared behind the target. Claws struck, more gears shattered.

Korvan pivoted.

"Hammerpulse."

Force rippled from his boots, a rolling shockwave over the floor.

The last dummy blew apart.

"Beacon of Dawn."

A corona bloomed, beautiful and reckless. The shadows were cast away and bands of radiant light pushed out from the head of the Staff.

Korvan let it whisk itself away before it could burn the yard too much.

"I told them you weren't typical."

Eris stood on the stair, coat open over training mail.

She stepped in. "You're commanding all three at once."

"I'm trying."

"No. You're doing."

Her eyes took in the wreckage. "When you arrived, Brusk dragged your stance, Vasha wrote her own orders, and Solace nearly drowned your conduit. Seems your trial in the wilderness taught you something. Well done Korvan," She said it with a smile.

He felt himself beam back at her.

She looked past him to the rings of the city.

"Don't let the compliment go to your head though. The work is not done. The nobles are whispering. Some fear you. Some would use you. Too many are watching. Already their games are in motion to lay claim to you."

"Which are you?"

"I'm your tutor. I'll protect you from both."

Her voice was matter of fact.

A pause.

"But, I cannot shield you from everything that is coming."

"What is coming?"

She did not answer. She nodded once.

"Your strength is not the question. The cost of what you've gained is. Remember that."

She turned for the steps.

"I think today, I'll have a coffee. Keep training Aric. You're good, but greatness lives in you."

Korvan faced his Veyrkin.

"You heard her."

Power climbed his spine.

"Prism Lance."

Light refracted through the circle. Training constructs softened and slumped.

Smoke thinned leaving ruined clockwork machines and smoldering wood.

His breath was even.

He looked at his Soulmark, he'd thrown more power today than he did during the fight in Feldmar's woods. He had barely touched his pool of Aethyr. Either Solace's Reservoir was growing or his own was.

"Come on," he said with a grin.

"Let's go again."

***

Wind tugged the pennants above Tower Meridian.

Eris watched from the parapet while Korvan moved far below. Staff swept. Soulmarks flared. Veyrkin cut clean geometry through dust.

Talmar glided above, owl eyes keeping count. Coryn paced the wall's base, dusk made muscle. Kaelith stood beside her, fiery mane banked to coals.

You haven't stopped watching him, Kaelith said.

Warmth pressed back through the bond.

"He reminds me of myself."

Kaelith's thought curled like flame.

He's touched by something. I can see the echo on his Soulmark.

Eris nodded.

"Do you think it is truly one of the lost Veyrkin?" She asked.

I think it likely, though the Aethyr has been strange around young Aric since he arrived.

Below, Korvan staggered once. Solace flickered.

He pushes harder than any Initiate she'd seen, in years.

If the high tables ever ordered her to stop him, she had not decided if she would.

***

The corridor outside Madam Ren's held a ghost, a voice Korvan hadn't heard in nearly a year.

"You walk like a soldier now. Almost didn't recognize you."

Varnrik leaned under an arch. Covered in Mine dust, stinking of drink. Eyes like old cuts.

Korvan's fists clenched so hard his knuckles popped, he felt his heartbeat thunder into his throat and his vision narrowed.

"What are you doing here." It wasn't a question.

"I want to know why it takes the Aethyrguard to drag you home. The boy coughs his insides out while you polish tower floors."

He stepped closer. Close enough Korvan could smell the stink of his breath mixed with years of alcohol.

"You used him. Poor little hero with a dying brother. What a story. Sure those saps ate it up."

Korvan's hands curled. The air thickened. Power crawled his spine unbidden.

"You sit once a week and call it love. He needed a brother. You chose a badge."

"I did this for him."

"No. You did it for you. Couldn't stand being nothing. Couldn't stand being like me. A nobody."

A jab of the finger. "You've got her eyes. She left because she was weak. Guess you're just like her. Weak, and running from your problems."

Heat climbed Korvan's arm. The spell rose to his teeth.

"Hammerp—,"

Solace cooled his spine. *Breathe.*

Vasha brushed his ribs. *This one smells off, little hunter, he is no threat to you. Do not do this.*

Brusk rumbled through him, the voice he needed. *Korvan good man. Korvan not cruel. Korvan protect.*

Varnrik must've seen the look in Korvan's eyes because he stepped into him. Korvan was rooted, his father bounced back.

"Maybe there's more of me in you than I thought boy," he accused.

"Go on," Varnrik said.

"Prove me right. Hit me. Give me a reason to get you expelled from your precious Aethyrguard you coward."

"That's enough Dad," Korvan ordered. He did not step back.

"You do not go near his door like this."

Korvan pulled his staff off his back and slammed it into the ground. A roar of Aethyr coursed through the alley, not a directed attack, just a display of strength.

"I could end you here. Oh and by the twin gods there is part of me that wants to lay into you the way you did to us when we were boys. To make you feel that fear I felt as a child. To make you feel helpless in the face of someone stronger. You wouldn't learn from it though, you'd just see it as having proved you right. That I'm a monster. That I'm just like you. Go home, wherever you call home now. I've got to visit my brother."

"You think caring makes you better than me?"

Varnrik tried to keep the heat in his voice but he'd already stepped a few steps away. Korvan saw it, the fear in his eyes.

"No dad, caring doesn't make me better. Acting on it does. You had every change to stop and love us. To help me care of him. To let me be a child. But you chose to drown yourself in a bottle. You chose to lose us. I don't break what I love to feel like I don't need it."

A few more steps, Varnrik was a shell of the monster Korvan had known. The man he was terrified of as a child was little more than a drunk now, more a danger to himself than anyone else.

"You're more me than her," Varnrik said.

Korvan raised his scarred palm. The old scar gleamed pale.

"While you slept, I kept a fire alive with this hand. I kept Caelen alive. I'm not you."

Korvan stepped up quick, borrowing speed from Vasha. He pressed coins into the man's pocket, enough Silverbrands for Vanrik to live happily.

"Use this coin, Dad. If you ever loved us, you'll get yourself better, and maybe just maybe, I'll give you another chance."

Spit hit the stones.

"Orders from a boy."

"I'm not a boy, I'm an Initiate of the Aethyrguard. I am bonded to three Veyrkin. I am an Aethyrbound Warrior. And I am your son. I am giving you a chance. Make different choices."

"I'll just come see him when you're gone."

Korvan whirled and came close enough that he felt Varnrik's mustache against his chin.

"If you touch him again Varnrik... No, you wouldn't. Not now. You're too afraid. You're just trying to goad me now."

Korvan turned and He walked.

"Goodbye, Dad," he whispered.

Behind him, glass shattered.

A scream split the air and fell into sobs.

He did not turn.

***

Madam Ren met him at the door.

"He's awake, he's better today too."

He walked ahead with a nod.

"Korvan," she called.

"He doesn't need savior all the time. Today, just be his brother."

She turned to her sweeping before he could respond. He glanced around and saw the large Calico resting in a basket in the windowsill. Green eyes met his own. They reminded him of Vasha.

His brother's room smelled of thyme and warm glass. Caelen sat propped on pillow.

"About time," he said.

Caelen looked up from the Clockwork machine he was tinkering with and went wide-eyed when he saw his brother's face.

"What happened."

"I saw him."

Caelen shook his head.

"What did you do?"

"Nothing. Everything. A lot of yelling."

"Good. He doesn't get that piece of you."

A cough climbed hard and deep.

Korvan steadied him the way he'd been shown. The brown bottle smelled of mint and bark, hold it over the mouth and count. Three in. Five out. Again. Again.

The spasm eased.

"Don't go to him alone again, take Sera, Thalen, Bren, anybody," Caelen said.

"I won't. He won't come near you again unless he upholds my requirement. Guess we'll see if he does."

"Tell me something that isn't him."

"Sera and I went on a date. I told her I loved her."

"About time, I like her Korvan," Caelen said.

His smile was small and real.

They let the room breathe.

"We're not broken, just bent," Caelen said.

"If I recall, bent is how you make wings," Korvan answered.

But Caelen had already drifted off to sleep. Korvan propped his feet up, resting them on the bed.

The sun had shifted, soft rays came in the window at odd angles. Caelen was building another small clockwork model. This one was much larger than the one before.

Caelen looked over at Korvan and grinned.

"You should see your face. I thought I slept a lot," He said through a cough.

"I'm ok. Don't start the worried face."

Korvan sat up, his muscles were stiff from the odd position of the chair, but he did feel better after the rest.

"Bren stepped away for a while. Said he needed time," Korvan said.

"Stepped away, you mean like Thalen, or?"

"Not like that no, he's pulled back from all of us. He's trying to face it all alone," Korvan said.

"Well, that should be your specialty than brother. From everything you've said about Bren, he's a good man. Keep trying, if anyone knows what he's feeling, it's you. How are you and Thalen now that he's back?"

Caelen stopped working, he grabbed a new book, his hands refusing to be idle. He started drawing something in it.

Korvan glanced up, trying to get a look. It was like their old glider, maybe, it didn't make much sense to him.

"Hey, no peaking. It isn't ready yet," Caelen said turning the book away.

"He's better, he helps me a lot, much more than I realized. I'm glad he's back."

"How about you and Sera, you love her huh?"

His tone sounded sweet, filled with happiness.

"She... is great. She sees so much, like someone gave her a way to look in my head. I'm doing better at letting her in, I'm trying to let all of them in."

"You? Letting someone in?" Caelen smiled.

"Miracles do happen."

The smile thinned. Korvan's own faded.

Caelen's eyes cooled.

"What did dad say that upset you so much?"

"That I used you to get in. That I keep you alive for your adoration and for applause of people seeing how good I am at protecting you. That I'm not any better than him."

He stopped before the next words could break him.

"Did you believe him?"

"No. Maybe. Some of it hurt. He knew what buttons to push."

"He always does, but Korvan, I know what you've given up for me. I've seen it for our entire lives, you're not perfect, you're stubborn, and reckless and gods are you hard-headed somedays. But you're my brother, you're a good man, and I wouldn't be here without you." Caelen reached for a tin under the blanket.

Korvan froze, his hands shook and his mouth had gone dry, his eyes flitted between the tin and Caelen's face. He had tears in his eyes.

"Like that time when we were Kids and you stole us some treats... I couldn't get them myself but..."

Two honey rolls lived inside, still warm.

"Eat."

They ate in silence. Sugar steadied them both.

Korvan admired Caelen. Despite everything he kept moving forward, each day, he did everything he could to get better. He was brilliant, Korvan didn't know how brilliant, but he was able to make Clockwork machines with little more than a manual and spare parts. That would get him into the best of apprenticeships. But what he admired most was that he always put on a brave face...

A brave face.

Madam Ren's words barged in, 'maybe today, just be his brother.'

Korvan took one last bite of the honey roll. It tasted just how they did when they were kids. A forbidden treat they couldn't afford.

He nodded to himself.

"Caelen. I've not been a good brother. Sure, I've taken care of you, but that's not the same. I don't want you to hide what you're feeling, not from me, never from me. I'm sorry you felt like you had to put on a mask from me so I wouldn't know how you felt. Whatever you want to tell me, I want to help you with it."

Korvan set his face and gave Caelen an earnest look. He grabbed his brother's cold hand and squeezed.

The brave façade cracked. Caelen began to tremble from something that wasn't the sickness. His inhales quickened and he slammed his eyes tight.

It didn't stop the fear.

"I'm so scared Kor," Caelen choked out. The words were thin and honest.

"I joke so it weighs less. I joke so I can keep going, so that it'll make it feel lighter. It doesn't. I don't want to be in these rooms anymore; I don't want potions and brews and everyone looking at me like I'm nothing more than death warmed over. I don't want to be hidden away from everything and kept put away... I don't want to die."

Korvan pulled him in.

Caelen broke.

"I'm so sorry Caelen... It's all right to be afraid. I am too. But someone reminded me that fear can't hurt us, not if we don't let it. I'm here, I'm not leaving you. I'm not letting go."

They held each other until the quiet turned gentle.

"You don't have to burn yourself to keep the fire lit anymore," Caelen murmured.

"Use the tongs sometimes."

Korvan sat back and looked at him.

"How do you know about that?" Korvan asked.

"I wasn't asleep. I pretended. I pretended to be a lot back then so you wouldn't know I saw you crying. I just wanted to make sure you wouldn't leave too. If I stayed awake... you stayed with me."

Caelen began to breath with a familiar rhythm.

Korvan set him back against the pillows and fixed the blankets around him.

"Of course you did. We're so similar, doing everything we could to keep the other safe or happy. Oh little hawk."

Korvan sat with him, holding his hand and listening to the calm breaths. He willed his Aethyr into Caelen, urging it to fix whatever was broken within him.

The sky darkened and began to grey again before Korvan left. He was spent.

Maybe it didn't do anything.

Maybe it would.

Sometimes the trying was the only thing left.

***

The Aethyrgate shimmered before them. Rune pylons braced the humming oval. Six Sentinels stood hard in ceremonial blue.

The Mid-Year Trial had returned.

Korvan stood at the platform's edge in light kit. Staff across his back. His Soulmarks swirled, filled with Aethyr.

Sera stood behind him, hands folded, Fennik at heel. She met his look.

"Step forward," the Arcanist called. "The Beyond awaits."

Initiates entered one by one. The rest of the two dozen of them that had made it through since the Harbor. Some had been removed by the edict, some had quit. Others were cut from lack of skill.

Korvan stepped. The Gate tugged his soul before his boot crossed. It felt like the lip of a current.

He passed through.

Silence on the far side.

A glade unfolded. Dew on wide leaves. A hush under green vaulting. The Beyond listened. Trees bent in reverent arcs. Light like a temple at dusk.

Sera came through. Then Bren. Then Ryn and Javek. None spoke. The rules were simple. Survive the Beyond. Find what calls to you. Return.

He was not here to bond again. He felt that truth.

But something waited farther in.

It felt like a question he had avoided.

It had begun to wake.

Chapter 24: The Mid-year Trial

The Veyrth'Kael had shifted.

What had been dream-forest and mist-ruin now held an edge, as if the land had grown teeth.

Korvan stood on a shale-colored path. Leaves shifted only when no one looked. The air just felt like pressure on his skin, and it was absent of any smell.

They'd walked for days without a map anyone trusted. Their faith placed squarely on Ryn and Javek. Land-marks changed color. Footprints erased themselves between steps.

Each time Sera closed her eyes, she pointed forward and said, "This way."

Bren went quiet and it was apparent something gnawed at him. His gait stiffened. Shoulders hunched. The hammer rode his back like extra weight; the shadow on him weighed more.

Ryn and Javek flanked, their falcons carving tight, uneasy circles far above.

Sera turned with a hand hovering above Fennik's ears.

Korvan's fingers opened and closed on the staff. He hadn't called the blade, but light moved under his skin as if listening.

The trail narrowed. Mirrored stones rose on both sides that reflected more than the enchanted forest around them, it reflected things within them.

In one: Korvan carrying Caelen through frost, feet bloodied, voice hoarse from prayers to gods he no longer kept.

In another: himself in the Trial ring, kneeling alone. No Veyrkin at his side.

The Beyond had mirrored before but this fidelity was something new.

Bren stopped at a stone and stared, jaw set. "It's not real."

Sera moved closer to Korvan.

"No," she whispered.

"But it is true."

He turned before the rock could offer him more.

"Come on, let's keep moving," Korvan said.

His voice came out rough. He didn't wait for reply.

Behind them, the stones shimmered once and turned blank.

Mist slid ankle-deep over the ground. Old statues leaned toward each other. They were faceless, eroded, half-buried with their arms outstretched.

At the far edge, where soil thinned and roots refused to go, stood a single hollow tree, split and blackened like a wound.

Bren took a step.

Korvan opened his mouth, but it went quiet.

A man stood beneath the tree. Older. Hardened. Cael'Lumar watch-leathers, dust-stained and faded.

His face hid in shadow.

Bren froze.

"...Garran?" Barely air.

The figure didn't move.

Sera didn't look up. She had knelt by Fennik, eyes on the moss.

"He died Bren, years ago now," she said, soft as rain.

Bren was halfway across when the figure turned.

Eyeless, just a glaze of wet black where a face should be.

It lunged.

Bren's hammer met the first blow and shuddered.

Something else moved, low, serpentine, rippling the mist. The statues groaned.

The wild Veyrkin came from the flank.

A Howler twisted too far, limbs at angles no body should manage. Eyes glittered with fractured gleam.

Bren's legs moved, he ran forward.

"Garran?"

The name cut his mouth.

The mist tightened. The hammer barely came up before it hit.

Claws raked his flank, four clean tracks ripping through leather, skipping ribs, opening the obliques. Bren's skin unzipped. The ground slammed his spine. Trees spun.

Light answered.

"Auryn's Edge," Korvan breathed, and the glaive flared into his hands. He cut a diagonal through the beast's chest; the wound hissed and smoked. The shriek was agonized.

Vasha dashed to the right, sliding past Korvan's hip. Hunger flickered through their bond as he sharpened with her.

Sera slid in on her knees. Hands firm at Bren's ribs. Fennik braced warm against him.

Bren stared at the sky.

Everything shook. Everything spun.

Korvan held the line. His glaive high and lashing out in protective strokes.

The beast circled once. Twice. Then vanished into the mist.

Bren pushed up slow, one hand to his side. Blood slicked his knuckles.

"He was right there," he rasped.

"I saw him. I felt him."

Sera didn't flinch.

"You did," she said, certain.

"But that wasn't him Bren, Garran died remember?" Her eyes held his.

Bren didn't answer.

His hand closed on moss and held.

A sound cracked inside him, too private for anyone else to hear.

They breathed. The breath after the spike. The kind that lets a body come back to itself.

Ryn and Javek appeared, their faces twisted between anger and relief.

Korvan lowered the staff, but didn't dismiss it yet.

Something watched.

The dragon stirred again, Korvan was certain now. An ancient pressure weighed on him.

A shiver went down his spine.

"We keep moving," he said, lower.

Bren nodded. Sera helped him stand. She bound the four tracks tight; red seeped through despite the wrap.

Moss thinned to scorched clay. Air grew thin. Ground split; stones rose like old ribs.

Behind, Bren lowered himself to a stone with careful hands. Fennik pressed warm to his thigh. Rok lingered, eyes troubled.

"Why'd it go for me?" Bren asked.

"Because you chased a shadow," Korvan said, flat.

"The Beyond doesn't forgive distractions, you know that."

Bren flinched. Fingers locked on his knee. He breathed until the flinch smoothed.

Ryn's voice came from the trees.

"Nothin' tracks right. Soot's elevation's off. She can't claw above the mist-line. She's all but blind."

Javek added, "Screech is seein' doubles. Images vanish when he fixes on 'em. Never seen him shake mid-flight. Somethin's messin' with things."

Korvan frowned. "You're Veilwardens, you have to be able to find the path."

Ryn stepped closer, voice dropping. "Can't say how far this mist goes. If it takes our Veyrkin, we're next."

Korvan didn't answer. The pressure in his chest deepened.

Sera knelt at the pool and set two fingers on the light.

It rippled like breath.

"This place is a test of belief," she murmured.

He felt it then, a subtle pull. The mist parted and revealed a grove of carved rings and etched runes. It was all clean lines and recognizable geometry.

A ritual site.

It should not exist here.

His breath locked.

"That's an Aethyrguard circle," he said.

Bren was already moving before the thought finished. Despite his wound, he went quick.

"I know the ritual," he said, voice steadier than he felt. "I want to do this right. I must know if I can."

"Bren, remember last time," Sera said.

He waved her away, Korvan couldn't help but notice that Bren's eyes settled on him.

Ryn cocked an eyebrow. "Don't see many volunteers for a binding. Not in this place. Feels like it's breathin' down our necks."

Javek nodded once. "Feels wrong and right both. Never seen anythin' like it."

Korvan stepped beside Bren.

"Then we follow the ritual," he said.

"We guide it. Together."

***

They all knew the rite. Five steps. Simple on parchment. Here though every step felt like a cliff. One misstep...

First: Invocation of the Fyrstrand.

Sera stood behind Bren and set her palm between his shoulders.

"Breathe," she whispered.

"You know the way."

Bren inhaled. His Aethyr answered. It was small, but honest and heavy.

Second: The Circle of Channeling.

Ryn scattered salt and runestones in swift arcs, words a rasp under breath. Javek worked with Sera to trace chalk glyphs over aethyr-ink.

Bren stood center. Boots rooted.

The ground had accepted something.

Third: The Sympathetic Mirror.

An obsidian disc in the center. Smooth, dark, pulsing faintly.

Bren stared.

Garran looked back. This time he didn't look like a faceless monster.

He was younger. A smile on his face, wholly unbroken.

"I see him," he whispered.

Korvan's hand settled on his shoulder.

"That's not him," Korvan said.

"It's you. Who you used to be. Who you're still allowed to be."

The obsidian shimmered.

Lightning chased the ring.

Fourth: The Anchor Mark.

The Howler slipped down the ridge.

Choosing.

Its wings crackled with static. The membranes hung between ribs of bone and silver thread. Talons sharpened like jagged stone. Only recognition in its eyes.

It stepped into the circle.

Bren didn't back away.

When claw met palm, he braced for pain.

The mark came like lightning.

A Soulmark burned across his collarbone. It was bolt-shaped, searing gold-blue. It bit deep, crawling across him as muscle twitched, then settled.

He didn't cry out.

He stood.

Ready, no longer afraid.

Fifth: The Binding Seal.

Korvan breathed the closing glyph. The light that rose didn't pour from the Veyrkin. It answered from within Bren, called by the circle, affirmed by the ground.

A second flare followed from Korvan, it was a golden light that flared around the fledgling bond.

Sera gasped. Ryn blinked hard. Javek swore soft and sincere.

Bren felt none of it.

The Howler vanished into his chest, As if a part of him had finally come home.

"I felt... something else," he murmured.

Sera nodded. "So did I."

The twins said, "Korvan, was that you?"

He shrugged, he'd only said the word of binding.

Fennik barked once, tail flicking. Rok grunted and pressed his weight to Bren's leg.

Sera wrapped him in a fierce hug.

"You did it," she whispered.

"You really did."

His breath broke, half laugh, half sob.

"Took me long enough."

Korvan clasped his shoulder.

"It was never about speed, I knew you could do it," He said.

Bren looked down.

The mark still glowed. It was warm.

"I thought I'd feel like someone else, I just feel whole," Bren said.

Ryn shot him a crooked grin. "Well, shit. Look at you. All bonded and shin-in'."

Javek bumped her with an elbow. "He earned it. Good on ya, Bren."

They stood there closer than before.

A quiet ring of light in the Beyond's cold shadow.

***

The pull found Korvan again.

He stepped away. No one stopped him. Sera met his gaze across the glade. Her look was soft, a question in her eyes. He shook his head.

She nodded and didn't follow.

He turned toward the stone arch at the clearing's edge. Glyphs pulsed faintly.

He stepped through.

The runes flared with welcome. Pale light traced each glyph in turn, striking an unknown cord.

Light folded inward.

One moment: Sera, Bren, Ryn, Javek, all shouting his name, boots pounding toward him.

The next: only silence.

The ground turned slick and black under his boots. Wet obsidian. No trees. No sky. Even his breath made no sound. He opened his mouth.

Silence.

He felt his pulse quicken, but he took several deep breaths like Cristos had taught. He had been here before in his dreams. This place wouldn't hurt him. His fear would only hurt him if he let it.

The dark moved.

Thought bled into air

His failures.

His fears.

His grief.

The silence listened.

Pressure gripped his ribs. Lungs locked. He staggered.

Couldn't speak.

Couldn't cast.

Couldn't flee.

Then the blows came. Old Wounds returning.

Caelen alone in a dim room, coughing blood into his hands. Reaching for someone who never came.

Sera turning after their kiss, unsure.

Thalen on Ashwing's back, wings beating him into the distance.

Bren hammering at dummies beneath twin moon, fading at the edges.

Davrin's Soulmark burned to ash. Another boy Korvan could not save.

The missive. Maedryn's eyes. The line he would not cross because it would make him a weapon, not a man.

And beneath all of it a single thought.

How many more will I fail?

You would carry the light, said the voice with no shape.

Yet you fear what it shows.

His knees hit stone. Only the weight of what he hadn't said to the ones he loved.

Thalen passed me. Sera believes in someone who doesn't exist. Caelen is slip-ping, and I grow stronger. Stranger. Other. What if power is all I have left to give? What if I am becoming the man I swore never to be?

His throat cracked.

No.

He steadied himself. He pushed with all his might against the darkness every fiber of him stretching out, grasping for anything to cling to.

He found it within.

He wasn't becoming Varnrik. He was breaking out of his shadow.

Brusk said he was good. Eris saw his potential. Madam Ren praised his sacrifices, Sera kissed him, Thalen came back. Caelen... Caelen loved him. Caelen saw all the sacrifices.

I am good. I've just been afraid of being happy.

"I didn't ask for this, but I will not be afraid anymore, I'll be better. Better for myself," he whispered into the dark.

No answer.

Silence echoed throughout the eternity of the realm he stood in.

Then. A single radiant thread.

It appeared before him, suspended in the void.

A simple light. Waiting.

He reached.

When you come to me again, you will name me. Or you will be lost to the darkness.

Pressure broke. The dark exhaled.

Sound returned.

The arch flared behind him.

He was still kneeling. Still shaking.

Still alone on the far side.

***

Korvan found them beneath a leaning pine, its trunk split and still steaming where lightning had bitten the bark.

Sera rose first. Relief stood her upright; scrutiny kept her steady. Her gaze measured his breath, the set of his shoulders, the pulse riding his Soulmarks.

Bren pushed to his feet slower, wincing, one hand braced on Rok's shoulder. He didn't speak. He didn't need to.

"You vanished," Sera said, quiet and sure. "The light swallowed you. We thought—"

"I was there, just somewhere you couldn't follow," Korvan answered, stepping through the last curl of mist.

They watched him like he might disappear again.

"I'm all right, No better than alright. I finally see how foolish I've been. I'm sorry I've been so closed off with all of you. You deserve better from me and from now on, I'm going to be better," he said.

Korvan felt warm, like some tension around his heart finally let go, an ache so old he forgot it was there. The sense of calm that washed over him made him smile and close his eyes.

"Korvan…"

Sera's voice wobbled.

A sharp crackle split the canopy.

A winged Howler cut low across the glade, static trailing off talons like fine wire. He banked once, a silver scythe.

Ryn's Shriekwing flared and complained. Javek whooped from below.

The creature moved more reptile than bird; the jaw ran long and jagged, built to crush, not carry. Lightning ran his wing-bones.

Not a Draconid like Ashwing. Older, stranger.

Korvan felt it, faint as memory: recognition riding the current.

"Stars above! He's a comet," Javek shouted.

"He near turned Soot into feathers," Ryn barked, half-laughing, half-terrified.

Bren didn't smile, but his chest lifted. His fingers settled over the new Soulmark at his collarbone.

"His name is Bolt," Bren said, voice tilted high.

Korvan nodded. "It fits."

Sera stepped closer.

"Where did you go?"

Korvan's eyes slid to the trees.

"There was a voice," He started.

Sera's breath caught.

"It showed me fears. Caelen alone. Thalen flying away. You turning from me. Bren left behind. Davrin. Maedryn. A reminder that I can't carry it all," Korvan said.

Bren folded his arms. "And you keep trying."

"Because I thought if I didn't, everything would fall," Korvan looked away.

Bren shrugged.

Korvan nodded once. "I must let go of the lie that it all rests on me. That I don't deserve to be happy. That I can let people in."

Sera's eyes misted and her hands went to her mouth.

"Letting go isn't failure," she said.

"It's making space. For what comes next."

He breathed, smaller. Quieter.

He stepped forward and pulled her into a hug.

"I'm ready."

Overhead, Bolt wheeled and screamed into the fog.

The path ahead shimmered.

They walked. Together.

***

A glade opened before them. Trees here were etched from with-in; bark shimmered, leaves shone like dew-spun glass.

Sera didn't stop.

Fennik paced her flank, the white sigils along his coat warming brighter with each stride.

The air vibrated like a song felt in the teeth, not the ear.

A spiral of stones rose from the moss. At its center, a pool reflected a sky no canopy should allow. Pale threads of light turned slow circles across the surface.

"Sera," Korvan said behind her, reverent without trying.

"I feel it," she whispered.

"Something here is mine."

The Beyond shifted.

Petals fell without wind. Where they touched, crystal flowers opened.

Bren let out a breath. "That's not normal."

"The Beyond is responding to Sera," Korvan murmured.

She stepped to the rim.

The water didn't mirror her. Her reflection stood upright in the pool, separate, composed. It lifted a hand and beckoned.

Fennik whined, soft and small.

"It's all right," she said.

She didn't touch the surface. She set her palm on stone.

The runes under her hand flared, gold veining outward in perfect threads.

Something moved in the trees.

It stepped into the glade without sound.

A Cervidae, but larger.

It came into the light.

They collectively inhaled. Javek gasped. All their eyes widened.

"Holy Fu...," Ryn's voice fell silent.

A Glacierhorn.

Its coat shifted silver, to emerald to sky-break blue. Antlers towered like crystalline spires, scattering rainbows in the light. A pair of glasslike wings unfurled and trembled as it caught the light. The eyes were colorless, but full of wonder.

Bren's voice went hoarse. "It's beautiful."

Sera turned toward it.

The creature tilted its head as it looked at her.

Then it sang. A clarion bell, one clean note that pierced like long-withheld grief.

She rose slowly. Hands trembled. Chest ached. Tears found their way.

"I see you," she said.

The Glacierhorn stepped closer.

Fennik went still.

They all forgot how to exhale.

Its wings unfurled. Light traveled its veins.

Sera reached.

Light answered from within.

Her Soulmark ignited; fully revealed. Gold bloomed along her forearm, threaded with mirrored loops and crystal veins.

Korvan stepped forward.

"Will you walk beside me, Glimmer?" Sera asked.

The creature did not vanish.

"I think it was always meant for me."

Korvan nodded. "So do I."

The seal didn't take.

Not yet.

Glimmer started to dim.

"I need the rite," she said, tears breaking again.

"Then we begin," Korvan said.

They moved as they had for Bren.

Bren scuffed the spiral. Korvan whispered light into the earth.

Sera stepped inside the ring. Glimmer waited. Fennik took his station behind her, tail still, head bowed.

"The bond needs three, a seeker, witness and the anchor." Korvan said.

He turned to Bren. "Seal it."

"Me, but I don't..."

"We trust you Bren, you've earned it."

Korvan looked at him, with all the sincerity he could force on his face.

Bren nodded. "All right. Let's do it right."

Sera lifted her voice.

"I do not bind by force. I call through the Aethyr. Will you walk with me, Glimmer?"

The Glacierhorn stepped once.

The glade pulsed with Aethyr.

The runes spiraled. Her Soulmark surged. Resonance rippled out.

Korvan didn't speak. But he felt it, the same as with Bren. His Fyrstrand unfurled invisible between them all. He looked down at his arm and saw it, parts of his own power tethered between Sera, Bren, and himself. Sera's was stronger, almost as strong as the Bonds with his Veyrkin. But then he noticed others, one like

Sera's, three, he recognized as his Veyrkin, and two more that had not fully connected.

Bren raised his hand and his voice rang true, "Myleir!"

The glade rang out. Light folded in toward Sera. Korvan felt another pulse and saw it this time, a flash of light, part of his power going along the bond to Sera. It... it sealed her bond.

Korvan's eyes went wide.

The light settled.

Into her chest. Into her soul.

The Glacierhorn bowed. Antlers kissed her brow.

When the light faded, Glimmer remained.

Sera's breath caught.

Bren whistled low.

"Never seen one like that."

Korvan went to Sera's side. "You did that."

"He chose me," she said.

"He saw you, exactly as you are." Korvan added.

The glade shimmered while the Beyond listened.

Korvan looked at her, really looked, and something behind his eyes let go.

"That was beautiful, and you are incredible." he said.

Color touched her cheeks; she didn't look away.

"Obsidian Tier," she said, palm on Glimmer's wing.

"He's a Wyrdkin Aspect. He doesn't follow the Disciplines; I can tell right away. He moves between them, amplifying them. I think he can draw through me and Fennik."

Glimmer tossed his head and chimed. It sounded like Joy.

"So... a pegasus cousin, but deer shaped?" Javek asked, squinting.

"Yes and no, Pegasi are built for war. Glimmer is... a guardian," Sera said, a faint smile rising.

Bren crouched at the edge of the clearing, fingers combing moss.

His voice changed. "Boot prints. Two sets. Fresh. Not ours."

Korvan joined him, a chill settling under the breastbone. "How, is that possible, other Initiates?"

"Maybe. But how did they get here?" Bren's hand slid to his hammer.

The scream cut the trees.

Human. Splintered by pain. It reached a fever pitch and fell silent.

Korvan ran.

Bren sprinted after; Sera kept pace. Overhead, Bolt and Glimmer worked the cloud-line with the Screech and Soot.

They crested the ridge and stopped.

A hollow glade lay below. Trees blackened at the roots ringed it like burned teeth. One Initiate stood rigid beside a broken Veyrkin it's limbs twisted and spent. At their feet lay another Initiate, sternum caved, steam lifting off a hole burned through rib and lung. Between them stood a Man.

He wore no visible symbols and Korvan couldn't see a Soulmark.

The man's leathers were worn to suede, unfamiliar sigils scorched and smudged along it. Magic clung to him like frostbite. No Soulmark glowed, but power did.

"Too late," the man said, calm as a lullaby.

He turned. His gaze gleamed with something fractured.

Bren stepped forward, voice flat. "Back away. Last warning."

He laughed once, tired.

"You think this is mercy? Look at you. Shackled and branded. You call that strength? It's a curse."

Korvan lifted his staff. "Give us your name."

"A forerunner," he said, soft and rotten.

"One who unlearned obedience. And you—"

His eyes fixed on Korvan.

"You're the Lightbearer. So, it is true. Even here, they whisper your name."

Korvan's gut went cold. The Aethyr snapped.

Power surged from the man. A wave of raw will.

The first blast hit Bren square on. He met it on the hammer-head; boots carved furrows. The second pulse took him off his feet with a sickening crunch as his armor split open. Bren was thrown into stone. Blood spattered moss around him.

"Aethyrwall!" Korvan barked.

Radiant force domed up. The third strike struck and fell harmless.

The rogue kept walking.

"Ah, so you do have some skill. Let's see it then."

He clawed the air. A jagged sigil flared. It streaked toward the standing Initiate who stood frozen in terror.

Javek moved.

Just speed and no plan.

The bolt hit him center chest.

His breastbone collapsed. His spine arched. He skidded across the ground like thrown lumber, rolled twice, and didn't rise.

"Javek!" Ryn's scream tore loose and kept tearing.

She bolted. Sera caught her wrist. "No."

The world narrowed. Ryn's voice kept breaking the space open.

The next strike came hotter.

Korvan answered on reflex, radiant force lancing to clip the rogue's balance by a heartbeat.

He heard nothing but Ryn's screams. He felt nothing but the clearing buckle.

The sky crackled above.

Raw Aethyr ripped into being. The ground blistered, bark curled, air warped.

Bolt dove.

Thunder cracked. The Howler took the spell head-on. It should have broken him. Instead, lightning coiled across wing-bones and sank like rain into sand. He shuddered and kept coming, charged alive.

Bren, pale and blood-slick, grinned through red.

"Bolt doesn't need to dodge that," he panted. "He's eating it."

The rogue faltered. A blink. Long enough.

Sera arrived radiant as a star, Glimmer at her side with crystalline wings wide. Spirals of runes flowered from her hands, mirror-fractals locking into a lattice. They bent the wild Aethyr to their will.

A bolt screamed toward them. Glimmer pulsed. The lattice turned it, snapping the spell into the tree line; rock detonated to gravel.

Another came, faster than before.

Sera lifted her palm. Soft light threaded her fingers. Glimmer amplified the motion; their magic wove together, not stacked.

The rogue gathered a knot of power, the earth around him buckled.

Korvan drew breath to cast...

Bren threw Bolt.

The Howler crashed into the knot and blew it in the rogue's face. The shock-wave flattened sound. The glade lurched. Vasha flashed from Korvan's shadow, shoulder-brushing his thigh.

Behind them, Ryn fell to her knees.

Javek's chest was a charred cavity, rib-edges glass-bright and cracking. The center burned through clean. His eyes stayed open.

Still blue.

Ryn sobbed and broke against him. The sound climbed out of some place words couldn't reach.

Not again... I won't let them get away with it again.

Korvan felt himself threaten to break, to give in to that fury boiling within, to let the predator out and hunt like Vasha.

But a golden thread hung in his memory. Chose him, or be lost to the darkness.

"Enough." Korvan's voice rang out as law.

"Radiant Binding,"

Golden threads knifed from the earth and lashed the rogue. He snarled and stripped one, but two held. Korvan stepped with Vasha's grace, reappearing behind him mid-cast.

"You serve a broken order and a lost cause, this doesn't make you worthy," the rogue spat.

"I don't care. I don't fight for them. I fight for what I love," Korvan said.

Solace rose from the mist, her feathers catching the light from Sera and her Veyrkin. Warmth flooded Korvan from his lungs to his bones.

"Beacon of Dawn." It rang as an edict.

Light burst to reveal and to sear. Shadow fled from the deepest corners. The rogue's shield spidered and shattered under the force.

"Gravitic Crush."

Weight fell. Soil split in rings. Ribs bowed. Air pressed from all sides. The man's sigils coughed and died to sparks. He fell to his hands and knees, as he was forced into the earth.

Judgment wore an Initiate's skin and he had an ocean at his call.

Breath returned to the glade in a ragged pull.

"It's over," Sera said, not lifting her eyes from Bren.

Ryn still wept, a raw sound without the shape of words. The cost always stayed.

The rogue trembled under the weight. Korvan kept it on him.

"Speak, make this mean something," Korvan said, stepping closer.

The man smiled, split-lip soft. "It already does. Just not to you."

"Give me your name"

"Not yours to take."

"What are you?"

"A shadow, we were the Aethyrguard once. Before it rotted," he said, eyes too sharp for broken.

"You killed an Initiate, you killed my friend, and you tried to kill more. You're a coward who attacked without warning," Korvan said.

"I stopped the shackling."

Korvan tipped his chin toward the sprawled Veyrkin.

"This?"

"A mercy, death is far kinder than debt," he whispered.

His right hand twitched. Thumb found the inside sleeve.

"Stop!" Bren barked.

The sigil flared.

Silver threads crawled his veins. Pupils vanished. Breath hitched and stilled.

He sagged, empty.

Ash curled from the mark and unraveled.

Korvan exhaled through his teeth, palm on Solace's neck, small circles without thought.

The silence deafened them all for a time.

They moved because there was nothing else to do.

Bren sat stripped to the waist while Sera rewrapped his ribs. Yellow-green bruises mapped his side. Breath came easier. Shadows lingered under his eyes. Fennik dozed against his hip.

Korvan set the staff and watched the dark. Solace hummed low. Brusk and Vasha ghosted the perimeter.

Ryn sat apart. Not far. Far enough.

Arms around her knees, hair curtaining her face. She hadn't spoken since the scream. Soot perched above—a black weight on a dead branch.

The rescued Initiate lay propped against a log. Breathing steady. Eyes too wide. A boy with a cracked bracer stared at his forearm. Where the Soulmark should have burned was a seared oval, edges dusted ash-gray. Something that was once sacred, now spoiled.

"You're safe now," Sera said, voice low.

"It's gone," he whispered.

"Your Fyrstrand isn't destroyed only wounded," Sera said.

"The connection's shallow. But give it time, you'll recover."

"What now?"

"Keep walking," Bren said, rough and certain.

"Stay alive. Remember you made it through what most don't." He shifted with a wince.

"You'll carry the scar. We all do."

Korvan nodded. "You can't give up, that's the most important part."

The boy didn't look lighter. He looked steadier.

Ryn didn't turn. But her hands stopped shaking.

***

Night fell hard.

Mist pooled at camp's edge like smoke without flame. The fresh Initiates slept with his head tilted forward, gone too deep for dreams.

Korvan kept watch. Solace coiled at his back, Vasha and Brusk watched the perimeter. Bren dozed near the coals, arms crossed, Bolt low-headed beside him.

Sera found Ryn at the tree line.

The girl hadn't moved. Javek's Shriekwing perched near, copper dulling, rune-light fading to a thin pulse. It hadn't made a sound since dusk.

Sera crouched and let the moment breathe.

"Ever seen one fade like this?" Ryn asked at last, voice brittle, not hollow.

"No," Sera said.

Ryn nodded once. "Figured."

Weight thickened the quiet.

"He weren't s'posed to die," Ryn said. "He was smart, and fast. Outtalked trouble before most could blink."

"He was funny, and always sweet to me," Sera added.

Ryn scrubbed at her face. Salt rimmed her eyes. "Maybe if I'd been closer. If I'd—"

"Ryn, no, none of us could've stopped that. We had no idea the rogue was that strong," Sera said, soft without bending.

"Don't matter now." Ryn's jaw locked.

"He's gone, an' I got a bird that won't sing and a heart that won't shut up."

The Shriekwing stirred. Feathers rustled. It lowered its head to Ryn's boot.

"You don't have to bury it yet," Sera said, a hand on Ryn's shoulder.

"Sometimes they hold on. Just long enough. To say goodbye."

Ryn's throat worked.

"I ain't got the words."

"You don't need them right now," Sera said. "Be here. That's enough."

The silence turned gentler. Memory slipped in where breath couldn't.

They ran the high fields of Feldmar again, dogs yapping, dust on tongues, Javek always two steps ahead yelling about sky beetles and treasure maps. Their mother's voice chased them out the door, all threat and laughter: If you break that fence I'll string your hides for shade!

"She's gonna murder us," Ryn had panted.

"Yeah," he'd grinned, mud-cheeked and bright, "but we'll die fast and free."

Back in the trees, the memory hurt. It steadied, too.

Ryn stroked Screech's dull plumage.

"He named him Screech, cuz the cries sounded like home. Momma screaming when we went places we weren't allowed."

She laughed once, crooked, then broke. "He always said we'd die old, fat, drunk on Midmonth wine. Stupid bastard. He always lied pretty."

Leaves whispered. Sera stayed. She didn't prune the grief.

She held the space as tight as she held her friend.

***

The Aethyrgate opened with a whisper.

Korvan stepped through first. Bren followed, carrying Javek. Sera came after, Glimmer and Fennik flanking her. The wounded Initiate stumbled in behind, pale and shaking.

Ryn last.

The Vault of Trials received them in clean silence. Lightstones hummed; anchored runes pulsed like order caged. Four Knights in obsidian tabards, two Champions, and Arcanist Hale stood waiting for them.

She didn't look up. "Report."

Korvan stepped forward. "Our group encountered a rogue within the Beyond. He killed one of us, before I stopped him."

"Explain," Hale said, gaze lifting and sharpening.

"A man, he had no Soulmark, no marks at all," Sera said, clipped.

"No Veyrkin?" Hale asked.

Korvan shook his head. "Him alone. He wielded the Aethyr like a cudgel, didn't work the Disciplines."

"A saboteur, rare, but not unheard of for the Beyond to send an echo," Hale murmured.

"That wasn't an echo," Bren said.

"He had a name. Conviction. He Killed himself before we dragged answers out of him."

A ripple passed the Knights. Barely there.

"Casualties?" Hale asked.

"I already said he killed one of our group. Two more dead, one human, one Veyrkin," Korvan's words were hot.

"Unfortunate but not disqualifying. Survival is sufficient," Hale said.

"You're fucking joking, that's the bar?" Bren snapped.

Silence erupted.

Hale didn't blink. "You are alive, Initiate Bren Halver. Iron-marked Howler bonded. Team defended, with only one lost. All in all a more than acceptable showing for your squad."

Bren turned, his eyes had grown wide and a crazed smile was on his face, "Acceptable. That's all you can say? Flame take the lot of you, my friend is dead, and you say it's acceptable."

He left.

A Knight shifted for pursuit. Hale stilled the movement with a hand.

Sera stepped into the quiet. "I bonded. Obsidian Tier. Wyrdkin Aspect. Glim-mer."

Heads turned.

"Confirm," Hale said.

Glimmer stepped out in mist-silent grace. Crystal hooves chimed. Antlers re-fracted halos across the vault. The wall glyphs flickered as he passed.

Hale shaped the verification sigil. Sera's Soulmark answered strong.

"Confirmed, Obsidian Prestige. Wyrdkin Aspect," Hale said.

Korvan heard a strange note in Hale's voice, something like longing.

Her gaze cut to Korvan. "Your squad keeps outpacing projections."

"Maybe the projections are obsolete," he said.

Hale didn't answer. "Escort the wounded. Tend to the body. Review to follow."

They moved.

Korvan watched the archway.

Bren was already gone. He looked longer at Ryn, she was stiff and looking at the spot Javek should've been.

The rescued Initiate bowed awkwardly to her and the rest of them. "Thank you. I thought we were dead."

Ryn didn't turn.

***

"Bren shouldn't be alone," Sera said.

"He's hurting worse than he admits."

"He won't talk yet, but I think he'll listen," Korvan said.

A figure stepped out of the shadows.

Eris.

Violet robes trimmed in iron-thread. Twin sigils sewn over her heart. Her eyes were sunken and rimmed in black.

"You're not dismissed," she said.

"We were going to Bren," Sera answered.

"He's safe," Eris said.

"The debrief is over," Korvan said.

"By order of the High Warden," Eris replied, "new bonds undergo Ritual Veri-ty. No exceptions."

Sera stiffened. "Arcanist Hale already—"

"That is for the records, what I do is truth," Eris cut in.

Korvan's voice dropped. "Now?"

"I must," Eris said. She didn't elaborate.

"What does it feel like?" Sera asked.

"Pain, pain for all involved," Eris said.

Korvan frowned. "For you?"

She didn't answer.

She led them through the winding underbelly of the Crown Keep, to a section they didn't recognize. It felt older than most of the keep, like the castle had been built around it.

"The chamber's ready," Eris said.

They turned down the side hall and entered a surprisingly small room.

Glyphs pulsed faint beneath stone scars. It was a ritual circle, but larger than any Korvan had ever seen.

Eris took her place. "When it begins, do not resist. Tell your Veyrkin, it will hurt."

Softer: "He reminds me of Kaelith, and Sera. I'm sorry."

Korvan stood at the perimeter and watched. Eris looked exhausted, she seemed utterly spent and about to fall.

Sera stepped to center. Glimmer hovered, wings pulsing in time with Sera's exhales.

Eris lifted her hands. A silver tether unspooled into the floor. Glyphs ignited in sequence.

Korvan tensed. He didn't move.

"By flame and form, by soul and strand," Eris invoked, "reveal the bond, or let it burn."

Light lifted. Sera gasped. Her Soulmark twisted against a foreign current. Glimmer shrieked, bucked, and nearly flew out of the circle.

"Stay," Eris said, voice tight with strain. Light bled from her cuffs as the ritual ate at her.

Sera planted her palm on Glimmer's flank. "I'm here."

The bond shuddered. Then it pulsed.

Mirrored light burst from Glimmer's core, wove through the glyphs, and stead-ied them. The ring didn't verify; it synchronized.

The bond held.

Eris dropped to one knee and caught herself.

Korvan went to her.

"Are you ok?"

"No," Eris said, sweat beaded on her forehead and her skin felt clammy.

Sera knelt beside Glimmer.

Eris nodded. "But now, no one can take him from you."

***

Night climbed the keep.

Korvan and Sera sat on a low bench beneath the stars. Marble tiles gleamed; the garden held its breath. Constellations wheeled like slow oaths.

Below, the Veyrkin played.

Fennik chased rune-light along the pool. Glimmer matched him, wings tucked, antlers scattering starlight. Brusk arrived and dipped a tusk into the water; Vasha leapt and scattered arcs.

Brusk nudged Fennik. Fennik trilled. Glimmer danced. Vasha boxed a drifting petal. Solace lifted her arms and spun a slow helix of light across the tiles.

"They're already in sync," Korvan said.

"Fennik's always been kind, but with Glimmer it feels easy, like he was always part of us," Sera answered.

"And you?" he asked.

"I thought I'd feel whole," she said. "I feel... relieved. Tired. A little terrified."

He brushed a strand from her cheek.

"Sounds like me," he said with a chuckle.

She leaned into his touch.

"You didn't have to stay and witness that," she whispered.

"Of course I did."

"Why?"

"I know how it feels to be alone with someone you trust and have them hurt you, Eris didn't want to, but she still hurt you. I didn't want you to be alone," he said.

She rested her head on his shoulder.

Below, the Veyrkin settled.

"They trust each other. I trust you Sera, I'm hoping you trust me too?" Korvan murmured.

Sera turned.

Her gaze was steady.

"Absolutely, I do. But it means more now because you asked," she said.

He saw her. Tension unspooled.

He leaned in. The kiss met hard. Heat and hunger. Ease and calm.

They stayed that way, wrapped in moonlight and each other.

Chapter 25: Knightmares

The bells rang at dawn. They weren't a sharp warning or a low toll of grief. They were a summons. Aethyr-forged bronze struck true; windows shivered; swifts burst from the upper towers.

The central spires of the Crown Keep swayed with quiet Aethyr. Veins of Aethyrglass took sunlight and spread it in rays. Banners drew breath on high balconies. Lantern halos braided into morning. Oil, salt, polished steel rode the air.

Korvan stood at the Heartspire's ceremonial platform in formal black stitched with silver. Starsteel pauldrons bit cold along his shoulders. Below, terraces filled in ring after ring. Elders in formal blue, merchants bright with dye, children lifted to see, Initiates shoulder to shoulder. The sound of the crowd rose and fell like surf. For one heartbeat, he felt small inside it.

He placed a breath like his lessons had taught him. The weight stayed. His chest moved anyway.

The Initiate tag at his breast was gone. On his right pauldron the bond-sigil burned fresh into starsteel. It should have anchored him. It didn't. Vasha watched at his left. Brusk held his right. Solace perched behind. The bonds pulsed low.

Cael'Lumar's inner court brimmed. Families. Scholars. Merchants, Nobles. Children on shoulders. Madam Ren stood with Caelen under a red awning. He had demanded to come. His smile was bright but thin.

Sera waited with the newly confirmed bondholders at the left. Robes immaculate, Fennik at her heel. To Korvan's right, Thalen stood in silver-chased pauldrons, a matched pair like Korvan's. Midnight lay like a poured shadow at his boot while Ashwing crouched beyond in patient stillness.

On the dais, High Warden Archion Dren lifted a hand. Silver hair bound tight. Robes austere. Twin glyphs of Flame and Stone glowed at his shoulders.

"Today," his voice carried.

"We recognize two who endured the Beyond and returned with power and fidelity. Their bonds hold; their names are written in flame. Though they have earned this early, this honor stands as proof of what the Aethyrguard may become."

Korvan heard the words and saw other things. Javek's still chest. Ryn's raw scream. Bren silent at the fire. Sera trembling under Eris's Ritual Verity and refusing to release.

But the one that haunted him was the rogue's eyes, bright with a surety of purpose.

"Step forward, Korvan Aric, son of Varnrik, bearer of bond threefold. Do you accept the mantle of Knight?"

Another breath was placed.

"I do."

"Thalen Ryst, Heir to House Ryst, legacy of the Aethyrguard and bearer of Wing and Shadow. Do you accept the mantle of Knight?"

Thalen's mouth edged toward a grin. "I do."

The brand kissed steel. When the light dulled, the etching remained.

"Rise, Knights of the Aethyrguard. Let your strength be a blade. Let your loyalty be a shield. For the Aethyrguard. For Cael'Lumar!"

Cheers surged. Bells answered. Banners climbed on the wind. Korvan didn't smile. He met the High Warden's gaze and found a look that weighed and measured. The speech felt like it had only just begun.

He left by the north colonnade. Oil and beaten steel hung in the Heartspire's tunnels. He rounded a curve and saw Sera in a spill of light, Fennik's runes throwing soft prisms across the wall. He lifted a hand.

"Knight."

Bren stepped into view and blocked the corridor.

The word landed heavy. Brusk shifted. Korvan quieted him with a palm.

Bren wore leathers and a careless cloak. The cut over his brow had yellowed. The new Soulmark at his collarbone glowed through torn wrappings like caged lightning.

"You went through with it," Bren said, voice scraped thin.

"I did. It was the right thing," Korvan said, straightening himself.

"Right," he said, a laugh that never cleared his teeth. "Do you really think they're right Korvan?"

"What are you saying?"

"People died. Javek. That rogue. Those kids in Feldmar, all those people," He tipped his chin toward the bells.

"We keep burying names. The tower keeps hiding them."

"That isn't on me."

"No." He stepped closer, voice low.

"But you don't stop them from rewarding you. Even if you failed to save people."

Korvan felt his gaze drop, his left hand clenched and he felt Vasha tense.

"That isn't fair Bren. You know I did everything I could. Javek, Davrin, they aren't my fault. I want to change the Aethyrguard. I want them to see we don't need the old rules."

Bren studied him. "Do you believe that? Or do you need it to be true so you can live with yourself?"

Korvan opened his mouth. No answer came.

Bren's eyes cooled. "Didn't think so."

He stepped aside.

"Go enjoy yourself, Knight," Bren spat it like a curse.

He vanished into dispersing robes and murmurs.

Korvan looked back to the light.

Sera was gone.

He drew a breath in, held it, let it go.

"Hold the line," he said under his breath.

***

The council chamber rose like a tall bowl. Sun fell through narrow slits; dust hung like quiet stars. Senior Aethyrguard formed a semicircle. Arcanists, Champions, a knot of Knights in obsidian. Two Champions flanked the dais.

Archion Dren didn't pace. He spoke like a man reading a ledger already proved.

"Effective immediately," he said, "the prohibition on unsanctioned bonding is rescinded."

Quills paused. Eyes narrowed a hair.

"This is no return to chaos. Each bond need not be tested nor each Soulmark inspected. Our art must grow with the threats we face. Flexibility is not surrender."

Archmage Maedryn lowered his quill. Eris stood to his right, hands clasped, face unreadable save for one tight muscle at her jaw.

Maedryn stepped forward. Copper thread at his cuffs held a coal-glow.

"High Warden, the decree you now rescind is barely thirty days old. Squads were dispersed. Some were cast out. Lives torn. Now we reverse. Should we not pause and ask why?"

Archion turned without heat. An old Soulmark glimmered faint at his collar. "The why is writ in the Aethyr. The Beyond has shifted. The Mid-Year trial has proven that we must adapt."

"And those cast out?" Maedryn asked. "Those who refused to bend? What becomes of them when rules change again?"

"They chose to leave, none were forced, no bonds were found that did not meet the rituals requirements," Archion said, softer, colder.

"The Aethyrguard moves forward. They chose to be left behind."

"You wanted this... you wanted to purge some of the order, to remove those you think too weak, or unwilling to serve," Maedryn pressed.

The room held its breath. The Aethyr seemed to take a pulse.

The High Warden turned and looked at the Archmage. He let himself smirk, The Archmage was no doubt the greatest threat to him in this room. In a straight fight Archion was not sure which of the two men would come out on top. No, if he were honest he knew Maedryn would, especially with Eris in the room. Archion and Maedryn had competed for years, rising to the pinnacle of their order. He knew Maedryn as much as Maedryn knew him.

"If weakness existed within our order, it was allowed in by those who offered positions. Our assessments need updated, requirements stiffened. If the weak were purged, are we not stronger for it? I offer direction, not compromise," Archion said.

Check, old friend.

He saw a glare flash across Maedryn's eyes. The Archmage knew he'd overextended and set himself up for the riposte. The Quiet Flame may have been the key dignitary of their order, but Archion was born to nobility.

Eris didn't move. Kaelith's shadow bent across the far wall. She looked to Maedryn. If Archion and Maedryn came to blows, no one would win.

Archion lifted a hand.

A Warden stepped forward with a scroll.

"Send the missive. The law is changed. Those who resist will answer to me."

No one asked what answering meant.

Ink settled.

New law formed.

***

Ashwing carved the blue sky. Each downstroke rolled muscle and pushed them along. His talons curved off the mid-wing joint in sickles. The barbed tail flexed once.

Thalen flew without fear. The air was cool along his cheek. Cael'Lumar unfurled beneath. Lines of ringed roofs, aqueducts the city's ribs, banners still trembling from the bells.

Knight. He'd done it. He'd really done it.

Movement below caught his eye: Korvan on a high walk above the second ring. Polished pauldrons. Cloak thrown back, standing looking out at the sea.

Ashwing spiraled and landed hard, talons gripped stone. Wings folded with a sound like sailcloth snapping.

"You looked like you were enjoying it," Korvan said.

"I was, don't love landing, but it's getting better," Thalen admitted, brushing grit from his sleeve.

"You always get better."

They stood with the city breathing under them.

"Congratulations," Thalen said at last.

Korvan watched him, wary.

"I mean it," Thalen added.

"Look I know, I hated you. Not for who you were. For who I wanted you to be. I wanted to be the best, and you threatened that. Then you started to leave me behind, like Lareth did," He looked away.

Korvan's mouth tightened.

"I was so jealous of you. You never had to prove you belonged. Everyone assumed it. I clawed for that. Then you left too."

Thalen huffed.

"I know. I'm sorry Korvan, I shouldn't have left. I got Ashwing out of it, but... leaving was the wrong choice. Will you forgive me?"

He watched Korvan's face work, the way it did when he tried to solve any problem, looking for a way that he could hold it all and leave none of the burden on anyone else.

What he did next made Thalen flinch.

He stepped forward and pulled him into a hug. His arms were strong, but comfortable. Thalen let out a gasp.

"Korvan..."

"I know Thalen. I think I've known for a long time. The jealous I felt was me not being sure if I wanted to be you... or be with you."

Thalen's pulse dropped, and his hands turned to stone.

"I'm working on being better, working to let myself be happy. I don't want to promise you something I can't keep," Korvan reached out his hand, an offering.

Thalen's own shook, was this really happening?

He took it.

Korvan's hand was somehow softer than he expected, but it was strong. A heat came from him that could only be the pool of Aethyr inside him.

Korvan continued.

"When we were in the trial, I saw tethers on myself. The smallest went to Bren, then Sera, my Veyrkin, Caelen and then two I didn't quite recognize, that were smaller than the others. Then when we were on the podium together, I felt it. I couldn't see it, but I didn't need to. It's you, and it bloomed to life as full as any of them. Something in me calls for you, and I know without a doubt that I want you in my life. I can't promise you I'll be perfect, or even be good at this. And well, I need to talk to Sera, just to make sure she's ok with it too."

Thalen laughed. A deep belly laugh that bounced off the walls and fell down the parapets.

"Of course you figured it out. You've seen me clearer than the others have."

Thalen shook his head, it felt like relief.

"If I'm given enough time, I usually figure things out," Korvan said with a grin.

"So, what now?" Thalen asked.

He looked down and realized they were still holding each other's hands.

"I talk to Sera, and make sure she's ok. Knowing her she's been waiting for us to figure it out. Then..." Korvan met his gaze, something lingered in his eyes Thalen didn't recognize.

"We figure it out, together."

Thalen felt his chest warm, and his heart sped up. His cheeks burned. He hadn't realized he'd been smiling.

"That, is a good plan," Thalen said.

"See, I knew you had it in you."

He said it with a mocking tone.

Korvan gave him a playful shove.

They stood together looking out over Cael'Lumar.

The city they were sworn to defend.

As Knights.

***

The day burned down. The city softened.

Sera climbed to the Garden Archives and took the high veranda. She folded her legs and let breath settle lower. Glimmer dozed near, crystalline wings tucked. Fennik laid his nose to her ankle. Gulls complained over the harbor. Bells flattened with distance.

Ceremony meant little to her. Titles even less. Let Korvan and Thalen the brand like an old scar. She had Glimmer and Fennik and a rhythm in her bones she was just learning.

Something else stirred inside her.

Bren's voice clung. The line of his mouth when he stepped in. The way his body fell. His flinch from her hands and the shrug that pretended it was nothing.

"Why couldn't I reach him?" she asked the air.

Glimmer stirred; antlers chimed against vine. Warmth rose through the bond, crystalline and patient.

"I know," she said, palm to his neck. "We did what we could. It still feels small."

She was built for sitting with pain until it softened. Holding fear without forcing it to change. Presence had always been her gift.

The horizon blurred where sea met sky. Somewhere out there, something was coming undone. Thalen rising. Korvan changing. Bren drifting.

She bowed her head to her knees and let the ache breathe.

Fennik edged close, a warm crescent at her hip. Glimmer leaned until antlers shadowed her shoulder.

"I'm not ready," she whispered.

The Aethyr stirred anyway.

***

Night had fallen and the city made small noises. Chain settling on a gate, a wheel's soft tick, laughter that didn't ask permission.

Korvan left the parapet. Down the back stairs, through a service hall, into a narrow gallery where the Heartspire opened on the inner gardens.

Eris waited. Kaelith's reflection rippled in the black pool like a fallen star learning to breathe.

"You were hard to find," she said.

"I wasn't hiding."

"You were, but none of us blame you. Congratulations are in order. You made a choice. One I imagine that you still struggle with."

There was no judgment in her voice. She glanced once at the steel pauldron and its clean bond-sigil.

"Bren thinks I'm just doing it for the fame and glory, but I'm trying to change things."

"He's grieving, his emotions are ruling him right now. But he isn't entirely wrong. It's ok to want some recognition for your efforts Korvan" she said.

He nodded, he knew that as much as he said his intentions were pure, he couldn't deny the feeling of achievement he felt.

"Ryn won't meet my eyes," He said.

"She may in time, either way, you don't get to ask that of her."

She nodded toward his shoulder.

"That Rank can open doors and shut others. Learn which you need, and which ones you must kick down."

She gave him a hard look.

He chuckled, Eris always was teaching him something.

"I don't know if I can."

"You can. The choice is if you will."

He waited.

"You'll receive formal orders soon. But the abridged version is you have field autonomy," she said.

"Outside the rings you choose your duties and go where you feel needed most. You'll be assigned initiates and a team if you wish. Your seal gets you through warded districts within the city. You can also requisition things through the Quartermaster."

She let a breath settle before she continued.

"It also chains you to rotation. Two nights each fortnight on Inner Ward watch. One dawn patrol along the Third and Fourth Rings. If there is a Breach, you are to respond. Escort detail. You also get to help train the newest Initiates. I can't wait to see that."

She gave him a wicked smile. Korvan cocked his head.

Is she teasing me? He thought.

"And missions?"

"Through me for now, I am still your overseer. I won't waste you on pageantry if I can help it."

He nodded, it was surprisingly... simple?

"What else?"

"Keep training," she said quickly.

"Knights who ease off turn lose all their edge. Spar when no one asks. Drill with Thalen; you outstrip him in the Disciplines, he still is your better with a blade. I'll work with you as often as I can, but as a Knight there are far more eyes watching and, pressures from others that I will not intervene as much."

Wind moved across the pool; moonlight broke through the clouds.

"You'll be asked for favors," Eris went on.

"Say no when you must. Say not yet when a flat no costs the wrong thing. You'll be invited to tables and told your presence proves inclusion. It proves utility. With High Warden Dren, bring a knife and a clear head."

"You really don't him do you," he said.

"I heard what he didn't say. This was a play for control. Don't mistake it for wisdom," Her gaze held his.

"Thank you, Eris. This feels early. But I couldn't have done it without you."

"It is early," she said. "You also earned it."

Something gentled in her tone.

"You carried more than your share, fought an enemy you weren't prepared for, and did your best to save yourself and your friends. I am proud of you."

The words landed hard. His smile came unguarded.

"I don't know what to say."

"You say, 'Thank you, Battlemage.'"

He chuckled, "Thank you, Battlemage."

"Go now. Enjoy yourself."

He nodded.

"Eris," he said.

"Yes."

"What if I fail?"

"You will. We all fail. Getting up and trying again, the learning from it? That is what defines us," she said.

He stood with that, then one moment more.

"That sounds like Cristos."

"My husband is an exceedingly wise man," she said.

Korvan felt his eyes go wide and his jaw gaped.

"Go. Go before someone asks you to perform," she added, softer.

He went.

***

Bren stood in a practice yard that shouldn't see use after curfew and used it anyway. He rolled his shoulder, set his feet, swung. Hammer down. Up. Down. The wrap at his ribs held. The mark at his collarbone glowed, cooled, glowed.

Bolt hunted the thermals above, a knife of storm slipping between tower shadows. He dove hard and never touched earth, yet the jolt landed in Bren's bones.

He wasn't angry. Anger would have been simple. He felt raw.

"You're not alone," Sera had said.

He lifted the hammer again.

"I know," he said into the dark.

"I know."

A laugh cut itself off with a hand. Someone kissed someone and decided to survive another day. Someone cried into a sleeve and refused to name it.

Bren swung until his arms failed. He held the hammer upright in both hands like a mast and waited for the deck to steady.

The bells had rung for someone else. They always rang for someone else.

***

In the Garden Archives, Sera fell asleep sitting up between Fennik and Glimmer, breath light and even. Glimmer watched while pretending not to. Fennik dreamed fox dreams, paws twitching, a small whuff.

On the high walk, Thalen leaned against Ashwing's warm chest and watched the last red slip off the clouds. Midnight pressed to his shin until he scratched the exact spot behind her ear that she preferred.

In the narrow gallery, Eris looked down at her hands until they stopped shaking. Kaelith's reflected fire went out when a gust wrinkled the pool. Iron and the scent of kelp rode the wind.

***

Korvan crossed the innermost court with his mantle in hand and his staff at his back.

He went to Madam Ren's. She was awake because she was always awake when her people needed someone to be. She answered at the second knock.

"He's sleeping," she whispered.

"He made the whole ceremony. The fit came near the stairs on our way home."

Korvan's throat closed. He nodded.

"Go on," she said.

He did as told.

Caelen slept with a hand on brass, crystal, and cog wheels. It was the small clockwork Veyrkin he'd been building, as if he had fallen mid-tinker.

Korvan leaned his head to cool stone and let his eyes burn.

Under the skin of the city, the Aethyr moved like tide. It didn't care for mantles or missives. It cared for truth brought to it.

He could live with that.

He would live for them.

Chapter 26: Warden's Price

They buried Javek in the Sealed Hall of Lost Bonds. Doors that never opened, opened for the living Initiates. But always welcomed the dead.

The pyre was built high, duskwood ribs laced with river-sedge and starbloom. Eris set the ward herself, fingers sure, voice low. It was a ritual that settled over the body in a thin pearl film. Clean oil and wild jasmine lifted with the spell.

Javek lay in the center, shrouded in white. A ceremonial sword at his chest. His Soulmark faint along the collarbone, pale ink at the brink of fire.

Initiates stood in ranks. Leather creaked. A cough died. These stones remembered other flames.

Korvan stood at the front. Thalen on his right, Sera on his left. Staff grounded in front of him. Brusk waited farther in the back beside the Initiate they had saved, Nivran.

His face was ashen, jaw locked tight. He leaned toward the boar for comfort.

Ryn stood closest to the pyre. She did not move.

Solid black dress. Bare feet. She offered no words, no tears came.

Bren stood beside her, thumb worrying a black thread at his wrist until the skin went pink.

Eris began. Gravel and grace.

"Javek Dacre of Riverpost. Initiate of the Aethyrguard. He was Loyal. Brave. He gave everything for one he didn't know. Let The Dawnmother welcome him and let The Keeper of Threads remember him. Always."

Silence took her next breath.

Thalen stepped in. "He was hopeless at drill counts. Never could remember the third beat. But he smiled, he always smiled. He was my friend."

Sera said, "He talked to my Veyrkin like old friends. Said the Aethyr sang in his dreams. He was my friend," Her voice thinned at the end.

Bren didn't look up. "He blocked a blow that what would have cut through any of us. Sometimes that's the work. He knew it. He did it. He was my friend."

Korvan took a step. "I didn't know him as well as I should have. That's on me. I watched him fight. I watched him learn, and I was always grateful to have him close."

He looked up at the ranks. "We carry him. All of us. And we make sure the next ones don't fall for nothing. He was my friend."

Ryn opened her hand. A carved feather lay in her palm, bone white, perfect. She knelt and set it on duskwood like setting a word you refuse to speak.

"Screech," she said, vowels pulled toward the floor. "That's his name. Bird-brained, loud as a kettle. Javek always said the noise kept the dark from feeling lonely. We were twins, I'm a whole minute older, but he was always in the lead, rushin' on ahead. He died like he lived. Rushin' ahead and being brave. He was my brother, but he was also my friend."

Eris flinched once. Small. Late.

"By the Flame's mercy, with the Twin Moons Protection. Let Javek Dacre rest, and know peace."

Korvan caught it.

Eris nodded toward the gathered audience.

Six torches lowered as fire kissed kindling and took. The flames rose Blue and Gold, the colors of Light and Memory, of Atheris and Kael'Thir.

Duskwood sweetened the air. Heat rolled like a gentle hand. The Hall listened.

Cristos stood in back, arms folded, head bowed. Lira of Squad Five, storm-thread braided in her hair, kept her eyes on flame.

Becca of Squad nine watched Ryn and didn't blink. Drenik and Soel of Squad Two held each other's shoulders.

No one spoke.

They all witnessed.

Fire fell to ember. Ember to ash. Boots blackened. Silence stayed heavy.

Ryn's tears could be heard like raindrops.

The gathered left soot behind and took the weight with them.

***

The debrief chamber was smaller than a courtroom and more dangerous. Oval. Windowless. Vellum scrolls lined the walls. Shelves held crystal tubes that glowed. Scrolls floated behind glass.

A scholar's crucible.

At its center: a blackglass half-moon table and one chair that made the spine sit straight.

Arcanist Kane Vor waited with stillness balanced like a scalpel. Gray on gray with seams of gold thread. An inkless quill hovered at his shoulder.

Korvan stepped inside.

"You may sit," Kane said. "This is not an interrogation."

It didn't comfort him. He sat. The chair made his back itch.

"You have returned from a second sanctioned Trial," Kane said. "Three Veyrkin, Reservoir, Bulwark, Howler, none sealed under Rite."

Korvan didn't answer, none of it was a question.

"No one in your squad carries that spread, none even in your year. You did not follow protocol."

The quill began to write on air.

"Relax," Kane murmured.

"I'm not here to revoke anything. I'm here to understand."

Korvan finally cracked, "Understand what."

"You."

Quill scratch on parchment and then back to hovering.

"I have questions, you will answer truthfully. I will know otherwise." He tapped the side of his head.

Korvan knew some people alleged that they could use Lightweaving to detect lies. He'd never seen anyone do it but Sera and that was because of Fennik, not her. Either way, it made his skin crawl.

"Have you experienced blackouts since the trial?"

"Yes."

"Voices?"

"Yes"

"More than one?"

"No. Only one."

A small nod. A box checked.

"Have you been compelled by this voice to do things, have you found yourself unable to resist it?"

"Not compelled. Called."

Several scratches.

"Continue," Kane said.

"I don't know what you want to know."

Kane peered over the top of his eyeglasses.

"Have you had Dreams?"

"Yes."

"About what?"

"That's for me to know. My dreams don't matter to the Aethyr-guard."

"That is false. Dream-resonance with a Veyrkin indicates a tether," Kane said, patient as a blade.

"It means there is yet another bond outside of the ritual."

Korvan said nothing.

"You told no one," He went on.

"The High Warden suspects only that something watches you. Your Fyrstrand shows as much."

Korvan's hands closed slow on his knees.

"And you didn't name it? Didn't bond with it?"

"It didn't give a name."

"That is uncommon," Kane said, and wrote that down.

"Now comes the part you won't enjoy. You are to be watched Knight Aric. We seek to understand how it is that you are able to bond in a way that defies the logic our order has known true for generations."

He shook his head, they'd all warned him. He was being pulled into the games whether he liked it or not.

"By who."

"Battlemage Eris Vale."

His breath ran out of him, his leg started to jump under his hand and he rolled his shoulders.

"She is not tasked to leash, She is merely to record and report on your... unique ability," Kane said.

Kane rose and collected vials from the walls. The quill scratched rapidly behind him.

"You are not prey Knight Aric. I also do not believe you are not a fool. You carry more power than is good for you and you know it. We know the Battlemage tells you more than she should. Regardless, you are an event. Events are measured and logged. Do not mistake your gifts for immunity to authority."

The door opened with a wave of the Arcanist's hand.

"Dismissed."

The upper tier held more air than people. Amber bars of light crossed stone. Korvan walked toward the mess hall on habit; steam and quiet argued there and he could sit between them.

Eris sat at the far end, her bowl smelled of mint and bone broth. A kitchen boy clattered in back. Two trays cooled, abandoned by their owners.

She didn't look up when he sat.

"You know," he said.

"I have known for a few days," she said.

"Is this what you were trying to protect me from?"

She met his eyes, and nodded.

"Yes. It seems that I failed."

A pot clanged against metal in the background.

"They think I'm dangerous."

"You are," she said, simple as fact. "They don't fear you now so much as what you could become. Three bonds. Power deep in your marrow. Left to drift?"

A small tilt of her head.

"You are not the first to bond so quickly, they haven't forgotten what happens when people like that lose control."

He looked at his hands. New scars over his knuckle. A pale crescent near the base of his fingers, an old burn that refused to quit.

"They aren't wrong. I know I'm dangerous, but I'll keep using it to help people. Just keep doing that work."

"That, is very wise."

"I've had good teachers," He said.

"There's more, I should've told you before," Korvan added.

Now she looked up. Full attention on him.

"In the Beyond during my first Trial I met something," he said and dropped his voice.

"You mentioned, some time back. Our first session after you bonded Solace."

"I didn't tell you all of it."

She gave him a curious look.

"It's a Veyrkin Eris. It's so strong. Stronger than anything I've ever felt."

She exhaled. "I see."

"You believe me?"

"It isn't about belief," she said. "But yes, I believe you."

She leaned back. Porcelain clicked.

"I'll match your honesty. Kaelith is Starlit Prestige. She is also not bound by the ritual's of the Aethyrguard. She came in storm and fire after a Breach nearly wiped by company. She is Stronger than most would believe too. Far more than I've shown."

Korvan blinked.

"You are the Gilded Knight, we all know you're powerful. You're saying there's more to her strength?"

"Power isn't only for showing, it is for choosing when to act."

"I know what it is to carry what strength the guard cannot explain," she said. "To be watched under the pretense of protection while people prepare to contain you. I am dangerous too."

She leaned in, drawing him close.

"No manual will teach you this. Power is a tool, it is used for change and when applied in the right ways it can be a blessing. But Authority? Authority is what makes the changes last. One requires you to play the game, one does not. I am Powerful. I am one of the strongest of the Aethyrguard. But I do not have the Authority to bring the change I should. I made my own choices. Sooner than you'd imagine I think you will have to decide for yourself the path you'll take."

He sat with it. He felt a heat in his chest, but cold lingered under his tongue.

"I want to be a good brother. A good friend. I want this city kinder for everyone."

"Then stay true to yourself. Do your part and I will do mine."

She stood and gathered her tray and dropped it for the wash.

She walked toward the door but stopped.

"Find me when the Dragon speaks again."

He didn't breathe for a heartbeat.

He hadn't said dragon.

Eris didn't look back.

"You aren't the only one with secrets, and I'm a very good listener," she said.

The door shut.

Korvan looked at his hands again.

The pale scar stood out against his tanned skin.

***

Clouds parted in slow whorls. The wind had a hint of smoke and the ever-present salt of seawater. Eris rode Kaelith; the Pegasus's silver-flame mane streamed.

Airships drifted beneath them as they were loaded for trade to distant lands. Eris always thought they were marvelous inventions. They had towers of aethyrsteel and woven crystal, chained by light to ringed platforms. Kaelith slid between them, folding a wing to knife a narrow seam of sky.

You are quiet, Kaelith said.

"The quiet helps me think," Eris said.

You are brooding again.

"No, I am planning."

There is no distance between brooding and planning for you.

Eris watched gulls shear a high current and vanish behind a trade zeppelin.

"I spoke with Korvan," she said. "He told me about the Dragon."

The word rang the air like a soft chime.

Kaelith didn't answer at once.

So a Dragon stirs.

"You knew," it wasn't an accusation.

I suspected. The Aethyr bends differently when one of his kind wakes. They carry the weight of first stars. A pause. *Did he give a name?*

Eris shook her head.

"No. He doesn't know it yet. Is it truly one of the first Veyrkin?"

Kaelith tilted into a higher stream, hooves skimming clouds.

The echo around him is immense, even without a bond. But I doubt he is that old, even the most powerful of the Veyrkin are not timeless. No, the Dragons, they are simply greater than most.

"Greater than you?" Eris asked.

She ran her palm, smoothing the warm line between Kaelith's withers.

Few are.

"The Guard won't understand."

They have long forgotten older ways.

They climbed, threading the upper towers. Below, Cael'Lumar's rings shimmered.

"I told him what I had to," Eris said.

You are protecting him.

"I'm preparing him."

For you, those are the same. I have known you for my entire life. It is unlike you to lie, even by omission. Why keep the full truth from him?

Eris's jaw tightened. She shifted on Kaelith's shoulders.

"Because admitting where I failed, I think it would break something in me."

Maybe it would finally let it heal.

They rode the silence and took in the views.

To the east, the endless sea. The west held different problems.

After a time, Kaelith angled down a rising current.

Do you believe others will turn? That they'll leave the order?

"Some already have. Others are waiting for an excuse," Eris said.

What about you?

"I'll stand with him," she said. "As long as he remembers who he is. If he forgets…"

Then I will stand with you.

They circled once more above the rings. Midday slid across gem-lit streets, casting long, fractured shadows.

"He isn't like the others," Eris whispered.

No. And neither are you.

***

The missive burned a hole in his pocket.

Bren sat beneath the weathered arch by the eastern barracks, where the cliff broke into open sea. Only things here were wind and salt and the hard truths he carried.

Prohibition on unsanctioned bonds: rescinded.

He read it again.

And again.

Dren's language was clean and measured. The meaning twisted.

Others in his year were already gone. Two left in the night without goodbyes. He didn't blame them. Not after the Beyond. Not after Javek. Not after watching trust unravel like wet thread.

The Aethyrguard frayed around them.

Bren leaned forward, elbows on knees, watching mist roll the lower cliffs.

He remembered Javek's laugh. Ryn's quiet. The boy wounded in the Beyond with the seared Soulmark asking if he'd ever be chosen again.

He remembered Korvan at the pyre.

'We carry him forward.'

Bren's throat tightened.

He understood what Korvan was trying to do. Fix it. Change it. Build something from broken pieces.

He was scared. Scared Korvan would lose himself. Scared Sera would shatter if the pull went wrong. Scared Thalen would drift away. Scared Eris would have to choose. Scared he would be left holding pieces when it fell apart.

He still couldn't walk.

The Guard had taken enough. Javek. Lareth. His faith. His clarity.

If he left now, it would win.

Bren stood. Wind snapped his mantle.

The sun pushed long amber rays across the sea.

He touched the black thread on his tunic; it was still knotted.

"I see what you're trying to build, Korvan. I just hope you can hold long enough," he said.

He turned toward the rising city.

He didn't tear the missive.

He folded it. Tucked it in his coat and started walking.

***

Far out in the sea, a dark line split the horizon.

A voice hung in the air.

Clouds thickened with slow intent.

Lightning flashed.

Thunder cracked.

A storm was coming.

Chapter 27: Buried Tethers

The assignment arrived without ceremony. Sealed orders from the Archmage's second scribe, a curt nod from the quartermaster. Grellfen's Gate had called for aid: "Aethyrgate breach response, low urgency," the script said.

Korvan did not trust it. None of them did. They rode at first light. Korvan, Sera, Thalen, Bren.

Ryn could not be found.

Two Knights, two Initiates a year in. More than enough for small breach.

The wind shifted like a restless animal. The road cinched as it climbed, threading brittle woods and old stone. Cliffs bracketed the path; wind poured down their throats. Hollow watch posts leaned along the ridge.

Late on the third day, the fortress rose.

Grellfen's Gate loomed with weather stained roofs. Pride dulled by stormy years. Corrosion veined the masonry, glassy striations in the stone.

Korvan rode point on Vasha. His cloak snapped in the cold. Sera paced on Glimmer, the crystalline cervid stepping with precise grace. Thalen circled on Ashwing, a clean arc through thinning cloud. Bren took the rear on a Guard mount, hammer high, shoulders tight. Rok loped at his knee with stone-plated ease.

The road stayed quiet.

Too quiet.

No townsfolk at the gate. One Guard waited wearing half-plate, his face pale. His Soulmark was cracked and bandaged. Overdraw had nearly broken him.

"We sent work a week ago, didn't think help would come so fast," he said.

"We're here, show us this Breach," Korvan said.

Inside, the town breathed silence. Shuttered windows. Barred doors. No wind through the alleys. Children watched with eyes too old.

At plaza-center, light twisted in strange angles.

A pane of Aethyrglass, the size of a ship's hull, had been set into the ground like a blade. It gleamed at impossible angles.

"Grellfen's Gate," the guard said, gesturing to the mirror, "The reason you're here."

"What's been happening? They said there's a Breach?" Thalen asked.

"Breach? No Knight, no breach. But odd dreams, and stranger happenings."

Korvan looked at all of them, eyebrows shot up.

A scream cut the square.

A pageboy stumbled from the side street and raked his cheeks bloody.

"They're dead. They're all dead!"

He dropped to his knees.

Korvan moved. Sera slid with him. Fennik's runes flared under her hands.

Bren stepped up, hammer raised—

and froze.

The beast fractured out of air, all wrong angles, and twisted joints, it dripped Aethyrblight as it moved. It burst from the mirror and coagulated into a wolf-shape with three hinged jaws, eyes shedding hollow light.

"Solace."

The Reservoir tore past Korvan, feathers flaring.

"Aethyrwall." Korvan's staff bit stone. A dome snapped up around the boy and Sera a heartbeat before the thing hit.

Two more wolf-like creatures appeared.

Bren surged.

Too late.

A hooked foreclaw raked Korvan's forearm. Flesh opened in three parallel burns; skin curled black at the edges; fat beaded and hissed. The air tasted like hot copper and scorched glass. He staggered. Solace shrieked in defiance, the paving cracked in reply.

Thalen struck from above. Ashwing's downstroke hurled a gale that shoved the monster off its line.

They drove them back. The beasts stuttered, flickered, and sank into mist.

Silence reclaimed the square.

Korvan looked at his arm, blood ribboning through his leathers. It stung but wasn't deep.

Sera pressed a palm to Fennik's chest. The fox's runes pulsed and Korvan's wound stitched itself.

"What. Was. That." Thalen said to no one in particular.

"This town has been remembering death for a long time, I think whatever is happening, this Gate is the cause," Sera said.

Korvan looked for Bren.

He saw him standing still.

Head bowed.

Palm to temple.

Knuckles white.

***

Night draped Grellfen's Gate in uneasy hush. The Aethyrgate hummed. Lamps jittered.

Korvan lingered at the plaza's edge, arm wrapped in fresh bandages. Solace crouched beside him, eyes the low blue of banked coals.

Ashwing's descent shook a banner loose.

"They don't know what hit them," Thalen said hopping off the Wyvern's back.

"The Gate's Guard are ghosts, there's Two Knights, and six initiates from a previous year stationed here and they can't tell me what happened, this is beyond strange. If you'll forgive the pun."

Korvan kept his eyes on the well where Bren sat hunched.

"He hesitated."

"I know," Thalen replied.

"You're not going to—"

"Not yet, I want to figure this out first, then get us home," Korvan said.

He felt his jaw tighten, and he shook his head slowly.

Cracked bells drifted from deep in the keep.

Sera approached with a tray and passed Korvan a flask. Fennik padded close, tail low, nosing the stones.

"The boy?" Korvan asked.

"Alive," she said.

"His mind broke. There is so much pain in him. Someone else's grief was poured into him."

Thalen's jaw flexed. "This gate has been here for ages. Its never acted like this, and if people aren't seeing their own ghosts, what does it mean if you already have..."

He didn't finish.

Bren hadn't moved.

"Someone needs to talk to him," Sera said softly.

"Yeah, it can't wait," Korvan said.

He crossed the square. Each step met more of his own hesitation than Bren's.

"You alright?"

No answer.

"You froze Bren," Korvan said, gentler.

"I saw Garran, In the glass." Bren said.

His voice sounded like it came from somewhere else. Like it had been hollowed out.

"Your old captain, the one from the mid-year trial."

Bren nodded. "He trusted me. I told him the path was safe."

He dragged a hand down his face.

"We buried him in pieces. I still hear the crunch his ribs made when the rocks fell."

Korvan sat beside him. Cold stone pressed against his spine.

"That wasn't today," he said.

"But he was standing right there, I saw him plain as I see you."

"It wasn't real Bren. But this is."

Korvan nodded toward the boy breathing on a blanket. Toward Sera watching.

"I can't be like you," Bren said at last.

"I don't want you to be me Bren. I want you to be Bren."

A beat.

"I'm here," Korvan said, quieter.

"I know."

Bren raked hair back.

"That's why it's harder. It's not you. It's everything else. It's—"

He didn't finish. Bren let his head drop. His shoulders rattled and went still.

Korvan let the quiet work.

Caelen had taught him when silence heals more than talk, sometimes just being there was all that was left.

The grey that happens before dawn crawled across broken stone.

No one slept.

Korvan and the rest of his squad stood in a defensive formation.

The gate was moving.

The tremor came first, a buzzing in the molars.

Solace lifted her head. She turned toward the obelisk.

It cracked.

Then it shattered.

Blighted light rolled out in a quiet sheet. Shadows twisted losing all shape. Half-forms flickered and died.

They came.

Echoes given a body.

"Form up." Auryn's Edge snapped to Korvan's hand, the glaive bloomed dawn-white.

Thalen fell from the sky. Ashwing's wings cut twin scars of wind. His spear punched a hound-echo through the spine and burst it to vapor.

"Flank."

"I've got it."

Korvan drove his palm forward. "Kinetic Lance."

Pressure spiraled and bore through a serpent-wraith, pinning it to a fountain lip and detonating stone into a wet, ringing rain.

Sera flashed left, Fennik and Glimmer at her sides.

Her hands came up and she shouted, "Wyrd Mirror."

A blight-twisted falcon dove. Its scream hit the shield she raise and broke itself upon it.

A piercing call split the field, then thunder followed.

Bolt hit wrapped in static. He howled, flung a slicing gust, and severed a spider-limbed echo mid-leap; legs thumped stone and evaporated, leaving only a smear of cold.

"Bren," Sera called. "With us."

Bren didn't move.

An elk-echo thundered at him, antlers tangled with bone and black tendrils. Too fast.

"Bren! Move!" Sera shouted.

He didn't.

Brusk rumbled to his side and checked the beast with a wet crack. Both spun from the impact.

"Dawnshard," Korvan called, and a spear of concentrated daylight nailed the echo mid-chest and blew it open.

More came.

Dozens.

Grellfen's grief roared.

Ashwing roared above. Wingbeats left precise targets that Thalen followed with his sword. Solace fell into Korvan's rhythm, Reservoir pulse synchronizing each cast.

"Left side's folding, BREN, Move your ass," Thalen called.

"I'll hold it," Korvan shouted.

He braced.

"Radiant Binding."

Golden chains knifed from the paving and lashed three malformed echoes mid-leap. Solace's feathers quivered at the pull of her Reservoir, but she kept close to Korvan.

Sera planted her feet. "Soulbind Grace."

Fennik pulsed white as he gave more, bracing two fallen Guards. His paws left little heat-marks on the stones

Bolt howled again.

"Thunder Reach!"

Bren's voice finally cracked the air.

A blue-white bolt trailed off his hammer and speared a wraith-lion. Its skull popped in the collision.

Their relief Korvan felt didn't last long.

The pane sighed and birthed another wave.

Every death Grellfen tried to bury walked back out. For each they felled, two pressed forward.

Thalen skimmed low on Ashwing, "Left side."

"I have it," Korvan said.

Another Radiant Binding.

More golden chains, more stuck targets.

Sera lifted both arms. Fennik burned, the little fox white hot. A wash of renewal broke, closing shallow cuts, steadying breath, damping the shake behind their ribs.

Bone writhed from the mist. A skeletal wyrm, vertebrae like beads of frost-fire. Sockets burned with hate.

Bren flinched.

"Shield up," Sera called, sigil carving air.

Bren froze.

Korvan didn't.

Auryn's Edge lengthened, haft a sunline. He blurred past Bren, set both hands, and drove the burning blade through the wyrm's skull. Light stuttered and the Wyrm broke before it could fully form.

"I'm fine," Bren panted, hammer low.

"You are not fine," Sera said, bracing him.

Echoes circled.

Korvan met Thalen's eyes. "I need your help. We must end this."

Thalen's nod was grim.

Pressure gathered from nowhere and everywhere. The square groaned as reality braced.

It stepped out of the shattered obelisk.

Bigger than any echo thus far, more robust.

Hooves shattered stone. Horns curled like cooling iron, roots still orange at the tips. Chest a fortress. Arms like trunks ending in claws that steamed where they touched earth. A bull's face. Human hate.

"Ash and silence," Sera cursed.

"A Minotaur," Thalen breathed.

"No." Korvan's eyes widened.

It charged.

Brusk met it. Impact boomed. The Bulwark checked it for one heartbeat, enough to save a life, and took a backhand across the square. Stone furrowed under him. He hit a wall, left a crater, slid down amid caved plates, breath thin and wheezing. He didn't move.

Ashwing dove. Thalen vaulted free midair. His longsword carved silver into the shoulder. Meat and bone parted. Black steam jetted.

The Wyvern landed, heavy, his tail snapped out like a viper. Once, twice, three times, each sting leaving a bulging puss within the Minotaur. It swung for Ashwing, who leapt out of the way.

It did not stop.

A sweep caught Thalen and flung him. His spine hit a pillar. His leg torqued. He dropped in a heap.

"Thalen!" Sera ran.

Ashwing roared.

Vasha blurred forward. Her claws finding seams and opening them. The beast roared and swung. It missed her by a whisper and drove a horn through a wall. She harried the Minotaur, just fast enough to keep out of its grip. But the Aethyrblight had driven it beyond any sense of fatigue. None of their Veyrkin seemed to do any more than anger it.

Korvan stepped into the square, eyes burning white at the edges.

"Solace," he whispered. "All of it."

The Reservoir opened.

Lightweaving braided to Forcecraft. Air thickened and glowed. Korvan lifted into the air in a lattice of his own making. Auryn's Edge reformed into a sun-white spear he had never called.

He hurled it.

The beacon hit center mass.

A heartbeat of nothing.

Rupture answered. Cracks raced along the minotaur's hide. The monster bellowed. Old mortar trembled. It tried to pull the plaza down with it. The cracks drew inward; stubborn hate stitched itself. Horns tilted.

"Enough!"

Korvan cut his palms down.

"Gravitic Crush."

The ground howled. Pressure slammed in layered rings. The monster's knees hit stone. Flagstones split. It shoved against the invisible yoke, muscle ropes standing, light veins pulsing its throat.

It pushed back.

It let out a roar that was more spell than anger. Half-dead echoes hurled themselves into the bindings. The Minotaur planted a hoof and stood into the weight, inch by inch.

Korvan narrowed to a thread. Solace poured. Heat climbed his mark, he felt his breath thin. He was dangerously close to the limit.

Thalen moved again, jaw set, one leg dragging behind. Ashwing screamed overhead. Thalen flung a spear. It hammered the knee of the Minotaur and buried itself deep. The joint buckled a fraction.

"Now," Thalen rasped.

Korvan answered.

"Beacon of Dawn."

Truth answered back.

Light cascaded in a widening circle. Whatever darkness hid within the monster vanished the moment his light touched it. The horrific echo began to unwind.

"Force Rend," Korvan breathed.

The world bent against his spell. The Minotaur split from within, only white rupture shredding the idea of it. In dying it tried to drag the square with it. Flagstones lifted and lifted toward the Breach.

Solace wrapped Korvan's ribs and burned the last fragments out of air.

Silence reassembled in pieces.

Heat crowded the plaza. Dust hung weightlessly in the air.

Brusk groaned under a hill of broken stone. Half his iron plates were gone. His barrel chest had folded in a cruel scoop. When he tried to rise, breath whistled.

"Stay," Korvan said, staggering to him.

Warm blood crept down his ribs from a slice he hadn't felt yet. His shoulder hissed around something sharp. He didn't look.

Thalen leaned into a pillar with teeth bared. His right leg bent wrong.

"Don't touch it," he grated as Sera touched it

"You already are," she said, kneeling.

Her hands shook. Light still came. Glimmer trotted up, wing-facets trembling. Fennik walked between the bodies, his paws dragged heavily.

Sera's face had gone pale. Sweat strung her temple. She hovered palms over Thalen's knee. "Breathe."

He did. Barely.

"Soulthread Stitch."

White-gold thread surged. Bone pulled true. Sinew spun back into line.

Thalen's jaw knotted, breath hissing.

She pivoted.

Brusk.

The Bulwark wheezed. Ribs had collapsed inward. Her motions slowed, stayed exact. Fennik pressed into her hip and gave all he had.

"Pulse of Renewal," she whispered.

Glimmer set a wing over her shoulders.

Brusk's chest rose deeper. The whistle softened. Plates shifted but were still broken. His breath steadied.

Sera swayed.

Korvan reached. She caught herself on scorched stone.

"One more, Not done yet," she said.

He peeled back his cloak. Blood slicked ribs and shoulder. Cuts had gaped to muscle, a shard of stone stuck out of him.

"Pulse of Renewal."

The worst edges drew together, inch by inch. Not perfect, but more than enough.

The spell took too much.

Sera pitched forward to her hands.

Fennik folded against her knee with a small fox-sigh. Runes flickered once and went dark.

She didn't cry.

She shook, her strength spent.

"We're alive," she said. Barely air.

Korvan watched her eyes. Exhaustion glazed them, and still they searched.

She blinked. "Where's Bren?"

Korvan turned.

The square was quiet in broken ways. Columns lay like fallen teeth. The fountain steamed over disheveled cobbles.

Bren's shape wasn't there.

He looked more.

Not by Brusk.

Not near Thalen.

Not at the camp's edge.

Sera stood, unsteady, and turned a circle. "He's gone."

Korvan rose on legs that wanted to fold.

Haggard. Bleeding. Exhausted. None of that mattered.

He searched for his friend.

***

He ran.

Boots slammed stone, then dirt, then stone again. Grellfen's walls blurred. Alleys smeared like water-streaked glass. The world tilted wrong.

He didn't stop.

He couldn't.

Not after Thalen went down. Not after the light swallowed the Minotaur and made it scream.

The scream still rang in his ears. Javek's. Then Garran's. Then someone else entirely.

Bren froze again.

He always froze.

The thing hadn't touched him. It didn't have to. The shape was enough to crack the seal he kept over fear and the Beyond and everything he'd buried under duty and oaths and the hammer he no longer trusted in his hands.

Shadows twisted at the edges of his sight. Not true ones. Not now.

He found himself under the shell of an old watchtower. No doors. No roof. Stone walls half-fallen, a drift of cold ash.

He collapsed to his knees, breath ragged. Hands over his face.

He wanted to scream. Nothing came.

Javek fell again and again, the same flicker of surprise before the spell struck. Thalen, proud and bright, hurled into stone, leg snapping. Brusk broken.

What if he hadn't stood? What if Korvan hadn't thrown that spear? What if Sera hadn't held?

"I'm not strong enough. I'm not like them," Bren rasped at the ground.

The words tasted sour.

He pressed his forehead to the ground.

"I see them every time I close my eyes. Every person I didn't save."

He didn't notice the tears until his fingers curled in the dirt, wet and shaking. Bolt wasn't with him. He had vanished when the glass shattered. Even he couldn't bear to be near Bren.

Maybe no one could.

He stayed there a long time, curled in the ruins while the Aethyr cracked and re-formed around him.

For the first time he could remember, Bren did not stand back up.

He broke.

Chapter 28: Caelen

He had always been too thin. Too quiet. Far too clever.

Ren told him of the the first time she found Caelen curled beneath a threadbare blanket on her apothecary floor, fevered and hollow-eyed, whispering broken numbers into the cold. He could not have been more than ten. She almost turned them away.

"Too frail," she muttered. "Too far gone."

Something in his stare stilled her hand.

She kept him alive by tincture and defiance. She held him through the shivers and coaxed spoons full of medicine past clenched teeth.

"You're not dying on me," she growled one night, wiping blood from his lips. "Not till I say so."

When he asked for paper and ink, she gave them. When he asked for copper wire and steel pins, she raised a brow and fetched them anyway.

By night he murmured formulae into the dark. By day she watched him build his hands back into himself.

He smiled and said nothing.

His hands shook too hard to hold a spoon. He refused her help. So he built.

The first brace was crude. Copper rings and string, scrap leather waxed and cinched to his forearm. It worked. He could eat again. He could write. Light returned to his eyes.

When she reached to adjust a strap, he swatted her hand.

"It's mine, I'll fix it," he said.

Ren nodded.

She began leaving her medical books open. Aethyr schematics. Neurological glossaries. Margins crowded by dead Arcanists. She said nothing, but he devoured those too.

At some point, He stopped calling her Madam Ren. Just Ren. Family didn't need titles, or that's what he'd told her.

Korvan was three years older.

In Caelen's earliest clear memories, Korvan stood slightly ahead, shoulder between Caelen and the door, back to the wind, pockets near-empty. Always his protector. His champion.

Korvan took any work that didn't need a man's years: hauling salt sacks until his palms split open, scraping barnacles until his knuckles bled, shoveling slag, mending nets, running messages uphill. He came home with little more than a mouthful of air, Ashers tucked into his boot where their father wouldn't see.

Varnrik learned to arrive first.

"Advance on the boy's hours," he would purr at the docks, breath sour.

Or he appeared on pay-night to 'settle accounts.' Sometimes an employer shrugged at Korvan and said, "Your father settled this week." On better days, a man pressed two Ashers into Korvan's palm and called it kindness.

Korvan never let Caelen get behind that man. He stepped between them. He took the words. He took the fists. When coin failed, he bartered repairs for food: hinges set true, latches mended, a kettle handle riveted tight. Anything for bite.

One night Ren came back to her shop and found faint blue leaking from under Caelen's door. Inside, a rotating lens tracked the stars, clicking slow and precise.

"It doesn't do anything yet, but it will" he said.

A month later he was moved into her house, half the cellar was a mechanical graveyard, the overflow of things he couldn't fit in his room. Spark-jumping relays. Coils. Gears stacked in careful towers. Ren pretended to hate the mess.

"You're clogging the air with metal."

"You're steeping rat-root in my kettle," he said.

He bartered diagrams to clockwork engineers for parts. Ren never acknowledged the coins he left on the mantle. Korvan sent what he could, folded small. He never asked permission. She never asked how many hours it cost.

Despite tinctures, check-ins, and scraped coin, Caelen faded. His will held like iron. His body kept the softness of wax.

"You were supposed to rest," Ren said.

"I'll rest when I'm dead," he replied, gentle.

"Korvan's out on a mission. His work matters. So mine has to matter too."

On the eve of his seventeenth birthday, a month into living alone, Caelen stood beneath the great gears of the old clocktower. It had been abandoned by the Crown Guard so he was able to rent it for pittance, Korvan paid, but Caelen had almost saved enough from what he'd been able to trade to pay him back, not just for the rent, but for the years of care with Ren.

He'd fixed the gears in the tower; the old cogs turned with patient weight. The wind brought salt through broken shutters.

Ren had protested the move. Korvan surprised them both. Let him have some sky, he said. Jaw set, eyes soft. Ren relented on the condition of daily checks.

Caelen knew it was a ploy. They were doing everything to strengthen him and still his body weakened. He needed a room that was his, a place to prove he could stand in it.

A knock came from the stair. Three short raps. Silence.

He took the steps slow. The tower stood empty. At the threshold sat a box with no messenger and no mark except a single seal: a stylized starflower pressed in time-worn wax.

He did not breathe until he was back upstairs. He did not speak as he set it on the table.

The latch yielded. Old wood. Edges smoothed by years of hands.

Inside lay a mechanical sphere. Familiar shape. Exquisite craft. Work by hands that understood his hands.

He pressed the central rune.

Brass petals unfurled. Light touched his face. A voice rose.

"Caelen. My brilliant son."

His heart misfired.

"I wish I could have stayed," she said, clear and trembling.

"I made a choice. I tried to pass on my gift to your brother. But the Aethyr does not give freely."

He sat without noticing.

"I didn't mean to hurt you, or him. I thought I could protect you both. You won't understand now. Maybe never. Your illness was my failure. A weakness that I never could fix."

His throat burned. His fingers shook.

"I know why you build. I see my hands in yours. That spark, is what I loved most about your father."

"I'm sorry. I believe in you. Tell Korvan thank you for caring for you both. And Caelen... I love you. I love you both. My precious boys..."

The sound sputtered and died.

He tried a dozen angles and a dozen tricks. It would not play.

He let it dim. Petals folded shut on a last mechanical breath.

He sat with it. He listened to the city breathe and the gears chew down his pulse. A coil on his bench sparked once and went quiet.

Dawn tolled. Storm-clouds rolled on the horizon, low and black. He looked at the unfinished schematic beside her gift, then reached for the next piece.

The Bestiary began out of spite.

Apothecaries called him brittle; their apprentices called him strange. Korvan called him brave and treated him like a man, which hurt in an unusual way.

He found a ledger too large for his bag and ruled it with a straightedge. He made columns for Aspect, Tier, Behavior, Territory. He drew a cutaway of a Howler's chest from memory and annotated the air sacs with neat ink.

Ren found the glossary under his pillow. "You'll run out of space."

"I'll build another one."

"Of course you will," she said, failing to hide a smile.

He collected accounts from anyone who spoke. Dock men who swore a Shriekwing stole their hats. A cook who lost ladles to something with too many hands. A retired Champion who smelled of wine and old leather but still described Pegasus withers with reverence.

He learned the weight of copper on a page. He learned how a drawing could teach someone who would never see what he had.

Then he started building them. Clockwork Veyrkin to accompany each entry. Scrap gears cut to fit, brass feathers burnished, sapphire pins set for eyes. Spring-wound and hand-balanced.

He had practiced on Brusk for Korvan, and with Vasha. But his first real test was Fennik. Small enough for his palm. Tail a bevel chain. Runes etched by a scribe's touch. He cranked the key, set the fox on the sill, and watched it trot three steps before tilting its metal head toward the sea.

Two days after the Heartspire bells, Korvan filled the doorway. He had changed so much. He had grown at least another half a foot. He'd gained significant muscle, he looked closer to a shipwright, or a smith, in size. But the muscle was all sharp. It made him look like a predator. Vasha's claws clicked on stone behind him, her long body coiling near the worktable, eyes half-lidded.

"You cut your hair," Caelen said.

"Eris said it made me look less tragic."

"I disagree, the wavey hair made you look like one of Ren's love story characters," Caelen said with a chuckle.

Korvan huffed. The laugh loosened his shoulders. He took in the mess, the draft work, the ticking fox, the brass feathers drying on cloth. He didn't touch. He never touched without asking.

"How are you?"

"Fine," Caelen lied with craft.

"Liar, you need to eat Caelen," Korvan said, setting down honey rolls.

"You remembered."

"I always do. I'm not always good at showing it."

They ate on the step. The sea threw light up Cael'Lumar. Vasha stretched and placed her broad head near Caelen's knee, there was a rumble in her throat.

He slid the first figure across the floor. A palm-length Vasha, sleek and jointed, each claw a perfect sickle. Korvan palmed it like a relic.

"I've catalogued her," Caelen said, tapping his ledger. "Howler Aspect. Argent coat. Amethyst eyes. Predation: silent. Affection: selective. She catalyzes your worst instincts. I recommend six feet between her and unfamiliar fingers."

Vasha slitted her eyes, pleased.

He looked at Korvan's

"It looks alive," Korvan said.

"She is," Caelen answered. "I just mirrored the full size version."

They didn't speak of Korvan's new rank. Or Javek. Or Varnrik. Not that day.

Sera came on a rain-washed morning with a basket too large for her frame. Fennik trotted in first, runes faint and friendly.

Caelen rose too fast. The room tilted, then steadied.

"Sit," Sera said.

She unpacked the basket: broth, bread, tea. Some tools he needed but never asked for. A new oilstone, fine files, a magnifier on a copper arm. She set everything with surgeon neatness.

"I brought your favorite treat."

"Which one is that?"

"All of them."

Her smile softened the room.

He showed her the ledger. She read with her thumb pressed to the page, as if steadying the words.

"Amazing. This is better than what we have."

"I only draw."

"This is much more than a drawing."

"That isn't all," she said, and tied a torque to the brace at his wrist. It had a pearl sheen and felt warm to the touch.

"I enchanted it with some of Fennik's strength. It'll help your symptoms, should make you feel strong. If there is an emergency break it, it'll pour my strongest magic into you."

He blinked hard and nodded once.

"You didn't need to, I'm sure it cost a great deal," he managed.

"I know, I didn't need to. I wanted to," she said.

He gave her Glimmer last. Antlers of cut crystal. Hooves that chimed when the mechanism walked. A wing that flared and folded with a lever flick. Sera lifted it like an egg and laughed, bright and unguarded.

At the stair she squeezed his shoulder.

Thalen arrived like an overdue apology.

He stood very straight in the doorway, mantle exact, hair wind-tamed. Ashwing loomed behind him like a living blade. He smelled of sky and bitter metal.

"You work here," he said, taking in the gears, the books, the cot with precise corners.

"I do."

"It's... clean," he offered.

"It used to be. I'm glad you came. Korvan talks about you fondly," Caelen said, mouth tilted.

Thalen brought a parcel. In it was precision tweezers, jeweled drivers, and watchmaker's springs. It was rare enough to still Caelen's hands. Tools a Noble's son could afford.

"Payment, for all the times you've kept him upright," Thalen said, awkward.

Caelen studied him. "You're kinder than you want believed."

Thalen's mouth twitched. "Don't tell a soul."

They spoke of Lareth once, then let the subject rest. Thalen asked sharp questions about the Bestiary's classification, aspects, and prestige, until Caelen laughed and made notes.

"So," Caelen started.

"So," Thalen said.

"You and my brother?"

"Fuck... he hasn't said anything?"

Caelen leveled his gaze at Thalen, a wry smile held.

"Of course. It's very new. There isn't anything really, Korvan and Sera must be aligned. I understand that."

"I know others have multiple partners, its not a foreign concept. But don't you get jealous?" Caelen's question was genuine. For all his expertise on machines, puzzles and his burgeoning knowledge of medical texts, emotions still were the thing he struggled with most.

"Sure, of course I get jealous. But jealous isn't a terrible thing by itself. Sera makes Korvan happy. She also offers him something I don't, and that I can't offer him. I'm jealous that I can't do that, but I am also thrilled that he gets it from her. Sera is an amazing woman and I'm proud to call her my friend. The times when being jealous is bad, is when you let it rule you or make yourself feel small, or act in a way that is harmful on purpose. The point really is, just like with your friends, they all give you something different, something unique. That doesn't make you any less than another because you're different."

Caelen nodded, and filed that away, "So, you want Korvan to be happy, just like you want your friends to be happy. Sera makes him happy, so that makes you happy, because he's happy?"

"That's a lot of happiness, but yes that's the heart of it."

Thalen's cheeks were flushed, and he rubbed the back of his head.

Caelen could appreciate that. He didn't really feel that way about people, he loved Korvan of course, he was grateful for Ren and everything she'd done. But this sounded quite different.

"Well Thalen, I'm glad my brother found you. He deserves all the happiness in the world. The things our father did... well that doesn't matter now. You make Korvan happy, which means I'm happy too. Thank you for making my brother happy."

Thalen's eyes watered for an instant before he snapped them shut. The noble's expression cracked, and Caelen felt like he'd offended him.

Thalen stepped toward him quickly his voice low, his hair fell around his face blocking his eyes, "May I hug you. Korvan said you like people to ask before they touch you."

Caelen smirked, and grabbed Thalen. He pulled him tightly. The Knight's core was shaking. Caelen's shoulder felt wet as tears dropped onto it. Thalen wasn't quiet as tall as Korvan, but still a head taller than Caelen was.

Thalen left lighter than he came. Caelen had heard the new thing between Thalen and Korvan. He saw it now in the careful way Thalen looked at the workbench, as if the room mattered because Korvan did.

Some nights the coughing came like a thief. He woke to copper at his teeth and the old bruise behind the sternum.

On those nights, the sphere came down from the shelf. He did not press the rune. He laid his palm on brass and felt for a vibration that would not return.

"I'm not a mistake," he whispered to the dark.

Bren did not knock. Of all Korvan's closest companions. He never came.

The morning after Thalen he added a page to a journal. This page was on mothers. On gifts. On matters of the heart as he had been taught.

The Bestiary thickened. He inked Vasha's gait with anatomical arrows. He logged Brusk's impact from memory. He sketched Solace's feathered arms from a dream of falling through gold and waking with a feather-print on his skin.

He asked Ren for sea-salt and graphite and rubbed the pages until they gleamed faint as bone.

On the inside cover he wrote:

Caelen Aric's Bestiary: Concerning Veyrkin and those who Tame them.

He finished the figures. Vasha, Brusk, Solace. Fennik and Glimmer. Ashwing and Midnight. He set them in a shallow case lined with old velvet and oiled wood. He left space for the one Korvan hadn't named. He'd tell Caelen when the shape arrived.

They had never all visited together. He arranged them side by side anyway and laughed at the small assembly. In brass and spring, they made a family he could hold.

Ren found him in the window's pale light with oil on his hands and softness in his mouth.

"Eat," she said, pressing a warm roll to his fingers.

"Yes, Ren," he said around a smile.

She looked at the case, the ledger, the torque bracing his wrist. "You've been busy."

"I'm trying to be alive," he said, surprised at how easily it came.

"Good," she answered, steady as a pulse. "Do that more."

Caelen stood and stretched until his ribs clicked. Outside, the sea flared white where it should be blue. A storm was coming. He set the case on the shelf above his bed, wiped his hands, and returned to the bench.

Gears turned. Light shifted over the tower floor like breath.

He wasn't better.

He wasn't worse.

He was making.

It was enough.

Chapter 29: Storm-Tide

The storm had no name. It came with intent.

Wind knifed the tiered walls of Cael'Lumar, ripping banners and driving rain sideways across the towers. Thunderheads spiraled with unnatural precision, veined in violet Aethyr. Too controlled for weather; too focused to be chance.

Korvan stood on the Second Ring's eastern watch wall, cloak plastered to skin, salt burning every breath. Stone ran slick under his boots. Far below, the harbor heaved in shapes, as if something old had turned over in its sleep.

This was no tempest. It was a herald.

Sera held his left. Calm-eyed, one hand on Fennik's spine as the Mender paced, runes guttering, brightening, guttering again. Vasha crouched at Korvan's right, silver and amethyst, tail flicking, rain bead-steaming along heat-hazed fur while she watched the black water.

Thalen checked Ashwing's tack. The wyvern's half-spread wings shone black, tendons quivering like drawn bowstrings.

The air thrummed. The wardline sang in a thin, uneasy pitch that made Korvan's molars ache.

"Storm's wrong, Ashwing can feel it. It's been called here by something," Thalen said.

Behind them, Initiates and Knights formed in staggered ranks. Rain flattened cloaks and silvered helms. No one spoke above the weather. Ryn stood lean and locked, braids darkening under the downpour. Soot carved tight circles overhead, ebon wings cutting water in a wordless warning.

A new presence stepped into the line.

Knight Sirene Malyka of Vara'Lumar: umber skin rain-bright, braids banded with dark gold. Inlaid obsidian sigils gleamed on her cuirass like night given geometry. Her Veyrkin, perched on her shoulder, an eagle hewn from prisms.

"Verdict sees it too," Sirene said, her voice held an accent like Cristos, but more rounded around the vowels.

Korvan nodded.

The Bastion Bell tolled.

Once.

Twice.

A third time, deep and final.

The bell's warning that something had come into the harbor.

Sera pushed her hood back. Her mouth thinned.

Verdict's wings spread. Refracted sigils leapt into the storm, rippled, then snapped.

"Whatever it is, it's coming," Sirene murmured.

The harbor answered with a tone too low to the wind. The ocean exhaled from beneath the ribs of the world. Korvan's Soul-marks throbbed out of time, every third pulse a skipped step.

Water drew outward, pulled by something.

The surface split.

One gleaming coil breached, then another, each as wide as a merchant-ship. Moss and barnacle clung to it. Luminous cracks pulsed beneath the skin like molten veins. Barnacled plates flexed and locked. Drowned nets hung like funeral veils from its spines.

The harbor wall, which had repelled all attacks for centuries, screamed when the body hit. Stone buckled. Anchors tore free. A whole section failed and went under with a sound like a city inhaling.

Out of the sundered maw rose the serpent.

The head was wrong: long-jawed, gills flared like sails, a crown of bioluminescent horns burning cold fire. One eye lay crusted in sea-rot and soft growth. The other glowed red with intent.

Vengeance had been given shape.

Orders cracked down the line. Along the quay, shield teams locked chevrons. On the terraces, Bulwarks took the foreground.

"Bulwarks front! Shields on flanks! Hold until ordered!"

Solace shimmered to Korvan's side, feathers of dusk-laced glass catching storm light. Warm gravity slid into his bones.

We are ready Korvan. This thing will not be our end. Solace's voice held a surprising venom.

Sera layered mirrored sigils, around as many as she could, Fennik moved tight to her heel, glowing steady. Thalen vaulted up; Ashwing's roar tore the sky, mighty wings flapped, the sound of sails fighting the storm. They lifted into the air and careened forward.

Korvan gave them both a glance but missed their eyes.

"Be safe," he whispered to them.

The serpent surged again, closer. A cutter capsized in its wake. Its tail scythed a stone bridge to chalk, figures pinwheeling. One struck a parapet spine-first, bone pushed wrong beneath skin and slid into black water. It learned as it moved; its next strike punched a ward-pylon first, it cracked with cacophonous bang.

Ryn went over first.

She dropped to the square, boots breaking water, and yanked two unbonded Crown Guard that had fallen from the masonry. One bled at the temple. The other gasped and coughed up water.

"They won't survive this," Korvan said.

Across the harbor the serpent opened its mouth.

Spear-teeth framed a gullet of red-violet light. Aethyrfire churned in its throat. Heat boiled rain to steam. The first breath would scour stone and marrow both.

"Move!" Korvan bellowed.

The sky split first.

Kaelith fell like star, golden light tearing the clouds. She struck the air between beast and city, hooves hammering invisible ground, chest to jaw. Radiance scissored the maw. The Leviathan's charge collapsed. The blast it had prepared erupted in its throat.

The serpent adapted, pulling back into deeper water so it could move better, it gathered another blast and prepared to fire once more.

Kaelith wheeled and Eris unfurled radiant bands that bridged broken wardlines. They held long enough for shields to set feet again.

Korvan didn't see the next pass.

He saw the clocktower.

Caelen's tower, high on the Harbor ring, windows blue with workshop light. The world slowed. The serpent slapped its tail, sections of the wall the size of houses flew across the city. The clock tower caught one of them. A tremor ran through it. The upper floor let go. Stone, wood beams, and glass began moving in one terrible shrug.

The sound hadn't reached yet. The image had.

"Caelen!"

He ran.

Solace surged with him. His cloak drowned. Vasha snapped from crouch to sprint, a silver streak at his flank, claws hissing on wet stone. He vaulted the parapet and threw Flickerstep mid-leap, he flashed forward in a burst of light vaulting through the air. Debris glanced off light like stones off a shield. He landed on a cracking stair without breaking stride. Faster now. Vasha's hunger laced his pulse; Solace's calm threaded the heat.

"Korvan!" Sera's voice cut thin through storm.

Behind, the serpent lashed, tail shearing quarried blocks from the seawall. Aethyr detonations strobed mist. Kaelith crossed again, laying ribs of light over the ring. Verdict's halos tightened above Sirene. Ashwing dived and climbed, carving air into blades.

Korvan ran.

Rain needled his eyes. Every footfall shuddered bone to hip. He pulled on Solace too hard; edges began to fray.

He didn't care.

His brother was in that tower.

A shockwave hit before it sounded. The tail slammed down-ring. The street split; cobbles spat into his shins. His head slammed hard into a beam, the world spun and he saw spots.

He got up anyway.

A second tone rolled out, too low for ears. Wards flickered, then failed along a terrace, light guttering

He pushed.

The clock tower groaned. Another brace gave. Figures skidded across the balcony. A lantern arced, brief and helpless, then went out.

"Just a little farther," he told the rain.

The ground lurched. A fallen beam blocked him. Stone screamed. Chips flayed his cheek. Korvan dragged power raw and snapped Flickerstep again—

Too slow.

The beam met his face. Debris shook loose and fell. The world narrowed to a crushing darkness.

***

Silence came back as a ringing in his ears.

Then nothing.

Darkness held him.

He felt like he was floating. The place felt familiar.

A spark.

Gold flickered in the void.

"Where is he?"

His voice could've cut stone.

"Where is Caelen?"

No answer. Only an ancient hum moving under skin.

He surged, though there was no ground to drive from and no sky to cut. Only pressure. Rage. Fear.

"You keep showing me power. Why do I feel helpless?"

Gold brightened and a shape coalesced.

A dragon stepped out of nothing: slate scales stitched with stars, wings curled like smoke, eyes wide and still as winter seas.

Korvan's fists closed. "Say something."

I hear your anger, the dragon said. *Fury cannot shield what you fear to lose.*

"I don't want a shield."

His jaw ached.

"I want my brother safe. I'm strong enough to do that. Now get the fuck out of my way so I can save him."

Orion tilted his head, unreadable and immense. *Then stop begging for permission.*

Korvan stilled, and he looked at Orion, the name had appeared in his mind. He swore the dragon smiled.

You are not a weapon forged by others. You are not your father's echo. You are not broken. The constellations in those eyes shifted. *You are mine. We do not choose lightly. But I have chosen you Korvan. You are ready. Come find me, and you will meet my true form.*

"I will, but first I save Caelen. I stop this monster. Then I'll come find you."

Korvan heard it, he wasn't asking, he spoke his truth.

Something like magic came from Orion. Korvan felt pushed, lifted with a speed he'd never known. His body mended and his strength returned.

I waited years for the right person, for you. It is clear I waited well. I will see you soon. Echoborn.

***

Kaelith tore the cloudbank in a sun-born arc.

Eris rode bareheaded. All who saw her thought her radiant and terrible.

Her hair streamed like molten wire. Her cloak cracked like judgment. Her gauntlets caught lightning and threw it back. The staff in her off hand sang. On each end a helix of force or light, runes blooming and fading.

Kaelith banked.

Eris stepped free of the saddle.

The sky bent to carry her, Beacon of Dawn blooming underfoot with each quiet breath. The storm was pushed back and the Leviathan recoiled at her light.

Sera's lungs seized for an instant. Around her, no one moved. All eyes turned up at the sun that had appeared over Lantern Harbor. Raindrops hung bead-still. The wind ceased howling. The noise of war retreated like the tide.

Gone was the woman of emotionless corrections, long lectures of honor and duty, of repeated drilling on endless forms.

The Gilded Knight had taken her place.

Eris lifted one hand and the Aethyr obeyed. Runes flared into orbit, a coronet of balanced moons. With the other, still gripping her staff, she snapped her fingers.

Kaelith answered.

A column of white-gold fire roared from the Pegasus' wings sundering the crown atop the Leviathan. Bone cracked. Horns splintered. The beast's scream drowned the Bastion Bell.

It came on anyway.

Gills flared like torn sails. The leviathan lunged, burning, crown shedding molten light into rain.

Eris did not blink.

She spoke a word Sera did not know.

Radiant Binding rose from sea and air. Dozens of bands began looping around neck and fore fins, cinching taught. Lightning wreathed Eris's staff. The storm didn't strike her; it fed her.

Kaelith galloped across light itself, Beacon of Dawn ringing like a smith-god's anvil, each step peeled reality thin.

The serpent lashed blind, overwhelmed by the light. Its tail scythed for the watch wall.

Sera braced and poured everything she had into her shield. Fennik's runes burned hot, Glimmer let out a thin sound.

The ward held. A thin cry in its stones, but it held.

Freezing rain hit her face. Iron on the tongue, her heart pounded in her throat.

Sera felt the lesson under spectacle, as she looked up she could see it. She wasn't sure how she could, Glimmer's knowledge of the Aethyr was flowing into her but, she knew it. Eris was holding back. She could do more, but she didn't want to damage the harbor.

Eris was in a different league. Only then did Sera realize how far that gap really was.

The serpent shrieked, bound, and wounded, but not yet broken. The crown sparked violet; infrasonic pressure rolled out, buzzing teeth and staggering casts. Fennik faltered; Sera clamped his ribs and pulled him close.

Below, the battle lurched. Knights barked clean orders. Castings cracked. Fresh squads pounded the tier stairs, water to knees. They had managed to push back the tide that was rushing in from the gap, slowly several of their larger Veyrkin had begun moving stones to form a barricade. She saw spells lay over them sealing the ocean out.

Sera's head turned, sparing a glance to the crushed street where Korvan vanished.

No movement.

Farther along the ring, smoke pulled up the cliffside. The clock tower burned itself into her thoughts. It was swaying and twisted by the storm. Lightning clawed it and the upper story folded.

Her stomach fell.

"Ash and silence," She cursed.

Then her mind caught up to her as the horror sank in.

"Oh no. by the Twin Gods. Caelen…"

On the plaza's broken lip, Sirene raised a hand. Verdict launched in prisms, a Wyrd Mirror lattice pulsing out in concentric panes, refraction scrambling the crown. It struck wide; the far quay cracked instead of the wardline.

Sera surged. Fennik and Glimmer flanked tight. Shields spooled from her fingers. She layered Halo Veil with Wyrd Mirror nested so stone would break where she wanted it to. Her forearms trembled. She did not stop.

Ashwing cut a hard arc. Thalen swiped with all he had, his blade carved into the beast's hide, leaving a gash across it. Ashwing spun, wrapping his wings in a spiral and they darted up. Thalen squeezed his thighs, clinging with everything he had.

Chaos though, tended to punish heroics.

The serpent slammed down in pain, a shrill scream from its gargantuan maw. The shockwave broke flagstones and pitched bodies. Two Initiates rag-dolled across the square; one hit shoulder and hip, socket popping with a wet crack, and slid under a cart.

Ryn didn't slide.

She was already moving. Rage pared her face to bone.

Not for glory.

For Javek.

For the days she believed the line would break if she didn't step first.

Her focus snapped past the serpent to a small shape behind a toppled stall. A child, curled and crying.

Ryn moved.

The math finished before Sera could shout.

The second tail came low through the smoke.

Ryn didn't scream.

Impact folded her midair, ribs collapsing around her spine. It threw her fifteen paces. She struck the wall with a snap. Blood threaded from her ears. Her Soulmark flared once in the rain like a torch in fog, then smoldered out.

"No!" Sera's voice tore thin.

The sound of a crow crying filled the sky.

Ashwing knifed down.

Thalen was two heartbeats late.

The child lived.

Ryn didn't.

Time buckled. Noise fell down a well. Sera's hands wouldn't stop because looking would change the world.

Soot dropped from cloud with ragged wings. He folded himself small beside Ryn, beak to stone, making a sound like a string fraying.

Another weight for the ledger.

No legacy to remember them, only her courage.

Thalen's jaw locked. Ashwing's membranes crawled lightning like veins hunting a heart. Across the field, Kaelith screamed bright and boiled stained-glass wards to vapor.

Eris turned at the sound.

Kaelith knelt next to a Wyvern, Next to Thalen. Her eyes followed.

She saw the body.

She did not look away.

The glyphs orbiting her reddened at the edges, her temper had finally found its glass.

The chains tightened. The serpent howled, until the sound was crushed from its throat. Runes hissed where light found purchase. It clawed for air and held nothing back.

The bindings didn't break.

Eris released them.

Her hand lowered. Deliberate. Final.

"Enough," she said.

The word hit harder than any cast.

"Let it crawl home. Let whoever sent it learn: while I draw breath, this city does not fall."

Kaelith touched beside Eris.

The serpent shuddered. Its blood poured in violet sheets. One horn sheared and spun end over end into harbor black. It's regal crown shattered, body marked by countless wounds.

It turned, broken and warned.

It hurled itself to sea with a convulsion that staggered the piers. Sheets rose. Pylons snapped.

The silence of aftershock followed.

Sera's hands trembled as the last lattice unspooled and died.

Kaelith's blazing eyes cut to Eris. The pegasus dipped a fraction. Eris exhaled slow. Her breath came hot, and her skin had a shimmer of its own.

A thought slid under Sera's grief like a knife:

Korvan and Eris both burned the same type of bright.

Sera turned toward the street where Korvan had fallen.

The rubble had shifted.

***

Bren didn't miss the moment.

He simply didn't move.

Rain needled the watch wall. The Bastion Bell shook marrow. The harbor ruptured and the serpent came threading out of thunder like a cathedral dragged from the deep. Its crown burned; its one living eye fixed the city as if it recognized a throat worth crushing.

He knew the drills. Shield the line. Anchor the young. Follow the Knights.

His boots stayed locked.

Sound crowded his skull: wardstones screaming, the sea's bass-hum, Sera calling placements. Beneath it, was an old pain. The sound of rocks collapsing, ribs caving, Garran's grunt cut short. The glass at Grellfen had shown him a corpse and called it a compass. His body still pointed there.

I am here, Bolt murmured through the bond.

Bren exhaled.

He saw the child behind the stall. Ryn saw her first and changed direction like a hawk.

Bren ran.

He did not reach her.

The second tail slid under smoke and wrote a lesson across the square. Ryn's body left the ground, arced wrong, landed worse. A fast, ugly fold. He felt her ribs go.

Soot dropped and went still beside her.

Bren's legs kept moving after use had gone. His hammer was a weight, not a weapon. He lost the child's shape, found her again by the sound a throat makes when it chooses not to cry. He put his body over hers because that required no thought.

He went to Ryn then, without remembering the choice. He knelt in rain and brick-dust. Her eyes were open. Still blue, just like Javek's. Her chest was a dent no one could hammer back. He put a hand on her cheek and left mud there because his hand would not stop shaking.

The serpent ripped free.

Eris opened her hand and let the chains fall.

"Enough," she said.

The beast turned, half-crowned and bleeding, and threw itself seaward with a spiteful lash. Stone failed. The harbor roiled. For a breath, the rain paused, as if impressed.

Bren felt Sera's breath thin with spent magic. He felt Bolt press shoulder to his back, a warm, living wall.

He had failed to be first, to be fast, to cast clean. He had failed to arrive while Ryn was still a person.

He closed her eyes with two fingers. The lids were grit-wet and soft. Soot made a sound that would break you.

"I'm sorry," he told her.

Small words. Honest anyway. All he had left.

He stood into a body too heavy for one soul, set the hammer on his shoulder, and looked over the ring. The city shivered under rain.

Bolt leaned close. *With you.*

He turned from Ryn and walked toward away from the harbor.

He couldn't stand it anymore.

There was still a child breathing under a stall, a fox whose runes guttered, a friend who would spend himself down to bone if no one pulled him back. He was late to all of it.

He went anyway.

A breath passed.

Then another.

He did not look back.

***

The world was sideways.

Caelen was too literal for metaphor, so the world being on its side was concerning. Stone pressed his ribs. Rain cut through the shattered window like thrown knives. Violet licked the torn sky. Something enormous moved the air in tides; the tower answered in groans.

He coughed. Blood strung his teeth with copper and heat.

Something had shifted wrong. Not bruised or displaced. Broken.

His spine.

He catalogued it the way he catalogued everything: loss of motor below the navel; numbness that somehow had an edge; breath shallow and fast; hands shaking, shock. Response protocol? None that mattered. Legs did not answer. Fingers might as well have belonged to someone else. He could move his eyes. That was all.

Sparks hopped from the collapsed relay frame. The Echo Lens lay canted on the ledge, rune-sheen ticking itself out of true. A ceiling strut had punched through the drafting table; oil bled across his blueprints.

That felt cruel. Ruining his work.

He tried to reach. Nothing happened.

This was how he ended. How ironic. He was certain his sickness would be the end of him. Instead a freak accident caused by a colossal Veyrkin.

He would have liked to see Korvan one more time.

Wind shifted, something settled above him.

Breathing became harder. Something must have settled.

Footfalls hammered the stair, too fast for caution. A door below tore against its hinges. A voice ripped up the shaft, raw and unhidden.

Then he saw him.

Korvan burst through the fractured arch, soaked, forearm bound and bleeding. He dropped to his knees and didn't touch at first, hovering and shaking as if contact might scatter what was left.

"I came as quick as I could Caelen."

He sounded out of breath.

"I'm here." Caelen meant to whisper. He might have only thought it.

Two shadows passed, circled once and then two familiar Veyrkin landed. Glimmer landed with grace. Ashwing landed heavier, talons skittering on grit, rain hissing off hide.

Sera hit the floor running. Thalen was beside her.

She wasted no words. Hands already lit, she slid in sideways and mapped him with a Mender's eyes: pupils, breath, blood, spine. Fennik pressed his warm skull under Caelen's wrist until the tremor evened. Glimmer arched a wing, facets alive with mirrored runes.

"Sera, his back," Korvan said, voice frayed.

"I see it." Her tone was steady enough to lean on.

The tower gave a long, tired shiver. A beam shifted.

Korvan's palm hit the stone, his eyes glowed with power and something determined. "Aethyrwall."

Raw force erupted, and the dust stopped falling. The creaking of the building ceased. He took the strain into shoulders and jaw. Light guttered through his Soulmarks and steadied.

Sera's work began.

It felt less like heat, but like a map redrawn over meat and nerve. A wrongness loosened, slow and precise. Pain rose like tide and took him whole for a breath, then changed shape.

Caelen gasped.

Not from hurt. From sensation below the injury, a presence like deep music returning to a room.

Something older than the pain stirred beneath his broken bones.

Her fingers moved fast. Faster than they'd ever moved before. She followed the Fyrstrand through marrow, calling the buried thread to meet her hands. Fennik gave, runes bright as he shouldered cost. Glimmer narrowed his light, focusing Sera's pull to filament-fine exactness.

Caelen felt a hairline click in his back: one, then three.

"Pulse of Renewal."

Sera said

Warmth blew through cold places. Blood that had pooled began to move. A phantom ache faded under a truer pressure.

"Hold," Sera warned, it sounded like she was talking to herself, she set her hands, thumbs braced.

"Soulthread Stitch."

White-gold spilled from palm to vertebrae, a seam running down his spine as if suturing a broken bow. The tower, the storm, the pain narrowed to that one line and the pull of her will along it. Fennik's glow faltered and flared. Glimmer's wings trembled. The Soulmark along Sera's forearms climbed and burned.

The beams above shift, I can hear them moving, Solace murmured at Korvan's skull.

Caelen didn't understand how, but he heard solace's voice.

"I've got him." Korvan's second hand joined the first, his face contorted with effort.

"Bulwark Engine."

Multiple pillars of force sprang around them, they braced and sank into the floor slightly before holding.

Thalen stepped beside Korvan and set his shoulder to the beam. Ashwing pushed in behind him and tried to lift too. Vasha appeared beside Sera, stabilizing her. Brusk crawled in with Caelen.

Weight settled where Korvan told it to. The braces bit. The tower listened.

Caelen's breath hitched.

Because the world answered.

He felt it: a thread rising through him. The Fyrstrand woke and wound his nerves. Every schematic he had drawn suddenly seemed a child's copy of this geometry that lived in his veins.

His left hand twitched. Then his right.

Sera didn't look up. Sweat fell from her chin to his ribs. She was beyond anything but the task at hand.

"What's...what's happening?" His voice scraped and broke. "Sera, Korvan..."

"Almost," she said through her teeth. "Almost there."

Another beam slid. The bracing moaned. Korvan bared his teeth and leaned into the cast, sweat salting his lips.

Thalen stepped closer to him, Both arms producing renewed purpose. Korvan gave him a brief nod.

"Aethyr Mend."

Sera's voice rang out.

The last edges of the damage drew together under her hands. The light she poured thinned and held. The flare went out like a wick pinched between wet fingers.

Silence fell.

Sera tipped forward into Korvan; he caught her with one arm, half lifting and half folding her toward him, every muscle in him bulged from the pressure of the ceiling.

Her eyes stayed open just enough to find Caelen's face.

"Move something," she whispered. "Anything."

Caelen stared up at the split sky. He told his body a simple thing.

Left foot.

It answered with a small, defiant shift beneath dust and blood.

His breath broke. His eyes flooded hot. He swallowed hard so the next words would be steady.

"Sera... what did you do?"

She blinked, slow. "I listened to what was broken," she said, voice thinned to thread. "Then I stitched it."

Fennik collapsed at his side with a fox-sigh, runes guttering to coals. Glimmer's wing dimmed by degrees before they dropped to his sides spent.

Korvan's hands were on Caelen's shoulders now, rain and dirt streaking his face, relief and terror making him look young.

You're here," Korvan said.

His voice cracked on the second word. "You're okay now."

Not okay.

Changed.

Caelen felt the room as if the tower were a machine he could finally hear: rafters taking load, stones swelling from pressure, the Aethyr relay still clicking down a pattern too complex. Beneath it all, the hum of the thread winding back through him, bright and patient.

Welcome, Echoborn, said a deep voice that was none of theirs.

He turned his head the fraction the world allowed.

Solace had appeared without sound. Her eyes held him. Feathers flexed, and glowed low blue at the edges, tasting the new shape of him.

"I see you," Caelen whispered, not sure to whom he spoke.

I have been waiting for you, she answered.

Chapter 30: Doubt and Dust

Rain held to stone like breath held too long. It beaded along split beams, ticked from the fractured ceiling, pooled in the gouges where the tower had tried to fold Caelen into the floor. His work lay in ruin. Bent gears, cracked lenses, wire spools fused to slag. The star lens had split clean down the center. Its glow was gone.

Korvan crouched beside the cot and gripped the frame until his knuckles blanched. He'd kept his hands there since they carried Caelen down.. He hadn't moved when Sera collapsed. He hadn't moved when Thalen said they should call for help. He couldn't make himself let go.

Caelen lay wrapped to the chest, lips dry but whole. Cuts had closed in a hurry. Pulse strong. Breath steady.

Across the room, Sera had been tucked into a chair, Korvan's overcoat over her for warmth and Fennik curled to her ribs. Glimmer stood just outside next to the sill.

"She shouldn't be breathing, Used more power than I've even seen you use," Thalen said, pacing.

He stopped.

"It wasn't only her," Korvan said, voice raw.

Thalen turned. "Solace?"

Korvan nodded and brushed damp hair from Caelen's brow. "She opened a conduit. Let Sera carry more current than she ever should have. Glimmer guided it for her. I have no idea how it happened."

"Through Caelen?"

"I don't know how. But yes, that's what it felt like."

Korvan kept his eyes on his brother.

Caelen stirred.

He flexed his fingers. Brow furrowed. He opened his eyes. They were clearer than they had any right to be.

"Still here?" he rasped.

"I'm not going anywhere," Korvan said.

Caelen blinked at the room, then the broken lens in the corner. "I liked that one."

"You nearly died," Thalen said.

"Close only counts in horseshoes, I'm still here," Caelen said.

Thalen looked at him like he was speaking a different language.

"Horseshoes is a game where you toss horseshoes at a post, the more that land on it, give you points, if you hit it that's a different amount of points, if you get close that's a point. Close only counts in horseshoes. It's not a good joke if I have to explain it Thalen."

Korvan laughed. He laughed a deep, rising belly laugh that defied the ruin around them. He laughed so hard he doubled over and his stomach began to ache.

After a few deep breaths, he looked. Thalen's face said that he thought he'd finally snapped. Caelen was stifling his own giggles.

"How does the rest of you feel, your spine was twisted all the way around." Korvan asked.

Caelen grimaced and looked under his blanket to see his legs in the normal position.

"Good as new." Caelen stared at his hands as if they were a new instrument. He lifted one.

The air answered with a taut, low hum. Light coiled at his fingertips. Precise. Unbidden.

He flicked toward the lens core. The broken shell jumped, hissed with displaced Aethyr, and rolled free of rubble as if called. A thread of violet-white traced its path and faded.

Thalen drew breath. "Wyrdforging."

"I didn't try to cast," Caelen said, startled.

"You just did," Korvan said, standing.

"Caelen, you did magic!"

"It felt…"

Caelen flexed again, and Korvan saw the feint outline of the Soulmark growing against his skin.

"Familiar. Like I've always known how to do it," Caelen finished.

Solace stirred in Korvan's bond.

Caelen, she said.

The light in the stairwell deepened.

Solace stepped through. Rain jeweled her dusk-feathers; her eyes held starlight drowned and reborn.

Korvan turned, "Solace—"

She didn't look at him.

The ancient raptor crossed the room and stopped beside the cot. Caelen's eyes widened. Understanding landed.

Solace lowered her head. Caelen lifted a trembling hand and touched her brow.

Light answered.

Lines wrote themselves into his skin. A Soulmark bloomed across his chest: radiant feathers circling mirrored thread, a spiral nested itself.

"What," Korvan whispered.

He understood at last the disharmony he'd carried since they'd bonded. Solace had never truly been his. She only entrusted herself to him. She had kept him alive long enough to bring her home.

Sera blinked awake through exhaustion.

Thalen took one step, jaw set, eyes gone sharp with confusion.

"Did he just bond with Solace?"

"Yeah… Yeah he did."

Korvan couldn't believe it. He no longer felt her. Losing a bond was supposed to be a horrific pain, but he didn't even notice her leaving.

Caelen exhaled and set his palm over the new mark, reverence on his face.

"She's mine?" he asked.

"She was waiting for you," Korvan said, "Somehow, she knew you'd be able to bond."

"So does this mean I'll have to join the Aethyrguard too?" Caelen asked.

"No, it means you can do whatever you want, little hawk."

Korvan reached out, in an offer.

Caelen jumped into his brother's arms.

The rain softened on broken stone.

The storm had moved on.

Everything else had shifted.

***

The High Warden's sanctum kept an engineered chill. A half-dome of crystal sulked in the rear wall, Aethyrglass dulled with smoke. Five pillars carved as coiled beasts watched with jeweled eyes, their pulses keeping time with the wardline.

Korvan stood straight at the black stone table, jaw set.

Sera beside him, composed, coiled.

Thalen at the wall, arms crossed.

Bren came last. No bow. No eye contact. He stood like a man braced against his own bones.

High Warden Archion Dren sat centered, Archmage Maedryn to one side, Eris to the other. Arcanist Kane Vor unrolled a scroll. His voice was clean as a blade.

"The leviathan breach was met with swift defense. Memory-Aethyr present, someone sent it to attack us. No living bond signature; an external cast on the thing. Eastern ring damage: extensive, contained. Civilian dead: twelve. Aethyrguard: One. Initiate Ryn Dacre. Three wounded. All considered, minimal loss of life for such a deadly assault. This was a clean victory."

The neatness grated.

Thalen stepped into it.

"It targeted children."

Eris flinched, so subtly if Korvan hadn't been looking at her he'd have missed it.

"This was clearly an escalation with the group you all encountered outside of Riverpost. This was a test of our resolve and how quickly we could marshal a defense. We will reinforce all the wards, especially those around the harbor and look to reinforce key locations of the wall."

The Archmage's answer felt important but didn't address Thalen's point.

Archion pivoted. "Korvan, what do you think?"

"It hunted people, it didn't seem to care about any of us until we got in its way, it wasn't after the Aethyrguard, it just wanted blood."

He tried to keep the heat from his voice, he wasn't sure how successful he was. Eris gave him a shallow nod.

"And what would be your response?" Archion asked.

Korvan searched for words.

Bren found his.

"Stop pretending this dies on a report."

Eyes swung to him. He stepped forward, arms at his side, head held high.

"We're not in control of this situation. If you keep waiting for a better moment, you'll be engraving more names on the memory wall than it has space for."

"You forget your place, Initiate," Archion said, a measure of heat touched the High Warden's words.

"No." Bren's mouth flattened. "I remember it. I'm done. This place isn't mine anymore."

Sera inhaled to say something that might hold him. Thalen held still.

Korvan stepped half a pace. "Bren—"

The man had already turned, but he held up a hand.

At the doors he paused, voice low and true. "I'm sorry Korvan, it's too late. I'll send for my things."

Bren looked back at Sera once. Only once. "Goodbye."

Archion didn't raise his voice. "Initiate Bren Halvor. Excommunicated from the Aethyrguard. Effective immediately, he is stripped of his rank and privileges."

Vor's quill hissed.

Sera gasped.

Thalen's head shook.

Korvan stared after his friend, darkness was all that was there.

"You will not speak of this beyond this room," Archion commanded.

Venom crept into his voice, "The Aethyrguard does not fracture."

Silence agreed because it had to.

***

They drifted to the familiar chamber that had been their over the last year. City lamps woke in the wet; amber washed the dome and didn't comfort.

"That was no Tantrum," Thalen said first.

"No, His heart finally broke," Sera said.

"We saw it coming," Korvan said, each word weighted.

"We hoped it wouldn't," Sera answered.

"Hope doesn't make a good defense," Thalen said.

"No, but it tells us where to stand," Korvan murmured.

They held their triangle.

Together, alone.

"That's three we've lost," Thalen said, tightening a worn strap.

"We get better, I don't know how you both are feeling, but I won't lose another friend," Korvan said.

He looked at them both.

They looked at each other.

They all agreed.

***

Bren didn't return that night or the next morning. By midday, a trunk waited under polite watch at the outer gates. Sealed.

Sera stood in the yard with her hands locked behind her back. Fennik lay at her heel, ears twitching at sounds no one else heard.

Korvan came on slow boots over wet gravel.

"He's gone."

She nodded. "I know."

"Are you angry?"

"Sad," she said. "And furious. But not really at him."

Korvan looked to the line where the sky and sea became hazy.

"We were supposed to face this together."

"Maybe he wasn't meant to carry it," Sera said.

Thalen's voice was soft, "He led better than any of us. Leaders break too. None of us found the right door to him. "

No one argued.

A bell rang, another summons.

"Before we go, I can't wait anymore," Korvan said.

They both stopped and turned.

"I wanted to do this Sera, just you and I, but I'm tired of waiting for the right time, sometimes you just have to do the thing. I care about Thalen too. He cares about me." He glanced at Thalen.

The noble had frozen in place. His eyes gone wide and mouth slightly open.

"I wanted to make sure you were ok, if we tried to figure out how to make it work. You and I, him and me. There's a lot more words, a lot more feelings, but..."

He stopped when he saw Sera's smile.

"I love you Korvan Aric. I want you to be happy. Of course I'm ok with you being with someone who brings you joy too."

Korvan's brain didn't quite keep up, "You... You love me?"

She laughed and her eyes did that squinty thing he adored, "You are so oblivious sometimes."

"It's one of the things that's so endearing about you," Thalen said, but looked at Sera as he did.

She turned to Thalen, "You're my friend Thalen, I want you to be happy too. I think we can figure all of this out. It won't be simple, but I think we can handle it."

Thalen offered her his hand, she took it, "Same is true for me Sera, I'm grateful to call you my friend."

Korvan's brain finally caught up with the rest of him, "This is going... much easier than I thought it would."

"You are being honest with me about your feelings, you are being vulnerable with something you want, and you stood up for someone you care about and protected their feelings too. Of course I'm ok when you approach it like that. Besides, its not like its frowned upon or anything." Her voice was so matter-of-fact. How could anyone argue.

"I don't deserve either of you."

"Don't say that," they said in unison.

"It isn't about deserve. You get our affection because you've given us yours," Thalen said.

"But come on, that Bell isn't going away and I'm sure its for us," Sera said.

They began to walk toward the summons.

"Do you think we'll see him again?"

Sera's voice was quiet as they walked.

"Yes," Thalen said, settling his cloak. "I only worry about where. And how."

Korvan lingered a breath watching them both, a warmth blossomed in him he didn't know was possible.

***

The morning after the storm everything smelled of damp stone and cut pine.

Caelen sat cross-legged on what remained of his cot, shoved against a safer wall. Below, crews shouted as scaffolds climbed the flayed edges. The old gearwork ticked on, scarred but alive somehow. The star lens lay split, its glow dead.

The deed lay open. Crown Guard seal heavy in wax. A "gift" for Korvan's bravery. He knew a bribe when he read one. Still the paper and the seal were real. For the first time in their lives, a home no landlord could snatch, and the Crown Guard even paid for the repairs. Certainty sat strange on him

Dust curled in a shaft of light. He tracked it with one finger, already inventorying salvage. Warped wire spools. Lens shards humming faintly.

Solace moved out of shadow.

She looked different than when she was with Korvan. She was slightly taller at the shoulder but remained, light and fast. Fine silken feathers, that were red along her limbs and darkened to black at her spine. The feathers caught light and the color shifted in unique ways. Her rear talons were long and precise. Spinal quills shimmered. Eyes like twin stars looked through him.

The bond pulsed, the strangest feeling he had ever had. It felt like the spark of inspiration before an idea strikes.

"You're sharper than I imagined," he said.

I have always been sharp. You were not ready to bleed.

He blinked, then laughed, dry and honest. "You sound like me."

You sound like you. I agree with your conclusions.

Her tail swayed once. He felt her map the room and his mind in the same measured passes. They didn't blur. They aligned well, his logic wrapped into her instinct.

His palm found the new mark at his forearm. It looked vaguely like feathers in a spiral around an open eye.

Rest my Caelen, she said.

"I did. I think." He rubbed his eyes. "Hard to tell."

You have cataloged rubble for two hours.

"Only the important pieces."

Define important.

He held up a cracked lens shard humming like a thin river.

"This one. It split in such a complex pattern, its beautiful."

She stepped closer and inspected it.

"I can feel that I'm changing. This power in me, its getting stronger by the hour," He swallowed.

I was never meant for Korvan. I steadied his heart because I could. But you are my reason.

"That's a heavy burden for a dying boy."

You are not dying. Not anymore.

Her brow neared his.

They kept quiet until it settled in like a friend.

He reached for a schematic and smiled, crooked.

"Then let's build something impossible."

***

Fog packed the eastern harbor thick as wool. Ropes creaked like old joints. Everything was quiet. Cael'Lumar had not yet roused.

Korvan stepped from the small sky skiff that had carried them. Another benefit of promotion. Access to the Aethyr-powered carriages. Sera followed, Fennik a russet crescent in her hood. Thalen last, Ashwing drifted between drafts overhead.

Sirene Malyka waited on the pier with Vara'Lumar's weight in her stance. Verdict perched on her shoulder. His eyes were strange, translucent, and prismatic.

"I hoped they would send you, didn't expect the others," Sirene said.

"They're my squad and I trust them with my life," Korvan said, glancing at Sera, at Thalen, at the Veyrkin that had never failed them.

She nodded them aboard the boat.

"We hunt ritual traces, a binding sigil. Anything that could've been used on that Leviathan. Thankfully, we have a lead, A harbor brig went quiet two nights before the serpent appeared."

Canvas sail snapped. The city bled away into fog as their barge rolled deeper into the sea.

They rolled along the waves, a slight bend to all their knees. When you grew up next to the sea, you felt born to it. Their legs were sure.

Korvan looked at Sirene, she was not fairing as well. Her face had a green to it, but she forced herself to remain composed.

Korvan couldn't bring himself to speak.

His mind ran on all the events of the last few days. Joy and heartbreak hung in equal measure. Bren, Ryn, Javek, the Leviathan, compared to Caelen, Sera, Thalen.

The more he thought about it the more it made sense, all of his life he had dealt with heartbreak and sadness, with the grief from his parents, the tragedy of his sick brother.

But...

Maybe that's the point. This last year had been the best year of his life. Of course, tragedy still happened. But he was still here, Caelen was ok, more than ok. Sera and Thalen were... his? It still felt bizarre to even imagine.

He chuckled to himself.

He got surprised and curious looks from everyone.

Something in his heart twitched, a great truth unveiled.

Just like the darkness cannot exist without light, there can be no joy without sorrow. All their efforts aren't about avoiding sorrow; they're about finding the people that make it worth fighting through.

He felt a strange feeling spread through him, a sense of sureness he'd never known.

For the first time in his life, Korvan understood. Home wasn't a place. Home was people. And he'd finally found his way home.

***

The derelict ship shouldered out of the mist.

Heat pricked Korvan's Soulmark, something waited for them.

The ship's hull was blackened. Timbers warped from a fire from within. Sail lines hung limp. A lone, torn sail flapped, its edges charred. No name visible on the prow.

Korvan boarded first. The deck creaked under more than his weight. The air felt cumbersome, filled with the memory of what had happened.

"Brusk, Vasha, you have to stay back. This deck won't hold all of us and you."

They didn't argue but settled on their skiff.

He looked to the space where Solace would have drifted.

The rest joined him.

"This was no normal fire, this was Flamecalling," Sirene murmured at a scorched coil. Her eyes had taken on the same look as Verdict's. Perhaps a gift the Seerbound offered.

Verdict hopped to the broken wheel and blinked. A pale-gold lens swept the deck.

"North hatch," Sirene said.

Sera lifted her hand.

"Gleamflame."

Soft lumen unspooled and pooled ahead.

They descended.

The scent punched them, Ash, burnt sap, and the distinct putrid stench of rotted fish. The lower deck held it like a sickroom. Hands and cloth went to mouths. It did little to help.

A dried blood trail looped careful arcs between crates. On the far wall, something burned deep. Runes, hundreds of them, arranged in unfamiliar patterns.

"That's new. Testing their binding?" Thalen asked.

Sirene didn't answer. Verdict hovered before the rune, wings stiff. Light rippled down. The Seerbound would reveal the truth.

The Eagle cried in pain and fell.

The rune flared.

Korvan's eyes burned, and his ears rang. When it adjusted, he saw a man screaming without sound. A Soulmark burning out of him like a name erased with a hot blade. A second figure in chains, body jerking. A third shape watching, still as a knife on a table.

The image faded.

Sera set her palm to her sternum.

Sirene's voice dropped.

"They are cutting Soulmarks out of people...," Sirene's voice was soft. Her eyes were wide, and a shaking hand went to her mouth.

"We saw it in person, they've been doing it for years. You should've seen how shaken Riverpost is," Thalen said, jaw hard.

"I came to Cael'Lumar to learn from my cousins here... but this. Vara'Lumar needs to know if this cult spreads...," Sirene's voice faded.

Above, the ship creaked.

Vasha's growl could be heard, *Little Hunter, I smell something foul. Be careful!*

He voice was hurried, and tense.

Korvan didn't have time to respond.

Shadows folded inward at the hold's center.

Something drew them in.

A figure resolved. An anchored echo, a working of illusion, of Wyrdforging.

They were tall and wore charcoal robes. A Half-mask of white aethyrbone covered their face. The other half was human, smiling. Silver chain marks coiled along their arms.

"Children of the Aethyrguard," the echo said.

Voice warped beyond anything recognized as human.

"You are so dutiful. So slow."

The figure tilted their head.

"You were never meant to arrive in time. This hull exists to rot. Like your oaths."

Korvan stood, rising to meet the specter.

"Who are you? What do you want?" They came out demands.

"We are what your Warden fears," the figure replied. "What your marks conceal. We are no longer bound by your antiquated rules."

The scorched rune showing the projection answered with a pulse.

"We are the Unshackled."

The rune glowed brighter, dangerously so.

Verdict flared. Refracted panes nested and snapped outward.

Korvan moved and stepped in front, a shield of pure force erupting between them and the rune.

The echo fractured, an acid colored light erupted sucking the heat out of the room. It smashed against Korvan's shield.

He bit his lip and thrust his arms out, pouring his all in.

Hands found him, one shoulder, the other.

He didn't look away.

He couldn't.

He had held.

Silence stooped back into the hold. It no longer felt empty.

"They wanted us to see, they wanted us to know who they are," Korvan said.

His jaw twitched and tightened.

He touched the scorched mark once more. It was still warm.

"The Unshackled. Sounds like they've officially declared war on the Aethyrguard," Thalen said.

Korvan nodded once.

"Come on, let's go give our report. There's nothing left for us here."

Fog closed around the skiff as it turned for shore. Behind them, the derelict ship eased back into the mist.

Korvan looked over black water toward the city.

"They'll listen this time."

Chapter 31: The Gift

The skiff came in quiet.

Korvan peeled off before the barracks steps. Rest wouldn't hold the line. His brother would.

He would not miss it this time.

A year ago, he'd let training grind the day to dust. He'd woken to a date and a hurt he couldn't take back. Caelen had been sick, but Korvan was still late.

This year a storm had chosen to rise on Caelen's birthday. Korvan wouldn't miss it. Not again.

He carried the gift in both hands. Some would consider it a modest gift. But it was more costly than anything they'd ever known. Korvan's promotion carried yet another benefit, ten Glimmers a month now, the gold-veined coin nobles used for luxuries. Rent in their old life had been six hundred Ashers if you paid on time. Six Silverbrands. One Glimmer weighed ten Silverbrands. To many it was a generous stipend. To Korvan it was a king's ransom. He hadn't touched a gold-veined coin until the quartermaster pressed his new pay into his palm.

It still felt wrong on his skin.

It meant Caelen would never go without again. They would never go without again. Not while he could stand.

Third Ring lanterns haloed the curve in amber. He knocked once on Ren's door. It opened before his hand fell.

Caelen stood there alive in a way Korvan had never seen him. Copper tool dancing between fingers. Solace a hush of light behind his shoulder. The old weariness had thinned; a bright mind had stepped forward.

"I knew you'd make it," Caelen said, eyes flicking to the wrapped box.

"I told you, leviathan or not, I wasn't missing it." Korvan's smile broke in the middle. "Happy birthday, little hawk."

He offered the bundle.

Ren's rooms smelled of medicinal root and solder. Charts adorned the walls. Soulmark schematics, projection arrays, a half-built containment ring. A brass sphere sat sealed on the central bench.

Ren hadn't changed the space after Caelen had moved. Her duty had teeth, but her compassion had longer ones.

Korvan's gaze latched to the sphere.

"Mom sent it," Caelen said. "Didn't have her name, but I know her seal anywhere. I missed whoever delivered it."

He set Korvan's bundle by the sphere. Solace nosed the package, then stood guard beside Caelen's hip.

"I primed it before the storm," Caelen added, mouth flattening. "Before the leviathan."

He pressed the center rune.

Petals parted with the softest click. Pale light deepened.

A voice came with it.

Caelen. My brilliant, impossible son...

The sound rolled over Korvan like a wave. A blade lifted from his ribs. His Breath stuttered. Old grief woke in his chest and ached.

I tried to pass my gift to your brother. Gifts are never without cost...

Caelen stared. Jaw locked. Hands steady but clenched.

Your illness... my failure. Not a curse. A consequence...

Korvan sat without meaning to.

Tell Korvan thank you for caring for you both. I can't imagine what he's done...

And Caelen. I love you. I love you both. My precious boys...

Light dimmed. Sound unraveled.

The kettle's slow tick returned.

Caelen found his voice first.

"That's the first time it's played again. It must've been waiting for you. I tried every latch and combination, never worked. But she left something else."

He unwrapped blue silk. A duskwood pendant lay inside, etched with a rune neither recognized.

"She said this was yours. It wouldn't work until you were ready."

Korvan reached. Fingers shook. The wood warmed beneath his touch. The rune pulsed. Aethyr moved through him. His Soulmark woke and pulsed erratically.

"She didn't leave us empty; she left us gifts. Simply distinct kinds," Caelen murmured.

"I thought we lost her," Korvan said, voice raw.

"I did too," Caelen said.

Night pooled.

Temple bells climbed the tiers.

Thalen and Sera had arrived, they carried baskets laden with all manner of favors. Thalen also had gifts that were wrapped in paper that sparkled, one for each person.

Ren's garden table now overflowed with spiced drinks, fresh fruits cut into festive shapes, roasted meats of different cuts and, Caelen's favorite, honeyed sweet rolls. Sera gave him a wink when she handed him a box of his own.

Korvan had told them earlier they didn't have to come, they insisted.

Out in the gathering court, Brusk shouldered Vasha, the great cat turned into a playful bow and pounced; Solace cut a small circle around the yard and returned to her post.

Midnight sat with Ren's Calico, Tangerine, and they lazily batted at each other in a mock duel of two great felines.

"It seems that no matter the size, all cats are warriors," Thalen said to Ren.

"Don't let him fool you. Tangerine is a big softy. I'd wager Midnight is in no real danger," Ren plucked a berry as she spoke.

Midnight looked at her and then at Thalen with an expression no animal face should have made.

Thalen laughed, a deep, rich rolling sound.

It had become one of Korvan's favorite things to hear.

"Thank you all for coming. For being here with Caelen and I to celebrate his birthday. We wouldn't have gotten here without you."

They all turned and looked at the brothers. Drinks were in hands, cheeks were rosy with laughter, drink, and too much food.

Caelen cut in, "Korvan's right, he's a sap, but he's right. Thank you, for everything. You all helped save my life in one way or another. I'll be forever grateful to each of you."

"Now who's the sap?"

Caelen made a face and then punched Korvan's arm.

The moon climbed high into the sky. Thalen and Sera excused themselves and Ren went off to rest.

Caelen and Korvan sat on the steps to Ren's tranquil garden.

"Let me try one thing."

Caelen's hands were careful and sure.

He turned the sphere.

"There's a notch here. Like a key bed."

Korvan nodded once and handed the pendant over.

Caelen slotted the pendant into the waiting seam.

The sphere opened.

A Harmonic hum rose through the ground. Aethyr pulled beams of light together, in a similar fashion, Korvan noticed, to the rune on the burned ship.

The space filled with an illusory image.

A figure stepped out of it.

Her Chestnut hair was bound in a loose braid laced with silver wire. Bracers looked like obsidian. A sigil on the breastplate that

Korvan immediately recognized. Authority lived in her bones the way music lives in a string.

Korvan stood abruptly getting a better view.

"She was like me," he said.

His voice was quiet and certain.

"She was Aethyrguard."

The projection looked at her sons.

"If you've found this, you're old enough to know."

Her voice was vibrant and laced with steel

"I am Champion Sigrid Gunnarsdottir. I am Aethyrbound by craft. Tamer of three Bonds."

"I believed in our purpose. I believed we could hold our world against threats within the Veyrth'Kael."

Caelen's brow flicked. Names tucked themselves into their proper drawers.

"Then I found him. Or he found me."

The light behind her changed. Vast wings folded the dark back on itself. Scales the color of starlight.

Orion.

"He would not bond," she said, but it didn't sound sad.

"I was already touched by Aethyr-blight. My Fyrstrand frayed and I continue to grow weaker. Thankfully, he saw my affliction. A binding would ruin us both. He also said I wasn't the right fit, despite the bruise to my ego."

"He gave me a truth I didn't want: Aethyrblight wasn't only in beasts. It had started to twist us."

"I brought it home. They said I was the threat, they said I met-tled in affairs that I shouldn't have."

She paced. The left fist clenched the way Korvan's did. The right brow arched the way Caelen's did.

"So I left."

Sigrid stepped closer.

"I wanted to give my power to you, Korvan. To pass on my talent without my curse. To make you formidable, so you could carve a life you deserved."

"And Caelen, our little hawk, you always saw the way things worked, how they were built, you are destined for such heights. You just needed time to grow wings."

Her mouth curved faintly.

"I failed. My ritual failed, it rebounded. Korvan got none of my strength, only my burdens. And Caelen. Caelen became corrupted in a way I could not undo."

Her head fell for a moment; she shook it slowly.

"If the Aethyrguard still hasn't said it aloud by the time you get this, know the blight has grown."

"I believe in you both. No matter where you have made it, I believe in the bond between you. Brothers first."

She breathed in, it was a ragged sound.

"If Orion still watches. Tell him I'm sorry I wasn't enough."

She looked beyond the scribing pane, then back, pulled by something they could not see. They saw it then, the corruption along her neck. That same twisted wrongness Korvan had seen on too many wild Veyrkin.

"You'll find my name in a sealed record if they haven't scrubbed my name. I was formidable. Peerless." A quick, rueful light crossed her face. "Except for one on my heels. Eris, if memory serves."

She knelt. The Champion put to the side and a mother leaned forward.

"My little hawk who sees everything. My Echoborn prince who protects everyone but himself."

"I love you. I am so proud of you both."

"A breath. Please take care of each other."

Her voice thinned.

"Korvan, you are older. Stronger. Hold the line for him, but hold it for yourself to. Caelen, be his conscience when his falters."

"You are more than you know. I wish I had more time. I wish I didn't have to leave you with more questions than answers. I wish..."

Her eyes closed. A tear ran. Then another. She didn't wipe them.

"I am sorry I left you with Varnrik. He tried to be good once, I hope he finds himself again. You bear his family name. You may hate me... I wouldn't blame you. You may not want to listen, but know, I did everything to keep you safe."

"Momma loves you."

More tears.

They weren't only Sigrid's.

"My babies."

She began to fade, slow and inevitable.

"My heart."

Breaths stalled, lungs burned.

"My sons."

Light held her smile at the end and then let go as the echo of Sigrid faded back into the shadows.

Silence returned.

Korvan's hands hung open. Caelen wiped at his face, failed, tried again.

They both sat with wet eyes, lips that quivered and the hum of old Aethyr that lingered in the stones.

They sat with it. Long enough to hear their breathing shift.

Korvan rose, moved to the bundle he'd carried in earlier, and set it on the bench. The cloth came away to a leather tube and a small pouch sealed in Guard wax.

"I should have brought this out when the sun was high," he said. "But it's still your day."

He uncapped the tube.

Vellum slid out, a stack of precise drafts. Spar cross-sections. A rib map that mirrored a wing. Angles annotated in a thin hand. Harness points and weight tolerances. A final sheet that showed the thing whole, sleek lines eager for the air.

Caelen's fingers hovered. "Korvan…"

"It's a glider," Korvan said. "Your old design, or as much as I could remember of it. It's just the plans of course, you'll pick every piece yourself."

He pressed the pouch into Caelen's palm. The weight settled deep.

"One Glimmer for materials," he added, mouth unsteady. "And a spare, to grow on."

Caelen laughed.

He set the coin down like it might bruise the table. He unfolded the harness draft and read the notes with moving lips.

Then he looked up.

"You're sure?" he asked, voice gone soft, the same tone it had when they were boys.

"You've watched sky your whole life. Time to touch it," Korvan said.

Caelen laid his palm on the vellum.

He nodded once and a mischievous grin spread.

"Then I'll fly."

Caelen turned and pulled Korvan in. The hug was fierce and unguarded.

"I love you, little hawk."

"I love you too, Kor."

Outside, the city shifted in its sleep.

Somewhere, bells argued about the hour and gave up.

Ren's kettle knocked softly with a bed time tea steeping.

Korvan took one of Sigrid's brass petals and turned it in his hand.

"We'll go to the Records and get every single piece of her story. I don't think she expected me to be...."

Korvan paused and looked down at himself.

Caelen answered, "All of that?"

"All of this," Korvan agreed.

"I had forgotten what she sounded like. It was nice to hear her voice again," Caelen said.

Korvan huffed.

"It sure was. What do you say we finish off those rolls Sera brought?"

"I thought you'd never ask," Caelen beamed.

They looked at the place their mother had stood.

Their mother's request of the young boy Korvan had been. Those words that had become a mantra played for Korvan again.

Hold the line.

Chapter 32: The Gate Between

Dawn arrived thin and unsmiling.

Mist walked the Crown Keep's ribs, beading on crenels, pooling in mortar seams, sliding down the old stone's throat.

Light cascaded into the hidden antechamber where Korvan's journey first began.

He did not come now as he did then.

Gone was the too-thin, hopeful boy that wore an oversized cloak. Now he stood tall, formidable, and prepared.

His new Knight's kit sat clean on his reforged frame. Tempered plates over a stitched gambeson, gorget snug, bracers laced taught. Across his back rode a new glaive, a lean killing curve rising from a saber-cat's sculpted maw. Silvered fangs cupping the first inches of steel in Vasha's honor. In his right hand, his mother's staff, his staff now, hummed against his palm.

Not only was he more than he once was. He was better.

Brusk waited behind, copper plates rustling in anticipation. Vasha paced the ring's edge, tail tip ticking. When her gaze slid across the saber-cat etching on the glaive, a low approval thrummed in her chest.

Korvan stepped into the Ritual Atrium, blacksteel pillars polished to a mirrored shine. Containment sigils breathed pale blue and gold along his armor. The great doors held, but the Aethyrgate beyond them pulsed in the stone.

Quiet. No Initiates clinging to breath. No prayer-hiss. Only echo, and what he had become to answer it.

Footsteps hushed down the stairs.

Thalen waited at the base. He wore no cloak, rain-dark braid short at the nape, new chain glinting under a travel surcoat, greaves cinched, buckles kissed flat. Sera stood beside him in tight riding leathers, bow unstrung at shoulder, a neat fletch at her hip. She had been drilling mounted shots from Glimmer's back; her stance said she meant to master it. Fennik pressed at her boot.

"We're going with you," Sera said.

Thalen checked a strap one last time.

"Like he could stop us."

Korvan let his jaw unclench.

"I wouldn't have it any other way."

The Aethyrgate throbbed.

The Beyond. No, the Veyrth'Kael, he corrected himself. Names carry power. The Veyrth'Kael waited for them.

Eris came down the spiral. Her hair looked tossed, and her armor jostled. She'd run.

Her voice carried sheathed steel.

"It feels so strange standing here, now after everything," she said, as if afraid to wake the place.

"Feels smaller," Korvan answered.

"Because you've grown."

He looked back and felt a hurt twist his heart.

"Bren's gone. I tried to find him. Thalen's scouted. He's not coming back... is he?"

Eris breathed out through her nose. "No. Not everyone who joins the Aethyrguard survives. Some meet a fate worse than death. We do our best for those that remain."

She stepped beside him, looked at the Aethyrgate first, then at him.

Korvan never realized he was taller than she was. Eris had always been larger than life. Standing there now, she looked just like another person that carried too much.

"Did you know her?" he asked.

A pause. Regret flashed across her face.

"Not well, but more than by rumor alone. Sigrid was fifteen years my senior. She was Powerful. Magnanimous. Affable. You have her eyes. Your names being different was a good distraction, no one batted an eye at a miner's son."

A brief smile cut and healed.

"But oh was stubborn. And rash, occasionally hot-headed. Like her son some might say."

"She was a great Aethyrguard Champion, Korvan and by all accounts an even better woman," Eris said. "Better than we deserved. She was role-model, as good as any I've ever had."

She turned to the gate. "I'll tell no one. It isn't my place. You have my word."

"You knew. You knew she was my mother."

"Eventually yes, I knew. The way you place yourself between the enemy and everyone else. Your hunger for the truth and fore fairness. I saw her grace in you."

A breath.

Her voice got quieter.

"I'm sorry. I did not stand up for her when she warned us of the Aethyrblight. I was young. I thought others knew better...."

He shook his head.

"You trusted your leaders... I forgive you, Eris."

He put his hand on her shoulder and squeezed. She put her hand over his and squeezed back.

A breach in protocol, a balm for their souls.

"What now?" she asked.

Korvan let the staff's hum find his lungs.

"Forward," he said.

He shifted the staff to his left hand and faced the sealed doors. Thalen came up on his right. Sera took his left. Their Veyrkin formed a horde behind them, a blend of wings, talons, claws, and tusks.

Korvan lifted the staff and traced a precise lattice in the air.

"I am Korvan Aric. Son of Sigrid, Knight of the Aethyrguard. Open. This. Gate."

Runes unlocked.

The chamber answered.

Lines of force kissed the pillars; the doors unlatched with a deep hiss.

"We'll be back Eris, count on it. And when we do get back, we'll change the world," he said without turning, "but first, I have a Dragon to find."

He walked in.

Back into the Gate Between.

Not an Initiate. Not a boy afraid of his own shadow. A son, bearing names dragged out of the night. A brother forging a life for himself and his family. A friend, guarding the ones who stayed. A lover, making a path for those that carried his heart. A Knight, obedient not to noise, but to something truer. Hope.

The Aethyrgate welcomed him.

No trial this time.

This time it would be a reckoning.

Somewhere beyond its unending light, a dragon waited.

He waited to recognize Korvan, to welcome him.

It seems after all, that the waiting isn't the worst part.

To Be Continued...

AFTERWORD

What can I say except, thank you.

Thank you for reading my story. This has been a passion project and an idea that has lived in my head in one form or another for a decade.

I hope you found a spark of light in these pages, and that the journey meant something to you.

If this story moved you, challenged you, or simply gave you a few hours of escape, I would be deeply grateful if you'd leave a review. Honest reviews help authors like me reach new readers and make it possible to continue telling stories that matter. Whether it's a few words or a full reflection, your voice makes a difference.

If you enjoyed the book, please also consider sharing it with friends, family, or anyone you think could use a little more magic in their life. Word of mouth is the true engine that keeps stories like this going, and every recommendation helps keep the world of *The Aethyrguard* alive and growing.

Thank you for giving this story your time and attention. I know how precious that gift is.

For every reader who turns a page, asks a question, or dares to hope alongside your favorite characters.

I see you, and I'm so grateful.

Hold the line,

Z.L. Coffman